SAY YOU REMEMBER ME

KINGS OF EDEN FALLS

SAY YOU REMEMBER ME

JUDY CORRY

Cover Design by Judy Corry

Edited by Precy Larkins

Proofread by Jordan Truex

For more info on Judy and her books visit: www.judycorry.com

Visit Judy's shop at: www.authorjudycorry.com

Also By Judy Corry

Eden Falls Academy Series:

The Charade (Ava and Carter)

The Facade (Cambrielle and Mack)

The Ruse (Elyse and Asher)

The Confidant (Scarlett and Hunter)

The Confession (Kiara and Nash)

Kings of Eden Falls:

Hide Away With You (Addie and Evan)

Say You Remember Me (Maddie and Ian)

Rich and Famous Series:

Assisting My Brother's Best Friend (Kate and Drew)

Hollywood and Ivy (Ivy and Justin)

Her Football Star Ex (Emerson and Vincent)

Friend Zone to End Zone (Arianna and Cole)

Stolen Kisses from a Rock Star (Maya and Landon)

Ridgewater High Series:

When We Began (Cassie and Liam)

Meet Me There (Ashlyn and Luke)

Don't Forget Me (Eliana and Jess)

It Was Always You (Lexi and Noah)

My Second Chance (Juliette and Easton)

My Mistletoe Mix-Up (Raven and Logan)

Forever Yours (Alyssa and Jace)

Standalones:

Protect My Heart (Emma and Arie)

Kissing The Boy Next Door (Lauren and Wes)

For all who've craved a love that whispers, 'I see you, and I choose you'—this book belongs to you.

PLAYLIST

"The Black Dog" by Taylor Swift
"But Daddy I Love Him" by Taylor Swift
"Used To Be Young" by Miley Cyrus
"Hurt Again" by Jillian Rossi
"Every Night" by Imagine Dragons
"Wildest Dreams" by Taylor Swift
"How to Be Your Friend" by Maddie Zahm
"Love I've Been Jealous Of" by Rachel Grae
"Nosedive (feat. Lainey Wilson)" by Post Malone
"Tired of Me" by Mikelle Dowse
"Inevitable" by Maddie Zahm
"Somebody to Someone (I Just Wanna Fall in Love)" by
Natalie Jane
"18" by Jillian Rossi
"Despacito" by Luis Fonsi & Daddy Yankee
"too young to be old" by Jax
"Bed Chem" by Sabrina Carpenter
"I Love You More" by Ryan Mack
"The Distance" by Evan and Jaron

"Eyes on You" by Michael Bolton
"Potion" by VOILÀ
"King of My Heart" by Taylor Swift
"Unconditionally" by Katy Perry
"Emily" by James Arthur
"Just Us" by James Arthur
"Lights On Kind Of Lover" by Maddie Zahm

1

———

MADDIE

"IS IT JUST ME, or are the guys in this club way better looking than everywhere else?" I asked my aunt Sloan as we settled into a corner table on the main level of The Garden, drinks in hand.

It was Friday night, and since I would be moving to the small town of Eden Falls, Connecticut where Sloan lived, in order to start my new job on Monday, she had decided to take me to one of her favorite clubs in the area to celebrate.

"It's definitely not just you," she said, a hint of a smile on her lips as she took a sip from her cocktail. "Why do you think I moved back here?"

"I thought it was because you loved teaching drama to rich prep-school kids?" I smirked before taking a sip of my gin and tonic.

"That's how I keep the lights on," she said, chuckling. "But living in a place where the men are as gorgeous as they are wealthy? It definitely makes weekends more interesting."

I glanced over at a group of polished businessmen chatting

near the bar, their tailored suits and easy smiles making them look like they'd stepped straight out of a magazine.

"So how many of those guys have you dated?" I asked, nodding toward the men closest to us.

"In that group?" Sloan's gaze slid over the six men. After a moment of consideration, she said, "Three."

"Nothing serious, though?" I asked, curious how my gorgeous aunt, who was only eight years my senior and more like a cousin to me, could still be single.

Seriously, what were all these hot men in Eden Falls thinking, leaving a catch like her alone?

"Not really. Not since I broke up with Marcus, anyway." She shrugged. "I mean, I dated the guy in the gray suit for a few weeks back in March. But when the timeline for when either of us wanted to have kids came up, we realized we probably weren't actually that great of a fit." She watched the guy with dark brown hair and glasses for a minute, the faraway look in her eyes telling me she was disappointed things hadn't worked out. "He's on more of a five-year plan when it comes to marriage and kids. But I'm already thirty-four, so I can't really afford to wait that long if I want to have a chance at having biological kids of my own."

"Dang, that sucks," I said, knowing just how important being a mom was to Sloan. "He's cute."

"He is. But it's fine." She waved the thought away, like it was nothing. "Not all of us can be the cool, young mom that you are."

"Yeah, right..." I chuckled. "Pretty sure having a baby during my senior year of high school isn't exactly something I'd recommend to most women."

Nope, getting pregnant in the backseat of a guy's car had definitely not been on my vision board back in the day.

But when I'd taken a pregnancy test during the spring of

my junior year and discovered the upset stomach I'd been dealing with for two weeks was actually morning sickness and not a weird case of the flu, all the dreams I had of attending a college a few hours from my home in Ridgewater, New York couldn't be easily realized with a newborn.

Yay for being a dumb, rebellious teen.

Oh well, at least I'd gotten the best son in the world out of it. He was definitely worth all the anxiety his unplanned pregnancy had caused.

"So tell me about your new job." Sloan shifted in her seat to face me instead of the eye candy standing nearby. "Is it the same position you interviewed for a couple of months ago?"

"No." I shook my head. "That was a front-desk position. This time I interviewed to be an assistant to one of the senior executives."

"Oooh, an executive assistant. You're moving up in the world, I see."

I nodded. "And the benefits are way better, too," I said, relieved that Grant and I would have good health insurance once the benefits package kicked in.

Raising a rambunctious eight-year-old kid who loved playing sports had me taking him to Instant Care way more times than I'd like to admit. Thankfully, he'd only actually managed two broken bones so far.

"Cheers to good health insurance." Sloan chuckled, raising her glass and clinking it against mine. "Geez, since when did we get old enough to get excited about boring things like that?"

"Way too many years ago for me," I said, thinking about how this was the first time in years that I wouldn't need to apply for Medicaid, food stamps, or subsidized housing since this new job would actually pay enough for me to fully support my little family.

"Well, I'm proud of you. And I'm glad you're moving here,"

Sloan said, her voice softening with genuine warmth. "It'll be nice having you and Grant close by."

"I'm excited too," I said, glad that I'd put my ego aside and applied for another position at Hastings Industries, even though they'd given the last position I'd interviewed for to someone else. "Now I just need to find a place to live."

"We'll figure that out," Sloan said, covering my hand with hers and giving it a pat. "And until then, you and Grant are more than welcome to stay with me. I didn't just redecorate my guest bedroom for nothing."

"Thank you," I said. "You really are the best."

My younger sister lived in New Haven with her husband, which was only about five minutes from the high-rise office building I'd be working in. But since they were expecting their first baby in November and had already set up quite a few baby things in their spare bedroom, I'd felt weird asking if my eight-year-old son and I could crash with them for an unknown length of time.

Sloan, on the other hand, had a nice little house in Eden Falls with a pretty good-sized backyard for Grant to run around in and get all his energy out. So even with the twenty-minute commute to work each day, it would be perfect.

I just hoped it wouldn't take too long to find an apartment of my own so that Grant and I could get the fresh start we needed.

"So do you know anything about this high-powered executive that you'll be assisting?" Sloan asked. "Is it one of the Hastings boys? Or one of the other executives?"

"It's one of the Hastings," I said, stirring my drink with my black straw. "I originally thought the CEO was looking for an assistant since I didn't realize there were multiple 'Mr. Hastings,' but the woman who interviewed me told me it was actually one of the CEO's sons."

"That sounds about right." Sloan smiled. "I mean, Joel is cool, but I would've been shocked if he was looking for a new assistant since I'm good friends with his current assistant and he's always gushing about how much he loves working at Hastings Industries." She took a quick sip of her margarita. After setting it back on the square napkin with the club's logo—a tree that resembled the tree of life from the Garden of Eden—she asked, "Do you know which son you'll be assisting? Is it Ian or Carter?"

"I think it's Ian," I said. "Maybe?"

The HR lady who had interviewed me had referred to him as "Mr. Hastings" so much during our interview that I had only caught his first name maybe once. But the name Ian sounded more familiar than Carter, at least.

"You're assisting *Ian*?" Sloan gasped, her eyes going wide.

"Yes..." I narrowed my eyes, wondering why she said his name like that. "Do you know him, then?"

"Oh, I know Ian all right." Sloan chuckled. "It's pretty hard not to know who Ian Hastings is when you live in Eden Falls."

"Because his dad is a billionaire?"

"Well, yeah, because of that too," she said, a sly smile lifting her lips. When she noticed my puzzled brow, she added, "Let's just say Ian *Heartbreaker* Hastings is quite popular around here...especially among the ladies."

"So he's a player?" I groaned, a sense of apprehension filling my chest. I did not need to work closely with another rich, playboy-type guy.

"Oh, he's definitely been a player in the past," Sloan said. Then seeming to sense my sudden unease, she added, "But he's a good guy. And an awesome businessman. I've never heard of his bad attention span with women ever interfering with his work. So I'm sure it will be just fine working with him."

"Yeah?" I asked, slightly wary since getting mixed up in

someone's relationship drama was not something I needed. Not when I was still recovering from the carnage my own previous relationship had put me through.

But hopefully, Ian would be pleasant to work for.

Though really, I was desperate enough to get a fresh start far from all the drama with my ex in Ridgewater that even if Ian turned out to be a tyrant, I'd probably still want the job.

I mean...I could always find another job if I needed to once Grant and I were settled, right?

***

"Someone's popular," Sloan remarked, glancing at my phone when it buzzed for the third time in a row. "Who's blowing up your phone? Some secret lover you haven't told me about?"

"You wish." I chuckled. "But sadly, no. It's just Lexi teasing me about something."

"Lexi's teasing you?" Sloan's blonde eyebrows knitted together. "About what?"

I shrugged and, in the most bored voice I could muster, said, "She's just trying to get me to do something dumb..."

"What kind of dumb thing are we talking about here?" Sloan leaned closer, curiosity evident in her green eyes.

"The kind of dumb that involves me *'kissing a hottie'* tonight," I said, using air quotes to emphasize the absurdity of the text I'd just received.

"What?" Sloan's eyes sparkled with amusement and intrigue.

I slid my phone across the table so she could read the text from Lexi.

Lexi: **Have you kissed a hottie tonight? Time's ticking.**

"Why is she asking you this? Did you tell her you were

planning to make out with hot guys while we were here or something?"

"No!" I squealed, my voice louder than intended. Glancing around to make sure no one was eavesdropping, I lowered my voice to a whisper. "It's just... I guess I've been complaining to her a little too much about how I never really got to date around in college and missed out on all the fun parts of being in my twenties."

"Since you were with the same guy for eight years."

"Yeah..." I took my phone back and turned it over, placing it face down on the table.

"And since you're only twenty-six and haven't actually tried dating again, even though you've been single for a year, Lexi is trying to knock some sense back into you," Sloan said, clearly thinking my little pity parties were ridiculous too.

Which, yeah, I got. Jaxon and I had called it quits a year ago, but instead of going out and having fun with guys on the nights Grant was with his dad, I'd opted to stay home. It was easier not to get my heart broken again if I didn't offer it to anyone in the first place.

"Anyway..." I sighed. "I guess Lexi is tired of me just complaining and not actually doing anything about it. So when I was leaving to come out with you, she told me that I wasn't allowed to see Grant again unless I *kissed a hottie* tonight."

"She's holding your son hostage?" Sloan laughed, clearly more amused by my sister's antics than I was. "And the ransom is you kissing a stranger at the club tonight?"

"That's what she said." I smiled despite myself. "But, I mean, it's not like she'll know if I do it or not."

"Oh, she'll know," Sloan said, a sneaky grin lifting her lips. "Because I'm going to be your witness."

"So you'll vouch that I kissed some dude so Grant can see his mom again?"

"Not exactly."

"Huh?" I asked, confused. "What do you mean?"

"I mean that I'm here to hold you to it. And if you don't follow through, I'll call Lexi and tell her that she can't let you inside her house again until I've seen you in the arms of a sexy man tonight."

"You'd keep an innocent little boy from his mother?" I gasped, not believing what I was hearing. Had my sister and aunt somehow teamed up on this?

"I've been trying to get you to bring back your boy-crazy side for months. So yeah, if I have to help Lexi and Noah raise your sweet little boy while you go out and sow your wild oats, I'll do it. It's for your own good."

"You're ridiculous." I rolled my eyes. "You guys can't kidnap Grant. I know where both of you live."

"You'd be surprised at the connections I have," Sloan said. "One of my former students disappeared from his fiancée for a whole year without anyone having any idea where he went. I'm sure he'd hook me up."

"Sounds like a *great* person to be connected to," I said wryly.

"He's a really great guy, actually. In fact, he owns this club."

"So does that mean he came back?" I asked, suddenly curious. "And did his fiancée forgive him?"

"They're getting married next weekend, so I'd say things turned out okay."

"Well, good guy or not, it sounds like this mysterious club owner is too busy with wedding plans to help you kidnap my son."

"Maybe." Sloan shrugged. "But regardless, you deserve to have some fun tonight. Plus, I saw the way all the guys were checking you out when we walked in. I bet there are more than a few who'd jump at the chance to help you fulfill your goal for the night."

"You mean *Lexi's* goal?" I corrected her with a raised eyebrow. I was definitely not the one who had come up with this crazy idea to walk up to a complete stranger and kiss him.

Sure, it was probably something I would have done in another life, before I suddenly had to grow up when I became a teenage mom. I'd definitely been a huge flirt back then, sneaking into college parties with my friends before we'd even gotten our driver's licenses.

But now? I doubted I even remembered how to flirt with a man.

"What about that guy over there?" Sloan asked, pointing to a blond guy in a navy-blue polo shirt who had just walked up to the bar. "He's cute."

I studied the guy's profile, imagining myself walking up to him and striking up a conversation. But when he turned to speak to the bartender and I caught a better glimpse of his face, I shook my head. "No, I don't think I could kiss a blond anytime soon."

"Too similar to Jaxon?" Sloan guessed.

"Yeah...definitely don't need to find someone who resembles my ex."

"So tall, dark, and handsome it is."

"Yes." I nodded. Then, not wanting to seem too eager, I quickly added, "H-hypothetically speaking, of course. I'm definitely not committing to talking to anyone, let alone kissing them."

"Oh, you're kissing someone tonight." Sloan chuckled. "It's happening."

"Ahhh." I shook my head and covered my cheeks with my hands as a sudden swell of anticipation filled my chest. "I'm not supposed to want to do this."

"But you do." Sloan laughed again, her eyes sparkling with mischief.

We spent the next few minutes casually scanning the room, weighing the pros and cons of different men as if we were at a farmer's market deciding which produce was freshest.

"What about him?" Sloan nodded toward a man walking toward a table to our left. He was tall, well-built, and had a very handsome face.

"He's cute," I admitted.

"And he's a brunette," Sloan noted, approving of the dark-haired prospect.

"So he must be perfect, then," I said. "Tall, handsome, and not a blond."

"I'd say it's time for you to go get your kiss from a hottie." Sloan winked. "I mean, time is ticking."

I rolled my eyes but couldn't suppress the small smile tugging at my lips. Maybe I was warming up to the idea after all.

"You really think I should do that?" I asked, my insecurities still needing reassurance.

I mean, did people actually just walk up to random strangers in clubs and kiss them?

I don't want to get charged with assault, do I?

"I think you deserve to have a few minutes of spontaneous fun," Sloan said. "Take a step out of your responsible, single-mom shoes and remind yourself what it's like to just live in the moment and chase something that feels good." Sloan shrugged. "And if you end up deciding that kissing hotties at a club was just a one-time thing, you don't have to do it again."

I nodded, taking in what she was saying.

This didn't need to mean anything big. I didn't need to take this super seriously or anything—it wasn't like the next guy I kissed would be my future soulmate, right?

I was just going to try something different, and if I discovered that kissing complete strangers was in fact as awkward as I thought it might be, I didn't have to do it again.

Or even step back into this club if I made a complete fool of myself.

Yeah... I breathed in deeply, hoping to calm my nerves. *I could be spontaneous for two minutes.*

"I think I'm gonna need a shot of tequila before I can do this," I said when another surge of anxiety bubbled up.

"Here, have my drink." Sloan pushed her margarita closer. "I'm friends with the bartender, and he always adds an extra shot to mine."

Even though I was already feeling pretty buzzed after two drinks, I quickly downed what was left of Sloan's drink.

"Remind me to hydrate after I'm done making an idiot of myself," I said, setting her glass back on the table. "I can't believe I'm actually considering this."

"Yay, crazy Maddie is back," Sloan teased, her grin wide.

I shook my head. "You're supposed to be the responsible one."

"Sorry, I'm a terrible influence." She shrugged with a mischievous glint in her eye.

Before I could respond, a man appeared on the staircase that led down from the VIP lounges above. Not just any man— *the* man.

The one you read about in books or see in movies, the kind that takes your breath away before you even realize you've stopped breathing.

He was tall; his dark hair tousled just enough to suggest he wasn't here to play by anyone's rules. A jawline so sharp it looked like it could cut glass, and shoulders broad enough to carry the weight of the world—effortlessly, confidently, like it was all part of his day-to-day.

But it wasn't just his striking looks that rooted me to the spot. No, there was a pull, a kind of magnetic charge in the air around him. He had an aura of control, of power, that made the rest of the crowded club seem like a fuzzy background.

This wasn't just a man who got things done—he was the kind of man who didn't even need to ask twice. The one people would turn to when things went south, and he'd handle it without breaking a sweat.

"Now *that...*" I whispered under my breath, my heart betraying me with a wild flip in my chest—a sensation I hadn't felt in years, "is a beautiful man."

My eyes roamed over him as he made his way down the staircase to the main level, taking in his custom-tailored suit, which clung to his toned frame, accentuating every powerful line of his body.

Even from across the room, there was something about him, something magnetic, that made me wonder if maybe Lexi's idea of me kissing a stranger wasn't so crazy after all.

"I can't believe I'm saying this," I murmured, unable to tear my gaze away as he strode toward the bar. "But I think I just found my guy."

"Wait, what?" Sloan's voice was distant, her eyes wide as they followed my line of sight.

It could've been the alcohol—or maybe it was just the sheer force of attraction—but when his eyes met mine, it felt like the universe paused. The room dimmed, the music softened, and all that existed was the pull between us.

He leaned against the bar, and when his gaze seemed to take me in more fully, an electric current shot through me, a tug deep in my chest that urged me forward. And when he sent me a smoldering look, one that promised trouble in the best possible way, I knew that if I didn't move now, I'd lose the nerve

—and with it, the chance to be alive in a way I hadn't been in too long.

"I'll be right back," I said, sliding out of my seat before Sloan could even think to stop me.

"Wait..." Sloan started to say something, but I could barely hear her over the pounding in my ears as I made my way toward the stranger, my palms damp with the thrill of what I was about to do.

The handsome man's dark eyes stayed locked on mine as I approached, and when I stopped in front of him, a slow smile spread across his lips.

"Hi," I said, striving to sound confident even though my legs felt like they might give out at any second.

"Hi yourself," he replied, his voice deep and smooth, sending a shiver down my spine. "And who might you be?"

I hesitated for just a moment before deciding that a little mystery wouldn't hurt. "Just someone looking to be a little reckless."

"Is that so?" His eyes gleamed with amusement as he leaned in closer.

"Yes." My breath hitched as I inched even closer, feeling the warmth radiating from him.

"Well, I'm sure I can help with that," he murmured, his breath warm against my ear. "Since Reckless is my middle name."

I bet it is.

And before I could second-guess myself, I leaned in and pressed my lips against his.

He froze momentarily, like he hadn't expected me to actually kiss him. But the initial surprise seemed to wash over him quickly because a second later, sparks ignited and his hand came up to my waist, pulling me against him as he deepened the kiss.

And oh my heck, I knew it had been a while since my last first kiss, but I was pretty sure I'd *never* had a first kiss like this before—one with instant heat, want, and adrenaline. His lips were firm, skilled, and he tasted faintly of whiskey and something sweeter, something I couldn't quite place.

I let my hand slip up his chest and neck until it rested against his jaw. His jaw was strong with just a hint of a five o'clock shadow. And I reveled in the feel of it. Jaxon had never been able to grow a beard, so the feel of this stranger's light stubble on my fingertips was a new sensation. One that I loved.

He was a man. Powerful and strong.

Sexy.

Man, he was so sexy. And with the possessive way he was holding me, I might just burst into flames.

For a moment, as heat swirled hotter and hotter in my veins, the world around us disappeared.

It was just him and me, wrapped up in the intensity of the kiss.

"Oh honey, I'm so sorry your mommy wasn't able to come home," Sloan's voice suddenly sounded in my head, bringing me back to reality. *"She internally combusted in the arms of a hottie at the club last night."*

And yeah, I didn't know how much time had passed, but I should probably come back to earth before something like that happened.

So even though I didn't want to, I slowed the kiss. When we finally broke apart, both of us were slightly breathless.

The stranger's dark eyes searched mine, a hint of something more behind his playful smile. "Well, that was unexpected," he murmured, his voice low.

I couldn't help but smile back. "Good unexpected, or bad?"

"Definitely good," he said, his thumb brushing lightly

against my waist. "Though I wouldn't mind knowing who just kissed me."

I bit my lip, debating whether to reveal my name, but then decided to keep the mystery alive. "Maybe you'll find out some-day," I teased, stepping back before things could get more complicated.

"I'll hold you to that," he said, his eyes promising this wasn't the last time we'd meet.

With one last smile, I turned and walked back to Sloan, my heart racing as I tried to process what had just happened.

2

———

MADDIE

I GLANCED down at the text Sloan had sent me ten minutes ago as I finished up the tour of my new workspace. Hastings Industries was in one of the newer high-rises in downtown New Haven. The building was sleek, modern, and frankly, a little intimidating. After spending the last few years working as a receptionist in a small, cramped office in Ridgewater, this was a whole new world.

Taking a deep breath, I typed out a reply to Sloan: *I haven't met him yet. Just got back to my desk after a tour. The HR lady says he'll probably call me in once his meeting is over.*

I set my phone down and took in my new surroundings. The office was more impressive than I'd imagined, with its modern décor, state-of-the-art technology, and a sense of efficiency that seemed to permeate the air. My desk was situated right outside Ian Hastings' corner office, which had floor-to-ceiling windows that offered a breathtaking view of the park below. The greenery and the cityscape beyond felt almost surreal, like a postcard come to life. It was the kind of view that made you feel like you'd made it, like maybe—just maybe—things were starting to come together.

And I needed them to come together. This job was more than just a paycheck. It was a fresh start for me and Grant. I glanced at my son's photo on my desk—a snapshot of him grinning with that gap-toothed smile of his, holding a soccer ball bigger than his head. He was my world, and this job was a chance to give him the stability we both needed.

Marsha, the head of HR, had been wonderful during the tour. She was a middle-aged woman with short, fiery red hair that suited her vibrant personality. From the break room to the conference rooms, she'd shown me everything, even the little things like where the restrooms were—a detail I appreciated since I drank water like a camel.

But what really struck me was the office space I'd be working in. My desk, with its prime location just outside Mr. Hastings' office, felt like the heart of the operation—like I was Donna, the legal secretary to the great Harvey Spector in my favorite show *Suits*.

And that view—oh, that view—I still couldn't believe I'd be working here.

Just as I was about to dive into my email, Marsha appeared at my desk. "Mr. Hastings is finishing up his meeting in the conference room now," she said with a warm smile. "He'll probably invite you into his office as soon as he sees you. I'm sure he'd like to get to know you a bit before going over what he needs from you today."

I nodded, doing my best to keep my cool as a thrill of anticipation shot through me. "Thanks, Marsha."

As she walked away, I busied myself with getting acquainted with the computer system, trying to ignore the fluttering nerves in my stomach. This was it. My chance to make a good first impression.

A few minutes later, I heard the sound of expensive shoes clicking on the polished floor. Looking up, I saw a group of men in tailored suits leaving the conference room. They looked important, powerful, the kind of people who made big decisions over coffee and conference calls.

My eyes scanned the group, and then—

My heart stopped.

There he was. The man I'd kissed at the club.

How could this be happening? I wondered as panic surged through me. Of all the people in New Haven, how could *he* be here?

My mind raced, trying to make sense of it, but there was no time to think. He was walking right toward me.

My instinct was to duck my head down, to pretend to be absorbed in my work, praying he wouldn't notice me. Maybe if I just—

But instead of hearing him walk past, I felt his presence stop directly in front of my desk.

Oh no. Please no. Please don't be who I think you are.

My heart hammered in my chest as I slowly looked up, hoping against hope that I was imagining things.

"Hi," he said, his voice smooth and all too familiar even though we'd only spoken a few sentences to each other on Friday night. "Marsha tells me you're my new assistant."

The blood drained from my face as reality hit me like a freight train. *This* was Ian Hastings. *My boss* was the man I'd kissed in a moment of wild spontaneity.

Not just kissed, but full-on made-out with.

I'd stroked the stubble on his jaw. Lost myself in the heat of his embrace.

How could this happen? How in the world had Sloan not stopped me before I'd gone up to a complete stranger and kissed him?

And why the heck hadn't she warned me about what I'd done before I showed up to work today, stupidly not having a clue that the one moment I'd decided to be reckless, it had been with my freaking boss?

When I met Ian's gaze, his dark brown eyes widened like he was only just then recognizing me.

Oh crap! This was not good.

Is he going to fire me on the spot for sexual harassment?

I mean, I hadn't kissed him in the workplace, and he'd seemed happy to take part in that kiss at the time...but with my luck, there was probably some sort of rule against throwing yourself at your future boss in a club.

I watched his Adam's apple bob as he swallowed hard. And for a moment, he just stood there, speechless, clearly as thrown off as I was. But then he licked his lips, seemed to gain his bearings, and then said, "Hi...I guess we've actually met before."

"Yes..." I nodded, desperately searching for words. "I, uh..."

But I couldn't finish the sentence because my brain was currently in the process of short-circuiting.

This can't be real. This can't be happening.

I'm so going to die.

Ian cleared his throat, seemingly trying to break the awkwardness. "Well," he began, his voice strained but polite, "it's nice to officially meet you, Maddie. Why don't we...uh... why don't we step into my office?"

I nodded again, unable to trust my voice. With shaky legs, I stood up, my heart pounding so loudly I was sure he could hear it.

As I followed him into his office, all I could think was that it was no wonder Sloan had been so anxious to hear if I'd met my boss yet.

She's so dead when I get home from work today.

I just hoped I'd still actually have a job when this meeting was over with.

3

———

IAN

WELL, *this morning just got complicated*, I thought as I led Maddie—my new assistant—toward my office, fighting to keep my steps steady and my expression calm.

Calm on the outside, at least. On the inside, my pulse raced like a hummingbird's wings, my mind spinning in a hundred different directions.

How was it possible that out of all the women at the club on Friday night, the woman who had reignited a spark I hadn't felt in...well, longer than I wanted to admit...was the very woman I couldn't afford to feel any sparks with.

Man, the universe really had a twisted sense of humor, didn't it? After nearly a year of feeling numb, the first woman to tempt me into breaking my ten-month celibacy streak had to be my new assistant.

My new and *extremely attractive* assistant.

I pushed open the glass door to my office, shoving those thoughts aside. *Professional.* I needed to stay professional. I needed to handle this like the executive I was—and the future CEO I hoped to be.

"Please, take a seat," I said, gesturing toward one of the chairs in front of my desk.

Maddie nodded and sat gracefully in the chair, but I could tell she was trying to appear calm in this awkward predicament we found ourselves in.

She looked...different in the daylight, somehow even more beautiful, with shoulder-length hair, a petite frame, and plump pink lips that—

Nope. I shook my head and moved my gaze away from her mouth before the memory of how her lips had felt as they'd moved with mine on Friday night could flash through my mind for too long. *Definitely don't need to think about that heated exchange right now.*

I shook my head and shoved the forbidden kiss aside, taking my seat across from her. Clearing my throat, I searched for the right words to start this meeting that was already so far off script.

But before I could say anything, Maddie's eyes—which I hadn't realized were crystal blue until this moment—widened, and she blurted out, "I'm so sorry about this weekend," her voice laced with anxiety. "I never do things like that—I swear! It's just that my sister practically threatened to kidnap my son if I didn't kiss someone while I was out. But I promise I had no idea it was you. Not the *you* you, at least. Not my future boss. I mean, I didn't even know what you looked like, and when I interviewed for the job, I thought I'd be assisting your dad, and he has much lighter hair, so I never imagined his son would be so tall, dark, and handsome—" She covered her mouth, her eyes suddenly going wide with horror as she realized what she'd just said. "Oh my gosh, I just called you tall, dark, and handsome to your face. I can't believe I said that. You're my boss. I'm sure you know what you look like, and that kiss, well..." She shook her head, her words tumbling over each other as she tried to explain. "It wasn't supposed to happen. Not with you. I promise, I—"

"Hey, hey," I interrupted, holding up a hand to calm her down. Despite everything, I couldn't help the chuckle that escaped me. "It's okay, really. It's an understandable mistake. And I can tell it wasn't some calculated attempt to seduce your future boss." I winced internally as the words left my mouth, realizing how bad they sounded.

Looks like we're both on edge.

I cleared my throat before trying again. "What I'm attempting to say—however badly I'm doing it—is that maybe we should just move on. We both know what happened, and we both know our intentions. So let's chalk it up to an interesting night and agree to avoid any more...mishaps."

"Okay." Maddie blinked, then nodded slowly, taking a deep breath as she tried to compose herself. "I'll try to move on." She hesitated for a moment, as if gathering her courage. "So...does that mean I still have a job?"

"Yes." A grin tugged at the corners of my lips, and I couldn't resist the chuckle that followed. "As long as you can still see me as your boss and not as some reckless guy who, on occasion, lets his guard down outside the office, then yes, you still have a job."

"Okay, good." Maddie smiled, relief washing over her features, and for a moment, the tension between us eased.

"So how about you tell me about yourself?" I said, leaning back in my chair, hoping to move our meeting into what an initial meeting between an employer and a new employee should look like. "Have you lived in the area for long? You mentioned having a son?"

"Yes." She nodded, seeming to relax at the idea of talking

about something less charged. "I'm from a small town in central New York state. Born and raised. But I have some family in this area and always thought it was such a beautiful place, which is why I applied for this job." She licked her lips, briefly glancing down at her hands. "Anyway, like you said, I do have a son. Grant. He's eight and the best thing to happen to me. And well..." She furrowed her brow like she was trying to think of what to say next. "I, uh, I have a bachelor's degree in interior design—not that I've ever really done anything with it aside from helping my dad with his remodel. And..." She bit her lip. "I don't know. I guess that's pretty much it. Except that I just wanted to say that I'm really excited to work here. I researched your company a few months ago and it seemed like a great place to work and, um," —she ran her hands down her skirt, in what I assumed was a nervous tic— "I promise to do my best and fulfill all my responsibilities to the best of my ability."

"Awesome," I said. "It's good to get to know a little about you."

Though I was somewhat surprised she was old enough to have an eight-year-old since she didn't look a day older than twenty-five. But I supposed she could be a little older than I had thought.

Or perhaps she had her son when she was a teen?

My mom had me when she was nineteen, so it could happen.

"And now that I know a little about you, how about I start by telling you a bit about myself?" I said, pushing aside the curiosity I had about my new assistant. "I grew up in Eden Falls—a small town just outside New Haven. I know you're familiar with that town, since... well, it's where we first met." I gave her a wink, a playful grin tugging at my lips. "Though I suppose I'm already breaking my own rule by mentioning that."

"Yes, I've spent a little time in Eden Falls." Maddie smiled at what would now be considered our inside joke, the tension in the air dissipating just a bit more.

"I'm also the son of the company's founder and CEO," I continued. "But I promise I didn't get this job through nepotism or anything like that." I smirked so she'd know I was joking. Even though I felt I was qualified for this job and worked hard to get where I was, being the oldest son of Joel Hastings did come with a lot of perks.

"Anyway, I'm mostly involved in mergers and acquisitions, handling investment properties, and, well, attending a lot of meetings—many of which you'll join me in." I watched her as I spoke, noting how her eyes followed my words with interest. "I also do quite a bit of travel—not always for business. I'm actually heading to Norway this weekend for a wedding. So I won't always be in the office. But there might be times when I'll need you to travel with me. To various conferences and such. I hope that's okay?"

"Marsha mentioned the possibility of travel when she interviewed me." Maddie nodded. "I have family nearby who's already offered to watch my son. And his dad has partial custody, so he can help out, too."

I filed that information away, my curiosity piqued about her situation—the dynamic between her and her son's father. Sure, she had kissed me on Friday, but you never knew the kinds of relationships people had these days. But it sounded like they were separated. Which was...good to know.

Not that I should care.

I definitely wouldn't be crossing those lines again.

Even if I've been imagining her soft lips whispering sweet nothings into my ear for half the time she's been talking to me.

I pushed the inappropriate thought away.

Man, I needed to get laid again. Ten months of celibacy was way too long.

But hey, at least my celibacy streak had come in handy for one thing. It had kept me from doing what I usually did on my nights at the club—a.k.a. it kept me from going home with whatever beautiful woman had caught my eye and exploring each other in a much more intimate setting.

Dang, maybe the universe actually did have my back this time. Sleeping with my new assistant would have been *much* different than an innocent kiss.

"Your main responsibilities this week will be getting familiar with the company and meeting the other executives and associates," I continued, grateful Maddie couldn't read my mind and was simply jotting down notes for herself into a navy-blue notebook. "I'll have my dad's assistant show you the ropes on some of the administrative duties and how to access the various training videos if you haven't already accessed them." I paused, trying to remember if I was forgetting anything. When nothing else came to mind, I asked, "Do you have any questions for me?"

She pressed her pink lips together, her eyes going up and to the right as if she was mulling this over. Then she said, "I can't think of anything right now."

"Okay, great. Then I think that covers everything for now."

"Okay, awesome," she said, jotting one more thing in her notebook before closing it. "Are there any meetings I should plan on attending today?"

I pursed my lips as I tried to remember what my schedule looked like. "I have a couple of meetings this afternoon. I think I can handle the one with Branson Financial on my own. But I'll definitely need you in my three o'clock meeting since there are a lot of moving parts that I'll need notes on."

"I'll be ready for that, then."

She stood, and even though I knew she could let herself out

of my office, I found myself standing as well, saying, "Here, I'll walk you out."

As I escorted her to the door, my eyes were drawn to the glass walls of my office. And when I looked at her desk just beyond the glass door, I realized just how perfectly the glass walls framed her desk.

Man, I really should've told Marsha to hire someone less stunning. Someone more like Rhonda, the sixty-something assistant who had just retired.

I really didn't need to be distracted by a set of pretty blue eyes and a petite-yet-perfectly-curvy frame.

But no, every time I looked up, I'd see her there.

Hopefully, once the initial attraction had passed, I'd be able to focus on my work without the memory of our kiss floating to my mind every few seconds.

"I look forward to working with you, Miss Stevens," I said, forcing formality into my tone as I extended my hand. Maybe using her last name would remind my brain to keep this strictly professional.

"I look forward to working with you, too," she replied, her cheeks flushing the most alluring shade of pink as she slipped her hand into mine. And the moment our hands touched, a spark of electricity shot up my arm.

Static from the new carpet, I told myself. Definitely nothing to dwell on.

Maddie stepped out of my office a moment later, and I gave her a nod before closing the door behind her. I turned back to my desk, determined to focus, but my thoughts refused to cooperate. Instead, I found myself replaying that forbidden moment from Friday night.

The memory of that kiss rushed back—how she'd felt in my arms, the way her eyes had lingered on mine just before she walked away. There was something in her gaze that made me want to lean in again, despite everything.

Why was it that the first time I'd felt a spark with anyone in nearly a year, it had to be with my new assistant?

I sighed and shook my head. This was going to be a problem.

And it was probably bad that I couldn't wait to see how it would unfold.

4

MADDIE

"BE GOOD FOR AUNT SLOAN TODAY." I leaned down to kiss Grant on the forehead, brushing his messy blond curls out of his eyes. "I'll be back before dinner, okay?"

"Okay, Mom." Grant, who was still nestled under his dinosaur blanket, grinned up at me, his eyes half-lidded with sleep. "Have a good day at work."

"I will," I promised, though part of me still couldn't believe that I was actually heading to this job—a billionaire's executive assistant. Since, after how I'd started things off, the fact that I was still employed felt like a minor miracle.

But now, in my second week, I was starting to find my rhythm.

Sure, I'd spent the first few days blushing like a schoolgirl every time Ian so much as glanced my way, but at least I hadn't done anything too catastrophic.

Not *again*, anyway.

Was I still slightly annoyed with Sloan for not giving me a heads-up that I'd hit on my boss before seeing him at work last Monday? Absolutely. But she claimed she didn't realize who I was kissing at the club until it was too late—and after seeing how thrilled I was after my epic kiss with a stranger, she hadn't wanted to burst my bubble.

Could she have warned me the next Monday morning before I left for work? Definitely. But was I mad about having two whole days to fantasize about the handsome stranger I'd kissed? Not really. Daydreaming about being back in Ian's arms at The Garden had been a pretty sweet escape while it lasted.

But despite letting me make a fool of myself with my new boss, Sloan had been an absolute lifesaver this past week, watching Grant while I worked.

With her summer schedule mostly free, aside from a few drama camps here and there, she'd stepped in to help until I could find a good summer program for Grant. We were on the waitlist for one in Eden Falls, and the director had texted me on Friday, hinting at an opening. So I was crossing my fingers that Grant would get in soon.

Once that was taken care of, the only thing I'd need to do was to find a place for Grant and me to live.

"Have a good day at work," Sloan said when I made it back downstairs. She was standing in the corner of her small kitchen, sipping her coffee by the window.

"I will," I said, grabbing the lunch I'd packed from off the counter. "Ian should be back from that wedding he went to, so hopefully, he didn't decide to fire me while he was away."

Sloan chuckled, a half-smile lifting her lips behind her coffee mug. "He probably hooked up with another Norwegian model while he was away, so I'm sure things will be fine and your little blunder will be far from his mind."

My jaw dropped at what Sloan had just said. When I could gather myself enough to give a response, I said, "I don't know whether I should be comforted or offended by the fact that you think my kiss with my boss is so forgettable."

"Oh, I'm sure it was a very memorable kiss." She waved her hand. "But we're talking about a billionaire playboy here. He's just wired differently than you and me."

"Well, then I guess I have nothing to worry about."

"You'll be fine," Sloan said. "He would be an idiot not to keep you on."

"Well, I appreciate your vote of confidence in that area," I said, still slightly bugged by the idea that Ian might have gone off and hooked up with random women over the weekend.

Even though I knew I really shouldn't care.

Since there was obviously no way him getting hung up on our stolen moment could ever go anywhere.

As I pulled my work bag over my shoulder, Sloan got a sly smile on her face. "Oh, before you go, I wanted to remind you—I'm having a few friends over tonight. Just a little backyard get-together with drinks, appetizers, and a fire."

"Sounds fun," I said, grabbing my keys from off the hook.

"It will be," she said, her grin widening. "You should hang out with us. Who knows, maybe someone who's *not* your boss will be there and catch your eye."

I rolled my eyes, slinging my purse over my shoulder. "I'm not looking for a man right now, Sloan."

She shrugged, unfazed. "You say that now, but you just wait until Theo shows up. He's a hot single dad. And while I know you say you're not interested in dating...we already know that the universe works in mysterious ways."

"Uh-huh," I muttered, heading for the door. "Well, have fun playing matchmaker without me. I've got to get to work."

"Suit yourself," Sloan called after me with a laugh. "But the offer still stands!"

I waved as I stepped outside, shaking my head as I made my way down Sloan's flower-lined walkway and climbed into my fifteen-year-old Subaru. The engine sputtered to life, a sound

I'd grown used to, and I pulled onto the road, beginning the twenty-minute commute from Eden Falls to the office.

Connecticut was breathtaking in the summer—the early morning sun bathing the lush greenery in golden light.

It was like something out of a postcard.

And as I approached the city where I would be spending my workdays for what I hoped to be many years, I couldn't help but feel a deep sense of gratitude for this fresh start. Getting to rebuild my life in such a serene, picturesque place felt like a gift I didn't even know I needed.

When I arrived at my desk, I glanced through the glass walls of Ian's office and saw that he was already inside. It surprised me a little, considering his plane had landed late last night. But Sloan had mentioned that despite his active social life, Ian was always dedicated to his work.

My only hope was that despite my initial blunder at the club, he'd see that I was just as responsible and committed to doing my job well.

I tucked my work bag into my desk drawer and opened Ian's emails, sorting through the ones that had piled up since Friday. As I was drafting a reply, I heard Ian end a phone call. I glanced up, and just like the first time I'd seen him on the stairs at the club, the sight of him nearly took my breath away.

Man, it should be illegal for anyone to look this good at work.

You are not allowed to have a crush on your boss, I reminded myself, trying to ignore the flutter in my chest as Ian walked to the window, his gaze distant and thoughtful. *You're a professional now. No silly crushes allowed.*

But even if I was trying to be professional, it was hard not to notice how he was a work of art, standing there in his perfectly tailored suit, with his brow furrowed and that sexy pout on his lips.

Maybe it was the fresh Norwegian air that had done it, or maybe he'd gotten a new haircut for the wedding he'd attended there. Either way, he looked better than ever this morning.

I shook my head, trying to push the thoughts away. *Who cares if he looks like he stepped off the cover shoot for the Sexiest-Man-Alive magazine issue?* I had work to do.

I couldn't afford to get distracted by the very man I needed to stay focused around. But even as I tried to convince myself with my new mantras that included things like "focus on the paycheck, not the playboy" and "salary over smoldering looks," I couldn't help but steal one last glance in his direction.

Yep, just because I'd told Sloan I wasn't interested in dating anyone right now didn't mean I couldn't still appreciate my beautiful view.

***

After finishing Ian's emails, I glanced at his schedule for the day. He had a few meetings lined up, one of which was a board meeting in just a few minutes. Since I was still new and he'd only been in the office three of the five days I'd worked here so far, I decided it was better to ask what he needed from me, rather than assume. So I stood, smoothed out my skirt, and walked over to his office.

Knocking lightly on the glass door, I watched as he glanced up from his computer and waved me in.

"Do you need me to attend any of your meetings today?" I asked, keeping my tone professional, even though just being around him still sent my pulse racing.

"Actually, yes." Ian leaned back in his chair, his dark eyes lingering on mine for a moment before seeming to take in my appearance. He licked his lips, then cleared his throat. "I-I'd like you to sit in on the board meeting that's starting shortly.

It'll give you a better understanding of the company and every-thing we have coming up."

"Okay, great." I nodded. "I'll grab my laptop and notebook."

I turned and headed back to my desk, feeling a small sense of relief.

So far, so good, I told myself. One interaction down for the week, and as long as I kept things professional, maybe I'd manage to keep up my streak of not throwing myself at my boss.

But when Ian stepped out of his office, and I fell in step behind him, my eyes couldn't help but drift up his tall frame and admire it as we walked down the hall together.

How tall was he, anyway? I was five foot five, and he had to be at least ten inches taller.

So...six two? Six three?

I'd never been great at guessing heights, but either way, his towering height just added to his overall appeal.

Which you don't care about, I reminded myself. *Since he's your BOSS.*

When we reached the conference room, Ian held the door open, gesturing for me to step inside. I took a deep breath and walked in, immediately noticing the polished, professional atmosphere. Several executives were already seated around the large rectangular table, all impeccably dressed and exuding the kind of confidence you'd expect from people who ran a multi-billion-dollar corporation.

At the far end of the table sat Ian's dad, Mr. Joel Hastings, a distinguished fifty-something man with an air of authority that could easily be intimidating—yet somehow wasn't. Beside him sat his wife, Dawn, a poised woman with warm brown eyes and rich brown hair. Her graceful demeanor matched her husband's presence, though there was a certain softness in her gaze.

Beside Ian's mother sat his younger brother, Carter, who was apparently a wiz with numbers. And even though he was only a year out of college, he was well on his way to becoming the company's chief financial officer.

And though this powerful family could have easily come off as the intimidating billionaires that they were, there was a warmth that emanated from them, making you feel oddly at ease in their presence. It was a rare mix of power and approachability—one that was as impressive as it was disarming.

Which probably helped them in negotiations with the companies they acquired.

I'd been curious about my new company's founding family last week, and not wanting to have any more mix-ups with who I should and should not recognize, I found Ian's social media accounts. It turned out that in addition to having Carter for a younger brother, he also had two other siblings who—you guessed it—were also extremely talented and good-looking.

Nash and Cambrielle didn't work at the company, though. Nash was an up-and-coming actor who recently had a small role in a movie alongside one of my all-time favorite actors, Justin Banks. And Cambrielle, who was the youngest in the family, had just graduated from Juilliard and landed a job as a professional dancer for the New York City Ballet.

With such an accomplished family, it was hard not to feel like an imposter in their midst.

I hesitated for a moment at the conference room's entrance, waiting for Ian to step farther inside. Then I followed him down the small aisle to the seats near the other Hastings family members.

As the meeting began, I did my best to stay focused, taking notes while the board members discussed quarterly progress. Much of it went over my head, but I tried to keep up. A few executives expressed concern about the numbers falling short of projections, but when the conversation shifted to the upcoming business summit in Boston, the mood lightened again.

I quickly scribbled "Summer Business Summit: Boston?" in my notebook, adding a question mark to reflect my uncertainty. Before I could fully process it, I felt Ian lean closer, his breath warm against my ear.

"I'll tell you more about the summit after the meeting," he whispered, his voice low and intimate. "I'd like you to attend with me."

My heart skipped a beat as the nearness of him, combined with the intoxicating scent of his cologne, sent my mind spinning for a moment.

Did he just say he wanted me to go with him?

A work trip with my incredibly attractive boss?

"O-okay," I stammered, trying to shake off the haze and focus back on the meeting. *This is a business trip, Maddie. Strictly professional.*

But my mind had other ideas, suddenly conjuring up scenarios straight out of the contemporary romance novels that I loved.

You'd think after everything, I'd have learned not to get carried away. But no, instead of focusing on financial reports and investor strategies, I was imagining all kinds of *forbidden* moments—a business trip that turned into something...more.

That's what I get for reading on the weekends Grant was with his dad this past year instead of going on dates, I guess. My brain seemed to be convinced I was living in a rom-com, especially after that kiss I'd shared with Ian when we first met.

I'd basically had the most unfortunate meet-cute with my future boss that anyone could imagine, and now my mind wasn't letting it go.

But this wasn't a romance novel. This was real life.

In real life, I needed this job to pay my bills and take care of my son. So imagining a scenario where we'd end up at a hotel and, whoops, there's only *one bed* left? Yeah, that needed to stop.

I sighed internally, shoving down yet another scene my overactive imagination was trying to formulate. One where Ian and I were snowed in at some remote lodge, forced to stay the night together and... No. I needed to stop this.

Besides, it was June. It doesn't snow in Boston in the middle of June.

The meeting continued, the voices of the executives fading into the background as I mentally slapped myself back to reality. Ian was my boss, and I had no business entertaining these thoughts. Not if I wanted to keep this job and not complicate my already complicated life.

By the time the meeting wrapped up, I'd managed to fill my notebook with semi-coherent notes—though I'd probably have to decipher half of them later.

"So, about that business summit," Ian said, glancing over at me as we walked toward his office behind a few of the other executives. "I was thinking I could fill you in over lunch since it's coming up in just a couple of weeks. There's a great Thai place next door."

"It's happening that soon?" I asked, trying to keep the surprise out of my voice. "Like, at the end of the month?"

"It's the last week of June." He nodded, his gaze steady. "Sorry I didn't mention it sooner. My assistant usually handles my schedule, and with your recent hire and my friends' wedding last weekend, things have been a bit hectic. But we should get you up to speed."

"Yeah, that makes sense," I said, my mind already racing with what I'd need to arrange for Grant during the trip. "I can join you for lunch."

The sandwich, fruit, and yogurt I'd packed could wait another day.

But the idea of this trip happening in just two weeks? That was fast.

I'd need to see if Jaxon could take Grant that week. And if he couldn't, maybe Sloan could help. Or Lexi?

"Great," Ian said with an easy smile, completely unaware of the logistical gymnastics my brain was already working through. "I've got a call in a few minutes, and then we can head down together."

"Sounds good."

He opened the door to his office, and I sat at my desk, trying to calm the strange anticipation thrumming inside me.

It's just lunch, I reminded myself as I pulled up a training video I still needed to watch. *Nothing to get excited about.*

Since again...my life was not a romance novel.

5

IAN

"READY TO GO?" I asked Maddie as I stepped out of my office about twenty minutes later.

She quickly logged out of her computer and grabbed her bag. "Ready."

We stood in silence as we waited for the elevator, the quiet stretching between us. After a moment, I cleared my throat. "Sorry if I seem a little off today," I said, my tone softer than usual. "I think I'm still jet-lagged from Norway."

"Oh?" She tilted her head, seeming surprised that I'd offered an explanation. "Were the layovers bad?"

"No layovers, actually. My family and I took my dad's jet." I managed a small smile, finding it refreshing that she hadn't known that I rarely travelled commercial. "So I should've slept like a baby, but it was a long weekend." I rubbed the back of my neck, the weight of the weekend still lingering.

When I'd agreed to "give away" my good friend Addison at her wedding, standing in a place usually reserved for a father, I thought it would be a simple, straightforward task. Walking down the aisle in front of their closest friends should've been easy.

And technically, it was.

But watching the woman who'd stolen little pieces of my heart vow to love and cherish another man for the rest of her life? Well...that was harder than I'd expected.

Not that I wasn't happy for Addison and Evan—I was. They were perfect for each other, and I wanted nothing more than to see them get their happily ever after.

But during that year when Evan had gone missing, I'd gotten...*confused.*

For a fleeting, hopelessly romantic moment, I thought that if Addison couldn't have her happy ending with him, maybe— just maybe—there'd be a chance for me.

"Who was the wedding for?" Maddie asked, pulling me from my thoughts. "A family friend?"

"Yes. I'm actually friends with both the bride and the groom," I said, deciding to sidestep the whole *falling-for-my-best-friend's-girl* thing. "But I knew the groom first—we're business partners."

Her dark eyebrows lifted. "Does he work here, too, then?"

"No." I chuckled softly. "He actually owns The Garden— the club where we, uh, met." I glanced at her, and the knowing look that passed between us reminded me that while my love life might be as dry as the Sahara right now, that kiss... Well, it was not easy to forget. "I'm one of the investors. It's a side project, separate from my father's company."

"Seems like a pretty successful side project." She smiled, probably remembering how packed the club had been that night.

"It's been a good investment." I nodded. "Anyway, it was a big weekend, a lot going on, and I didn't get as much sleep as I should have."

I noticed her studying me for a moment, like she was trying to read between the lines. But since I really didn't need anyone knowing why I was feeling slightly heartbroken, I didn't explain further.

Sometimes it was good to remain a little mysterious. Especially if I wanted to maintain the facade of a boss who had his crap together.

The elevator doors slid open, and we stepped inside. It was crowded with business professionals from the floors above, forcing us to stand close. When Maddie's arm brushed against mine, I caught the subtle hitch in her breath and felt a smirk tug at my lips. That spark from The Garden? Yeah, it was still there.

Even if it *really* shouldn't be.

We stepped out into the lobby when the elevator hit the main level. Resisting the urge to place my hand behind my new assistant's waist to steer her toward the exit, I walked just a step ahead of Maddie to lead the way.

"I have a standing reservation here for Monday lunches," I said, holding the door open for Maddie as we stepped into the restaurant. "So the hostess should have a table waiting for us near the back."

As we waited for the hostess to greet us, I inhaled deeply, letting the familiar aroma of curry and spices wrap around me like an old, comforting friend. The restaurant was unassuming but elegant, with warm lighting that created a cozy, intimate atmosphere. The décor was minimalist—dark wooden tables, vibrant artwork of Thailand's landscapes on the walls, and bamboo accents that gave the place an authentic touch. It wasn't flashy, but the calm and welcoming energy made it feel like an escape from the high-pressure world I found myself navigating each week.

"Mr. Hastings!" The owner, Saylee, a petite woman with

graying hair, lit up as soon as she saw us, her smile bright and welcoming. "What a pleasure it is to have you here today."

"I can't seem to stay away," I said with a chuckle, knowing my weakness for their cuisine. "Your yellow curry is addictive."

"I'm glad you think so." She beamed up at me. Then casting a quick glance at Maddie, she said, "Let me show you and your guest to your table."

We followed Saylee down the aisle, weaving through tables of business professionals deep in conversation. I didn't miss the curious glances Maddie and I were getting—the way some eyes lingered a little too long. It was a familiar scene, part of the package that came with being Joel Hastings' son.

And, of course, my dating reputation didn't help.

I could imagine the Nancys and Lindas of New Haven speculating, wondering if Maddie was my latest fling. She certainly fit the type I'd often gone for: petite, shoulder-length brown hair, striking blue eyes.

In other words, *gorgeous*.

But I rarely mixed business with pleasure, and given her professional blouse and pencil skirt instead of the figure-hugging and cleavage-flaunting dresses my usual dates wore, it should've been obvious to anyone watching that this was strictly a business lunch.

"Do I have a wardrobe malfunction I didn't know about?" Maddie whispered, stepping beside me as she glanced at the table of twenty-somethings gawking at us. "Because they're all looking at me funny."

"No," I said, briefly inspecting her white blouse and gray pencil skirt before glancing toward the table she was eyeing. When I found a few familiar faces looking our way, I scrunched up my nose and added, "Sorry, that's probably my fault."

"It is?" Her eyebrows knitted together.

"Yes. I briefly dated the woman in the red dress," I said under my breath. "I think she and her friends are just curious about who you might be to me."

"Oh." Maddie's eyes widened as she did a double take at Tennille and her friends. "So they probably don't realize I'm your assistant?"

"Probably not."

"Which means they probably hate me?"

I chuckled. "I think that's a safe bet."

"Oh goody," Maddie muttered under her breath. And I had to resist the urge to pull her closer—to protect her from the prying eyes.

We reached our table, tucked slightly away from the crowd but still within view of those watchful stares. My gaze wandered to Tennille again, her long blonde hair and icy-blue eyes standing out. And just as expected, she was staring right at us, her perfectly manicured nails tapping rhythmically against her wine glass as she whispered something to her friend.

We'd met at a party last summer, and after hitting it off, had spent a whirlwind weekend in Costa Rica. The fling had fizzled almost as quickly as it started, but the jealousy in her eyes now suggested it had left more of a mark on her than I'd realized.

Which was part of my problem—too many brief flings leading to too many hurt feelings.

It was why I'd decided to cut myself off from all of it last August after I returned from my trip to Italy.

Okay fine, if I was being *really* honest, losing hope of ever having a chance with Addison *may* have also dulled the thrill of chasing after anyone else, especially after realizing how empty my superficial hookups had been. Getting my hopes up with my best friend's girl had shone a spotlight on everything I'd been missing.

Which was why my kiss with Maddie at the club had blindsided me. It was my first real flirtation since I'd sworn off those reckless impulses, my first slip-up in nearly a year.

And at first I'd thought it might be a sign—like maybe the universe was giving me the green light to get back into the dating game. That I'd learned my lesson and could pursue the captivating woman who'd shocked my black heart back to life.

But nope, it was simply a test. A cruel twist of fate since the woman I'd kissed in that moment of weakness was none other than my new assistant. About as off-limits as she could be, and a harsh reminder that I really needed to keep my hands to myself.

But even if I felt lonely at times, it was a worthwhile sacrifice since my performance at work had never been better. I hoped that by this time next year, when my dad announced his plans to take on more of a part-time advisor role at the company, I'd be the obvious choice to fill his shoes.

Which was just another reason why the business summit had to go well. It wasn't just about boosting our company's image—it was about showing everyone that Hastings Industries was still a force to be reckoned with in the business world and stronger than ever.

So instead of letting my mind drift to the drama of my past, I turned my focus back to Maddie. She had paused beside me, seemingly debating which seat to take.

"Here, let me get that for you," I offered, moving to pull out the chair closest to us.

"Oh. Th-thank you." Her eyes widened as though she wasn't used to anyone doing something as simple as pulling out a chair.

Had her ex not done things like that for her?

"Of course," I replied softly. Our eyes lingered for a

moment, and when a faint pink flush rose to her cheeks, I couldn't help the pull of attraction I felt.

She really was so pretty. Beautiful, yet somehow approachable in a hometown girl kind of way.

And though I had typically chased after flashy, shiny women in the past, this sweet single mom from a small town... Well, she rattled me.

And I was rarely rattled by anyone.

As I helped her into the chair, the faint scent of her perfume—citrusy and light—drifted between us. It was subtle but intoxicating, and though it was probably the same scent she'd been wearing when she'd kissed me at The Garden, it felt familiar for another reason.

Out of nowhere, a flicker of the past surfaced: a girl I'd met on a beach during spring break of my freshman year of college. Her face was blurred by time, but the scent—or maybe just the feeling of that moment—brought it back.

Weird. I furrowed my brow as I took my seat, trying to pin down why the memory had suddenly resurfaced when I hadn't thought about it in years.

Had the girl on the beach worn the same perfume as Maddie?

Possibly. Scents had a strange way of embedding themselves in memories.

But before I could dwell on it, Saylee appeared with menus, pulling me from my thoughts. "Here you go," she said. "Will you be having your usual, Mr. Hastings?"

"Yes, please." I nodded, grateful for the routine since my mind was a bit scattered at the moment. "And for my guest..." I glanced at Maddie, who was flipping through the menu. "Do you like curry?"

"I've actually never had it," she said with an insecure look in her eyes.

"You haven't?" I asked, surprised since yellow curry was basically a staple food of mine.

She nodded. "I probably shouldn't admit it, but McDonald's is more of the go-to restaurant for me and Grant these days."

"Ah yes. I suppose that makes sense," I said, grinning at her candidness. "I remember being quite fond of their five-star cuisine when I was younger."

In fact, Maddie would probably be surprised that for a while there, back before my mom fell in love with a billionaire, it was the only type of restaurant we could afford.

"Their chicken nuggets are the best," she said. "But..." She glanced down at her menu briefly. "If you say you're addicted to the yellow curry here, then I suppose I should give it a shot."

"Great choice."

"And how spicy would you like that?" Saylee asked Maddie as she jotted down our orders on a small notepad.

"Uhh..." Maddie's eyes widened as she looked to me for guidance.

"I'd recommend starting with number one," I suggested. "It's good for beginners."

"Ok, I'll try the number one spicy," Maddie said to Saylee.

Saylee smiled, taking our menus. "I'll have those ready for you soon."

When we were alone again, Maddie leaned back in her chair, her gaze flicking around the room again. "So do people always stare at you like this?"

"Pretty much." I chuckled, running a hand through my hair. "You get used to it after a while, though."

"I don't think I ever would," she said, her eyes growing wide.

I shrugged. "It comes with the territory. Between the family name and a few high-profile exes, people like to speculate."

"That must get exhausting." Her lips twisted into a thoughtful frown.

"It can be." I nodded, surprised by her understanding. Most people assumed I thrived on the attention—and, sure, there had been times I'd soaked it up. But Maddie seemed to see through the act.

As Maddie's eyes softened, her voice dropped to a more sincere tone. "It must be hard to figure out who's genuinely interested in you and who's just...curious."

"You could say that." I held her gaze for a moment longer than I intended, the candidness in her words striking a chord.

"I'll admit," she added, her voice quieter, "that after finding out you were my boss last week, I did a little research so I wouldn't embarrass myself again." She looked down, brushing a stray lock of hair behind her ear. "And well...it made me think about how hard it must be to live under a microscope and have so many people having an opinion on what you're doing."

She'd researched me?

I could only imagine what kind of stories she'd come across —those "billionaire playboy" headlines weren't exactly flattering.

Yeah, I certainly hadn't been thinking of my future reputation back when I was jetting off on weekend trips with beautiful women, chasing the thrill.

Looking back, I realized it had been more than just a thirst for adventure—it was an addiction. A way to drown out the emptiness that had always been there.

If I could get enough women to want me, then surely I mattered, right? Surely I was someone worth chasing.

Deep down, I knew what I'd really been trying to fill—that hollow part of me that had never healed after my biological father lost interest in seeing me, or when Margot decided to throw in the towel on me.

Every fling had been a way to prove my worth, to convince myself I was someone worth staying for.

There was probably some case study out there about trust-fund kids like me who were numbing their loneliness with sex and extravagant trips. Heck, maybe there was one on me already.

"It's not all bad," I said with a half-smile, trying to ease the tension. "But you're right." I cleared my throat, shifting in my chair as I decided to be a bit more honest. "All the attention and constant scrutiny does make genuine connections complicated."

Maddie's eyes met mine, a flicker of understanding passing between us.

And for a moment, it seemed like she was about to say something more, to possibly share something real about herself. But before she could, Saylee returned with our drinks, breaking the spell.

"Here you are," Saylee said, placing a glass of water in front of Maddie and a tumbler of sparkling water in front of me. "Your food should be out shortly."

"Thank you," we both said at the same time.

Saylee left again, and the comfortable silence between us resumed. I leaned back in my chair, studying her as she sipped her water.

"So," I said, shifting the conversation toward safer ground, "I know I invited you here to talk about the business summit—and I promise we'll get to that—but since you've apparently learned everything there is to know about me from your internet research..." I winked playfully. "I think it's only right that I get to know a little more about you."

"You want to get to know me?" She blinked, sounding genuinely surprised that I'd be interested in her story.

"We'll be working pretty closely, so I think it's a good idea to become better acquainted." I shrugged, keeping it light. "You're about to get a front-row seat to all the details of my life —the good, the bad, and the ugly—so it's only fair."

"That makes sense." She nodded.

I smirked, unable to resist adding, "Plus, it will help me with my new goal of actually getting to know a woman before inviting her out of town."

Her eyes widened, briefly shocked by what I'd said. But being quick with a comeback, she got a smirk on her lips and teased me right back by saying, "Are you trying to convince the ladies at that table over there that you've turned over a new leaf?"

"Partly." I chuckled, liking that even though we barely knew each other, there was an easy energy between us. "But mostly, I'm trying to prove it to myself."

"It is good to have our own backs, I suppose."

"It is," I said, thinking that as a single mom who had just moved away from her hometown with her son, she probably had to have her back more than I could guess. "So, when you're not at the office helping with my every demand, or making McDonald's runs with your son, what do you do for fun?"

"Honestly? Not much." Maddie laughed softly, the warmth in her voice genuine. "Between work and being a mom, there's not a lot of time for myself."

"I guess I can understand that," I said, thinking of the stories my mom had shared with me about being a single mom for that year before my stepdad came into the picture.

"But when I do manage to steal a few moments," Maddie continued, "I like to read. And bake. Cupcakes, mostly."

"Cupcakes, huh?" I grinned. "What's your specialty?"

"Pumpkin chocolate chip," she said, her eyes lighting up. "With cream cheese frosting."

"Are you a 'fall girlie' then?" I asked, familiar with the small corner of the internet where women shared their love of everything pumpkin spice.

"I'd like to say that I enjoy every season," she said, biting her lip. "But...I may go just a little overboard with the autumnal vibes once September hits."

"Those 'ber' months are pretty great," I said, having a fondness for that time of year myself.

"Are you sure you're not a fall enthusiast?" Maddie raised her eyebrows in surprise. "Because only a fall enthusiast would use such a term."

I chuckled. "So maybe I have a secret fall Instagram account of my own."

"Wait, seriously?" She furrowed her brow.

"No." I laughed. "If I did, you would know about it since you would be the one managing it for me."

She chuckled. "I guess that sounds about right."

"Anyway, you'll have to bring some of your pumpkin cupcakes to the office one day," I said. "We can have a special Autumn Equinox party or something."

"I can't tell if you're joking or not..." She narrowed her eyes.

"About pumpkin chocolate chip cupcakes with cream cheese frosting?" I asked. "Never."

Before she could respond, Saylee reappeared with our food, setting the plates in front of us.

"Here we go," Saylee said as the fragrant spices swirled up, filling the air. "Enjoy!"

"Thank you," I said, picking up my spoon to dig in as Maddie eyed her plate.

She leaned in for a cautious sniff, her eyes wide as if unsure what she was in for.

As she took her first bite, I watched the subtle change in her expression, her pink lips parting slightly in a way that I knew I shouldn't find attractive but did.

"Oh my gosh," she said after a pause, her voice full of surprise. "This is incredible!"

"Told you." I grinned, pleased by her reaction. "Once you start, there's no going back."

Maddie chuckled, taking another bite. "I think you might be right."

6

<hr>

MADDIE

IAN and I ate in comfortable silence for a moment, the easy-going, flirtatious vibe we'd had going ever since we met simmering just beneath the surface.

And even though I was starting to think that Ian probably just had the type of personality that oozed charisma whether he was trying to or not, I was having a hard time remembering that this charming, confident, and extremely attractive man was my superior. My boss.

That this man who had asked me about my hobbies and invited me to bring him baked goods was the same man who could fire me on the spot if I ever got my role in his life confused.

"So," I said, picking up my water glass, taking a small sip to ease the flutter of nerves in my stomach, "we should probably talk about the summit, right?"

"That is why I invited you here, I suppose," he said with a smile, setting down his spoon and seeming to gather his thoughts. "So, basically, the summer business summit in Boston is something I've been attending for the past three years. It's a pretty big event with about seven hundred attendees—primarily business owners hoping to grow their companies. And though I've taught a few classes at this particular event each year, this time I'm actually giving the keynote on Friday morning."

"Oh, wow," I said, my eyes going wide. "That sounds like a pretty big deal."

"It is." He nodded, a modesty in his tone that I hadn't expected. "I was honored to have been asked to speak."

Ian was only twenty-eight—just two years older than me—so either he really was phenomenal at what he did at Hastings Industries, or he was given a lot of clout because of his dad being a billionaire.

Though, after seeing just a tiny bit into what he did during my short time at his family's company, he did seem to be extremely competent. And if his reputation for charming women was any indication for how good of a salesman he could be, I was pretty sure he could sell a luxury yacht to someone living in the desert.

"Anyway," Ian said, drawing my attention back to him, "I'll be giving a presentation on 'How to Thrive in Any Economy' and then answering a few questions in the Q&A afterward."

I nodded, thinking that topic sounded like a really good one.

"The conference staff should be handling most of the setup and tech for my speech, so you can just sit in the audience and watch during that time if you want." He paused, seeming to remember something. "Well, actually, if you notice any good soundbites, if you could jot them down with the timestamp, that would be super helpful since our marketing team will be posting several short-form videos to my social media platforms, which they'll also add to my YouTube channel."

"Wait." I blinked, surprised. "You have a YouTube channel?" How had that not come up in my internet search last week?

"Technically, yes." He chuckled softly. "I mean, it's not live yet. But I've been stockpiling content for a few months, and my team is hoping to have it up and running by the summit."

"That's awesome," I said, trying to mask my surprise. Apparently, Ian had layers I hadn't even scratched the surface of yet.

"It's a passion project of mine," he said, his cheeks flushing slightly. "A way to help make business education more accessible for all kinds of business owners."

"That's actually really generous of you," I said, thinking most people would probably try to keep their business secrets behind a paywall.

"Well, I wouldn't call it completely generous," he said with a light chuckle. "Sure, I want to help people get better at business, but there's a selfish angle, too. If I can teach business owners how to grow their companies before they partner with Hastings Industries, it means they'll be that much more viable when we invest in them."

"Sounds like a genius plan to me."

"Thanks," he said, a flicker of genuine appreciation in his eyes. "I hope it works out. But if it completely flops, I'll just set all the content to private and pretend it never happened."

"I'm sure it'll be a hit." I laughed. "I know I've only worked with you for a couple of days, but from what I've heard around the office, you're pretty great at what you do."

"That's because I bribed them to say nice things." He smirked, leaning in slightly.

"Well, that makes sense." I couldn't help but like how down-to-earth he was despite coming from a world so completely different from where I'd come from. "And when is the summit, exactly?"

"Oh, sorry, I should've mentioned that first." He chuckled again, his eyes crinkling at the corners. "It starts on the last Thursday of this month."

I opened my phone to check the calendar. And when I saw how soon the last Thursday of the month was, my heart skipped a beat. "So it starts on the twenty-fourth?"

"Yeah." He nodded, taking a sip of water as if it wasn't a big deal.

Oh crap. That's next week!

Panic bubbled up in my chest as my mind spun through the arrangements I'd need to sort out in order to attend with him.

Ian must have sensed my sudden apprehension because his brow furrowed. Then, as if realizing the same thing I was, his eyes went wide and he said, "Oh sh—. That's next Thursday, isn't it?"

I nodded.

"Sorry about that. I think going out of town made me lose track of what day it actually is." He sighed. "Do you think that'll still work for you to come?"

"Y-yes, it should be...fine," I said, knowing that I couldn't afford to screw this up. And then, realizing it would be Jaxon's weekend with Grant, I added, "My son will actually be with his dad that weekend, so I'll just see if he can take him a couple of days earlier."

"Good." Ian looked relieved. "Your room should already be reserved. My old assistant handled all that when I was first booked. My keynote is on the second day, and that's the only thing I absolutely need to be at, but I'll be networking and meeting with clients the rest of the time."

"That makes sense," I replied, trying to take mental notes. "You said you're hoping to bring in quite a few prospective clients?"

"Yes." His expression sharpened with focus. "I tend to catch the interest of a lot of people at these things."

"I bet you do." Then I realized he'd meant it in terms of catching their attention in the form of them wanting to do business with his company and *not* in the romantic way my brain seemed to want to focus on way too much. So I cleared my throat and quickly added, "I mean, I bet this is a great way to bring in clients."

"It is..." He chuckled, his eyes crinkling at the corners like he knew I'd been thinking about how his good looks probably turned a lot of heads. "There will likely be quite a few companies hoping to work with us after the summit." He licked his lips before leaning forward. "That's where I'd like your help. Since it's hard for me to keep all the faces and names straight and remember each of my conversations, I'll need you to be right there with me taking notes."

"Okay, I can do that." I nodded, liking the idea of being useful.

"Of course, there will be a few companies that I'll know immediately that I don't want to continue a relationship with. So we'll come up with a special hand signal or something. Like, if I tug on my ear, it means I like them, so you should put a star next to their name in your notes. And if I don't think I'd want to work with them, I'll rub my nose, like this." He flicked the end of his nose with his pointer finger to demonstrate. "And you can put an exclamation point next to their name."

"Okay." I nodded. "Ear tug and star for good, nose brush and exclamation point for no." Then just because I didn't want to accidentally mix the signals up, I quickly pulled out my notebook from my bag and jotted it down.

"Anyway, I'm thinking we can drive up together on Wednesday afternoon and come back Sunday morning," Ian continued, and I quickly wrote down *Wednesday through*

Sunday in my notebook. "I should already have a few lunches and dinners scheduled with clients in the area, and then there will be a couple of mixers at the bar in the evenings." He paused for a moment, letting me jot down what he was saying.

When I was done writing, he added, "These things are usually pretty laidback and just a good time to touch base and strategize."

"Do you usually go to these things on your own?" I asked, glancing up from my notes. "Or should I plan to attend the dinners and mixers with you?"

"If you're up to the long days, I'd definitely like to keep you close."

And while I logically knew he was talking about keeping me close in a professional sense, my stomach flipped at his words—for a second, my mind drifted off to those same fantasies I had earlier, thinking about how it would be nice to "stay close" at the hotel during this business trip with my sexy boss.

Get your mind out of the gutter, Maddie, I mentally scolded myself, knowing Ian definitely wasn't planning to keep me close in *that* way.

Ian continued to go over a few more particulars, mentioning that there would also be some time where I could explore the city on my own during the summit since he didn't expect me to spend every waking minute with him.

"But it will definitely be a full three days," he said after explaining everything. "So I hope you're up to it."

"I'm used to being on the go all the time with my son, so I'm sure it shouldn't be too bad."

"Good." He smiled, that easy charm of his returning as he leaned back in his chair. "I'm looking forward to seeing how it all plays out. It's always fun to switch up my work schedule a bit."

"Definitely," I said, thinking that someone as dynamic as he was probably thrived in these kinds of settings.

Was it weird that I was almost bubbling with excitement over the idea of seeing a different side of my boss? And that the idea of putting in extra hours with him during those few days thrilled me?

Yeah...it was probably weird since at my old job, just making it through the forty-hour work week had been rough.

But there was something to be said about working a job that you actually enjoyed. (And yes...working *with* people you enjoyed being around.)

"Anyway, I think we've probably gone over everything I can think of. So, if you're ready, we can head back to the office."

"Yes, I'm ready," I said, gathering my notebook and pen from off the table and slipping them back into my bag.

Ian asked the waitress for the check when she passed by, and once everything was settled, we walked out of the restaurant side by side, the afternoon sun warming my skin as we headed back to the office.

"Any fun plans for this evening?" Ian asked as he pushed the button on the elevator that would take us up to our floor. "A McDonald's run with your son, perhaps?"

"No chicken McNuggets are in my plans, sadly," I said, adjusting the strap of my bag on my shoulder. "Actually, my aunt is having some people over tonight and was teasing me about trying to set me up with one of her friends. But since I'm still trying to recover from my last dating blunder, I'm pretty sure I'll just hang out for a bit before sneaking off to watch a movie with Grant or something."

"Your last dating blunder?" Ian raised an eyebrow, his grin playful. "Is that what you've decided to call the night we first met?"

"Yes." I chuckled, shaking my head. "I mean, thankfully, I haven't added any others to my list since then."

"Hey." Ian nudged me with his elbow, amusement dancing in his eyes. "At least the last blunder made for a fun story."

"One which I will be keeping to myself, thank you very much." I shot him a look, trying to hide my own embarrassment.

He chuckled, his grin widening. "Oh, was I supposed to keep it a secret? Because I'm pretty sure it made for quite the entertaining story last week when I told my family I'd accidentally made-out with my new assistant."

"Wait..." I froze, the blood draining from my face. "S-so does everyone know what happened?"

Was that why his mom and dad kept looking at me during the board meeting this morning?

Oh crap, oh crap, oh crap.

They probably thought I was one of those girls who tried to sleep her way to the top.

"I'm kidding," Ian said, holding his hands up like he knew I was on the verge of a heart attack. "The only person I mentioned it to is my friend Owen since he was asking about the girl I'd hit it off with at the club."

"He saw us?" I groaned.

"He did."

"So does that mean there were probably a lot of people who saw us?"

"It's nothing to worry about." He laughed softly. "I mean, it's not like it was anything the patrons of The Garden haven't seen me doing before. I'm sure we just blended into the scene at the club."

Nothing he hadn't been seen doing before.

As in...he probably kissed random girls at the club on a weekly basis.

Ugh, why did the idea of him hooking up with random women bother me so much?

"But you said your friend mentioned seeing us...?" I asked, my brain apparently wanting to reassure itself that our kiss had been at least somewhat noteworthy among the dozens of make-out sessions Ian had probably already had this summer.

"Well, that's just because Owen was bartending that night and he notices things like that."

"Okay..." I sighed, not exactly the reassurance I was hoping for. But it would make sense that Ian would assume I was worried about being seen kissing him at all since that was what I *should* be most worried about in this situation.

I shouldn't be wondering how memorable it was for him and how our stolen moment ranked among all the other kisses he'd had recently.

"Trust me, no one else will remember." Ian put a hand on my shoulder, giving it a reassuring squeeze.

And while I knew he was trying to calm me with the gesture, it only made my heart skyrocket further.

Because yeah, Ian Hastings was touching me. Like it was no big deal.

Like it was a completely normal thing to do.

And he didn't seem to notice the way my pulse was suddenly racing because after letting his hand drop, he continued by saying, "And besides, you have that cute friend of your aunt to look forward to meeting tonight. Any gossip about us will be forgotten once they see you strutting around Eden Falls with a new hottie."

"Har har." I rolled my eyes, trying to push away the butter-flies fluttering in my stomach.

"Hey, you never know. It could be your lucky night." Ian grinned, the mischievous glint in his eyes unmistakable.

"I highly doubt that," I muttered, still feeling the heat from where his hand had rested on my shoulder.

The elevator doors slid open, and as we stepped inside, all I could think about was how I liked the flirtatious banter with Ian way too much.

Which meant, I should probably consider talking to Sloan's "single dad" friend tonight. Because even if I wasn't exactly looking to date right now, it wouldn't hurt to at least try and get someone else on my mind. Anything to help distract me from the undeniable pull I felt toward my boss.

7

MADDIE

"IF YOU KEEP COOKING us meals like this, I'm going to be less motivated to find a place for Grant and me to move into," I teased Sloan as I loaded the last plate into the dishwasher, still stuffed from the garlic butter chicken, roasted vegetables, and rosemary potatoes she had made for Grant and me.

"It's all part of my evil plan." Sloan grinned as she pulled a fruit tray from the fridge to carry into the backyard where her friends would all be gathering in a few minutes. "After years of only cooking for myself, it's been nice having you two around. You're the perfect taste-testers for my new recipes."

"Well, if you keep this up, we may never move out." I chuckled as I closed the dishwasher.

"I'll hold you to that." She winked. Then after glancing at the clock on the stove, she asked, "Hey, everyone should be here soon. Would you mind pulling the charcuterie board out of the fridge and carrying it out to the backyard?"

"Sure." I nodded, opening the fridge and spotting the tray of meats and cheeses neatly arranged on a wooden board. "I'll bring it right out."

The evening air was warm when I stepped outside a moment later, but thankfully, not too humid. Sloan's backyard was cute—a cozy patio with a built-in fire pit, outdoor string lights glowing softly overhead, and a patch of grass where Grant and I had kicked around a soccer ball a few times this past week.

As I set the charcuterie board on the table, I glanced up to see Grant walking toward me from the side of the house, holding the stick he'd been carving.

"Hey, Grant," I called over to him, knowing he sometimes needed a heads up before transitioning into a new activity. "Aunt Sloan's friends will be here soon, so you've only got a few more minutes to play outside before we need to keep out of the backyard."

"Okay," he said, not looking up from his stick. And I couldn't help but smile at my cute little boy, his hair messy with a few leaves stuck in it like he'd climbed a tree to retrieve the stick he was carving.

I'd just gotten a call this afternoon from the summer program we'd applied for and heard that he had gotten in, which was such a relief.

I had worried about making him start over with new friends at a new school in a brand-new town, but hopefully, with the summer program having a lot of kids in it from the elementary school he'd be attending this fall, he'd be able to make friends before too long.

"Two more minutes, okay?" I called to Grant, just to remind him before heading back in.

He didn't respond, but that was typical—eight-year-old boy selective hearing and all.

I was about to head back inside when Sloan appeared in the backyard, leading three people behind her. There was a woman with dark red hair, another with a short blonde bob, and a man with curly auburn hair and glasses.

Sloan waved them over to me. "Maddie, these are my friends Rosalyn, Jennifer, and Freddy," she said, pointing to each of them in turn. Then gesturing to me, she said, "And this is my niece Maddie who just moved to town."

"Nice to meet you, Maddie," Rosalyn said with a warm smile.

"Nice to meet you, too," I said, bobbing my head and smiling at each of them.

"Anything we can help with?" Freddy asked, glancing around the backyard.

Sloan shook her head as she looked over the setup. "I think we're good. I just need to grab the wine from the fridge."

"I can grab that for you," I offered quickly. No need to make her run back inside when I was already halfway there.

"Thanks, Maddie," Sloan said gratefully. "There should be three bottles on the bottom shelf."

I headed back inside toward the kitchen, but just as I was about to walk in, the doorbell rang. Sloan probably couldn't hear it from outside, so I went to get the door. When I pulled it open, I found myself looking up at a handsome man who was probably close to thirty with chestnut-brown hair and green eyes. He stood there, holding a bowl of what looked like cheese dip in one hand and a bag of pretzel crisps in the other.

He blinked at me, looking surprised, then glanced past me at the house as if double-checking he was at the right place.

"Are you one of Sloan's friends?" I asked before he could say anything.

He nodded, his shoulders relaxing. "Yeah."

"Great! I'm Sloan's niece. She's just out back," I said, stepping aside so he could walk through.

"Thanks," he said, still seeming a little thrown off but grateful.

As he headed outside, I made my way back to the fridge, grabbed the bottles of wine Sloan had mentioned, and carried them out to the backyard.

Sloan and her friends were all chatting around the fire pit, lounging in the patio chairs she had arranged. After placing the wine bottles in the ice bucket next to the wine glasses, I glanced over at Grant. He was sitting on the grass, ripping out handfuls of it to add to one of his grass piles.

Oh no. Not again.

I hurried over to him and crouched down, keeping my voice low. "Hey, buddy, don't rip out Aunt Sloan's grass, okay?"

He looked up at me, the brown eyes that he'd inherited from his dad full of innocence, like I hadn't already asked him not to rip out Sloan's grass three other times since moving in. But thankfully, he dropped the handful he'd just torn out and seemed to decide that he would stop...for tonight, at least.

"Is it time to read books now?" he asked, seeming to notice only then that we weren't the only people in the backyard.

"Sure." I nodded. "We can read a few books before the movie." Since yeah, if my boy who had struggled with reading this past school year was asking to read books with me, I was for sure going to take him up on it. "Let's go pick out some books."

Grant took a moment, glancing at his stick and pocketknife on the grass nearby. Knowing how tempted he might be to start carving indoors if he brought the stick inside, I said, "How about we leave the stick outside for the night? You can finish your masterpiece tomorrow, all right?"

He picked up the stick that currently resembled what my brain really hoped wasn't supposed to be a phallic object. After standing up, he carefully set it on the edge of one of Sloan's planter boxes.

"Maddie, you should come hang out with us!" Sloan called out as we walked past her and her friends.

I bit my lip, unsure of what to do. Sloan's friends all looked like they were a few years older than me, closer to her age. But even if I wasn't sure how much I'd have in common with all of these thirty-somethings, it *would* be nice to have some adult time. Aside from Ian, most of my co-workers lived in New Haven, and I hadn't really talked to anyone from Eden Falls yet.

But then, I glanced down at Grant and knew I should probably spend some time with him before he called it a night.

"I'm going to read a few books with Grant first," I told Sloan, feeling torn. "But I might be able to come out later while he watches a movie."

"Perfect," Sloan said with a warm smile.

I smiled back and led Grant inside.

"All right, buddy, go pick out a few books for us," I said when we made it to Sloan's cozy living room.

Not needing to be told twice, he darted over to the coffee table where Sloan kept a basket of books. Once he found a few favorites, we settled on the couch. I couldn't keep the grin off my lips when he opened up Dr. Seuss's book *Fox in Socks* first since it had always been one of my favorites, too.

I mean, who could resist the fun challenge of reading all those tongue twisters as fast as possible? Definitely not me.

And now that Grant was becoming a better reader, I could tell he was getting into it, too.

We were just getting to the part about the Tweedle Beetle battle when there was another knock on the door. "Hold on a sec, buddy," I said, sliding off the couch.

I padded across the carpet and when I opened the door, I found the guy with glasses and curly hair that Sloan had pointed out at The Garden as one of the guys she'd dated briefly standing next to another guy with slick, jet-black hair.

"Hi," I said, offering a smile to them both, curious why she'd invited an ex over. "You must be here for Sloan?"

"Yes." The guy with jet-black hair held out his hand. "I'm Owen. I used to teach at the school Sloan works at."

"Owen, huh?" I asked, shaking his hand, thinking his name sounded familiar for some reason. Had she mentioned him before?

"And I'm Bash," the other guy introduced himself. "I'm guessing you're the niece Sloan mentioned moving here."

"Ah, yes. That's me." I nodded. "My son and I are staying with her for a little bit until we find a place of our own."

"Well, welcome to Eden Falls," Owen said. "I hope you'll enjoy living here."

And I might have just been imagining things, but there was an amused look in his deep brown eyes that I didn't understand.

Had I missed something?

After a brief, awkward silence, I cleared my throat and stepped aside. "Sloan's out back. You can head through the house if you'd like."

They thanked me and walked inside. I watched them go, still wondering why Owen had acted like he was in on an inside joke I didn't know about.

Maybe he was just an eccentric guy and I was just reading into things?

Shaking it off, I returned to the couch where Grant was waiting patiently. We finished reading a couple more books before I took him upstairs to brush his teeth and change into his pajamas. Once he was ready, I grabbed my iPad from the dresser in the room we were sharing and got him cozy on the bed, setting him up to watch a movie.

"Remember, you've got your new summer camp tomorrow, so as soon as the movie's over, it's time for bed, okay?" I said, kissing him on the head after switching on the lamp next to him.

"Okay." He nodded, his eyes already glued to the screen.

But even though he'd said he'd turn off the screen once the movie was over, I knew my devious little boy well enough that I quietly set a timer on my phone to remind me to check on him, just in case he tried to sneak in another show after it ended.

After one last look at the cute boy who had given me a reason to keep going even when things had sometimes been unbearable over the past few years, I turned off the main light above and then headed back down the stairs.

As I stepped outside, the warm evening air greeted me, along with the sounds of happy conversation and the crackle of the fire. The sun was just starting to set, painting the sky with breathtaking streaks of pink and orange. The whole scene felt like something out of a movie, peaceful and perfect.

Sloan spotted me lingering on the back steps. Waving me over, she called, "We saved you a chair!" before pointing to an empty seat between the blonde woman I'd met earlier and the guy who'd brought the cheese dip and pretzel crisps.

"Perfect," I said, stepping onto the patio. "Just let me grab some of those amazing appetizers first."

I made my way to the table full of goodies, the smell of campfire filling the air. I helped myself to some fruit, meats, and cheese, then poured a glass of wine, hoping it would help settle the nervous flutter in my chest.

"Hey! I'm Jennifer." The blonde I'd briefly met earlier turned to me with a bright smile when I took my seat. "Sloan mentioned that you're actually moving here and not just visiting. Do you mind if I ask what brings you to Eden Falls?"

"Oh, of course," I said after taking a sip of my wine. "My

grandparents are actually from here, which I'm sure you must have guessed since Sloan is my aunt. Anyway, I've always really liked it here, and so when I saw a job listing at an office in New Haven a while back, I decided it was time to take a chance on living here."

"Oh, I love that," Jennifer said. "I'm also a transplant. I grew up in Wisconsin but have been here for about five years."

"That's cool."

I was about to ask her what had brought her here since Wisconsin was pretty far away, but then Jennifer asked, "So, where do you work? I work at an office in New Haven, too, so I wonder if I've heard of your company."

"I work at Hastings Industries," I said, tucking some hair behind my ear.

"Hastings Industries?" Jennifer's eyes lit up at the name. "Well, I'm definitely familiar with that. I don't know how anyone in Eden Falls couldn't know about that company."

"You're Ian's new assistant, right?" a male voice said from the other side of Jennifer. When I looked to see who had asked the question, I found Owen leaning forward, his eyes lighting up in recognition.

"Yeah..." I furrowed my brow. "I work for Ian Hastings."

And then, it hit me. Ian had mentioned having a friend named Owen who was bartending at The Garden the night we met. And when I saw the knowing look in Owen's eyes, like he was probably thinking about the kiss he'd apparently witnessed me giving his friend, my cheeks suddenly flamed hot.

"So, how have things been going with Ian anyway?" Owen asked. "Last I heard was that things got off to an interesting start."

My face grew even warmer. *Why is he asking me this?*

Was he trying to do some sort of detective work for his

friend? To see if I was going to talk about our now forbidden meeting in front of all of these people?

Not knowing if I should really be super open about anything, since it was a possibility any slip-up could get me fired, I forced a smile and tried to tread carefully as I said, "It's going all right. Some...awkward situations when you first start somewhere new, you know? But he's a good boss."

"That's good to hear," Owen said, his smile widening. "Ian's my best friend, so it's nice to know he's treating you well. If he gives you any trouble, let me know and I'll whip him into shape."

I chuckled awkwardly. Okay, so maybe this hadn't been a test at all.

Maybe he just wanted to know if his friend was a good boss.

"So, where are you from?" the guy on the other side of me asked. "I'm Theo, by the way."

"Hi, Theo," I said, thankful for the shift in the conversation. "I'm actually from a small town in New York called Ridgewater."

"Ridgewater, you say?" he asked, like he was trying to decide if it rang a bell. "What part of New York is it in?"

"Central New York. Between Syracuse and Ithaca."

"Ah, nice."

"So, how do you know Sloan?" I asked, seizing the moment to turn the focus off myself.

"I actually first met Sloan at the academy." He smiled, revealing a cute dimple that I hadn't noticed before. "I was a house dad at the boarding school—got free room and board while I was in law school."

"Smart." I chuckled, appreciating his practical side. "Not a bad deal at all."

"I thought so," he said with a grin. "It kept me from racking up student loans, at least."

Was it weird that I found it oddly attractive that Theo had gotten his law degree without any debt? Because yeah, after being married to a man who couldn't hold down a steady paycheck, a man who knew how to avoid debt was definitely a turn-on.

With Jaxon, money always seemed to slip through his fingers. We were constantly scrambling to pay the bills, always one step behind.

I hadn't necessarily married him for financial stability since we were so young when we got married, but a little extra cushion would've done wonders for my stress levels through the years. There's only so much robbing Peter to pay Paul you can do before you had to face reality and make the hard choices.

I took a deep breath, pushing away the familiar frustration that always bubbled up when I thought about Jaxon's failed business ventures and empty promises.

That chapter was closed now. And even though I was still working to pay off some of the debts he'd stuck me with, I had a good job now and his financial irresponsibility couldn't hurt me anymore.

"And what do you do now?" I asked. "Are you using that law degree you were working on?"

"I am." He nodded, licking his lips. "I'm a corporate lawyer now."

"Oh nice," I said. But since the extent of my knowledge of what corporate lawyers did came from binging *Suits* a few years ago, I asked, "What exactly do you do?"

"Essentially, I'm the legal expert who ensures businesses operate within the boundaries of the law and navigate complex legal situations."

"Oh, of course. That makes sense," I said, even though his

explanation was a little over my head. "That sounds like a lot of responsibility."

"It is," Theo said, nodding thoughtfully. "Definitely keeps me on my toes, but I like it."

I smiled at that, appreciating his down-to-earth demeanor. We continued chatting for a bit, the conversation light and easy as the warm evening breeze carried the smell of campfire and the low hum of voices around us. It felt nice to relax, to feel like I was starting to make connections in this new town.

But then, just as Theo was starting to tell me about his two-year-old daughter, the sound of the back door opening drew my attention. And when I turned to see who was joining the party, my breath caught in my throat.

Because it was none other than Ian.

What was he doing here?

Had Sloan invited him without telling me?

I had no idea. But based on the surprise that flickered across my boss's features when his brown eyes locked with mine, he hadn't expected to see me here, either.

"Ian!" Owen said, raising from his seat when he noticed his friend. "You made it!"

Had Owen invited Ian, then?

And was that before or after he realized I was here?

"You and Bash said it was the place to be tonight," Ian said, stepping onto the patio and walking toward Owen with a confident stride. "So of course I had to swing by."

"Here, you can sit by me," Owen said, gesturing to the seat between us that Jennifer had deserted when she'd gone inside to escape the campfire smoke.

Ian glanced at the empty chair beside me, hesitating for a second before nodding and saying, "Sounds good."

I shifted in my seat, acutely aware of how close he would be sitting. The last time we'd been this close in a social setting, things had escalated quickly. And since I was slightly tipsy from the wine, I wasn't so sure I'd be able to keep my cool.

Not with the way my body was reacting to his mere presence.

"Didn't expect to see you here," Ian murmured as he took the seat beside me, his arm brushing lightly against mine. And while his tone was casual, I could tell that he was just as caught off guard at seeing me here tonight as I was to see him.

"Yeah..." I swallowed, trying to act like his close proximity hadn't just sent my pulse racing. "I could say the same for you."

For the next few minutes, the conversation flowed around us, but I barely heard a word of it. All I could focus on was the way Ian was sitting so close, his presence sending my thoughts into a whirlwind. His familiar scent of sandalwood and something distinctly him enveloped me, stirring up memories of our kiss—of the way my heart had pounded against my chest in that one stolen moment.

I didn't dare glance at him again, afraid he might see right through me.

But then, when Bash made a joke and the group burst into laughter, Ian leaned in, his voice low so only I could hear. "So does this mean that Sloan is the aunt you mentioned earlier today?"

"Yes." I nodded. "She's my mom's youngest sister."

"Interesting," Ian said. "When I saw you walk back to her at the club, I just assumed you two were friends."

He'd watched me walk over to Sloan after our kiss? Why did the thought of his gaze following me all the way across the club suddenly make me feel breathless?

But trying to appear unfazed by that idea, I said, "No, she's just my cool, young aunt who's letting me crash with her for a bit."

Ian leaned even closer, and in an even more hushed tone,

he whispered, "Is Theo the guy she's trying to set you up with?" before nodding at Theo who was now chatting with the woman on the other side of him.

What?

"You said earlier today that your aunt was planning to set you up with one of her friends tonight."

"Oh, right," I said, my mind scrambling from his nearness and the way his warm breath felt on my ear. "W-we were just talking."

"Well, Theo's a cool guy," Ian said with a shrug. "I mean, not quite as awesome as myself, but since we can't exactly go down that road, he's a good second choice."

My jaw dropped, and I stared at him, stunned. *Did he seriously just say that?*

Had my *boss* just suggested that he was a better option?

My pulse quickened at the thought, and for a split second, I forgot where we were, lost in the implications of what he'd said. But coming back to my senses, I said, "Well, I guess I should feel honored you consider yourself the gold standard." I gave him a sidelong glance, trying to keep my tone light. "But as you pointed out, we definitely can't go down that road."

His lips quirked up into a small, teasing smile. "Doesn't hurt to acknowledge the obvious, though, does it?"

I swallowed hard, trying to ignore the way my whole body was buzzing just from this flirtatious interaction.

His confidence, his easy charm—it was almost enough to make me forget that he was my boss, and that as tempting as this banter was, it could only lead to trouble.

"No, I suppose not," I said, forcing a casual shrug even though my heart was racing. "But I think you might be overestimating yourself."

Okay, what was I even saying? I really needed to stop it

with these comebacks or I was going to end up with some kind of disciplinary action for sure.

But instead of firing me on the spot, Ian's eyes flashed with amusement. Then leaning in close enough that the warmth of his breath brushed my cheek, he mumbled, "If I didn't know better, I'd say you were trying to challenge me."

"Maybe..." I shrugged, feigning calm even though I was all shaky with nerves.

"Well," he said, licking his lips. "It's just too bad that you work for me. Otherwise I'd be more than up to the challenge."

My heart stuttered as I imagined what it would be like for him to make good on what he was hinting at—to take my hand and pull me away from the group so he could show me once more what it was like to get lost in his embrace.

To continue what we started that first night we'd met and leap down the path we might have taken if I hadn't been sitting at the desk outside his office the next Monday.

Would he have pursued me? Would he have contacted Sloan that very day and asked how he could get in contact with the mysterious girl he'd seen her with the Friday before?

Ah, I really wish I could have found that out. Because even if I wasn't ready for something serious, another stolen kiss with this man—this magnetic, impossible man—might have been worth the risk.

But that can't happen, I told myself, reining my fantasies back in. *Because no matter how tempting he is, keeping your stable job is what you actually need right now.*

So instead of saying something reckless like, *Maybe breaking the rules would be worth it just this once,* I met his gaze and said, "It's too bad we'll never know if you're the superior choice, since proving that would involve breaking all sorts of rules."

"Yes," he said, his expression shifting as his gaze flicked down to my lips. Then bringing his eyes back to mine, he mumbled, "It really is too bad."

8

———

IAN

"DID you guys happen to catch Alessi's show while you were in Norway?" Bash asked Owen and me as we all stood near the refreshments table in Sloan's backyard, sipping our drinks. "Because as weird as it is having my ex write breakup songs about me, I'm kinda bummed I didn't take time off to go to the wedding with you guys and catch her performance."

"You two dated for like, what, two months? Almost five years ago." Owen shot him a look, nudging him in the ribs. "You sure you're not just wishing those hits are about you?"

"Who else would the lyrics *'Under the firework sky, your eyes meet mine, a secret spark ignites, but we're out of time'* be about?" Bash smirked, undeterred by our more practical friend. "We literally started dating after that Fourth of July party on Ian's yacht. Who else was she igniting secret sparks with?"

"You've really dissected her new album, haven't you?" I chuckled, taking a sip of my whiskey. "But did you also consider that there were plenty of us on that yacht? I mean, what if she was eyeing Owen? Or, I don't know, someone even hotter like me?"

"You think she wrote a song about you?" Bash scoffed, rolling his eyes. "Yeah, right. Plus, I seem to recall you two being too busy with your dates that night to notice any looks from Alessi."

"Pretty sure my date was mad at me that night," I said, recalling the Fourth of July party Bash was talking about. The one where we'd all planned to stay overnight on my parents' yacht, but instead, I had to take my date back to shore in the middle of the night because, in her words, she couldn't stand to look at my 'ridiculously perfect face' anymore since it 'didn't come with anything beneath the surface.'

Yeah...that one had stung a little—hurt my fragile player heart.

"Fine." Bash raised his hands in surrender. "So maybe you weren't charming your date that night. But do you seriously think it's more likely for the song to be about you over me?"

"Okay, so it's probably not about me," I said. And I probably should have just left it at that. But since I could never resist pushing Bash's buttons, I had to add, "But that still doesn't mean it's about you, either. I mean, for all we know, those forbidden glances could've been between her and Miles."

"Miles?" Bash stared at me like I'd just suggested something heinous. "You sicko. He's her *stepbrother*."

And man, the scandalized look on his face was totally worth it.

"Okay, fine," I said, unable to keep in my laugh. "So, maybe there's a *small* chance the number one pop song in the world right now is about you."

"Thank you," Bash said, his expression turning smug. "I'll sleep soundly tonight now that that has been settled."

"Good to know," I said, taking another sip of my drink.

"And to answer your original question," Owen chimed in,

"sadly, we weren't able to catch Alessi's concert over the weekend since we had to fly out first thing Sunday morning."

"Ah, too bad," Bash said, nodding. "Miles told me he was going. Said they were gonna sightsee before she heads to Vienna for her next show."

Owen nodded. "Is Miles taking their parents to Vienna for her next shows, too?"

"I think so," Bash said. "At least I think that's what he said since he doesn't have to be back in Connecticut for the Sentinels training camp for a few more weeks."

They were just diving into a conversation about Miles's NFL team and their playoff chances with him as the new quarterback when Maddie's laugh cut through the air.

And even though I'd purposely left my seat beside her earlier because the sexual tension had already been too thick between us this evening, I had to know who had made her laugh.

Dare I hope it was Sloan or Jennifer making more jokes tonight?

But nope, when I glanced her way, I instantly regretted it because instead of finding her engaged in girl talk with the other ladies like I'd hoped, there she was, sitting close to Theo. Like they'd just picked up where they'd been before I'd joined the party.

Ugh was the only word that came to mind as a twinge of jealousy twisted in my stomach.

Why did I suddenly want to go sit next to her again? She was my assistant. I should know better than to get involved with someone I worked with. Yet every time I got within a few feet of her, it was like all my common sense evaporated and I couldn't stop the flirty comments from slipping out.

Why did I even come here? I didn't have time for garden parties this week.

Not when I was supposed to be working on my presentation for the summit, reworking the section that had been driving me nuts for weeks.

But of course, when I'd gotten Owen's text about Sloan's party, I'd jumped at the chance to ditch my work and clear my head.

Except now, standing here, all I could think about was Maddie.

I glanced at Owen, and when I saw him smirking at me as if he could read my thoughts, I couldn't help but wonder if he'd invited me here for some weird entertainment.

Was this whole thing planned?

Turning toward him, I crossed my arms and asked, "Why'd you invite me to this party anyway? You trying to set me up for an awkward situation with my assistant or something?"

"Nah, man." Owen blinked, all innocent-like, before shrugging. "Bash and I just figured you've been working too hard. Thought you could use a night with friends."

I gave him a look that said I wasn't buying it for a second. Bash caught my expression and grinned before raising his hands in mock surrender. "Okay, fine. Maybe when Owen told me that Sloan's niece is the girl we saw you making out with, we might've been a little curious to see how you two acted around each other now that she's your assistant."

"You guys are evil," I muttered, rolling my eyes.

"Hey, we gotta get our kicks and giggles somehow," Bash said with a shrug, completely unapologetic.

Owen leaned in a little closer. "You do seem to be in better spirits than you were at Addie and Evan's wedding, though. Are you sure you two are keeping things...above board?"

"Of course we are," I said, though my mind drifted. *Am I actually in better spirits now than I was at the wedding?* I had a good day today, I couldn't deny that. And yes, a lot of it had to do with the dynamic between Maddie and me. It was fun. Easy, even.

I glanced back toward her again. She and Theo were still chatting like old friends, smiles and laughter flowing effortlessly between them.

Was that how she was with all guys? Had things been so easy between us because it was just how Maddie was?

Not that it should matter, I reminded myself. Maddie was an employee. Nothing more.

I took a slow sip of my whiskey, letting the warmth settle in my chest. But when I flicked my gaze back to Owen and Bash, I noticed them both watching me, amusement all over their faces.

Yep, they'd totally caught me staring at her.

"Shut it," I said before either of them could get a word out.

Which just made their smirks even bigger since they were clearly enjoying the fact that I was hung up on someone I couldn't touch.

Man, I really should've stayed home tonight.

I walked into Sloan's kitchen, carefully balancing a few wine glasses in my hands after most of her guests had said their goodbyes.

Yep, even though I probably should've left the party two hours ago, somehow I stayed until the very end and was now even helping with the cleanup.

"Ian, you really don't need to help," Sloan said, glancing up from the charcuterie tray she was currently drying off with a towel. "I know you've got work early in the morning."

"It's fine," I said, stepping beside her to set the glasses near the sink. "Just because you hosted doesn't mean you need to be left with all the work."

Wow, I was really leaning into this domestic role tonight, wasn't I? Usually, I had staff to handle post-party cleanups for me, but after seeing Theo help put away the table and chairs, I'd apparently decided to turn over a new leaf.

And even now, ten minutes after Theo and everyone else had left the party, I was still here, trying to play the better man.

Because I liked to help my friends... And definitely not because I was hoping to catch another glimpse of my cute assistant before heading out.

"Okay," Sloan said, a grateful smile lifting her lips. "If you really don't mind helping, I'd appreciate it if you could use those tall genetics of yours and put this in the cupboard above my fridge."

"Of course," I said, grateful for the excuse to linger longer. So when she handed me the long, rectangular board, I opened the cupboard she'd indicated to stow it. "How did you get this out in the first place?" I asked when I'd completed the task, glancing at Sloan who stood nearly a foot shorter than me.

"Um..." She made a face like it should've been obvious. "Us non-tall folk have these weird contraptions called stools to reach the places you giants take for granted."

"Us giants?" I chuckled. "You make it sound like I'm freakishly tall."

"Aren't you, like, six-two?"

"Six-three," I corrected, fighting a smile.

"Yeah, well, even if that's the average height for the men in your close circle, that's still pretty tall to us regular humans," she teased.

"I guess you're right." I closed the cupboard and checked my watch. It was nearly eleven.

Where was Maddie? Had she fallen asleep when she'd

gone upstairs to tuck her son in? She'd disappeared up there almost an hour ago.

I sighed. Maybe I should head home. Staying any longer would only make it extremely obvious that I was just trying to steal another conversation with Maddie.

I was just about to reach for my keys in my pocket and call it a night when the creak of footsteps sounded on the floor above.

Is she still awake after all? I wondered, my heart kicking up.

And so, even though I knew I was probably making my intentions really obvious, I glanced over to the wine glasses I'd left on the counter and asked Sloan, "Where do you keep the dish soap? I'll hand-wash those glasses for you."

Had I ever hand-washed a dish in my life before?

No... But it couldn't be that hard, could it?

Sloan chuckled. "You really don't have to do that. I can toss them in the dishwasher tomorrow."

"It's nothing," I said, moving toward the sink to make my point. "Besides, there's nothing better than waking up to a clean kitchen, right?"

"I suppose there isn't." Her lips quirked up into a half-smile, like she could see right through me. "All right, the soap and sponge are under the sink."

I was just reaching for the sponge when I heard another soft creak, this time on the stairs.

She's coming down after all.

Anticipation thrummed in my veins, and I straightened a little too quickly.

Sloan must have noticed because after giving me a knowing look, she said, "If you feel like drying the glasses, too, the dish towels are in the left drawer."

"Perfect," I said, trying to keep my tone casual even though my focus was already shifting toward the stairs.

And then, just a moment later, Maddie appeared at the bottom of the steps, her gaze sweeping the room before landing on me. My attention sharpened the moment I saw her, and from the way Sloan's Cheshire-cat grin grew, she definitely hadn't missed it.

"Well, I think it's about time for me to head to bed," Sloan said with a mischievous lilt in her voice. "Ian was so kind to offer to wash the rest of the dishes so we can wake up to a clean kitchen. Isn't that thoughtful of him?"

"Oh, you don't have to do that." Maddie stepped farther into the kitchen, thankfully missing the obvious hints Sloan was dropping. "I came down here to finish cleaning up."

"Perhaps you two can work together, then?" Sloan raised an eyebrow.

Maddie looked at me and shrugged. "Okay, sure."

I nodded, trying to keep my cool, even though the idea of spending a few more minutes alone with her had me far more excited than it should have.

9

IAN

COME ON, *Hastings, get it together.* I took a breath, giving myself a mental shake as I stepped up to the counter. *It's just washing dishes, not closing a multi-million-dollar deal.*

I grabbed the first wine glass from the counter, trying to act like I'd done this a million times and not like I'd always had a housekeeper to wash my dishes for me.

I mean, it's not like it's rocket science? How hard could it be?

"So, what's the trick?" I asked. "Any special technique I need to know?" And while I'd tried to keep my tone casual, the slight tremor in my grip betrayed me.

Why was I suddenly so jittery? I'd been alone with plenty of women through the years, so why was I suddenly so nervous to be alone with this cute, single mom?

"It's not super complicated." Maddie gave a soft laugh, stepping up next to me. "Just warm water and a little soap. But be careful, the glasses can get slippery."

Her voice was light, teasing almost, like she found it

comical that a twenty-eight-year-old man would be so inexperienced with washing the dishes.

Which, yes, was quite ridiculous, now that I thought about it. But since I'd offered to help clean up, I needed to figure this out.

So I picked up the sponge, added a little soap and water to it and started scrubbing the inside of the glass.

"There, you've got it," Maddie said, leaning in closer to peek over at my work. "Easy-peasy."

But when her shoulder brushed mine a second later and I felt the warmth radiating from her, something in my brain must have short-circuited because before I knew it, my grip fumbled and the glass slipped right out of my hands, hitting the side of the sink before shattering into pieces.

"Ah sh—" I started to say before reaching down to pick up the glass shards. But my depth perception must have been off because I ended up slicing the edge of my palm against one of the jagged pieces.

"Ahh!" I jerked back, wincing as a sharp stinging pain shot through my hand.

"Oh no!" Maddie's voice rose, her hand flying to my arm. "Did you cut yourself?"

"I think so." I held my hand up for her to see. And yep, there was a small trickle of blood on the edge of my palm.

"Okay, it doesn't look too bad," she said, inspecting my cut with concern etched on her face. "But let's get a closer look to make sure you don't need stitches or anything like that. "

She turned the water up, guiding my hand under the stream. The sting of the water hit hard, making me almost wince again, but her fingers were gentle as she inspected it.

"I don't think it's too deep," she said, her voice soft but firm. "Just a surface cut. But we'll need to make sure it's clean before we bandage you up."

And she must have switched into full mom mode because instead of having me wash my hand myself, she grabbed some foaming soap and gently did it for me. Which was...surprisingly nice. I hadn't had someone care for me like this in...well, probably not since I was a kid.

She pulled a paper towel from the roll beside the sink and carefully wrapped it around my hand, applying warm, steady pressure to the cut. It was only then that she seemed to realize how nurturing she'd been.

"Oh my heck!" She gasped, her eyes going wide as she looked up at me. "I totally just went into mom mode, didn't I?"

"Maybe." I chuckled. "But it's okay."

A beautiful flush crept up her cheeks as she shook her head. "All right, well, just hold that there for a minute. I'll get the first aid kit."

"Smooth move, Ian," I muttered under my breath when she disappeared down the hall.

What kind of idiot can't even wash a little wine glass?

An idiot named Ian. That's who.

Maddie returned a moment later, carrying a small first aid kit. Okay, it was more like a survival pack, really—fully stocked with everything you'd ever need.

"That's quite the first aid kit." I raised an eyebrow as she flipped it open.

"Well..." Maddie smiled. "When you've got a rambunctious eight-year-old, it's a necessity."

"Sounds like he's a lot like my brothers and me." I chuckled, remembering myself at that age. "Always finding trouble."

"Oh, definitely." She laughed softly. "Now, let's take a look at that cut."

I extended my palm, and her eyes softened as they landed on the thin, half-inch slice along the edge of my hand. She rummaged through the bandages in her kit before selecting one. "I think this one would do, don't you?" she murmured.

"It looks perfect to me," I replied, though I hadn't really looked at it—I couldn't seem to tear my eyes away from her.

Her wavy hair was down, slightly mussed in the back, like she'd been lying in bed beside her son, maybe telling him a bedtime story or singing softly as he drifted off. Her eyeliner wasn't as crisp as it had been this afternoon when we sat across from each other during lunch, but it still framed her eyes beautifully—those blue, blue eyes that seemed to glow in the soft light of the kitchen.

She took my hand again, dabbing ointment onto the cut. And even though it was something simple, something a nurse might do without a second thought, in this quiet kitchen, it felt different—intimate. Her fingers brushed against my skin, and each time she let go, warmth lingered, making the moment feel heavier, more charged than it should have.

"There," she said softly, smoothing the bandage into place. "That should help."

"Thank you." I glanced down at my hand, needing to look away from her face before I was tempted to brush that stray lock of hair behind her ear.

She looked down again, too, and noticing the small scar near my thumb, she gently grazed her finger against it. "What's that from? Have you cut yourself doing dishes before?"

"No." I chuckled, my voice quieter than before, the memory of how I'd received that scar coming to the surface. "That's from my, uh..." I stopped, needing to clear my throat, which had suddenly become froggy from the emotions this memory brought up. "It's just from when I was a kid."

"What happened?" she asked, her gaze softening as she looked up at me.

I hesitated, feeling the warmth of her hand still wrapped around mine.

And even though I'd stopped myself from explaining more a moment earlier, the memory itself wasn't actually bad. It was a good one. One from a fun day with friends in a place I'd once felt loved.

The only thing that made this memory sad now was just that the memories made at that place had stopped.

Stopped because I hadn't been wanted there anymore.

Stopped because I'd been replaced.

But looking down and running my fingers along the old scar, I said, "I used to build forts in my bio dad's backyard with some neighbor kids when I stayed with him."

"Your bio dad?" She frowned. "Does that mean Joel Hastings isn't your biological father?"

"He's my stepdad." I nodded. "He and my mom got together when I was like five."

"Oh."

When she still seemed confused, I added, "I'm sure it's probably confusing since my last name is Hastings now, but I was Ian Hawthorne until I was eighteen."

"Oh..." Her brow furrowed then, like she was trying to figure out how that worked.

"Yeah, uh..." I swallowed. "My bio dad wasn't really that involved once he got remarried and had a couple more kids. So when I was eighteen, I decided to change my last name to reflect the man who had actually raised me."

"So you and your bio dad are estranged?" she asked.

"Basically." I nodded. "When I realized the only times we even talked was if I made the first move, I decided to do a little experiment to see just how long it would take for him to reach out. And well...it's been about twelve years since I've heard from him."

"Twelve years?" Maddie's eyebrows raised. "Dang. That sucks."

"Yeah." I nodded again. "He doesn't even live that far from here. Just twenty minutes away in New Haven." Her eyes widened like she was stunned that a parent who lived so close would choose not to take an active part in their child's life. But I shrugged and said, "It's okay now. I mean, I used to be really mad about it—hence the last name change. But it is what it is."

"His loss," Maddie said. And for a moment, it looked like she might reach out to touch my arm in a comforting way. But seeming to rethink it, she put her hands behind her back instead. After a moment, she met my gaze again, saying, "I guess I can relate somewhat, though. I haven't seen my mom since second grade."

"What?" My eyebrows shot up, surprised we'd have something like this in common.

She nodded. "Yeah, she just up and left one day, leaving my dad with three little kids to raise on his own."

"And you never heard from her again?"

"Nope," she said with a sigh. "My brother was curious about her when he was in high school and ended up finding out that she was in a folk band. But when he went to one of her shows and tried to talk to her, she basically blew him off and told him she had closed that chapter of her life and didn't want anything to do with us."

"Wow." My jaw dropped. And while I could understand a little of what she was saying since I'd been neglected by my own bio dad, he hadn't outright disappeared. I could call him up and he'd probably even be up to grabbing a beer together if I wanted to.

He'd just been too lazy to keep up the relationship.

"And this is Sloan's older sister?" I asked, trying to figure out how their family dynamic worked.

"Yeah." Maddie nodded. "We still had a relationship with my mom's parents and all her siblings. My mom just went no contact with everyone."

"Well, she's missing out," I said, wishing I had better words. Because even though I barely knew Maddie, I could already tell that she was someone worth sticking around for.

"Thanks," she said, drawing in a deep breath. "It sucked at first. But my dad is amazing, so my siblings and I really lucked out with him. He's the best grandpa, too."

Her voice wavered slightly as she mentioned her dad, and I caught a hint of emotion flickering across her face. There was probably more to that story—maybe about how her dad had stepped up to help a lot when Grant had been born, since considering how old her son was, she most likely had him in high school.

How had that been for her?

Before I could dwell too much on it, she cleared her throat and said, "Anyway, you never finished telling me how you got this scar." She nodded toward the old mark on my right hand. "Is it an epic tale?"

"Not exactly epic," I said with a grin. "But I was pretending to be a pirate at the time, so that's pretty cool."

"So cool," she echoed, her grin matching mine.

"Basically," I continued, "my friends and I were playing in our homemade fortress, and I had the brilliant idea to slide down the makeshift ramp we built. My hand ended up getting caught on a rusty nail on the way down, and voilà, I got this beauty of a scar."

"You were quite the daredevil, huh?" she teased, eyes twinkling.

"I did tell you that Reckless was my middle name, didn't I?" My grin widened as I remembered our very first conversation.

"Yes," she said, her voice softening as a hint of bashfulness crept into her expression. "You certainly did."

Our gazes locked, the air between us becoming electric. For a moment, I wanted to be reckless—to pull her into my arms and taste her lips slowly, deliberately. And when her eyes flicked down to my mouth, I couldn't help but wonder if she was thinking the same thing.

But before I could figure that out, she took a step back. In a light-hearted tone, she asked, "So...how often do you wash dishes by hand?"

"Honestly?" I rubbed the back of my neck, feeling a flush of heat rise to my face. "I'm not sure I've ever really done it. I've always had a housekeeper to handle that."

Her eyes widened, and a soft laugh escaped her lips. "So you weren't just being playful when you asked me what the trick was to washing dishes? You really didn't know what you were doing."

"Yeah," I admitted, feeling my cheeks redden. "Apparently, I'm a bit of a man-child."

"Well, at least you pay the people who help you avoid certain tasks," she said as she put the lid back on the ointment, putting it away. "That's definitely better than just being lazy and expecting a girlfriend to be your lover and your mom."

"From the way you say that, I'm guessing you might have experience with being someone's romantic partner and mothering them."

She scrunched up her nose. "Do I sound that bitter?"

"Not exactly." I chuckled. "But it does make me think you must have carried a lot on your shoulders in the past."

She sighed. "My ex really liked the idea of us sticking to the traditional gender roles in our home."

"So you didn't work while you were together?"

"Oh, I worked full time, too." She laughed lightly, even

though she didn't seem to actually think her situation had been funny at all. Then shrugging, she said, "I don't want to bore you with the nitty-gritty details, but well, we didn't have what I would consider a fair balance of responsibilities. And even though I was the one paying most of our bills since his various business ventures never really turned a profit, I also handled most of the household chores and made sure Grant's needs were taken care of."

"Is that why you're no longer together?" I asked, hoping to sound simply curious and not like I was judging her for not being married anymore.

"It definitely contributed to it," she said. "But no, there were a lot of other things, too." She looked like she might explain more about what led to her and her ex's divorce, but then she seemed to have second thoughts and left it at that.

So instead of prying for the details that she seemed to want to keep private, I asked, "Were you together for long?"

"We were together off and on for about nine years." She sighed. "We met when I was in high school and had fun. He was nineteen, so I thought it was exciting to hang out with an older guy. But we weren't really exclusive at that point." She picked up the wrappers from the bandage and tossed them into the trash bin under the sink. "We tried to make things work when I found out I was pregnant, but even then, we were so young that it was pretty rocky. We didn't even move in together until Grant was two."

Which was probably why she'd mentioned her dad being a good grandfather since it sounded like he'd probably been her main support system during that time.

"But I don't know," she continued, grabbing the ointment from the counter and tossing it into the first aid kit. "We were probably never really well matched. We tried to make it work because of Grant, but if I hadn't gotten pregnant so young—

before I really knew who I was and what I wanted out of life—we probably wouldn't have tried to make it work in the first place."

"Hindsight is always twenty-twenty, right?"

"It definitely is."

We were quiet for a moment, and I couldn't help but think that Maddie was such a strong woman. She was only twenty-six but had already been through so much and carried so much responsibility on her shoulders. Raising a child from such a young age while I could barely keep a plant alive without help.

I probably seemed so immature in comparison.

Sure, I was able to support myself—the privileged life I'd been blessed with helped me a lot in keeping the different cogs in my life spinning. But Maddie was raising a literal human. And from the sound of it, she had to do a lot of that on her own.

"I feel bad I wasn't much help tonight." I glanced at the sink, still full of dishes, and felt a bit useless. "In fact, I probably just made even more work since I broke one of Sloan's glasses in the process."

"It's fine," Maddie said. "I can handle it."

"I know." I sighed, tipping my head to meet her eyes. "I just — I wanted to be helpful, but now it's even later, and I know you have work early in the morning."

"It's really fine, Ian." Maddie chuckled. "I probably shouldn't have said all that about living with a man-child because I can tell you're now worried that I'll think you're a man-child, too. But I don't. So what if you don't hand-wash dishes? That's fine. You at least know how to load a dishwasher, right?"

"I do," I replied, probably a little too proudly.

"Then don't worry about it." She laughed. "Sloan was planning to throw everything in the dishwasher tomorrow, anyway."

"You don't think she'll send me an angry text when she

discovers I didn't actually leave a spotless kitchen for her to wake up to?"

"I can't promise that..." she said. But when a smirk lifted her lips, I knew she was teasing me.

"Fine." I couldn't help but laugh. "I'll go home and try not to have nightmares about turning into a man-baby in a diaper."

Maddie blinked, her brow furrowing. "I'm sorry, what?"

"Sorry! Weird joke." I quickly waved my hands, regretting the image I'd just put in her head. "Forget I said that."

"It's fine." She laughed. "But...I think you may have just cured me of thinking you look hot in every scenario."

I froze. *Wait, what?* My brain replayed her words, and I stared at her, stunned.

"Oh my gosh, I—" Maddie's eyes widened in horror as a hand flew up to cover her mouth. "I forgot for a second that you're my boss and that commenting on your looks is totally inappropriate."

"It's fine." I grinned, feeling her embarrassment wash over both of us. "But for the record, I once dressed up as Cupid at a Valentine's party as a prank...and I rocked it."

"I bet you did." She smiled, relieved that I wasn't upset. "I just know that I, uh, haven't exactly made myself indispensable at work yet. So I'd really like to keep my job."

"You're fine, Maddie. If I can't even wash dishes, do you really think I'd survive without an assistant for long?"

"Maybe not..." She laughed, her shoulders relaxing. "I definitely don't mind having a little job security."

"You do," I said, probably too earnestly.

And I probably shouldn't tell her that she could make all kinds of flirty comments and I'd still want to keep her around.

"Anyway," I said, shaking the thought away, "I should head out so you can get some sleep before work."

She nodded. And I might have been imagining it, but she

almost seemed disappointed that I was leaving. But the look was gone a moment later, and she said, "Let me walk you to the door."

She led me out of the kitchen and into the living room. When she opened the door, I pulled out my keys and unlocked my car. The headlights of my Bugatti flickered, catching her attention.

"Wow." Her eyes widened, her jaw dropping slightly. "That's...a fancy car."

I shrugged, feeling a little self-conscious. "It gets me from place to place."

"I bet it does." She laughed, shaking her head. "Probably gets you there pretty fast, too."

"That it does."

10

————

MADDIE

I SAT at my desk on Tuesday morning, scrolling through Ian's inbox. Most of the emails were routine—quick replies, confirmations, nothing requiring much brainpower. Which was a relief, because even after a solid seven hours of sleep, my mind was restless this morning, buzzing with the events of last night.

Yeah, last night had been...unexpectedly good. Not only had I made a few new friends at Sloan's party, but I'd also really enjoyed the surprise conversation I had in the kitchen with Ian.

There I'd been, just planning to help Sloan with a bit of cleanup after getting Grant to bed, when I walked in and found my boss standing at the sink, attempting to wash the dishes.

A half-smile tugged at my lips as I remembered the way he'd asked for tips. Knowing now that he rarely did things like that, it was kind of adorable that he'd tried to help out.

Even if he'd been completely terrible at it.

Oh, Ian. I chuckled to myself as I clicked the next email. *You are something else.*

And if he kept doing thoughtful things like that, I might just end up with a full-blown crush on him.

Not that I had any illusions about where this could go. Because even if he wasn't my boss, a high-powered billionaire like Ian Hastings would never be interested in a small-town girl with a kid.

Sure, there was this delicate attraction between us, like a thread waiting to be pulled. But we both knew it couldn't go anywhere, so the undercurrent of romantic tension between us was just something to make the workday more exciting. No expectations, no complications—just a little harmless fun.

I focused back on the emails on my screen. As I was about to click the one from the Boston Summit's team, a new email suddenly pushed through from someone named Margot Cavanaugh.

Wait... My fingers hovered over the mouse as I stared at the name. Was this...*the* Margot Cavanaugh?

Could this really be the famous socialite I'd seen splashed across headlines and social media a few years ago? The same Margot Cavanaugh who'd graced magazine covers and runway shows, the great-granddaughter of Reginald Cavanaugh, the oil tycoon?

My curiosity spiked, I clicked on the email. Before diving into the message, I checked the email address—*margot@everstoneenergy.com.*

Everstone Energy was her grandpa's company. So yep, this was definitely her.

I swallowed, my heart thudding as I refocused on the email's body, wondering what she might want from Ian.

Hi Ian,

I'm sure you're surprised to see an email from me as it has been a long time since we've last spoken. But I saw that you'll be speaking at the summit in Boston next week, and since I'll be there, representing my grandfather's company, I wanted to reach out.

I know things didn't end well between us—mostly because of me—but I've been thinking about our time together lately and if you're open to it, I'd love the chance to catch up while we're in the same location. Maybe clear the air?

Let me know what you think.

-Margot

I read the message again, trying to decipher the tone. Was it a professional catch-up or something of a more personal nature?

From what she said about things not ending well between them, it made it seem like this might be a more personal message.

Had they been friends at one time? Or had they dated?

The last I'd seen of her on social media was all the gossip surrounding her breakup with the professional hockey player she'd been dating for several years.

But maybe she and Ian had known each other before that?

Maybe in high school? Or college?

I furrowed my brow as I tried to decide what I should do with this message. Normally, if I could see Ian was in between tasks, I would just pop my head in his office and ask how to handle it. But he'd been working on his presentation all morning and had the smart glass of his office walls switched to their frosted setting, signaling he was not to be disturbed.

So instead of doing anything about this email, I marked it as *unread* for the moment and jotted down a reminder on a sticky note to ask him about it later.

Around a quarter to noon, the door to Ian's office finally opened. When he stepped out, his warm smile instantly sent a flutter through me, causing my mind to flash back to last night—those stolen moments, the lingering tension between us, the way our gazes locked and held, unspoken words hanging in the air.

"Can't believe it's already lunchtime," he said, his dark hair slightly tousled like he'd been running his hands through it all morning. "I've been buried in that presentation for hours."

"How's it going?" I asked.

"Good, actually." A grin spread across his face. "I think I finally figured out that part I've been struggling with."

"That's great," I said, and I meant it. Seeing him light up like that made something inside me warm.

"Any calls I should know about?" he asked, leaning against the edge of my desk.

"Just one. From the Everett Group. They asked if they could move their meeting back to four o'clock instead of three. Since you didn't have anything scheduled then, I made the switch."

"Perfect." He nodded. "Anything else I need to know about before I head out to lunch?"

"Just one more thing..." I hesitated, unsure how to bring up the email since I didn't know what he would think of it. But deciding to just go for it, I said, "I took care of most of your emails this morning, but there was one I wasn't sure how to handle."

His eyebrows lifted. "Yeah?"

I nodded and licked my lips. "It's from Margot Cavanaugh."

"M-Margot?" His expression changed at the mention of her name, something unreadable flickering in his eyes. "She—" He licked his lips. "She emailed me?"

I nodded, trying to keep my tone casual. "She mentioned she'll be at the Boston Summit and wanted to catch up. I wasn't sure if you wanted me to schedule a meeting or if it was something more...personal."

Ian's brow furrowed, and he seemed to pause, as if trying to make sense of why she would reach out. After a moment, he said, "I'll handle that one."

"Okay," I said, wanting to ask more but knowing it wasn't my place. "I'll move it into the personal tab for you to respond to later."

"Thanks. That will be great." He glanced at his watch. As if seeing that it was later than expected, he drew in a quick breath and said, "Well, I better head out. Mr. Paloski's probably already waiting for me across the street."

"Right. Your lunch meeting." I smiled, trying to push down the swirl of curiosity and confusion the email had stirred in me.

Had he seemed unsettled by my mention of the email?

Or was I just projecting things because I was so curious?

Once Ian left, I logged out of my computer and went to grab the lunch I'd left in the break room yesterday. I found a quiet corner near the window and sat down to eat my sandwich and yogurt. But as I ate, my mind kept drifting back to Margot Cavanaugh and why she'd be emailing Ian.

Knowing I wouldn't be able to settle down until I'd satisfied my curiosity, I pulled out my phone and typed "Ian Hastings and Margot Cavanaugh" into the internet browser's search bar.

It took a moment, but then my screen populated with a few different articles. The first from about nine years ago with the headline: **Future Power Couple No More: Ian Hastings and Margot Cavanaugh Call Off Engagement**

My breath caught as I read the last word. *Engagement?*

Ian had been engaged? I stared at the headline, the words blurring for a moment. *To Margot?*

I clicked on the article, and as soon as it loaded, I started skimming, my pulse quickening as I took in the details.

For the past two years, Ian Hastings and Margot Cavanaugh have been the picture-perfect couple, turning heads everywhere they went. Ian, the dashing heir to the Hastings business empire, was the charming businessman-in-the-making, while Margot, a glamorous socialite and model, seemed destined to become one half of the ultimate power duo. Their relationship, which began during their junior year at a prestigious boarding school in Connecticut, captivated the public, especially when Ian proposed two years later while the two were students at Yale.

From the outside, their relationship appeared flawless. Together, they graced red carpets, charity galas, and even made it to the cover of Style Magazine's *"Top 10 Couples to Watch." They were young, successful, and seemingly madly in love—a match made in high-society heaven. But just as quickly as their fairytale seemed to be unfolding, it came to a shocking halt.*

Fans and followers were stunned when news of their breakup broke, mere months after their engagement. While Ian and Margot have yet to comment on the reason behind the split, sources close to the couple suggested that their relationship began to unravel after Margot was spotted out with the hockey star Rhys Applegate since the two were seen together just weeks before the breakup announcement.

I stared at the screen, my heart sinking a little as I scrolled past a photo of Ian and Margot in their red-carpet glory. He looked so happy there. So in love.

How had it been to go through such a public heartbreak at such a young age? It was hard enough having your trust shattered in private, but for the whole world to watch it unfold? That had to cut deeper than most people could understand.

My thoughts drifted back to how vulnerable I'd felt after Jaxon betrayed me—after putting all my hopes and plans into our future together. The humiliation, the pain, the feeling that the rug had been yanked out from under my life.

And Ian had been—what? Nineteen?—when everything fell apart for him. When the woman he'd asked to marry him had gone on to date someone else.

No wonder he hasn't had any serious relationships since then. Having your trust betrayed like that—by someone you thought you'd spend the rest of your life with—broke something in you. It made you put up walls. Made you scared to get hurt again.

Was this why, if what Sloan had told me was true, none of Ian's relationships seemed to last more than two weeks? Was he so averse to getting his heart broken again that he decided to never really give it to anyone at all?

I'm reading into it too much. I sighed, shaking my head. Just because we'd both been hurt didn't mean we were the same.

I'd known him for less than two weeks. There was no way I could know what he'd gone through, or what had made him the way he was now.

Plus, this was an article from a gossip magazine. So who knows if any of this was even true. It could all just be speculation from someone hoping to make a lot of money off a juicy story.

Still, my heart went out to the younger version of him. Because Ian Hastings—the suave, confident businessman everyone admired—had been burned.

Just like anyone else.

My mind drifted back to the email. Margot had mentioned she'd been thinking about Ian a lot lately and wanted to catch up.

Was "catch up" code for "make up?"

Was it bad that I really hoped it wasn't?

11

______

MADDIE

THE BUZZ of my phone pulled me from the chaotic packing I'd thrown myself into as soon as I got home. It was Wednesday afternoon, the day before the Boston Summit, and Ian had let me off early so I could get ready for our trip. I'd been jittery all day, not sure what to expect from the weekend.

Was I nervous? Probably more than I should be, considering I wasn't the one giving a presentation in front of hundreds of people. But I knew how important this event was for Ian, and I wanted to be as supportive as possible.

He'd mentioned picking me up at Sloan's house around two, so when my phone buzzed, I half-expected it to be a message saying he was outside.

I grabbed my phone off the bed and opened the text.

> Ian: Running a little behind. Could you meet me at my house instead? I'll send the address.

I exhaled. At least I wasn't the only one behind schedule.

But he wanted me to meet at his house? My curiosity immediately spiked.

Where did a man like Ian Hastings live? Was it some sleek, modern apartment with a perfect view of downtown? Or maybe something bigger—a house?

He was a billionaire, after all.

Or did he live with his parents? I remembered Owen joking about them sharing the pool house at the Hastings Estate after college, but that was a while ago.

Deciding I wouldn't figure that out until I was actually at the place, I just texted him back.

> Me: Sure! I'll head your way.

Within seconds, his address popped up. I tapped it into my navigation app and grabbed my bags, excitement bubbling under my skin.

My first big work trip.

After years of working in a small-town office, I was stepping into the big business world, attending a huge conference with one of the biggest powerhouses in the industry.

Sure, I was just an assistant to said powerhouse and not an actual player in the field, but it was still surreal.

"I'll see you on Sunday, okay?" I told Grant when I made it downstairs with my luggage. He was sitting in the living room with Sloan, doing a puzzle at the coffee table while he waited for his dad to pick him up. "Come give me one last hug."

Grant jumped up from the floor, and I set my bags down to bend over and give him a hug and a kiss.

"Have fun on your trip," Grant said, hugging me back. "I'll miss you."

"I'll miss you, too," I said, my heart squeezing in my chest.

Even though his dad and I had been trading off days with

him over the past year, Jaxon usually having Grant on the weekends with me having the weekdays, it was still hard to be separated from my little buddy after so many years of having him all the time.

But I knew Grant would be well taken care of. And despite the way Jaxon and his new girlfriend had gotten their start, Janica was also really sweet with Grant, and I knew she loved him, too.

"I'll see you soon," I said again, knowing I needed to get out the door since Ian had hoped to be on our way to Boston before rush-hour traffic hit. "I love you."

"I love you, too," Grant said.

I gave Sloan a quick hug next. After saying my goodbyes, I picked up my bags again and headed out the door.

As I drove through the streets of Eden Falls toward the neighborhoods on the north end of town, the homes around me started to grow in size—first modest, then sprawling.

And okay, wow. There are some beautiful houses out this way.

Every turn I made brought me closer to what I imagined must be the fanciest house I'd ever been to. By the time my GPS announced I was almost there, the street was lined with enormous, manicured homes that looked straight out of a magazine.

Did Ian still live with his parents, then? Because I really couldn't imagine a bachelor needing a house like any of these.

My navigation app told me to turn onto a stone driveway with a huge gate. And after double checking the address, I clicked the button to buzz whoever was monitoring the gate.

"Hello, how can I help you?" a deep voice asked from the speaker in the box.

"I'm here to see Ian—uh, Mr. Hastings," I said, unsure how

I should refer to him. "My name is Maddie Stevens. I'm his assistant, and he said to meet him here."

"Of course, Miss Stevens," the voice said. "Come on in."

Just a moment later, the huge wrought-iron gate swung open for me. As I drove down the tree-shrouded drive, I couldn't help but feel like I was suddenly in a movie, heading to a rich billionaire's house for the first time.

Which yeah...I guess should fit since I was literally doing just that.

As the trees thinned and the house came into view, I gasped. It was breathtaking, like something straight out of a storybook. The home had the elegance of an English country manor, with a soft blue shingled exterior accented by natural stone. The expansive two-story structure looked brand new yet timeless, the kind of place that demanded attention, just like Ian. Stone chimneys rose from the roofline, and a porte-cochère arched gracefully over the driveway, leading to garages tucked behind the house. Copper gutters gleamed in the afternoon sun, adding a touch of luxury to the picture-perfect scene.

As I slowly pulled up, unsure where to park, Ian stepped outside the large, navy-blue-painted front doors, his phone pressed to his ear. He gave me a quick wave and gestured for me to drive through the porte-cochère. I followed his lead, pulling into a spot by the garages.

And wow, my well-loved Subaru had never looked so out of place before. Hopefully, Ian's house staff wouldn't have my car towed while we were away.

Ian appeared around the corner just as I was climbing out of my car, still on the phone but smiling apologetically.

"Sorry, I got stuck on a call," he whispered. "You can hang out inside. It won't be too long." He nodded toward the side entrance.

I followed him inside, stepping into a beautiful mudroom

with a cozy bench and shelves neatly organized with shoes. It felt...strangely homey. Not the cold, ultra-modern bachelor pad I had half-expected.

Did Ian live here by himself? Because as we walked down the hall, I almost expected to see a couple of kids that were Grant's age running around since it was so warm and welcoming. Like a family lived here.

He led me into the living room, a beautifully furnished space with soft lighting, fine art on the walls, and furniture that looked both expensive and comfortable. There was a gorgeous marble fireplace as the focal point of the room, and in the corner, a grand piano sat gleaming beneath the sunlight filtering through the windows.

Does Ian play the piano? I wondered.

I couldn't picture it, but then again, there was so much I still didn't know about him. I turned my gaze to the large windows, noticing a breathtaking view of the backyard—lush green grass, tall trees swaying gently, and a luxurious pool and hot tub nestled in one corner. It was the kind of backyard that felt like it belonged in my wildest daydreams. The kind of home I'd fantasized about one day living in, even though I knew it was far out of reach for someone like me.

I sighed softly, letting the fantasy fade. *You'd have to get a massive raise to ever live in a place like this,* I told myself before I could get too many ideas about having a home like this.

I turned away from the window, and after taking in the gorgeous chandeliers above, my gaze landed on the built-in shelves near the fireplace, adorned with books and minimal décor. I stepped closer, curious what kinds of books Ian might have on his shelves. But before I could inspect them, a digital photo frame caught my eye.

I stepped closer, wondering what kinds of memories Ian had on display. The first few photos that showed on the screen were from his childhood. There was a much younger version of him, he was maybe ten or so, standing proudly next to his stepdad with a basketball in his hands. Then came a photo of Ian as a teenager, wearing a tuxedo and laughing with Owen and another friend, looking like they were ready to go pick up their dates for the prom.

A small smile tugged at my lips as the images flickered across the screen. One photo showed him with his mom in a modest kitchen, the two of them mixing something in a bowl. *That must have been before the billionaire days*, I mused, my chest tightening at the reminder that Ian hadn't always lived the life of luxury. Once upon a time, it had just been him and his mom—much like Grant and me—navigating the world together as a single-parent family.

The slideshow shifted to more childhood moments: a younger Ian at various events, his smile wide and carefree. Then came more recent photos—him on a yacht with friends, laughing with his sister, their faces scrunched up in goofy expressions. My heart warmed seeing this lighter side of him, so different from the powerful, focused man I worked with. There was something refreshing about catching a glimpse of Ian when he was carefree, happy, and just being himself.

And then...my heart stopped.

The next photo was different. Ian looked younger, probably college-aged, but what really caught my attention was his hair. It was buzzed short and bleached blond—a sharp contrast to the dark brown I was so used to. My breath caught in my throat as the image tugged at something deep in my memory.

A flash of a distant memory surfaced—me sitting near a bonfire on the beach next to a boy with buzzed, bleached hair. The night was warm, the air thick with the smell of salt and firewood, and I could almost hear the laughter and waves in the background.

9 Years Earlier

The bonfire flickered against the inky sky as I trailed behind my cousin Izzy and her college friends. The familiar scent of salt-water hung in the air, mingling with the wood smoke as we walked through the sand toward the beach party. It was spring break for them, but for me? It was more like an exile. I'd been shipped off to Sweet Water, North Carolina by my dad, who figured that living with Aunt Reese would somehow straighten me out after the trouble I'd gotten into back home.

His plan? Get me away from Jaxon, the college guy I'd been sneaking around with.

Joke was on him, though, since that problem wasn't going away anytime soon.

Not unless the baby I was secretly carrying magically disappeared.

Yay *for that pregnancy test I took on Monday coming back positive.*

A pang twisted in my stomach, and I instinctively rested my hand there as we neared the bonfire. Izzy had begged me to come tonight, told me it'd be fun to hang out with her friends. And sure, this time last week I would have been thrilled to go a party with a bunch of college guys.

But now? Well...as much as I'd wanted to seem older and grow up faster, discovering I was pregnant when I'd barely turned seventeen wasn't exactly how I'd wanted to "grow up."

Would I even be able to graduate now? Or was my dad going to disown me and I'd be forced to drop out of school to get a job and raise my kid?

Yeah, he was going to be so mad when he found out.

Maybe I just wouldn't tell him. Maybe I could convince

Aunt Reese to help me keep the baby a secret and, I don't know, she could help me figure things out?

Okay, probably not. She had already been way too nice to let a "troubled teen" move in with her family in order to get straightened out.

I pushed those thoughts away and headed for the drink table, licking my lips at the sight of the big jug of strawberry lemonade. I reached for a cup, ready to ladle some in. But just as I was about to pour it into my cup, I overheard one of the guys nearby saying, "Yeah, I added a little extra to it. Should be strong enough to get the party started."

Which probably meant it was spiked with vodka or something.

I hesitated, still considering filling my cup since spiked lemonade was fun at parties. But then, the few brain cells I had left kicked in and I grabbed a water bottle instead.

Yep, even if I'd been stupid enough to open my legs for an older guy, I at least knew that alcohol and pregnancy were not a good mix.

I twisted off the cap and took a long sip, the cold water sliding down my throat as I tried to ignore the tightening in my chest. Pregnant at seventeen. What the hell was I supposed to do with a baby?

And if I did go back to Ridgewater and tell my dad, would Jaxon step up? Or was I going to be raising this baby on my own?

Why had I been so stupid? Sneaking around with him had been thrilling, fun even, but now? The regret was suffocating. Was it horrible that I'd been praying for a miscarriage, hoping that fate would spare me from this mess? I shuddered at the thought, guilt slamming into me. But at least it would be easier than the other option I'd been toying with—stepping in front of a car and ending it all.

I shook my head, trying to push the darkness away. This was supposed to be a distraction. I'd figure out how to tell my dad later. That his grand plan to send me to Aunt Reese's to keep me out of trouble had failed spectacularly since I'd gotten pregnant before I'd even come.

Blowing out a breath, I wandered away from the drink table, sipping my water and gazing out at the bonfire. The flames crackled, sending sparks spiraling into the cool spring air. It was a perfect night—not too cold, not too warm.

If only I was in the mood to enjoy it.

I spotted Izzy sitting on a log with her friends, laughing. For a second, I thought about joining her, but before I could move, a guy stepped up beside me. "You here for spring break, too?" he asked, his voice casual.

I glanced at him. He had a buzz cut, bleached blond hair, and dark eyebrows that didn't quite match, making me guess his natural color was much darker. He was cute—really cute—but since looking at a cute guy for too long had already gotten me into trouble at a party before, I shifted my gaze back to the fire.

"Yep, I'm here for spring break," I lied easily. No way was I telling this guy who looked like he was probably nineteen or twenty that I was a junior in high school.

"Same." He smiled, and I could feel his eyes on me. "Which school do you go to?"

"SUNY Cortland," I said automatically, spitting out the name of the college I'd been hoping to attend before everything went sideways. "What about you?"

"Yale."

I raised an eyebrow, impressed. "Ivy League, huh?"

"Yeah." He shrugged as if it wasn't a big deal.

"So, what are you studying at Yale?" I asked, wanting to keep the conversation on him and far away from my own life.

"Business," he replied. "You?"

"Interior design," I lied again. It was something I'd always dreamed of doing, but now...who knew if that would ever happen.

"That's cool."

I forced a smile, but my mind was already drifting back to the baby. What was I going to do? College seemed like a distant fantasy now.

Before I could get lost in my thoughts again, his phone buzzed, and I noticed him glance at the screen before groaning.

"Not someone you want to talk to?" I asked.

He sighed, slipping his phone back into his pocket. "It's my ex."

"Oh?" I tried to sound casual. "Recent ex?"

"Yeah. Dated for a few years. Thought I was going to marry her, but she cheated, so...it's been a mess."

I winced. "That sucks."

"Pretty pathetic, right?" he asked, glancing sideways at me.

"No," I said quickly. "It's not pathetic to get cheated on."

"Thanks." He smiled, though it didn't quite reach his eyes. "I appreciate that."

There was a quiet moment between us before he nudged my arm with his elbow. "So, what's your story? You looked pretty deep in thought when I came up to you. Any exes you're avoiding?"

"No exes," I bit my lip. "At least, not a serious ex. But well..." I hesitated. "I think I can top your sob story."

"Oh, yeah?" He raised an eyebrow, intrigued. "I doubt it."

"No, really...it's pretty bad."

"What is it?" he asked, his eyes darting back and forth as they searched my face. "Are you in some sort of trouble?"

"Kind of. I mean, my dad is probably going to kill me when he finds out. But—" I took a deep breath, feeling a tightness in my chest. "I, uh...I took a pregnancy test a few days ago. And it came back positive."

"Oh, sh—" He stared at me for a second, eyes wide. "Are you serious?"

"Yeah," I muttered, feeling the weight of the truth settle between us. "I wish I wasn't, but...I'm pregnant."

And I realized then that it was the first time I'd actually said those words aloud.

I was pregnant. A teen mom.

A statistic I never thought I'd be.

And with those words now out there in the universe, shared with a complete stranger no less, my throat tightened and my eyes burned as if the tears had been waiting for this moment to break free.

Don't cry, I told myself, swallowing hard and trying to push them back. But it was like holding back a flood with a paper dam.

"Hey," he said softly, noticing my sudden distress. "You wanna take a walk? Get closer to the ocean?"

"Yes." I nodded quickly, grateful for the suggestion since I really didn't need an audience to my breakdown. "Yes, please."

So he took my hand and pulled me with him toward the water, the waves crashing softly in the distance. My hands shook, and my heart pounded, but it wasn't from the cold. It was the fear that had been sitting in my chest ever since those two pink lines appeared. The future that felt like it was slipping further away with every step I took.

And as soon as the tide hit my toes, I couldn't hold it in anymore. The tears spilled over, fast and hot, before I even realized what was happening. I covered my face with my hands, embarrassed and overwhelmed. Ugh, why did I have to break down in front of a stranger?

"I...I'm sorry," I stammered between sobs, my voice crack-ing. "I don't know what I'm doing."

I felt his hand hover near my shoulder before he gently placed it there. "You don't have to apologize," he said, his voice low and kind. "It's okay."

But I couldn't stop the tears. They just kept coming, every-thing inside me unraveling. For the first time since I found out, I couldn't hold it together. I couldn't pretend to be fine.

Because in reality, I was...lost. So freaking lost. It felt like I was drowning and that I may never come up for air again.

The boy shifted beside me awkwardly, like he didn't know what to do, then asked, "Would you, uh...want a hug?"

"Mm-huh." I nodded, not trusting myself to say more. And before I knew it, he pulled me into his arms.

He held me close, his warmth radiating through me as I buried my face in his chest. And even though I didn't know this guy from Adam, somehow, for the first time all week, I felt almost...safe.

Like, maybe for a moment, I wouldn't have to carry it all alone.

We stood like that for a while, the waves crashing in the back-ground, and when my sobs quieted, he pulled back just enough to look at me. "Do you wanna talk about it?" he asked gently.

"Not yet." I shook my head.

He nodded, respecting that, and sat down in the sand next to me. "Okay. Well, in that case...let's talk about something else. Like, uh...cats."

I blinked through my tears, caught off guard. "Cats?"

"Yeah, you know...pets. Do you like them? Ever thought about getting one?"

"Actually..." A small, broken laugh escaped my lips, and I wiped my eyes. "I've always wanted a cat."

"Really?" His face lit up. "What would you name it?"

"Satan, of course," I said without hesitation.

"Satan?" He sputtered in disbelief. "You'd name your cat Satan?"

I couldn't help it—I laughed again, this time for real. "Yep. I mean, imagine yelling 'Come here, Satan!' or 'Get back inside, Satan!' at the top of your lungs for all the neighbors to hear. They'd wonder what was going on at my house."

"That's actually amazing." He laughed with me, his grin wide and genuine. "And now I kind of want to steal that idea."

"Okay," I said. "But you have to wait at least five years. Give me a chance to use it first."

"Deal."

The heaviness in my chest loosened, the weight of everything not gone but momentarily lighter. When we stopped laughing, he looked over at me, his eyes soft and understanding.

"You're going to be okay, you know," he said quietly, his voice steady and sincere. "I know it feels like your world's crashing down, but...you'll figure it out."

***

"Sorry about that," Ian's voice came from behind me, pulling me out of the memory. Chills raced across my arms, and for a split second, I could've sworn his voice sounded exactly like the boy from the beach.

No...it couldn't be. Could it?

I replayed the details in my mind. He'd gone to Yale, right? And he'd mentioned a girl—someone he thought he was going to marry—who had cheated on him. Just like the article I'd read about him and Margot.

But it couldn't be. The odds of us both being at the same

beach in North Carolina, at the same time, nine years ago... It felt impossible. Coincidences like that didn't happen.

And yet, something deep inside me tugged at the idea. Maybe my memory had blurred his face with Ian's over the years, but the more I thought about it, the more I couldn't shake the feeling. What if...after all this time, the boy who had comforted me when my world was unraveling had somehow become the man standing in front of me now? The man giving me a job at another pivotal moment in my life.

"I think I'm ready to head out," Ian said, not seeming to notice my mind was racing a hundred miles a minute. "You ready?"

"Yes," I replied, my mouth thankfully functioning while my mind raced.

"Great," he said, his voice steady, while my heart still tried to piece together a puzzle I wasn't even sure was real. "My car's in the garage."

12

——

IAN

I WALKED beside Maddie as we headed toward the spot where her car was parked, the early afternoon sun casting a soft glow over the leafy trees above. I'd already stowed my bags in the back of my Bugatti, so when we reached her sedan, I moved ahead, grabbing the bags from her trunk.

"Oh, thank you," she said, as if surprised that I'd assist her.

"No problem," I said before leading her to the garage where my car was waiting.

I'd considered having Alex, my driver, take us so I could get some work done during the drive. But after days of prepping for this summit, I needed the quiet hum of the road to calm my fried brain, so I told Alex to get the Bugatti ready for me to drive instead.

Besides, being in the car with her, just the two of us, felt... better. (For reasons I wasn't allowing myself to analyze, of course.)

The click of the trunk opening echoed as I placed her bags inside beside the luggage I'd put in there earlier.

"You all set?" I asked, closing the trunk.

"Yep, ready," she replied, her voice soft but steady. She slid into the passenger seat, and I couldn't help but glance at her again as I started the engine. She still wore the same white blouse and red skirt she'd been wearing at the office earlier.

I'd been slammed with work over the past week so we hadn't had any more moments like the one we'd shared in Sloan's kitchen. But even if I had been all work and no pleasure lately, I had definitely noticed that her red skirt hugged her curves *very* nicely.

"So," I said, pushing my thoughts away as I eased the car out of the garage, "I'm not sure how much you looked into the hotel we'll be staying at. But it has a cool and artsy vibe, not to mention a great location—lots of restaurants within walking distance. Which is nice, because I hate driving in big cities." I flashed her a grin. "Must be the small-town boy in me."

From the corner of my eye, I caught a smirk forming on her lips, and it did something to me—something I couldn't quite explain. But since I was curious about that smirk, I asked, "Why are you looking at me like that?"

"Looking at you like what?" she asked, all innocent.

"Like you're silently mocking me," I said, winking so she'd know I was being playful.

"It's just..." She chuckled softly. "When I think of you, 'small-town boy' isn't exactly what comes to mind."

"Okay, fair enough. I do travel a lot." I laughed, feeling some of the tension drain from my shoulders. "But I stayed in Eden Falls for a reason."

"How long have you lived in your house?" Her gaze turned to me, her expression soft. "Is it just you there?"

"I had it built recently," I said, glancing at her with a slight smile. "Before that, I was living with Owen—two grown men crashing in my parents' pool house after college. Real adult stuff."

She laughed. "I'm staying with Sloan right now, so no judgment here. Plus, I bet your parents' pool house is a little fancier than most."

"It was," I admitted with a grin. "Anyway, about two years ago, one of my friends got engaged, and seeing him buy a house and get ready to take that step made me realize that I should probably grow up a bit more, too. So I started thinking about building my own place. My dad sold me a piece of land, and after a long process, the house was finally ready this spring."

"So did you just move in?" she asked, her eyebrows lifting.

"Yeah." I nodded. "The basement's not fully done yet, but I moved in the first part of May."

"Well, from what I saw, it looks like you've got it pretty well set up."

"Thanks to the design firm I hired," I said, shaking my head slightly. "I tried to be involved in the beginning, but by the time we got to picking furniture and finishes last September, I realized I had no idea what I was doing. So I told Cara—the designer—to make it look like the kind of house someone could raise a family in."

She gave me a look, the kind that said she wasn't expecting to hear that. "So you're thinking about having a family, then?"

"Yeah..." I swallowed, feeling bashful for some reason. "I'm sure I don't seem the type, but I'm getting close to thirty now, and I guess I've had some things happen that made me realize dating a different woman every week isn't actually all that it's cracked up to be."

"A different kind of lonely," she said, seeming to understand.

"Yeah..." And when I met her eyes, I got the feeling that she might have experience with that as well. Being with other people—a romantic partner—but not really feeling seen.

"So are you saying you don't just let random women come

up and kiss you at the club every weekend?" She raised her eyebrows, a playful smirk on her lips.

"Actually..." I chuckled, feeling a bit of heat rise in my chest. "Believe it or not, that first night we met was actually the first time I'd done something like that in almost a year."

"Really?" She blinked, visibly surprised by my admission.

"I know you probably saw all kinds of stories about me out there," I said, knowing my dating life had been plastered across the internet—gossip headlines loved to exaggerate. "But I've actually been trying to be better."

Trying to be the kind of man who could deserve the kind of woman that I wanted.

"Well, good for you," she said, her voice sincere.

We were quiet for a bit, the hum of the car and the occasional blur of trees outside the window marking the time.

But then Maddie turned to me again and asked, "Do you have a timeline for when you're going to get that family to go with the house? Or are you more focused on your career right now?"

I thought about it for a moment, leaning back in my seat. "I've been really focused on work this year—trying to clean up my image with the board since I was definitely too far on the other end of the spectrum for a while. But once I get this new content creation project off the ground, I'd like to start thinking about settling down."

"So for now you live in that huge house all by yourself?" she asked, her voice quiet, as if she somehow sensed the loneliness I'd been feeling more lately.

"No roommates, no pets." I tried to keep my tone light, but the truth of it tugged at me more than I cared to admit. "I've thought about getting a dog or maybe a cat, but I travel too much. It wouldn't be fair to leave them alone."

"That makes sense." She nodded, her expression understanding. "Pets are a big responsibility."

"Yeah," I agreed, though my thoughts drifted to her. I imagined the weight of raising a child on her own, the responsibility she carried every day. "But not as much as raising a kid. I can't even imagine balancing all that. You make it look easy."

She laughed softly, shaking her head. "Well, I'm glad it at least looks easy."

I glanced over, catching the faint blush on her cheeks. There was something undeniably captivating about her in that moment—the strength she had, the way she carried herself despite everything life had thrown at her.

"You figured it out, though," I said quietly, my voice dipping lower. "And while I haven't met your son, I have no doubt he's a pretty great kid. His mom certainly is."

Her eyes softened, and she turned away for a moment, looking out the window as if trying to compose herself. When she looked back at me, there was a vulnerability there that tugged at something deep inside me. "Thank you for saying that," she whispered. "I do my best."

"That's all any of us can do, right? Our best at any given time." I paused, glancing at her again. "Some days it feels like we're barely keeping our heads above water, but at least we're still fighting."

She nodded, and her eyes lingered on me for a heartbeat too long. And I felt it again—that pull, the quiet gravity between us that seemed to grow stronger the more time we spent together.

We pulled up to the hotel a while later, its sleek, modern exterior standing out against the bustle of the Boston streets. I handed the valet the keys, and as we stepped inside, Maddie's gaze swept over the murals and sculptures that decorated the lobby.

"This place is beautiful," she murmured, her awe evident.

"It's a good spot," I replied. "Close to everything you need. Which is important when you hate driving in big cities."

She smirked, glancing at me sideways. "You're really trying to lean into that small-town-boy charm, aren't you?"

"I might be trying to change that first impression you got of me just a bit." I chuckled.

"I don't know why," she said. "It was a pretty great first impression. On my end, at least."

"That it was," I said. And when our eyes caught for a charged moment, I wondered what might have happened if we'd been able to build on that first impression. If she hadn't been a new employee and I'd been able to meet her again at Sloan's party without the boss/assistant dynamic being an issue.

I'd probably have asked for her number, and not being able to play it cool, asked her out the next day.

Then who knows, maybe instead of talking about settling down in the next couple of years, I'd have already been on my way to getting that family I wanted.

And now you're just being delusional, Ian, I told myself before I could get too far in that daydream.

Those kinds of love stories only happened in the movies.

"How may I help you?" the hotel clerk asked when Maddie and I stepped up a moment later.

"We're here to check in," I told her. "There should be two rooms under the name Ian Hastings."

"Of course, Mr. Hastings," the woman said, typing something on her keyboard. "May I see your license?"

I handed her my license.

"Okay," the woman said, looking at her screen once she'd pulled my information up. "It looks like I have you down for one of our luxury suites as well as a king-sized room. Is that correct?"

A sudden wash of guilt passed over me at the idea of my getting a luxury suite when Maddie would be in a regular room. So making a split-second decision, I cleared my throat and asked, "Actually, do you have any other luxury suites available?"

"Oh, you don't have to do that," Maddie whispered beside me. "I don't need anything fancy. A regular room is more than enough."

But I shook my head. "You'll be working long hours; you should have a nice place to relax in at the end of the day."

"I'm really fine with a regular room," she said.

But I turned back to the hotel clerk and asked again, "Do you have another luxury suite available?" And then, since I had the sudden desire to keep Maddie close, I added, "Preferably one next to mine."

The girl went back to her screen. After a moment, she said, "We do have a suite next door to yours. But it will be an additional charge, and I see your current rooms are being covered by the conference..."

"That's fine. You can just charge me for the upgrade."

"Oh, no, Ian." Maddie gasped. "I can't ask you to do that."

"It's really no problem," I said, glancing sideways and taking in the shock in her blue eyes. "I want to do this for you."

"Okay..." She sighed, relenting, but still seemed uncomfortable with the idea of being pampered. Which made sense since from what she'd told me about her past, it sounded like she hadn't really had anyone take care of her in a long time.

The clerk finished making the room adjustments and then handed me our keys, giving us instructions on how to get to our rooms.

The hallway was quiet, the dim lighting casting a soft glow over the walls as we reached our doors.

"This is you," I said, stopping in front of Maddie's door and handing her the key. "If you need anything before dinner, you know where to find me." I nodded to the door just left of hers.

She nodded, our fingers brushing as she took the card. And even though it was just a simple touch, it sent a jolt through me.

Her eyes met mine, and for a second, I wondered if she felt it, too—the electricity humming between us.

"Thanks, Ian," she said, sounding almost breathless. "For doing this for me. It's way too generous."

"It's the least I could do." I nodded. "I'll see you in an hour for dinner."

"See you," she replied, offering a small smile before slipping into her room.

I stood outside Maddie's door for a moment longer, my pulse quickening from that brief touch of her hand. As I headed into my own room, I realized I wasn't just looking forward to dinner because of the deal I was about to close—Maddie was quickly becoming the reason. And for the first time in a long time, I found myself wanting more.

13

MADDIE

I WALKED into the suite and was immediately speechless. The room was massive, like something out of a magazine. Gorgeous chandeliers hung from the ceiling, casting a soft glow over the plush sitting area with its velvet couches and a sleek coffee table. A wall of windows led to a balcony with a breath-taking view of Boston's skyline. I could already see myself soaking in the oversized tub in the luxurious bathroom or sitting on the balcony with a glass of wine.

Pulling out my phone, I snapped a few pictures of the room and sent them to my sister and sister-in-law.

> Me: Guess where I am?

Their responses were almost immediate.

> Lexi: WHAT! Did you marry a prince or something since we last saw you?

Juliette: How in the world are you staying somewhere like THAT? Spill, girl!

I grinned and quickly replied.

Me: My boss upgraded my room.

Juliette: Your boss got you that room!? So are you dating now?

Lexi: You're welcome for telling you to kiss a guy at the club.

I rolled my eyes and typed back.

Me: No, it's not like that. We're not dating. We've been keeping things professional.

Well, mostly. Our relationship might be a little more flirty than with my previous bosses but...a little friendly banter was okay in the workplace, right?

Juliette: You're delusional. No boss has ever upgraded me to a luxury suite!

Lexi: Make sure to let us know when he kisses you again. I want all the juicy details.

Me: He's not going to kiss me. So don't hold your breath for that update.

Lexi: Whatever you say...

Juliette: Well, I hope you have a great work trip. Have an extra glass of wine for me in that glorious tub.

Both Juliette and Lexi were expecting babies at the moment. Juliette and my brother Easton's baby was due in just a few weeks, so they'd both been sticking to mocktails when we got together for our girls' nights.

I answered a few more of their questions about the trip and then I went into the bedroom to unpack some of my things. After placing my toiletries in the bathroom, I stood at the closet, debating which dress to wear tonight. I didn't have the funds to buy a bunch of fancy dresses for this event, so it was likely that I might stand out like a sore thumb among all the other company owners attending the business summit. But I hoped what I'd brought would be good enough.

For tonight's dinner, which we would be having with Mr. Kwan—the CEO of a tech company that Hastings Industries was hoping to work with—I settled on a navy-blue dress that was simple but hopefully elegant.

After touching up my makeup and fixing my hair, I slipped into the dress. It fit well, and even though this was just a dinner for work and not a date, I felt a flicker of nervous excitement as I checked myself in the mirror. My phone buzzed.

> Ian: I'm ready to head down whenever you are. You ready?

A thrill shot through me, and I quickly replied.

> Me: Ready.

Less than a minute later, there was a knock at my door. I opened it, and there was Ian, standing tall in a navy suit that was tailored to perfection. He looked...well, devastatingly handsome as usual. His eyes swept over me, and for a moment, he seemed almost...speechless?

He cleared his throat and said, "Should we head down?"

"Yes," I managed, feeling suddenly breathless. The way he was looking at me sent a warm, unfamiliar sensation through my chest.

I grabbed my purse, and with slightly wobbly legs, we made our way to the elevator. As we waited, Ian glanced sideways at me, a hint of warmth in his gaze. "I really like that dress," he said.

"Thank you," I replied, smiling.

He tilted his head slightly. "Pretty sure we're a perfect match tonight."

I furrowed my brow, momentarily confused, until he extended his arm beside my waist, indicating his suit. "My suit and your dress—they're the same color."

I laughed. "Well, look at that."

The elevator arrived and we stepped inside. The few other times we'd been on an elevator together, there had always been other people with us. But this time, it was just the two of us.

We were alone.

My pulse quickened as I remembered a scene from the book I'd been reading last night—where a girl and her boss were stuck in an elevator. They'd been fighting their feelings for weeks and the sexual tension was so high they were about to explode. I had been internally screaming for them to finally just confess their feelings and kiss, and just when I thought the author was going to torture the characters—and me—for another chapter or two, the handsome boss had taken his secretary in his arms, pressed her against the elevator wall, and kissed her.

And man, the heated kiss did not disappoint. In fact, I'd gotten a little hot and bothered myself as I imagined finding myself in a similar situation with a sexy man.

And yeah, when I realized I'd been picturing myself and Ian as the two characters in the novel, I also realized that I should probably take a break from reading boss romances for a bit. Just until I'd gotten my attraction to my own boss under control.

Though I still had a few chapters left to read in that one, and since I liked to finish what I started, my swearing off boss romance novels might just have to wait until I finished the last chapter.

The elevator dinged, stopping at the fifth floor. And before I knew it, a big group was suddenly piling in, squishing Ian and me into the back corner.

"Sorry," I said, my cheeks flushing when I found my back pressed firmly against him. "Tight fit."

"It's fine," he said, his voice froggier than usual as he shifted slightly. But we were packed in here like sardines in a can, so when he attempted to adjust our position, his hand brushed across my butt.

"Sorry," he muttered. "I promise that was an accident."

"No worries," I whispered, cheeks burning as I tried to ignore the fact that this was practically another scene straight out of that book.

The elevator reached the main level, and I breathed a sigh of relief when we were able to step into the lobby.

"I think the restaurant is this way," Ian said, his cheeks still slightly flushed as he led me toward the glass doors to our right.

He held the door open for me to step inside the restaurant where we were meeting Mr. Kwan at six thirty.

"Looks like it's a busy night," Ian said, glancing around the bustling space as we stepped into the small line of people waiting to check in with the hostess.

"Do you think Mr. Kwan is already here?" I asked.

He scanned the room briefly, then checked his watch. "We still have ten minutes until our reservation. He usually likes to arrive right on time."

As we waited, I took in the low hum of conversations, the soft clinking of dishes, the elegant chandeliers above casting a warm glow. It was easily the fanciest restaurant I'd ever been in.

Curious about the kind of cuisine they served here, I stole a glance at a nearby table. I wasn't a particularly picky eater—the only things I didn't really eat was seafood and mushrooms. But before I could get a really good look at the entrees, I felt Ian suddenly going stiff beside me.

I turned to look at him, wondering if something was wrong. And when I inspected his face, his gaze was fixed at the front of the line. When I followed his line of sight, I saw what had caught his attention: a tall, willowy woman with blonde hair wearing a sleek designer dress and standing beside an older man surrounded by what looked like a security detail.

At first, I thought she was just a twenty-something woman on vacation with her much older, wealthy husband. But when she glanced back and I got a better look at her face, I realized we were looking at none other than Margot Cavanaugh and her oil-tycoon grandfather.

14

IAN

DON'T PANIC, I told myself the second I caught sight of Margot. *Just look away and maybe she won't see you.*

Because if I just avoided eye contact, maybe the girl who had ripped out my heart and stomped on it nine years ago wouldn't notice me in the crowd. Though, just in case, I edged closer to Maddie, hoping the tall guy ahead could shield me from her view.

But when I risked a quick glance, Margot was already watching, her gaze steady as our eyes met. She gave a small smile and leaned over to say something to her grandfather before heading straight toward us. *Great.*

My mind raced. Could I dodge this? Maybe just take an "urgent" call and step away? I was sizing up my options when Maddie leaned in, her voice low. "Did you ever email her back?"

"I didn't," I mumbled. "I deleted it instead."

Definitely not my most strategic move. I should've just replied with a curt "Not interested." Then maybe she'd know I had no interest in revisiting the past.

Maddie's eyes widened a fraction, her expression unreadable.

Was it pity? Probably.

Which yeah, it was pretty pitiful that after nearly a decade I was still this rattled by the sight of my ex-fiancée.

But since Margot was almost upon us, I needed to push away my stupid feelings and at least act like I was unbothered by this unfortunate circumstance.

So forcing a smile, I used the most enthusiastic voice I could muster and said, "Margot? Is that really you? What are you doing here?"

"I'm here for the conference," she said, opening her arms to give me a quick hug.

And even though I didn't really want to hug the woman who had broken my nineteen-year-old heart, I gave her a quick embrace.

"So, what brings you to the conference?" I asked. "I think the last I heard you were doing some modeling."

"Yeah, I did that for a while." She nodded. "Still do shoots here and there. But I'm actually working with Everstone Energy now and thought this event would be useful training for our team."

"Oh, awesome. It is a great event."

Okay, my nerves were making me sound *way* too enthusiastic about everything. I needed to dial it down just a bit.

"It's been a good change, and I'm enjoying the work." She looked at me, biting her lip briefly like she was gauging something. Then licking her lips, she said, "I actually tried to email you last week."

"Oh, really?" I asked, feigning confusion.

"I saw you were giving the keynote on Friday and thought it might be nice to catch up. But I'm sure you and your staff have been swamped." She eyed Maddie briefly, then continued. "My own assistant struggles to keep up with my inbox these days."

Was that supposed to be a dig at Maddie? An attempt to make her seem bad at her job?

Not about to let that fly, I gave Maddie a quick look before meeting Margot's gaze again. "Sorry about that. I'm sure my assistant put it in my personal folder—nothing slips by her. But I've been so busy prepping for the summit that I haven't had the chance to catch up on emails."

"It's fine." Margot tsked, waving it off. "Just thought we could grab lunch or dinner while we're here. It's been so long."

"It has been." I frowned as if I was mentally juggling my schedule. "Though, honestly, I don't think I'll have time for something like that with all the client meetings I already have lined up." I gave an apologetic smile. "Gotta keep our CEOs happy."

"What about after one of the mixers?" She tilted her head. "I've seen all those photos of you in the tabloids. You can't pretend like you don't make time for fun after hours."

"Ah, yes..." I chuckled, trying to appear unfazed even though I didn't like that she was bringing up my past. "I have made quite the splash in those tabloids. Not quite as infamous as you, but..."

Her eyes widened, as if my words had hit their intended mark.

But then I finished with, "But, sadly for the photographers, I won't be up to my usual shenanigans this year."

"Really?" Her eyes narrowed, unconvinced.

Without thinking, I slipped an arm around Maddie's waist, pulling her closer as if it were the most natural thing in the world. "Nope, those days are long gone," I said, my mouth somehow moving faster than my brain. "I've realized it's much more rewarding to spend my evenings with my...fiancée."

Oh crap! I'd meant to say "girlfriend," maybe even "date," but nope, there it was, right out there in the open. My *fiancée*.

"Your...f-fiancée?" Margot's gaze flicked between Maddie and me.

"Yes," I replied, hoping Maddie would catch on quickly and I wasn't about to face-plant with this little lie. "Sorry, I should've introduced you." I gestured to Maddie with what I hoped looked like confidence. "This is Maddie, my beautiful fiancée. Maddie, this is Margot, an old friend."

"Nice to meet you, Maddie," Margot stammered, her shock unmistakable. Her gaze flickered back to me, as though sizing up the whole situation. "I didn't realize you were engaged. Usually, your flings are all over social media, so it's strange I haven't heard of this until now."

She'd been keeping tabs on me?

Well, good. She was the reason I'd started those careless flings in the first place.

But instead of saying any of that, I pulled Maddie closer and said, "I've been keeping a lower profile this year. Trying something new." I glanced at Maddie, and while she looked slightly taken aback by the sudden turn of events, she seemed okay with playing along. "And as it turns out, settling down with the right woman suits me."

"Settling down?" Margot's eyes widened, like she couldn't believe what she was hearing.

Maddie chuckled lightly beside me. "You can't blame me for wanting to keep him all to myself, can you?"

Margot's expression was almost comical as she looked Maddie over, clearly sizing her up.

Maddie was so refreshingly real and down-to-earth that I could understand Margot's disbelief. She didn't fit Margot's image of my usual...well, type.

But that was just fine. My usual type was a lot like Margot and I was finding that I didn't actually like that type anymore.

But when Margot's gaze went toward Maddie's left hand, like she was looking for an engagement ring, I quickly took Maddie's hand in mine to hopefully conceal the fact that her ring finger was undecorated.

When I looked at Margot, her eyes narrowed, like she suspected something fishy was going on. But then I saw that the hostess was starting to lead her grandfather to their table, so with one final smile, I said, "It was great seeing you again, Margot. I hope you enjoy your dinner."

Margot's shock was still written all over her face. But she nodded, mumbled a goodbye, and headed back to her grandfather.

As soon as she was gone, I loosened my grip on Maddie's hand and was almost weak with relief as I exhaled, "Sorry about that. I panicked."

"It's fine," she said softly. Then seeming to notice Margot glancing back at us, she slipped her hand into the crook of my arm, giving it a reassuring squeeze. "Exes are complicated."

"That they are."

15

MADDIE

"THAT WAS A GOOD MEAL," Ian said, his hand brushing lightly against mine as we left the restaurant after our dinner with Mr. Kwan and his wife, Mei.

"It really was," I said. Good company *and* delicious food.

I'd ordered the buttermilk roasted chicken with mashed potatoes and green beans, and the chicken was so juicy and tender, I'd savored every bite.

"I hope you didn't get too bored with all the tech talk." Ian glanced back at me as he pushed open the restaurant doors and waited for me to walk through. "I know it was probably a lot."

"Not at all." I shook my head, smiling. "It's actually interesting, hearing about everything that's coming next. Makes the future feel a little closer."

"Glad to hear it wasn't too boring," Ian said. "And yes, it was fun to hear what Mr. Kwan and his company are working on."

Another couple exited the restaurant behind me, so Ian held the door open for them. Once they had gone ahead, we continued down the walkway toward the elevators.

"And sorry again about the whole 'calling you my fiancée' thing in front of Margot," Ian said, an apologetic expression on his face. "I think my brain jumped ship for a minute and it would seem that having my ex-fiancée in front of me caused the word to blurt out."

"I figured it was something like that," I said. Had I been surprised to suddenly be referred to as my boss's fiancée? Of course! But I could definitely think of worse things than having someone think I had caught the attention of such a handsome and powerful man.

And as long as we didn't bump into Margot again, and she kept our meeting to herself, there really shouldn't be an issue with one person thinking I was engaged to my billionaire boss.

"I'm guessing you must know all about my past with her, then?" Ian asked, his brown eyes studying me.

"Just a little," I admitted, feeling my cheeks heat at being caught, once again, in my curiosity about him. "I didn't know you two were connected until her email came through. But..." I bit my lip. "I will admit that I did a quick search after seeing her email and saw a few news articles that mentioned you two had been engaged during college."

"You really didn't know about it until last week?" Ian's gaze narrowed, like he'd expected his history to have been common knowledge to everyone. "It was all over the tabloids back then."

But I shrugged and said, "I think I was in high school when it happened. And since my dad didn't allow me to have social media until I was eighteen, I pretty much lived in a cave."

Though, if Ian really was that same guy I'd met on the beach back then, I guess I possibly *had* known about it. I just hadn't known it was him or that he and his ex were famous enough to have their breakup all over the entertainment news media.

No wonder he'd wanted to avoid her calls.

"Well, in case you're wondering, it was a messy breakup," Ian said. "And in the midst of it, I basically did the girl equivalent of cutting bangs and ended up bleaching my hair before buzzing it off."

He'd bleached and buzzed his hair after his breakup? My heart stuttered as his words hit me and the photo I'd seen earlier at his house flashed through my mind. Because there was no way that that photo being taken right after his breakup could be a coincidence, right?

That the guy on the beach, who had the same hairstyle that Ian had just described and was also going through a breakup with a girl who had cheated on him, would look so similar to Ian at that time.

"Trying to picture me with blond hair?" Ian asked, apparently assuming I was suddenly speechless at the idea of him with light hair.

"Um," I said, my mind scrambling as I tried to decide if I should tell him that I was pretty sure I may have actually seen his bleached hair in person.

But before I could decide how to say it, we rounded the corner—and there she was.

Margot. Standing by the elevator doors.

My stomach dipped.

"Hello," she said when she noticed us, her voice syrupy sweet. "Fancy seeing you two again."

And before she could get too close of a look, I reached for Ian's bicep, tucking my fingers under his arm to keep my left hand out of sight.

Because yep, apparently our little "engagement" facade was starting round two. Right now.

Fantastic. Lexi and Juliette were going to love this when I told them later.

The elevator doors opened, and the three of us stepped

inside. I clung to Ian's arm a bit tighter than necessary as he tapped his keycard on the reader and pressed the button for our floor.

Once "10" lit up, he stepped back, giving Margot room.

She tapped her card, then paused. "Oh," she said, raising an eyebrow in surprise. "Looks like we're on the same floor."

Of course we were. She probably had one of the big suites, too.

Was it too much to hope we were at the opposite ends of the floor?

We were silent as the elevator began its ascent, the quiet almost amplifying the tension. But when I caught Margot peeking a glance our way, I knew I had a part to play. So trying to look as natural as possible, I leaned my head against Ian's shoulder and just hoped she couldn't somehow hear how fast my pulse was racing.

"Tired?" Ian mumbled into my hair, his tone warm and affectionate, perfectly in character for the moment we were trying to portray.

"Yeah," I said softly. "I know I said I was going to take a bath earlier, but I think I'll just head to bed."

I was tempted to add something about him keeping me up too late the night before—just to rile Margot up—but since I probably shouldn't say something like that to my boss, I just left it at that.

The elevator pinged when it reached our floor and the doors opened.

"Have a good night," Ian told Margot, nodding for her to step out ahead of us.

"You, too." She nodded curtly before exiting.

Ian and I held back, lingering just outside the elevator as we watched Margot walk down the hall. But instead of continuing to the far end of our floor like I'd hoped, she stopped at the door just across the hall from ours. And when she glanced back at us as if waiting for us to go into our rooms, I knew she was most definitely watching to see what we did next.

Had she somehow found out which room Ian would be staying in and had requested to be close by?

Because this was just way too much to be a simple coincidence.

My eyes flicked up to Ian's, silently asking, *What now?*

"Don't take this the wrong way," he murmured, leaning close enough for me to feel the warmth of his breath on my ear, "but I think I'm going to need you to come into my room with me."

Oh boy. This night had to be breaking all sorts of company rules.

But since Margot seemed to be taking her time at her door, digging inside her purse as if she'd lost her key, I really didn't see another way out of this.

So, instead of stopping at my room like I had the first time we'd gone down this hall together, I followed Ian a few steps farther to his door and waited for him to unlock it.

The light on the keypad flashed green, and after taking a deep breath, I followed Ian into his hotel suite.

"Well, that was close," Ian said, sighing heavily once his door had clicked shut.

"Close?" I looked back at him, arching a brow. "That was nearly an ambush."

"Yeah." Ian chuckled, his gaze meeting mine. "It does seem like that."

"Do you think she knew where you were staying and asked for a room close by?" I voiced the question I had earlier.

"I have no idea." He ran his fingers through his dark hair,

tousling it. "We've literally had no contact since we broke up. So it would be strange if she did."

"I guess so..." I bit my lip. "...unless her real motivation for coming to the conference was to meet up with you. Possibly reignite the spark you once had."

"Well, she might want to catch up, but I have zero desire to even visit memory lane with her." He crossed his arms and blew out a breath. "So as far as I'm concerned, she's just another random hotel guest across the hall from us."

He really thought he'd be able to avoid her all weekend?

Because, with the few short interactions they'd already had, and the whole fiancée charade he'd accidentally started, I doubted it would be as easy as that.

"I get that you want to ignore her," I said, understanding his desire to keep the past in the past. "But as much as you want that, she's clearly planning to keep an eye on you. Which means that now that she also thinks I'm supposed to be your fiancée, she'll be watching me, too."

"I guess you're right." Ian sighed, letting his shoulders droop. "I really should have just replied to her email and told her to buzz off."

"It certainly would have been easier than what we've already done so far." I chuckled.

"Sorry about that." He shook his head, a guilty look filling his eyes. "And now she thinks we're sharing this room."

I nodded slowly, acutely aware that we were standing in his room together, just a short distance from his bed.

Was I going to have to stay in here tonight?

Wearing this dress as a nightgown since my stuff was locked away in the room next door?

As if reading my thoughts, Ian said, "I should probably just knock on her door and fess up to this whole thing, shouldn't I? Tell her I wanted to have a little fun pretending I was engaged for a bit, but that we're actually only here together because of business."

"You really want to do that?" I asked, thinking about how uncomfortable I'd feel doing that if I was in his situation.

"Well, it's not like I can ask you to pretend to be madly in love with me all weekend, forcing you to sleep in my bed...just so I can save face now, can I?"

My breath hitched at the idea of sleeping in his bed. And on instinct, I looked around the room, curious if it was similar to my room next door.

And that was when I noticed something on the wall just behind me. A door.

"Actually..." I said, stepping closer to the door to see if it was what I thought it might be. When I turned the lock and opened it, I found that there was another door just on the other side of it.

I glanced back to Ian. When he seemed to realize what I was looking at, a slow smile lifted his lips and he said, "Do you think these doors connect our rooms together?"

"I think so."

"So..." He tapped his chin thoughtfully. "That means that if one of us can get into your room and unlock that door from your side, we could actually keep up the ruse that we're both staying in here by just using this door."

"Uh-huh." I nodded slowly, considering it.

"Yes, this could work," he continued, seeming to form a plan in his mind as he paced. "We could make Margot think we're always together, while still allowing you to have your own space and that downtime I promised you."

"And if Margot keeps watching us..." I said, feeling the tension in my shoulders ease slightly as this new plan formed, "we can just use your door anytime we need to come and go."

"Exactly," Ian replied. He turned back toward the door that

led to the hall. After peeking through the peephole, he said, "No one is out there right now. So if you give me your keycard, I can just sneak into your room real quick and unlock the door."

"But what if she comes out and sees you?"

He looked around the room. Seeming to have an idea, he stepped past me. After inspecting the room quickly, he walked toward the mini bar and picked up the ice bucket sitting on the small countertop.

"I'll take this with me, and if Margot happens to open her door and sees me trying to get in the wrong room, I'll just pretend I went to get ice and accidentally stopped at the wrong door."

"Good idea," I said, thinking this might actually work.

So with the ice bucket tucked under his arm, he held out his hand for my key. After retrieving it from my purse and handing it to him, I said, "Good luck."

Then once he was at the door, he took a quick glance down the hall to ensure the coast was clear before stepping out.

I watched the door close, my heart thumping faster than it should for such a simple plan.

But then, less than a minute later, there was a soft knock sounding from the adjoining door.

Yay, he did it, I thought to myself as I stepped toward the door. *I won't have to sleep in this dress after all.*

I found Ian leaning casually against the doorframe when I opened the door, looking like a Greek god with a victorious smile on his face. "Ta-da."

And I couldn't help but laugh at the ridiculousness of this situation. It was like I was back in high school again, sneaking around with college guys behind my dad's back.

Only, this particular guy was way hotter than the guys I'd partied with back then.

If only my sixteen-year-old self could see us now.

Ian handed me back my key, and after returning the ice bucket to the counter above the mini bar, he asked, "So, are you really okay with pretending to be my fiancée while we're here? Because I know it's a huge ask and probably not at all what you envisioned when you agreed to come here with me."

"Will you fire me if I say no?" I asked, mostly joking though a small part of me worried my job could actually be on the line.

"Of course not," he said. Then inspecting my face better, his brow furrowed with concern, he asked, "Is that why you played along so well before? Because you thought your job would be in jeopardy if you didn't?"

"I actually didn't have time to think that deeply about it," I said. "I was panicking right along with you."

"Fair enough." He studied my expression, his gaze searching, as if trying to read what I wasn't saying. Then he took a step closer, his hand reaching for mine. "So, what do you say, Maddie Stevens?" His voice dropped to a low murmur. "Will you be my fake fiancée while we're in Boston?"

When his brown eyes met mine with an intensity I hadn't seen before, a wave of heat spread through me. And when his gaze briefly dipped to my lips, I couldn't help but think that if he kept looking at me like that, I'd probably agree to just about anything he asked.

"Yes," I managed, my voice barely a breath, betraying my sudden nerves. "I'll be your fake fiancée."

"Thank you." He lifted my hand to his lips, his kiss soft and warm against my knuckles.

And oh, when his gaze locked on mine in that moment, I suddenly felt like I might just melt into a puddle at his feet.

This man. He was way too charming for his own good—and I could understand why he never had trouble getting women to fall for him.

But it's just an act this time, I reminded myself. *He's just getting into the character of a doting fiancé.*

He let my hand fall gently, then stepped back. "I'm sure we'll need to go over the particulars of our little arrangement so we can make sure we're on the same page. But since I've already commandeered so much of your evening, I should let you go. We can work out a game plan in the morning."

"Okay," I said, nodding—though part of me really didn't want to leave him yet.

"I know the conference starts at eight o'clock, but I don't really need to attend anything until our lunch with the people from Urban Pantry, so maybe I can order room service for breakfast and we can go over everything then?"

"Sure," I said, my mind still needing to catch up with everything going on.

"Perfect," Ian said. "Just look over the menu tonight and text me what you want, and I'll call in our order when I wake up."

"Oh, shouldn't I be doing that?" I asked. "Since I'm your assistant."

"You're my fiancée this weekend," he said with a wink. "So I'll take care of it."

"Okay." Though it still felt weird having my boss being the one to take care of things like that for me.

"We'll figure out the game plan for everything else in the morning." He stepped forward, the signal that it was time for me to go back into my room for the night.

So I went through the doorway connecting our suites and made ready to close the door.

"Goodnight, Maddie," he murmured, his gaze holding a warmth that made my heart skip. "Sleep well."

"Goodnight, Ian."

And as I closed the door connecting our suites, I couldn't

help but think that being Ian Hastings' fake fiancée was already proving to be far more thrilling than anything I'd done in a long time.

I just hoped that when the weekend was over, my heart would remember that any feelings I may or may not catch for my handsome boss would have to remain fake.

16

______

MADDIE

A KNOCK SOUNDED on the door attached to Ian's room just a few minutes after eight o'clock. Having overslept, since I'd apparently forgotten to set my alarm last night, I'd been rushing around in a panic to get ready before my breakfast meeting with Ian.

Because yeah, even though I'd be pretending to be his significant other this weekend, he was still definitely my boss, and therefore, would probably still expect me to be on time and professionally dressed for the meetings we had scheduled.

When I opened the door, I expected to find Ian standing there wearing a suit and tie, since that was all I'd ever seen him in. Instead, he was dressed in a T-shirt and shorts, like he'd decided to take a quick run or hit the gym before breakfast.

Which made sense, I guess. The kind of muscles he had didn't just show up without effort.

"Sorry, I wasn't sure if I should text you or just knock on this door," he said, his eyes warm as he glanced down at me, seeming to take in the white blouse and pink skirt I wore. "But breakfast just got here, so we can get started whenever you're ready."

"I'll be right there," I said. Then I grabbed my phone and a notebook and followed Ian into his room.

His room looked much the same as it had the day before, the only real difference being that his bed looked slept in now.

"This way," he said, gesturing toward the open balcony doors. So I followed him out to the small table he'd set up, complete with white linens, silver domed platters, and coffee that steamed invitingly in the cool morning air. "It's a nice morning," he said, giving a nod toward the sun-kissed Boston skyline. "I figured we could enjoy it out here."

I stepped onto the balcony, breathing in the summer air, and the city seemed to stretch out beneath us, bathed in soft sunlight, the traffic below distant enough to add a gentle hum to the calm.

"You can sit here," Ian said, pulling out a chair for me. Once we were both seated, he lifted the lid on my plate, revealing a fluffy omelet folded around fresh veggies and melted cheese, exactly what I'd ordered.

I glanced at his plate and noticed he had the same food. "Looks like we have the same taste."

"Your order sounded so good," he said, his cheeks coloring slightly, "that I may have been forced to copy you."

I reached for my coffee, smiling to myself as I added a splash of half-and-half and a drizzle of honey. Stirring, I took a tentative sip, savoring the warmth that slowly spread through me.

"So," I began, setting my mug down, "what's the plan for when we're around your clients? Am I supposed to do the fiancée thing during those meals, or stick to the assistant role?"

"Good question," he said, patting his lips with his napkin. "I think for the client lunches and dinners, it's best if I introduce you as my assistant and keep things professional, since that's how they'll know you going forward from this weekend."

"Makes sense." I nodded, thinking that sounded like a good idea. "Just keep things how they were at dinner with Mr. and Mrs. Kwan, then?"

"Yes, exactly." He smiled. "I mean, if we were actually engaged, we'd probably keep it low-key at work, right? My parents have always handled things that way, at least."

"What about the conference and the mixers?" I asked. "Should we just do the same with those, too?"

"Margot will probably be at a lot of those," Ian said, scrunching up his nose. "And while I hope she won't be constantly watching us, I think it would probably be best if we acted more like a couple during those events."

"So with clients, I'm just your assistant," I said, tilting my head thoughtfully. "And at the mixers, I'm the assistant that you couldn't resist asking to marry you."

"Yes, something like that." His eyes crinkled at the corners, seeming to like how I'd worded it.

"I really got my claws into you quickly now, didn't I?" I asked playfully, cutting into my omelet with my fork. "Worked for you for only two and a half weeks and you couldn't resist proposing that I stay by your side forever."

"I mean, clearly," Ian said with a chuckle, playing along, "one look into those beautiful blue eyes of yours and I was hypnotized."

And when his gaze flicked across the table to meet mine, I couldn't stop the heat from rising up my neck and coloring my cheeks.

Unable to hold his gaze for longer than two seconds, I looked down at my plate again. Trying to push my blush away, I asked, "Do you think we should put any sort of guidelines in place? Just so we kind of know what each other's boundaries are, PDA-wise."

"Ah yes." He cleared his throat, his gaze focusing like he'd gotten lost in thought for a moment. "That's probably a good idea." He paused, taking a sip of his coffee. "So...how are you with PDA in general? Do you like it, or prefer to keep things private?"

"I'm fine with little things. Holding hands, staying close," I said. "But anything more than a quick peck in public is crossing more into territory I'm not super comfortable having onlookers witness."

He raised an eyebrow, a playful glint in his eyes. "So kissing me in front of everyone at the club was out of character for you?"

I laughed, rolling my eyes at his flirtatious tone. "Believe it or not, that was a one-time thing. At least since I've been an adult."

His smirk softened with curiosity. "Were you a wild teen?"

"Well..." I said, my thoughts drifting back to that chapter of my life. "Considering I got pregnant during my junior year of high school, I'd say I was just a *little* wild."

He stilled, taking that in with a thoughtful nod. "So you were pregnant during your junior year?"

"Yeah," I said, my voice a little quieter. "I found out that March, and Grant was born in October of my senior year."

"That must have been a crazy time," he said, his tone gentle, and I appreciated that it didn't sound like he was judging me for getting pregnant so young.

Not everyone reacted so kindly.

"It was," I replied, swallowing as I thought back. "I remember feeling like my life was over. But my dad—after the initial shock—was amazing. He flew me home from North Carolina, and he and my siblings really went above and beyond to help me out. I never could have graduated without their help."

"North Carolina?" he asked, his brow furrowing. "Did you use to live there?"

"Yeah." I nodded, heat creeping up my neck as I remembered that fateful night on the beach. "My dad sent me there for a couple of months to live with my aunt in a town called Sweet Water. It was supposed to keep me from 'getting into too much trouble.' But little did we all know, I'd already found trouble before I'd even moved there. I just hadn't taken the pregnancy test yet."

Something flickered in Ian's eyes when I said that. And when his gaze seemed to search mine, like he was trying to match my face with a memory, I couldn't help but wonder if he was remembering that night on the beach, too.

He swallowed, his Adam's apple bobbing with the movement before he asked, "So you found out you were pregnant while you were in Sweet Water?"

"Yes..." I swallowed, suddenly shaky with nerves. "I-it was right around my cousin's spring break and..."

But before I could finish that sentence, a knock sounded on Ian's door, interrupting the moment.

Ian glanced at the door, slightly startled. But then, seeming to return to the moment, he shook his head and said, "That must be my family's jeweler."

"Your family's jeweler?" I blinked, not expecting him to say that.

How fancy did a family have to be in order to have a "family jeweler" who would travel to see you this early on a weekday?

He gave me a playful smile as he stood and set his napkin on his chair. "I asked to have some engagement rings delivered for you to choose from."

17

———

IAN

AS I CROSSED the room to see who was at the door, my mind spun, tangled with the revelation Maddie had just dropped. *Sweet Water, North Carolina.* That was where she'd taken her pregnancy test.

Was it possible she was the girl I'd met on the beach? Could the girl I'd worried about through the years, hoping she would be okay after seeming so lost that night, actually be Maddie?

That night had been memorable, if fleeting—just two teenagers hanging out on a starlit shore, talking about the different sob stories we were currently wading through. She'd told me she was in college, visiting Sweet Water for spring break, just like me.

But had that been a lie? Had she only pretended to be in college to fit in with the crowd, thinking she'd never see me again? I remembered catching a hint of her perfume last week; the scent stirring up the memory of that night. I thought it was strange at the time that I'd suddenly been thrust back into that memory as it had been years since I'd last thought of it, but maybe it hadn't been so strange after all—maybe it had resurfaced because I'd actually been reunited with that girl and just hadn't realized it.

I opened the door, managing a smile for Mr. Calvin, the jeweler who'd handled my family's jewelry needs for as long as I could remember. "Thanks for coming on such short notice," I said, shaking his hand and inviting him in.

He chuckled, following me inside. "When a Hastings family member calls, I've learned it's best to answer."

"You're probably right." I laughed. "Diamonds and us—seems like a family tradition."

"A tradition I'm more than happy to help you keep." He winked.

"Go ahead and get settled in here," I said, gesturing to the sitting area. "I'll call Maddie in."

He began arranging everything he'd brought in his briefcase, opening it to reveal a couple dozen rings that sparkled under the lights.

As he continued to put everything in its place, I stepped out onto the balcony where Maddie was still finishing her breakfast.

"Hey," I said. "Could you come inside for a minute?"

Curiosity flickered in her eyes as she followed me back in. I introduced her to Mr. Calvin, and she gave a polite nod. For some reason, I felt a strange flutter in my chest, a mix of nerves and anticipation, even though this wasn't anything as serious as a real engagement.

"If you'd like to sit down," I said, motioning to the sofa, "you can take a look and see if there's anything you like."

Maddie's eyes went wide as she took in the collection spread before her. "Wow," she whispered. "I don't think I've ever seen real diamonds that big up close before."

"They're something, aren't they?" I chuckled. "I asked Mr.

Calvin to bring some similar to the size of the ring my brother Carter got his fiancée last year, so...here we are."

She bit her lip, eyes sweeping over the rings, each one a masterpiece. "They're all so beautiful. I don't even know where to start."

Mr. Calvin stepped in, asking her about her ring size and preferences. They went back and forth, narrowing it down until she finally settled on a few options with gold bands, ones that kept the design simple yet elegant, just like her style.

"Would you like to try these on?" I suggested, nodding toward her hand. "Just to see how they look on your ring finger."

Maddie hesitated, as if trying on an actual ring was crossing some invisible line.

Deciding she might need some help, I reached for the nearest ring, one with a thin gold band and a massive, oval-cut diamond. I paused as I offered it to her, silently asking if it was okay. She gave me a shy nod.

My heart thumped unexpectedly as I went through the motion of placing the ring onto her ring finger, and I braced myself for that old, familiar dread—the PTSD of my previous failed engagement.

But the hot flashes and panic I was waiting for didn't come. Instead, there was something entirely different: a strange, poignant longing.

As if, for the first time in nine years, I wanted to actually settle down and get engaged.

Like maybe what I'd told Margot was truer than I thought and I actually did want to find someone to share the day-to-day moments with more than I'd let myself admit.

Maddie turned her hand, watching the diamond catch the light. And after a brief moment, she said, "I really like it."

When her gaze met mine, just inches between us, I

couldn't stop my heart from pounding. She was so...breathtaking. And there was just something about an engagement ring on her finger that seemed right.

I swallowed, my voice dropping as I murmured, "I like that one, too."

For a beat, we held each other's gaze. Her lips parted, cheeks flushed in a way that made me want to touch her, to reach out and brush my thumb across her cheek. But before I could get too lost, Mr. Calvin broke the silence, asking, "Do you think this is the one?"

Maddie blinked, looking back at the other rings. "Maybe..." But after looking back and forth between the ring she wore and the other remaining options, she pointed to one with a diamond-encrusted band and asked, "Could we actually try that one, too?"

"Of course." Mr. Calvin nodded, lifting a radiant-cut diamond ring from its place. "This one's new—a four-carat piece I made earlier this month." He handed it to me, and I carefully slipped it onto her finger, my chest tightening as the diamond settled in place.

Maddie stared at it, breath catching, and whispered, "I—" She bit her lip, glancing at Mr. Calvin, then back at me. "I think this is the one."

I swallowed, meeting her gaze, and said softly, "I think it is, too."

"Congratulations again, Ian." Mr. Calvin smiled, shaking my hand after we'd settled up. "She's a beautiful woman. And I know it's probably not my place to say, but...I think she'll suit you better than any of the others I've seen you with over the years."

"Thank you, Mr. Calvin. I..." I blinked, momentarily caught off guard by his words and their meaning. But then, managing a confident smile, I finished with, "I'm just so thankful to have found her."

Mr. Calvin nodded approvingly, then left with a small wink, promising his discretion with our secret engagement. Saying that until Maddie and I made our formal announcement, he wouldn't mention this meeting to my family.

Which would definitely be good because I did not have the slightest idea how I was going to explain getting engaged to my assistant a mere three weeks after meeting her.

Well, meeting her again, I supposed. I was more sure than ever that we'd met for the first time long ago.

I closed the door behind Mr. Calvin and when I turned back, Maddie was waiting in the living room, looking slightly curious about the exchange I just had.

But since I wasn't ready to dive into what he'd said about Maddie being better suited for me than my previous flings, I looked out to the balcony instead where my breakfast still sat and said, "I guess my omelet is probably too cold to finish now, isn't it?"

"Probably," Maddie said. "But I can reheat your plate if you like." She tilted her head, smirking. "I know fancy billionaires like yourself probably don't have to use these strange contraptions called microwaves that us normal folk use and love, but I promise it'll still taste pretty good reheated. I eat second-day scrambled eggs all the time."

"Well, in that case..." I laughed, liking her playful mockery of my pampered lifestyle. "I'll let you handle it. I never learned to use a microwave, anyway. All those buttons are just too complicated for a spoiled trust-fund kid like myself."

She laughed at my comment, giving me a teasing grin as she grabbed my plate and gingerly put it in the microwave. "Now, just watch me make some magic happen," she said before making a big show of pushing a few buttons and pressing *start*.

"Amazing," I said. "What witchcraft did you just perform? Whatever would I do without you?"

"Probably call room service for a new omelet," she said.

And I couldn't help but grin because she was exactly right.

As my food warmed, Maddie's gaze went back to her left hand. And after playing with the ring with her thumb, as if checking the fit, she said, "I'm glad Mr. Calvin got my size right when he was picking rings to bring. Because with a diamond this heavy, I'd hate for it to slip off my finger and lose it."

"Yeah, that's a big diamond." I nodded, looking at the size of the rock on her finger. Then, suddenly worried it may have been too extravagant, I asked, "Do you think it's too much?"

"Too much?" She raised an eyebrow, her blue eyes going wide like my question surprised her.

I pointed at the ring. "I mean, if you were picking out an engagement ring for real, would you go for something like this?"

"A four-carat, custom-made diamond ring?" Her eyes glimmered with humor. "Yeah, I doubt any man interested in marrying me could ever afford a ring like this, Ian. This thing is huge."

"Fair enough," I said, laughing. "But if you did happen to meet a wealthy guy and fall in love, would you get a ring like this? Or something different altogether?"

"I don't know..." She looked down at the ring again, her eyes seeming to watch the way it sparkled as she tilted her hand this way and that. "I guess if money wasn't an issue, I'd probably be happy to wear a ring like this. It's gorgeous."

"Did you pick out your ring when you got married before?" I asked, suddenly curious what her ex had gotten her. "Or did your ex surprise you?"

"I actually never got a ring," she said. She must have noticed my confused expression because she added, "Jaxon and I never actually got married."

"Oh...I thought..." I let my words trail off, realizing I wasn't sure if she'd ever actually said she'd married her son's father. Trying to recall if she'd ever mentioned being divorced, I finally said, "Sorry, I shouldn't have assumed."

"It's fine," she said with a slight shrug. "I think most people would assume something like that, especially since we share a kid and were together for so long." She took a deep breath, and her shoulders seemed to sag as she let it out. "But Jaxon never asked. And after so many years, it just...wasn't a priority. We were too busy raising Grant and keeping our heads above water to worry about planning a wedding."

I watched as her gaze drifted, a faraway look in her eyes, and I guessed that there was probably some disappointment there. Most little girls dream of a wedding day, and Maddie had never had hers.

I shifted, rubbing the back of my neck. "If I'd known this was your first time wearing an engagement ring, I would've put a bit more effort into the proposal."

Her eyes brightened at my attempt to lighten the mood, and she let out a little laugh. "Well, since none of this is even real, I guess I'll let it pass."

The microwave beeped, and Maddie pulled out my plate, studying it for a moment before looking back at me. "Normally, I'd poke a finger in the middle to check if it's hot enough, but I'll spare you that."

"How thoughtful of you."

She smirked, handing me the plate. "I do try to be thoughtful now and then."

Taking her suggestion to heart, I poked the center of the omelet, feeling it was warm enough. "Looks like your trick works," I said, wiping my finger clean. "Might even come in handy if I ever crack the code on using a microwave."

She laughed, settling into the chair Mr. Calvin had vacated, crossing her legs and watching me. "Now the real test is whether these reheated eggs are still edible."

I took a bite of the omelet. "Not bad," I said when it didn't taste too much different from the bites I'd taken earlier. "It's actually better than I expected."

"Told you leftovers rock," she said with a wink.

"Do you have leftovers a lot?" I asked, curious.

She shrugged. "Sloan and I share kitchen duties these days, but back when I was in Ridgewater, I doubled recipes just to have leftovers. It saved me from cooking every day."

"Smart."

I finished off the plate and set it on the coffee table. Then leaning back against the cushions, I decided we should probably get back to the conversation we'd been having earlier and said, "So, before Mr. Calvin showed up, I think we were talking about setting some ground rules for this whole thing, right?"

Maddie tucked some hair behind her ear. "I think that's right."

"And you said you're not super into PDA, right?"

"Our first meeting aside? Then, not really..." She looked at me intently. "What about you?"

"Well..." I said, the back of my neck suddenly feeling hot. "I may have leaned more to the other extreme in the past." Which was basically code for me having the inability to turn away from a good make-out session with a beautiful woman if the mood struck. "But I can definitely see the prudence in toning things back a bit. It would have certainly helped me keep my name out of the tabloids in the past."

"Being discreet isn't nearly as exciting to report on, I suppose," Maddie said with a grin.

"And we both know what a fame-whore I've been in the past." I winked. "But...in case we run into Margot or anyone connected to her..." I cleared my throat, keeping things as casual as I could. "Would you be okay with me holding your hand again? Kind of like I did last night?"

She nodded, a soft smile touching her lips. "I think that'd be fine."

"What about putting my arm around your waist?"

"That's fine, too," she said, her voice steady, though there was a hint of pink on her cheeks.

"All right," I said, nodding. "Good to know." I hesitated, glancing sideways at her. "What about a kiss on the cheek? Is that okay?"

She blinked, and her smile softened. "I think that should be fine. Kisses on the cheek are sweet, anyway."

"Good. Then I think that's as far as we'll need to go in public. We want this to seem professional—no hands all over each other."

Her blush deepened at my mention of us having our hands all over each other and looked away. Which only reminded me of the delicate situation we were in.

Sure, she'd agreed to pretend to be my fiancée this weekend, wearing a ring and letting me keep her close. But I needed to be careful not to get reality confused with make-believe.

Because playing pretend with someone I was already so attracted to was a recipe for trouble—like tempting fate to pick up where we'd left off that night we first met.

And before I knew it, my mind betrayed me, flashing images so vivid it was like she was already in my arms.

I could feel the weight of her leaning into me at the bar, her lips just inches from mine, her breath warm and unsteady as her eyes searched mine with that unmistakable spark. I imagined drawing her closer, feeling the way her body would press against mine, every inch of her soft and willing as our mouths finally collided in a kiss that felt as inevitable as it was explosive.

We wouldn't stop there; I'd lean in, whispering something about not wanting the night to end, about bringing her somewhere private. She'd nod, maybe with that shy smile she'd flashed before, the one that always tempted me. And in the next second, we'd be alone, behind closed doors in a room like this, where I'd lift her into my arms, our lips meeting in hungry, dizzying kisses as I carried her to the bed, ready to taste her laughter and every inch of her that she'd offer me.

Nope. We're not going there. I cut off my fantasy before it could continue further down that forbidden path.

Maddie was my assistant. She was a *mother*.

And I was not going to even entertain the idea of treating this situation like I had other relationships in the past.

We might be about to fake an engagement, but the last thing I wanted was to make her life more complicated than it already was.

"So...should we come up with a story?" Maddie's voice broke into my thoughts, thankfully oblivious to my momentary lapse. "You know, in case someone asks how we met and fell in love, or...how you proposed."

"Yeah." I cleared my throat, focusing my gaze back on her face. "Let's come up with something good."

18

MADDIE

MY HEART GAVE a little leap as Ian helped me out of his car and handed his keys to the valet. We'd gotten through today's client meals without anyone so much as glancing at the huge rock on my finger, but now that we were back at the hotel and about to walk into the summit's first big mixer, I had a feeling that things were about to ramp up. Margot would be in the same ballroom as us, and even if we didn't actually end up interacting with her face to face, she could be watching us at any moment, and I needed to be convincing in my new role as Ian's fiancée.

Ian glanced over at me, his mouth pulling into a small smile as he took my hand, a spark of confidence settling in his eyes. "It's showtime, my darling," he murmured, giving my hand a reassuring squeeze. And even though I knew it was all just for show, the butterflies fluttered around in my stomach from the gesture.

Ian's hand was strong and warm, and though I'd tried so hard to be a strong, independent woman through the years, there was something comforting about holding his hand. Like maybe, even if it was just for tonight, I didn't actually have to handle everything on my own.

The ballroom was filled with a warm, golden glow when we walked in. String lights were woven throughout the decorations. Little tables dotted the room, each one perfectly set up for a private conversation or a cozy gathering, and two bar stations offered a variety of drinks, including the evening's signature drink—a watermelon margarita.

My mouth practically watered at the thought, partly because I loved watermelon margaritas and partly because a little social lubricant wouldn't hurt to help me settle into this night.

"Shall we get our drinks?" Ian asked, nodding toward the line at one of the bars once we were inside.

"Sure," I said, glad he was happy to make it our first stop.

As we queued up, Ian turned to me, his tone suddenly playful. "So, are you the type of fiancée who wants her man to order her drink for her? Or do you prefer to order for yourself?"

"Honestly?" I asked, scrunching up my nose. "I don't think anyone has ever offered to order for me before." Jaxon certainly never had. "But I guess I've sometimes thought it might be nice to have a guy take charge—in a respectful way, of course."

"Of course." Ian winked. "Respect is a must."

"What about you?" I asked.

"I usually order my own drinks, too." Ian tilted his head, amusement flashing in his eyes. "Oddly enough, my dates haven't offered to order for me in the past, either."

"Very funny." I rolled my eyes, nudging him. "You know what I meant."

"Oh, you mean if I like to order for my date?"

I nodded, curious despite myself.

"It depends on the woman, I suppose." He shrugged. "If

she likes it, I'll go for it. If not, that's fine, too." Leaning in, he added, "But tonight, I'd be happy to do it for you."

And I didn't know why, but the way he said that, with his shoulder gently brushing against mine, sent a rush of warmth all throughout my body.

Yeah...I was pretty sure I wouldn't mind having Ian Hastings take care of me for an evening, if for no other reason than to just have a night off from constantly being on watch for my own safety and security.

We made it to the bartender, and after placing his arm around my waist, Ian ordered two watermelon margaritas, sending a warm tingle through me.

The entire day we'd been keeping things low-key, almost businesslike. But now that the sun was slanting through the windows, the day transforming into night, he was leaning into his fake fiancé role, committing more fully to our little ruse.

With our drinks in hand, we strolled deeper into the ballroom, Ian guiding me by the hand around the tables and nodding at familiar faces until we stopped in front of a tall, dark-haired guy whose green eyes lit up at the sight of him.

"Drake Prewitt!" Ian said, clapping him on the shoulder. "Fancy seeing you here."

"Ian, my man, it's been ages!" Drake said, pulling Ian in for a quick hug.

"It has been," Ian said, patting his friend on the back. "Much too long."

"And who is this?" Drake glanced over at me when they stepped apart, curiosity in his eyes.

"This is Maddie." Ian set his hand on my waist again, pulling me close.

"Nice to meet you, Maddie." Drake extended a hand, his expression warm.

"Likewise," I replied with a smile, shaking his hand.

Ian's gaze lingered on me, and I thought I caught a flicker of hesitation, as though he was considering whether or not to introduce me as his fiancée.

But seeming to decide against it, he instead explained to me, "Drake and I go way back. Met in high school and then continued on to Yale together."

"Practically grew up together," Drake said with a chuckle.

"That we did." Ian's brown eyes sparked, like he was remembering something from their past before he asked, "So, what brings you here? I don't think I've seen you since college."

"I'm here with my mom's company." Drake gave a casual shrug. "Trying to pick up a few nuggets to help us level up."

"Nice," Ian said.

"Yeah, just trying to be half as successful as you." Drake smirked, and I got the feeling that there had always been some healthy competition between the two. "But all that aside, I've got to say that I'm really looking forward to your keynote tomorrow." Drake's expression turned into admiration. "I still remember how you wowed everyone in Professor Calhoon's class with your presentations. You were the king of persuasive pitches back then."

"Glad you're looking forward to it." Ian laughed. "I'm hoping it'll be decent."

"I have no doubt it'll be awesome," Drake said, clapping him on the shoulder. Then looking at me, Drake added, "I always tell everyone that Ian has the Midas touch because every idea he's had seems to be golden. But I'm sure that since you seem to be close, you already know that."

I was just trying to come up with a response when I caught sight of a familiar woman with polished blonde waves approaching us from the corner of my eye.

Margot.

Okay. Looks like it is really showtime now.

"Well, isn't this a blast from the past?" Drake said good-naturedly when Margot stepped into the space between himself and me. "All of us here at the same event—it's like a mini-college reunion."

"Yes—" Margot's gaze flicked from Ian to me, her eyes sharpening when she seemed to catch a glimpse of the ring on my left hand. "But with one big addition—Ian's beautiful fiancée."

The comment landed like a spark. "Wait—" Drake's eyes widened, darting to Ian and me. "You two are engaged?" He looked genuinely surprised. "Congratulations! That's... Wow, that's amazing."

Ian pulled me in closer, his warmth grounding me as he spoke with practiced ease. "Thanks, it's still pretty recent. We're still getting used to the idea ourselves."

"That's fantastic. It's about time you finally settled down. I remember back when..." Drake trailed off, a flash of embarrassment crossing his face as his gaze instantly darted between Ian and Margot, as though he'd been about to mention something about their own previous engagement.

"I figured I'd take a note from you, Drake, and try settling down a bit." Ian gave my waist a little squeeze, his voice smooth and warm as he took control of the conversation. "My dad used to tell me that marrying my mom was the best thing he ever did for his career—said it helped him focus and kept him from always chasing the next fling. Until this past year, I thought he was just saying that to keep me from using his jet so much, but it turns out...finding the right woman actually does a lot for a guy."

"It's true." Drake grinned, nodding in agreement. "Marrying Cassia has been a game-changer for me. Nothing like finding the right person to keep you grounded."

"So, how did you two meet, anyway?" Margo asked, an

almost challenging look in her eyes. "I mean, we usually find these things out on social media since Ian's always had such an exciting following. But he's been surprisingly quiet about this."

She was asking me? Instead of Ian?

Ugh.

But since Ian and I had known this question would come at some point tonight, I reminded myself of the story we'd practiced earlier that morning. "It's nothing too exciting, I'm afraid."

"Oh?" Margot asked, arching an eyebrow.

"Yes, so basically, I applied for a job at his company several months ago and when I was leaving my interview, I ended up in the elevator with the most charming man I'd ever met."

"Me, of course." Ian winked playfully, playing along with the story.

"Of course," I said, chuckling lightly like I was remembering how enchanted I'd been that first time I'd supposedly seen him. "Anyway, the elevator was apparently having issues that day and we ended up getting stuck between floors for a while. Ian, being the gentleman that he is, noticed that I was on the verge of a panic attack since I'm quite claustrophobic. And to keep me from getting too anxious, he struck up a conversation to distract me from what was going on."

"He's a proper knight in shining armor, yes," Margot said, an almost impatient tone in her voice. "And I assume he swept you off your feet immediately and then gave you the job you'd interviewed for earlier that day."

"Actually no," I said.

"No?" Margot's eyebrows knitted together, clearly taken aback.

I nodded, giving her a polite smile. "I mean, I was pretty enamored with him from the start, but the job I originally interviewed for was in a completely different department. And, unfortunately, I didn't get it."

Margot's mouth opened, then snapped shut as she processed this. "But I thought you—" She stopped herself abruptly, her gaze flickering between me and Ian with renewed suspicion.

And it made me wonder if she'd done some digging in the past twenty-four hours, and perhaps discovered we actually did work together, leaving her confused by my story.

Which, of course, was why Ian and I had crafted this carefully laid-out backstory. If anyone did want to dig into my employment with Hastings Industries, they'd find out I'd indeed originally interviewed back in March but didn't get hired until a few weeks ago.

"Anyway," Ian interjected smoothly, picking up the narrative, "once the elevator was finally back in service, I knew I wanted to see Maddie again—soon. So I got her number and arranged to meet up. It was a little tricky, since she lived a few hours away. But we managed to have our first date shortly after, and made it work whenever we could."

I nodded along, caught up in the story we'd rehearsed. "Eventually, I decided to apply for another position at Hastings Industries just to be closer. This time, unbeknown to either of us, it was actually for the position of Ian's executive assistant."

"And, of course, she got the job," Ian said, giving me a proud smile and a quick wink. Like our working together had been inevitable.

"Well..." Margot's expression twisted into something sly and almost condescending. She looked at Ian and said, "This girl certainly moves fast, doesn't she? Sees the Hastings prize and doesn't waste any time locking it down."

But Ian chuckled, unbothered by her jab, and with a hint of mystery in his tone, he said, "Actually, that's the real twist in our story. I'd been so burned in the past by women just looking for a piece of my family's money that I never told Maddie I was a Hastings. She thought I worked for a different company in the building. She didn't find out that I was a Hastings until her first day at work when we both got the huge surprise that she'd been hired as my assistant."

"Are you serious?" Drake asked with a chuckle, his eyes wide like he found the coincidence as amusing as we had since at least that part of the story was true. "That's almost too crazy to be true."

"I know," Ian said. "We were shocked, to say the least."

"Yeah," I said, joining in. "I'd planned to surprise him with getting a job in New Haven, since the long-distance thing wasn't sustainable with how deep our feelings were for each other. But man, did we both get the shock of our lives that first day."

"That we did." Ian glanced at me, his eyes sparkling as if remembering our true origin story. "A very happy surprise, though."

"So your whole relationship was based on lies and deceit?" Margot asked, not nearly as excited about our story as we were. "What a great foundation for a future marriage."

"I wouldn't say that," Ian quickly cut in, his gaze steady. "We knew all the things that mattered. The only thing she didn't know was the family I came from. But everything else between us was real. We knew each other's hearts..." His voice dropped to a pointed calmness, before he finished by looking straight at Margot and adding, "Unlike some relationships I've had in the past."

And I had to resist the urge to smile, because seeing Ian take a subtle dig at Margot felt oddly satisfying.

He turned to me then, his eyes warm. "And to be honest, I'm just grateful it was Maddie who was in that elevator with me that day." He squeezed me closer, brushing his thumb along my hip in a way that sent a thrill through my system. "From the outside, I get that it might seem fast, but I've never been happier—and I can't wait to start our future together."

Margot's smile grew tight, her gaze darting between us, clearly feeling the weight of Ian's attention on me. Finally, she cleared her throat. "Well, I should say hello to a few other people. It was great seeing you again, Drake." She nodded toward him, a smile on her lips that didn't reach her eyes. Then glancing back to Ian and me, she said, "Enjoy your evening, you two."

With that, she excused herself.

19

———

IAN

"WANT TO HEAD OUT?" I asked Maddie after finishing a conversation with the owner of a wig company about two hours into the mixer.

"Sure." Maddie shrugged, her blue eyes glittering from the soft light of the chandeliers above. "I'm good with whatever you want."

"Okay, good." I sighed, the tension I'd been holding in my shoulders all evening releasing slightly at the idea of escape. Because after two hours of handshakes, introductions, and Margot's relentless gaze, I was spent.

Not to mention the fact that my nerves about tomorrow's presentation were also creeping in.

So taking Maddie's hand in mine—a gesture I was starting to enjoy more than I should—I led her out of the crowded room, leaving our glasses on a tray by the door.

"Are you always so popular at these events?" Maddie asked once we'd made it to the foyer that led toward the elevators. "Or do you think you had more people coming up to you tonight because of your keynote tomorrow?"

"I usually talk to a lot of people at these events," I said as we walked past a painting of a fox in a wooded landscape. "But the line was new."

"Yeah, that line was crazy." Maddie looked up at me, and with a teasing glint in her eyes, she added, "Who knew my fiancé was such a hot commodity?"

"Well, apparently you did...since you moved towns and got a new job just to be closer to me." I winked.

"Do you think Margot bought our story?" Maddie asked in a hushed tone, glancing around quickly to make sure Margot wasn't following us.

"I couldn't tell you," I said with a shrug. "It's been nine years since we spoke, so honestly, I have no idea what's on her mind these days."

"Makes sense." Maddie nodded, though from her expression, I sensed she might've been looking for some reassurance.

So I quickly added, "But regardless of whatever Margot might think, you were incredible tonight. I'm pretty sure Drake will be expecting a wedding invite any day now."

"Glad I did okay." She blew out a breath, like she actually had been anxious about her performance.

I gave her hand a squeeze. "You were perfect."

I let my gaze linger on her face, momentarily lost in how she looked just then. The thought of brushing that stray lock of hair behind her ear had been on my mind all night—a move I could have played off as part of the act, if not for how real the impulse felt.

And having her by my side tonight, steady and supportive, had been a rare kind of comfort. Usually, I attended these events solo, or with my last assistant who was thirty years older than Maddie and who would often turn in after dinner.

But tonight, Maddie had been right there, making everything easier, even if I'd done most of the talking.

"So, what happened with you and Margot, anyway?" she asked, pulling me from my thoughts. "I know she cheated, but were there warning signs?"

"Honestly?" I turned slightly, meeting her gaze. "I didn't see it coming at all."

"So it was a complete shock?"

"Yeah..." I was about to go into it, but when we reached the elevators, a small group joined us. So instead of telling her my story with an audience, I instead pulled Maddie close when we got on the elevator—only for our little ruse, of course—and wrapped an arm around her, my hand settling at her waist. I could feel the warmth of her back against my chest as she tensed slightly, and for a moment, I wondered if her little intake of breath was just for show—or if she was having a reaction to being this close to me.

The elevator climbed, each floor ticking by too fast. The small group got off on the fourth floor, leaving us alone. My arm was still wrapped around Maddie's waist, and though we no longer had spectators for our little show, neither of us moved.

When the elevator doors closed again, Maddie looked up at me, her eyes holding a spark that seemed to match the rush in my veins. And for a moment, all I could hear was the quiet hum of the elevator and her soft breathing, quickening with each passing second.

I leaned in slightly, lowering my voice. "Is it wrong that I like holding you close like this?"

Her lips parted as her eyes searched mine—for what, I couldn't tell. But then, with a hesitant smile, she shook her head and whispered, "Only if it's wrong for me to admit I like it, too."

And that was all it took for the air between us to thicken, my pulse racing faster with every second.

Even though I knew I was pressing my luck, I let my hand

glide a little higher up her side, my fingers tracing the curve of her ribs, feeling the warmth of her skin beneath the thin fabric.

This woman... She felt too good.

So good that all I wanted to do was pull her close, to let her fit perfectly in my arms. The idea of pressing her gently against the wall, claiming her with a kiss that would linger far longer than necessary, hit me with an intensity that surprised me. If she really were my fiancée, if we weren't just pretending, I could pull her to me, let my lips explore the delicate skin along her neck, feel her shiver against me.

Unable to resist, I brushed a lock of hair behind her ear—the one that had taunted me all evening—exposing the soft line of her neck. My hand stayed there, hovering as I felt the thrum of her pulse beneath my fingertips.

Was that her heartbeat racing? Or was it mine?

She tilted her head back, her gaze going to my mouth. And the soft, shallow breaths she took were like unspoken words, filling the silence with a kind of plea. The look in her eyes invited me closer, closer than I should be, closer than I could let myself go.

One kiss. It would be so easy to lean in, to let my lips find hers, to get lost in that softness and let go of the self-control I'd clung to for weeks. Just a fraction closer, and I could finally feel her against me, let the scent of her become something I couldn't forget—

The elevator jolted slightly, slowing as it approached another floor. Maddie tensed, and I forced myself to pull back, the rush of longing tempered with an edge of frustration as the doors slid open and a man stepped in, glancing briefly at us before turning to press his floor number.

I let my arm drop but kept my hand lightly resting on her hip, unable to let go entirely. She stayed close, leaning into the small space between us as if she, too, wasn't ready to break whatever had sparked here. The man frowned at the panel, realizing his mistake.

"Oh, wrong way," he muttered, shaking his head.

I managed a chuckle. "Guess you'll have the place to yourself in a second. We're almost out."

The elevator reached our floor, and as we stepped off, I slid my hand into Maddie's. Her fingers tightened around mine, and I knew I wasn't alone in feeling that lingering, electric pull.

As we reached my suite, I fumbled for the key card, stealing a glance at her. The moment hung between us, and I wondered if she was thinking about how close I'd come to kissing her back there—if she wanted me to finish what I'd started.

The door unlocked with a soft beep, and as it swung open, I found myself saying, "Hey, it's not too late... Want to get cozy and hang out? Maybe watch a movie?"

And I could have done a little dance when her face lit up and she said, "Yeah, that sounds nice. Let me just change into some pajamas first."

So after she'd slipped through the connecting door to her room, I grabbed a T-shirt and shorts from my bag and changed. Then, for good measure, I went to my bathroom and used mouthwash before brushing my teeth.

You know...just because I liked having fresh breath. Not because I was expecting anything.

Then, stepping back into my room, I took a deep breath and settled onto the couch, trying to look as casual as possible despite the pounding in my chest.

A minute later, Maddie reappeared in the doorway connecting our rooms, wearing a pink cami and shorts, cheeks slightly flushed.

"Sorry, this is all I brought for pajamas," she said, looking a bit self-conscious.

"No need to apologize," I said, trying not to stare too openly, though it was difficult. "They look...perfect."

She tucked a leg under her as she sat on the opposite end of the couch, and I busied myself with the remote.

After a moment, she spoke. "So, you were starting to tell me downstairs... Do you mind sharing more about what happened with you and Margot?"

I glanced over, meeting her gaze. "I guess it's probably time that I tell you the non-tabloid version of my breakup, isn't it?"

"Only if you want to share," she replied, her voice warm.

I leaned back, exhaling. "If you were my real fiancée, you'd probably know everything about it by now, right?"

She nodded. "Probably."

I took a breath. "All right. So basically, we met in high school and were high school sweethearts and then ended up going to college together."

"So, pretty serious at a young age?" Maddie asked, her gaze softening.

"Yeah..." I sighed. "Anyway, she was the first girl I'd seriously dated, and so when we'd been together for two years and I was more in love with her than I'd ever been, I decided that the next logical step would be to get engaged."

"How old were you?" she asked.

"It was fall of our freshman year at Yale, so I'd just turned nineteen."

"Pretty young still."

I nodded. "My parents, bless them, saw how serious I was and tried to suggest that I cool things off a bit. Trying as tactfully as they could to tell me it might be good to date around a little before pledging my heart to the only person I'd dated for the rest of my life."

"Which I'm guessing you ignored since, just like me, you thought you knew better at that age."

"Exactly." I chuckled. "Parents are never wiser than us when we're teens. They're too out of touch."

"Seriously," Maddie said, laughing with me. "I mean, sneaking around with older guys is so fun. Only the dumb girls actually get pregnant."

"So we were basically on the same wavelength back then." I smirked, liking that we could both joke about the dumb choices we'd made when we were younger.

"Basically."

"Anyway," I continued, "Margot and I dated all throughout the fall of our freshman year, and I was so in love. Of course, now that I'm older and have had several more relationships, I know we weren't nearly as mature as we'd thought we were. But it felt good, and I was happy with her."

"It's nice to feel good with someone."

I nodded. "Then that December, I bought a ring, and the night after our last finals, I took her out to dinner at our favorite restaurant in Eden Falls. And being the romantic idiot that I was, I ended the night by taking her on a walk around my family's neighborhood to see the Christmas lights, ending in front of my parents' house where I had the words, 'Will You Marry Me?' lit up on our front yard."

"Aw, that's actually really sweet, Ian," Maddie said, looking at me with big eyes and pouty lips, like I was a cute little teddy bear.

"Well, I'm glad you at least think so."

"Did Margot not like it?"

"I don't know...she kind of got a terrified look in her eyes. I thought she was just nervous and excited at the time. But after everything that went down, I kind of wonder if she just went into shock and only said yes because she knew our families were spying on us through the window."

"Did your engagement not last for long, then?"

"We were engaged for about three months before the news broke about her sneaking around with Rhys Applegate." The professional hockey player who she would go on to date for the next five years.

"And did you not know about her cheating on you until it was in the tabloids?"

"Yeah..." I rubbed my arm and sighed. "Based on some things I've heard since then, I kind of think they might have been texting back before we were even engaged."

"What?" Maddie's eyes went wide.

"Yeah." I nodded. "I looked like a real idiot."

"You were in love with her, Ian," Maddie said, her eyes full of empathy. "It's normal to believe the best about someone until you have concrete evidence that proves otherwise."

"I guess. But I don't know. I just felt so stupid to think that I was actually going to marry her."

"It happens to the best of us." She shrugged. "Believe me, I understand that more than you probably know."

Which made me wonder, once again, about her and her ex. She'd said they weren't well matched and that she'd shouldered a lot of the workload that came with building a life together, but there had to be more to the story.

"So, did you immediately break off the engagement when you found out about her cheating?" Maddie asked. "Or did you try to make things work for a bit?"

"We actually didn't have much of a breakup," I said, rubbing the back of my neck.

"You didn't?" Maddie furrowed her brow, confused.

"Yeah. As soon as I saw the pictures of her and Rhys splashed all over the tabloids, I cut her off. No calls, no texts. Just...nothing."

"You never confronted her?" Maddie's jaw dropped. "Did you even get your ring back?"

"Nope." I shrugged. "Who knows, maybe she keeps the ring on her dresser as a reminder of what a fool I'd been."

"So yesterday was the first time you've seen her since you were together?" Maddie lifted an eyebrow. "You really didn't break up in person?"

"Apparently, back then, I was quick to cut people out of my life when they disappointed me," I said, realizing only in that moment that I'd basically done the same thing with Margot that I'd done with my dad the year before.

"So...do you still just ghost girls, then?" she asked. Her tone was casual, but I could tell she was really curious.

"Define ghosting..." I hesitated a beat, knowing I was likely about to look bad in Maddie's eyes.

She shrugged, keeping her tone casual but still curious. "I mean, I know you've had...relationships since Margot. But do you just disappear on women if things aren't exactly what you want?"

"Look, I'm not perfect." I scratched my neck, feeling a bit of heat. "Yeah, I've ghosted some women. If it was just a weekend thing, it didn't seem necessary to go through a whole...exit speech."

"Ian..." She frowned, disapproval clear in her gaze.

"Hey, I never claimed sainthood." I chuckled, raising my hands in surrender. "There's a reason I earned that 'billionaire playboy' title."

She narrowed her eyes at me, her lips tugging into a faint smirk. "And have you pulled that trick recently?"

"I haven't ghosted anyone in about a year." I met her gaze, holding it. "So, consider me a reformed man."

She laughed. "I guess it's easier when you're not dating."

"Touché," I said, smirking. But the way her expression softened, her eyes dropping to the floor as if she were turning something over, stirred a different kind of tension.

"So...if I hadn't shown up at your office that Monday after the club, but we ran into each other again somewhere..." she trailed off, looking up at me through her lashes.

"I probably would've asked you out." The answer came more naturally than I expected.

"Really?" Her gaze snapped to mine, her curiosity sparking something brighter between us.

"Yeah," I replied, meeting her stare, wanting her to know I meant it.

She paused, then tilted her head, looking almost doubtful. "But if we had gone out, would I have just gotten ghosted, too? Or maybe a polite 'too busy' text after a date or two?"

"You think I'd lose interest?" I frowned, surprised that she'd assume that.

She looked away, her fingers picking at a loose thread on her shorts. "I've seen the women you date. I don't look like them. I have a kid. It wouldn't be hard to assume you'd change your mind once you knew all that."

I wanted to protest, to tell her she was wrong, but the words caught in my throat. After a moment, I murmured, "I'd like to think I'm better than that..."

She gave a small smile, eyes still lowered. "Well, since it's all hypothetical and that first date never happened...I guess we'll never know."

That thought gnawed at me, and I was about to say as much when her phone buzzed. She glanced down, and her eyes brightened. "It's Grant," she said, already standing. "I should take this."

"You can take it here," I said, trying to hide how much I wanted her to stay. "I need to look over my notes for tomorrow's presentation, anyway."

She nodded, a big smile lifting her cheeks as she answered her video call.

And I didn't know what it was, but seeing her light up like that at the prospect of talking to her son did funny things to my insides.

"Hi, Grant," she said, her voice taking on a happy and nurturing tone. "How are you doing, buddy?"

And even though I just wanted to sit there and listen in on her conversation, so curious about what her son was like, I made myself get up from the couch and go into the bedroom area of the suite to look over my notes on my bed.

I grabbed my AirPods from my nightstand, planning to play the instrumental playlist I usually listened to when I needed to focus at work, but instead of turning on the music, I found myself listening to Maddie.

Her laugh rang out, light and warm, and curiosity itched at me. What was Grant like? Did he have her blue eyes? Or did he get his eyes from his dad?

I glanced up from my notes, watching Maddie as she smiled at her phone screen. If I had kids, I hoped they would get her eyes.

Wait. What?

I caught myself mid-thought, feeling a jolt. I was thinking about my kids having Maddie's eyes?

Man, this fake engagement was messing with my head.

But as she asked Grant about the movie he'd gone to with his dad that day, I couldn't shake the pull I felt to her. Talking to her son was probably the most relaxed I'd ever seen her. I could tell she really loved him.

How had her ex never married her? The man must've been blind or...just plain stupid. Because a woman like Maddie—she was the kind you didn't let go.

She laughed again at something Grant said, and I just watched her from across the room, feeling the strangest sense of wanting to know everything there was to know about her.

20

———

MADDIE

AFTER WRAPPING up my call with Grant, I turned to find Ian standing by his bed, putting his laptop away. His eyes softened as he glanced over, crossing the room back toward me on the couch. "How'd it go? Is Grant doing all right?"

"He's doing great." I nodded, feeling the warmth that only comes from talking to my son. "He's spending the evening with his dad and his dad's girlfriend. They took him to the movies, which he was pretty excited about."

Ian's eyebrows lifted slightly. "How long have you and your ex been...separated?"

"A little over a year." My voice felt steady, though I wasn't sure why talking about Jaxon with Ian made my chest tighten.

"And he has a girlfriend now?"

I nodded, feeling that old, familiar ache. "She's actually his high school sweetheart." I tried to sound casual, though I knew it came out more bitter than I intended.

Ian frowned, clearly confused. "Wait, I thought you said you met him in high school?"

"*I* was in high school when we met. But he was a couple of years older and dated Janica before that."

"So were they on a break when you met? Or...?"

"He was single as far as I knew," I said, since Ian seemed to be wondering if I'd been the "other woman" in Jaxon and Janica's relationship back then. "When they graduated high school, she left for college in another city. Jaxon stayed behind in Ridgewater and worked for his dad while taking a few classes. He and I met at a college party when I was sixteen. We hung out and hooked up a few times—nothing super serious. But then, well, I got pregnant on accident and...I guess I trapped him with a baby."

"He told you that you trapped him?" Ian gasped, seemingly surprised with my wording.

"He didn't use those exact words." I shook my head. "But, with how everything turned out, it just seems like me getting pregnant just delayed him from getting back with the girl he actually wanted to be with."

"You couldn't have gotten pregnant without his help," Ian said. "I mean, I don't know if any protection was involved. But you didn't just spontaneously get pregnant. This wasn't another case of immaculate conception. It happened because his sperm wasn't contained."

An awkward laugh bubbled out despite myself, and he shot me an apologetic look.

"Sorry," he said, a sheepish smile lifting his lips. "That came out a little too blunt."

"No, it's...it's fine. I guess I never thought about it that way."

"Yeah, I guess it's been important for me to take responsibility that way, regardless of what my partner has going on birth control-wise," Ian said, an unexpected vulnerability in his eyes. "I mean, I may have been a bit of a man-whore, but at least I knew that if I wanted to do my part in avoiding fatherhood before I was ready, I needed to keep everything under wraps."

And I knew I must have looked shocked in that moment because he put a hand on my knee and playfully shook it as he said, "Sorry. I forgot you're one of those sweet, small-town girls."

"Yeah, and you were supposed to be a small-town boy," I said, my jaw dropping. "But man, those city-slicker vibes are coming out tonight."

We both laughed, but the moment of lightness faded as I returned to the darker memories. "Anyway, I think I told you that we didn't actually move in together until Grant was two since things were pretty rocky between us at first. But then, I don't know, even though things weren't super easy, I guess I always thought that deep down, we'd be able to work."

"Hey, Grant is what, eight?" Ian asked. "That's a pretty good run. I mean, there are tons of couples who don't make it even that long. My mom and bio dad didn't. I certainly never have."

"I guess," I said. "But I don't know... With how everything turned out, it just feels like I kept him from living with the woman he actually wanted."

Ian looked like he wanted to say something, but since I didn't actually like telling this story and wanted to get it out as quickly as I could, I hurried to say, "A couple of years ago, Jaxon and Janica reconnected online. And, well... Jaxon must've decided the grass was greener on her side. They met up one night when she was in town and, uh, he just...didn't come home."

"What?" Ian's jaw clenched, his deep brown eyes sharp with disbelief.

I nodded, remembering those horrible days. "I thought something awful had happened—my first thought wasn't even that he was with someone else. We had a fight the day he went missing. So I assumed he'd gone to his parents' place to cool off since he'd done that before. But when he didn't answer my texts or come home the next night, I checked his location. Saw he'd stopped sharing it with me, and so I called him. No answer. I called and called, and finally, he texted back."

My throat tightened, the memory of his words still stinging.

"He said he was sorry, that he was a failure and a burden. And that Grant and I would be better off without him since he always just messed everything up." I swallowed, feeling the rawness of it all over again. "Anyway, I immediately got worried because this wasn't the first time he'd said something like that. He'd been in a bad place a year earlier and talked about...you know, not wanting to be here anymore."

"Oh no..." Ian reached out, resting his hand gently on mine.

"Yeah." I nodded, tears pricking at my eyes as I remembered the feelings of helplessness that had crashed over me.

The fear and panic.

"Anyway, after sending me that text, he turned off his phone." I blew out a breath. "And since I couldn't track him, I really panicked. I posted on social media, begged people to look out for him. I was terrified. Thought he was going to do something drastic, if he hadn't already done it. I even filed a missing person's report."

"Oh, Maddie," Ian said, scooting closer on the couch and pulling me into his arms. "I can't even imagine—" He stopped, seeming to search for words, before saying, "What a nightmare."

I nodded, sniffling as I tried to keep it together. With trembling lips, I managed to say, "It was literally the worst three days of my life."

"Three days?" Ian leaned back to look at me, so much

concern and feeling in his eyes. "You didn't hear from him for three days?"

"Yeah." I drew in a shaky breath. "Eventually, he showed up. Told me he'd been with Janica. Just...holed up in a hotel, acting like it was some kind of honeymoon."

Ian's arms tightened around me. "All the while you'd been going through hell, thinking he might be gone for good."

I nodded. "I felt like such an idiot for freaking out so bad." I scoffed, wiping at my tears. "I mean, I was relieved he was alive. But there was no coming back from that."

"I can imagine."

"Anyway, he packed his things and moved in with her after that. And we've been splitting custody of Grant ever since."

Ian was silent for a beat, but when I looked up, his face was full of tenderness. "I'm so sorry you went through all of that. You didn't deserve any of it." He paused, his voice low and certain. "You're incredibly strong, Maddie. Any man would be lucky to be with someone as amazing as you. And he was an idiot for not seeing that."

"Thank you." A faint smile touched my lips, a feeling of warmth blooming in my chest at his words. "It...really did suck. But I still have Grant, at least. And he's worth everything."

We sat together quietly, the weight of what I'd shared sinking in. I leaned into Ian's shoulder, feeling an unexpected comfort in his presence. It was something I hadn't felt in such a long time.

After a while, he pressed a soft kiss to my forehead, his touch so gentle and perfect it made my heart flutter. "Still want to watch that movie?" he asked, his voice low, almost hesitant, as if he didn't really want the moment to end.

I glanced at the time on the clock across the room. "It's late. You probably need to get a good night's rest before your big presentation tomorrow."

"You're a *terrible* influence, Maddie." A slow smile spread across his face, and his brows arched teasingly. "Always trying to make me responsible."

I laughed softly, the sound breaking the tension in the air—just a little. "Someone has to. I hear your assistant is slacking these days."

"Hmm," he murmured, pretending to consider. "She *has* been sneaking into my room in pajamas. Very unprofessional."

We both laughed, but neither of us moved to get up. Instead, Ian shifted slightly, pulling me closer until I was tucked against him, his arm draped over my shoulder. I let myself lean into him, the warmth of his body comforting, grounding, despite the storm of emotions churning inside me.

His fingers began tracing light, lazy lines along my shoulder, and I had to fight the thrill that shot through me with each pass. My heart picked up speed, thudding harder with every slow, casual stroke of his hand. Then he leaned down again, pressing another soft kiss to my forehead.

This time, it felt different—longer, more lingering. Like he was trying to tell me something with the simple press of his lips.

I breathed in his scent, fresh and warm, with just a hint of something woodsy and masculine that made my pulse race. My gaze drifted to his lips without meaning to, and before I could stop myself, I found myself wondering what he was thinking. What he wanted.

As if he could read my mind, Ian tilted his head, his voice quiet as he mumbled, "I keep forgetting we work together...and that we probably shouldn't be sitting in my room like this."

My breath hitched at the way he said it—soft, low, and laced with something deeper. It took me a moment to gather my thoughts, but with my voice barely above a whisper, I admitted, "I'm having a hard time remembering that, too."

Ian's eyes locked onto mine, dark and intense, his gaze

sweeping over my face and finally settling on my lips. My heart hammered, and I swallowed, trying to keep my thoughts from slipping too far into the realm of "what if."

"But maybe it's okay to be like this," he murmured, his hand still resting on my shoulder, his thumb grazing the bare skin just above my collarbone. "You're my fiancée this weekend, anyway."

I smiled, barely able to think straight under the warmth of his touch. "I am wearing your fancy ring," I whispered, lifting my hand slightly so it caught the light.

His eyes followed the motion, and when he looked back at me, something in his expression deepened, softened—but somehow sharpened, too. "It's probably only right that we practice being close like this...you know, just in case we have to ramp up our PDA tomorrow," he said, his voice low and gravelly.

"I think you're right," I managed to say, my voice no more than a whisper, as I could barely breathe in that moment. "Just to make sure we know what we're doing."

He hesitated, and for a second, the room seemed to go completely still. And then, slowly, he leaned in, his hand lifting to cradle my face as his lips brushed against mine.

The first touch was gentle, tentative—like he was savoring the moment as much as I was. His lips were warm and soft, and he tasted faintly of mouthwash—like he'd intentionally freshened his breath before I came back to his room.

Like he'd almost been hoping for this.

But this is just pretend, I tried to remind myself. *None of this can go past this weekend.*

But my mind didn't seem too concerned about reality in that moment since the thought drifted away as soon as his fingers threaded themselves into my hair, pulling me closer to him.

He kissed me again, firmer this time, and I felt a soft, aching warmth bloom deep in my chest. I couldn't stop myself from responding, pressing my lips against his, feeling the shift in his breathing—slightly heavier now, more ragged.

One of his hands slid from my shoulder, his fingers trailing lower, gliding down my back in slow, deliberate strokes. Each touch sent tiny sparks down my spine, heating my skin and quickening my pulse.

I melted into the kiss, letting the world narrow to just him— the way his mouth moved against mine, the way one hand tangled in my hair, cradling the back of my head as the other pressed warmly against the curve of my lower back, drawing me impossibly closer. My mind scrambled to remind me that this was temporary, that it couldn't go anywhere.

But logic was no match for the sensations coursing through me—the tenderness of his lips, the gentle graze of his thumb brushing against my cheek, the strength in the arm holding me securely against him.

And for once, I didn't want to be sensible. I wanted this moment. I wanted *him*.

I could think about everything else some other time.

His kisses deepened, growing more insistent, each one unraveling what little control I had left. Before I knew it, Ian shifted, his movements deliberate yet gentle. In a heartbeat, I found myself lying back against the couch, his solid frame above me, his weight pressing into me just enough to leave me breathless.

There wasn't an inch of space between us now. His chest pressed against mine, rising and falling in perfect rhythm, the wild thrum of his heartbeat echoing my own. Every part of him was intoxicating—the heat of his body, the faint brush of his breath, the way his lips moved against mine with a hunger that left me reeling.

I hadn't even realized my fingers had tangled into the fabric at the back of his shirt, clutching him like I couldn't bear to let go.

He pulled back slightly, just enough for his forehead to rest against mine as we both struggled to catch our breath.

"You're making it really hard for me to be a gentleman right now," he murmured, his voice low and ragged, laced with a quiet awe that sent my pulse racing even faster.

And I knew I should probably say something back, but my brain must have been short-circuiting or something because I literally couldn't form words.

The hand that was tangled in my hair shifted to trace a slow, deliberate line along my jaw. His thumb brushed over my bottom lip, the soft caress sending a shiver through me, my skin tingling with anticipation.

His gaze dropped to my mouth, and my heart lurched in response. And since I couldn't seem to speak, I decided to speak to him in another language. To tell him with my kisses that I really didn't care if he was that much of a gentleman with me tonight.

21

———

IAN

THE MOMENT MADDIE'S lips touched mine again, the rest of the world faded away. I couldn't think straight, could barely even remember my own name. All I knew was the feel of her beneath me, soft and warm and willing, her breath catching as my tongue gently grazed against her lips to deepen the kiss.

She tasted incredible, like something forbidden and perfect, and I couldn't stop myself from sinking deeper, pressing myself closer as if she might slip away. Her perfume wrapped around me, a soft, intoxicating blend that made me feel like I could breathe her in forever and still not get enough.

I hadn't planned on this. I hadn't planned on Maddie taking up so much space in my mind, my life.

But somehow, in the short time I'd known her, she'd captured me, piece by piece, before I even realized what was happening. The way she laughed, the tender love in her voice when she talked about her son, the vulnerability she tried so hard to hide—I couldn't help but care about her. More than I'd ever intended.

And that terrified me.

Because if I wasn't careful, she'd probably go and steal every single piece of my heart.

But here, in this moment, with her body so warm against mine, I let myself forget my own warnings—just for a while. My fingers traced along her jawline, brushing over the delicate curve of her cheek, her skin warm and impossibly soft beneath my hand. She leaned into me, and my heart lurched, a fierce ache pounding through my chest.

It wasn't just desire—it was something deeper, something that made me feel like if I let her go now, I'd regret it for the rest of my life.

I tilted her head slightly, giving myself the chance to explore further. My lips left hers, trailing a slow, deliberate path down her neck. The faint, intoxicating scent of her perfume filled my senses as I nuzzled into the hollow of her throat. She let out a soft, breathless sound that sent a thrill coursing through me, making it impossible to stop.

The curve of her neck, the warmth of her skin beneath my lips—it was overwhelming, almost too much. My hand moved to the small of her back, pressing her closer to me as I kissed the sensitive spot just below her ear. Her pulse thrummed against my lips, quick and unsteady, matching the wild rhythm of my own heartbeat.

Everything about her was consuming me, and I wasn't sure I wanted to come up for air.

I wanted to pull her closer, let this kiss turn into something more. My thoughts flicked to the bed, just a few feet away—it would be so easy...carrying her over, laying her down, and letting us both get lost in each other completely. My hands tightened on her waist, the heat between us growing as I smoothed my fingers along the skin just above the hemline of her shorts.

I hadn't been with a woman in such a long time. But going

there with Maddie...it almost seemed so right. Like maybe I'd waited this long because I was meant to wait for her.

For this moment right here.

But no—I shouldn't be thinking about that. Going that far wasn't just something you can come back from.

And Maddie had already been through so much. She'd been hurt by people who should've protected her, trusted her, loved her.

She had a son.

A life.

Responsibilities I never had to consider before.

And though she was strong—man, she was stronger than anyone I'd ever met—I could sense the fragility in her, too. She was tough, yes, but there was a softness, a delicate thread woven through her that I knew I couldn't risk breaking.

And she deserved so much better than a fling or a meaningless night. She deserved the world.

I felt her fingers against my neck, threading into my hair, pulling me closer, and my resolve nearly crumbled all over again.

I wanted her so badly, wanted to let go and forget everything that made this complicated. The ache was almost unbearable.

But I knew I couldn't.

Or rather, I *shouldn't*.

So instead of deepening the kiss further and taking her down the path I was so tempted to travel, I slowed the kiss. Letting the intensity between us simmer down to something sweet, something that I hoped told her what I couldn't say aloud yet—that I cared about her, that I wanted to be more for her than I'd ever been for anyone else.

That I was so scared that I was going to screw everything up.

My thumb traced gentle circles along her waist, easing the both of us out of the whirlwind.

I forced myself to break the kiss, leaning my forehead against hers, my breathing still unsteady. For a moment, neither of us moved, our breaths mingling in the small space between us.

"Maddie," I whispered, my voice hoarse. "You... That was..." But I couldn't finish the thought since words couldn't explain how I felt in that moment. So overwhelmed by the strength of the feelings I was having right then.

I didn't think anyone had ever made me feel the way Maddie did.

But she seemed to understand what I was trying to say because she just looked up at me, her eyes soft and full of something that made my heart twist as she whispered, "I know..."

And I suddenly wanted to tell her everything. Tell her that she was changing me, that I didn't want this to be just for show.

But I held back, afraid that if I went there now, I'd never be able to hold back again.

So I pressed a kiss to her forehead, lingering there, hoping she felt everything I wasn't ready to say.

Because this wasn't just a fake weekend fling. Not for me, at least.

Not anymore.

And that scared me more than anything.

22

———

MADDIE

I WOKE up to sunlight streaming through the curtains of my hotel suite, the memory of Ian's kiss from the night before blooming in my mind like the first rays of dawn. Turning onto my side, I clutched the pillow, a soft smile spreading across my lips as fragments of the night replayed in my mind.

The way his hands had held me, like I was something precious.

How his lips had moved with mine, stealing my breath with every kiss.

I couldn't remember the last time I'd been kissed like that.

Like I was beautiful.

Like I was special.

Like I mattered.

Mattered to a man who had the entire world at his feet—a man who could have anyone he wanted. But in that moment, on the couch in Ian's hotel suite, he hadn't wanted just anyone. He'd wanted *me*.

A flutter of nerves stirred in my stomach as I turned onto my back, staring at the ceiling. Was it possible that I'd totally interpreted everything wrong and was seeing things the way I wanted to? Yes, it definitely was since we *had* started that kiss under the pretense of it being practice for the fake engagement we were pretending to be in.

But I don't know...with the way he'd looked at me—his eyes burning with something that mirrored the ache in my chest.

With how he'd been so genuine and present and had really seemed to get as lost in the moment as I had...it just felt too real to be part of some act.

But if I was wrong...if it was all fake and I was fooling myself into believing Ian Hastings—one of the most powerful, sought-after men I'd ever met—could actually want someone like me...then he deserved an award. Honestly, give the man his Oscar.

But yeah...here's to hoping most of the acting talent had gone to his brother Nash, the *actual* actor, and not Ian.

My phone buzzed on the nightstand, pulling me from my thoughts.

Ian: Going to run through my presentation one more time this morning. Want to head down together around nine to meet Kacie and Brock?

I smiled, my heart giving an annoyingly giddy flutter. Kacie and Brock must've arrived in Boston last night to prep for filming Ian's presentation. The video would go on his YouTube channel later, showcasing his polished, confident self—the version of him the world saw.

I typed back a quick reply.

Me: Just woke up, but I'll be ready by then.

His response came almost immediately.

> Ian: Perfect. I left my adjoining door unlocked. Come in when you're ready.

I stared at the message a second longer than necessary, my mind catching on one very specific detail.

Had he left the door unlocked all night?

The thought lingered, tempting and dangerous. Could I have opened my door at any moment, stepped into his room, and...?

I shut that train of thought down fast. *No, Maddie. You absolutely should not be thinking about sneaking into Ian's room in the middle of the night. That would be wildly unprofessional.*

Though, considering I'd been making out with my boss less than twelve hours ago, maybe "professional" had already gone out the window.

Shaking my head, I climbed out of bed and headed for the shower. I chose an emerald-green dress that fit me just right—the one that always seemed to earn me compliments. It wasn't overly fancy, but I always felt confident when I wore it...which was something that I'd need today.

Ian was going to be front and center, and if I was going to be by his side all day, I wanted to feel like I at least fit in by his side just a little.

By the time I was dressed and ready, my nerves had settled into a quiet hum. Anticipation buzzed under my skin as I smoothed my hands over the soft fabric of my dress and stepped toward the adjoining door.

For a moment, I second-guessed whether he'd actually said for me to just enter whenever. But after double checking our texts, I inhaled deeply and opened the door.

My breath hitched when I stepped inside and saw Ian standing near the fridge with a bottle of his favorite sparkling water in his hands. He stood there in a perfectly tailored designer suit, the kind that looked like it had been made just for him—because, let's face it, it probably was. The dark gray fabric framed his broad shoulders and tall physique flawlessly, the sharp cut emphasizing his lean, powerful build. His dark hair was slightly tousled, like he'd run his fingers through it instead of bothering with a comb, and his deep brown eyes...

Well...those eyes did funny things to my insides every time they looked my way.

"Morning," he said when he noticed me, his voice low and warm, a small, easy smile tugging at his lips.

I swallowed, willing my voice to work. "Morning."

And just like that, the hum of anticipation turned into a quiet roar, filling every corner of my chest.

He put his water back in the fridge and turned to face me. "Let me just grab my things and then we can go."

He strode across the room to the desk area, slipping his laptop into his leather bag. Then he looked at the mirror on the wall behind the desk and adjusted his tie. As he gave his reflection one last check, I couldn't resist taking him in—the sharp cut of his jaw, the strong lines of his shoulders, the way he carried himself with a quiet, commanding confidence.

He looked like he belonged on the cover of some magazine, the kind of man who could walk into any room and own it without trying.

But it wasn't just his looks or his presence that drew me to him. Beneath all the polish and power, Ian had a tenderness about him, a kindness that didn't fit the image of the billionaire playboy the world seemed determined to see.

Watching him now, I was more certain than ever that he was the boy who had comforted me on the beach all those years ago. He couldn't know how much that moment had meant to me. At seventeen, I'd been terrified, struggling with a secret that felt too big to carry alone. Ian had been the first person I'd told. And even though it could have gone so wrong—he could have been judgmental like so many other people in Ridgewater had been when they eventually found out about my pregnancy —he'd thankfully been a safe space that night. He'd been a gentle listener, a strong shoulder to lean on.

And even though he hadn't swooped in to save me like some superhero in the movies, he said exactly what I'd needed to hear in that moment. He told me I'd be okay. That even though it felt like my world was falling apart, I would figure it out.

Those words had been everything. Not promises of miracles, not empty reassurances—just the steady reminder that I was stronger than I felt, and that I could take it one step at a time.

He didn't know it, since I'd never gotten the chance to tell him, but Ian was the reason I found the courage to call my dad a few days later.

I could still remember how terrified I'd been, my heart racing as I whispered, "Dad... I'm pregnant." But Ian's quiet strength had become my own in that moment. His kindness, his belief in me, had given me the courage to say those daunting words to my ex-drill sergeant father. And in the years since, even as I navigated the hardest moments, I'd held onto that strength like an anchor.

"Ready to head down?" Ian's voice broke through my thoughts, low and steady, grounding me in the present.

I turned toward him, smoothing the fabric of my dress out of habit, and froze when I saw the way he was studying me. His jaw slackened slightly, his gaze running the length of me from head to toe.

"You..." He cleared his throat, blinking a few times. "You look amazing, Maddie."

Heat rushed to my cheeks, and I quickly looked down as I adjusted my work bag on my shoulder. "Thanks."

He smiled, stepping closer, his presence steadying yet electric all at once. "Shall we?"

I nodded, meeting his gaze again and giving him a tentative smile of my own. "Yeah," I said softly. "Let's go."

For a moment, his deep brown eyes searched mine, like there was something he wanted to say but hadn't quite found the words for—possibly something about what had happened last night. But even though the air between us shifted, heavy with unspoken questions, he seemed to decide it was not the time for that conversation because without a word, he stepped closer and reached for my hand instead.

Which, really, was probably all the conversation we needed. The simple gesture saying more than words ever could. And as the soft weight of his hand stayed firmly in mine as he led me out of his room, hope stirred in my chest.

Because maybe—just maybe—this wasn't the start of something fake at all.

The green room was quieter than I'd expected, the stillness broken only by the soft, rhythmic sound of Ian's footsteps as he paced across the carpet. His usual air of confidence was absent, replaced by something I hadn't thought I'd ever see: nerves.

Ian Hastings didn't seem like the kind of man who got nervous. Over the past few weeks, every time his presentation had come up, he'd been calm and self-assured, never breaking stride. But now, with just fifteen minutes to go before he was supposed to take the stage, the tension in his broad shoulders and the faint crease in his brow gave him away.

But, oddly enough, it made him even more endearing.

In the corner, I'd been chatting quietly with Kacie and Brock, Ian's videographers, as they finalized their camera setup. One positioned on stage right, the other shooting from the front. They'd decided to add the graphics from Ian's slides during editing to make the final video look sharp and professional.

We wouldn't be able to release the recording until six months after the summit, thanks to the contract Ian had signed. But it was exciting to think that if Ian's new YouTube channel went viral someday, I'd have played a small part in setting this up.

The faint sound of applause from the ballroom next door interrupted our conversation, signaling the end of the previous presentation.

Kacie and Brock exchanged quick nods before turning to Ian.

"We're heading out to get everything set up," Kacie said, offering Ian an encouraging smile. "Break a leg out there."

Ian returned the smile, but the tension in his expression didn't fully fade. "Thanks."

As Brock and Kacie left the room, I walked over to Ian, my heels sinking slightly into the carpet with each step. He stopped pacing when I approached, his dark eyes landing on me with a mix of anticipation and something I couldn't quite place.

"Do you need anything from me?" I asked softly.

He tipped his head to the side, a flicker of amusement crossing his face. "How confident are you in your ability to teach for an hour on how business owners can thrive in any economy?"

I let out a startled laugh. "Not confident at all."

He chuckled, the sound low and warm. "Okay, well then…

maybe just send me all the good vibes you can and hope I don't look like an idiot up there."

"You're not going to look like an idiot." I smiled, hoping it came across as reassuring. "I haven't had the chance to see one of your presentations yet, but I heard what Drake said about you in college. Something about how your talks always left everyone impressed. I'm sure you'll do great."

"Those classes were about a tenth the size of this event."

I shrugged. "Still...I'm sure you'll nail it." Then, unable to resist, I added, "And if all else fails, don't people always say to picture the crowd naked? Supposedly it helps."

"You want me to picture *everyone* naked?" Ian's brows shot up, and his lips curved into a wicked grin. "Does that mean I have permission to include you in that?"

"I—uh..." Heat rushed to my cheeks, my face burning as I scrambled for a response.

He chuckled, holding up a hand. "Sorry, I probably shouldn't have said that. But...I think that actually helped my nerves a little."

"Picturing me naked?" I blurted before I could stop myself, my voice high and squeaky.

His grin widened. "No. Just joking about it did. I was actually a gentleman in my head and haven't tried doing that yet."

Yet? As in...he might try doing that later?

"Well..." I swallowed hard, my words catching in my throat. "I'm glad you're feeling better."

Before either of us could say anything else, two conference organizers stepped into the room. "Mr. Hastings, the tech crew is ready for you," one of them said with a polite smile.

"Okay." Ian nodded, straightening his suit jacket. As he followed them toward the ballroom, I stayed close behind, my heels clicking softly on the tiled hallway floor.

At the edge of the stage, Ian paused, turning back to me.

His nerves seemed to resurface for just a moment, and I acted before I could overthink it.

Standing on my toes, I pressed a quick kiss to his cheek. "Good luck," I whispered, my voice barely audible over the hum of the crowd filtering in.

Ian turned his head slightly, his eyes locking on mine. The air between us shifted, heavy and warm, as if the rest of the room had melted away.

"Thanks," he mumbled, his gaze lingering a second longer before he stepped onto the stage.

I slipped into a seat on the far side of the front row, pulling out my phone to record some footage for his social media accounts. My heart raced as I focused the camera on him, anticipation buzzing under my skin.

Ian Hastings might have been nervous, but as the spotlight hit him and he started to speak, it was clear to everyone in the room that he belonged up there.

23

———

IAN

"THAT WRAPS up our time for questions," the conference chairman said, taking the mic at the end of my keynote. "Let's all give Ian Hastings a big round of applause for the incredible insights he just shared with us. I know my mind was blown more than once."

The crowd erupted into applause, the sound swelling until people began rising to their feet.

A standing ovation.

I let the satisfaction settle in my chest, scanning the nearly thousand faces looking back at me with enthusiasm. I'd worked hard to prepare for this moment, and it seemed like the effort had paid off.

But as people swarmed toward me, shaking my hand, offering thanks, and peppering me with follow-up questions, my focus shifted to just one thing: Maddie.

Where was she?

Strange, wasn't it? How quickly she'd become so integral to my life. In such a short time, Maddie had wedged herself into my world, her presence so natural it was hard to imagine her not being part of my future.

I spotted her weaving through the crowd a moment later, her face lit with the kind of smile that made my heart lurch.

"Make some room, please," I said, gesturing for the crowd to part.

The sea of people parted, and when Maddie finally reached me, I didn't hesitate. I pulled her into my arms, ignoring the curious glances from those still lingering around us.

"You were incredible!" she gushed, her voice bubbling with excitement as she looked up at me. "Seriously, Ian. That was amazing. I'm so proud of you."

She's proud of me.

And while the standing ovation had felt amazing, hearing her say those words meant somehow more to me. Leaving me feeling unsteady, like the ground beneath me had shifted.

We pulled apart, but I kept her hand in mine, needing the connection as I turned back to the crowd. There were still people waiting, their expectant expressions reminding me that I wasn't off the hook just yet.

"I've got about ten more minutes," I announced, "and then my fiancée and I have lunch plans."

A ripple of surprise rolled through the group, followed by a flurry of glances aimed at Maddie. A few people openly searched for a ring, and for a brief moment, I questioned my choice of words.

Should I have thrown that out there when our engagement isn't even real?

But the thought faded almost as quickly as it came. It was out there now, and surprisingly, I didn't mind.

In fact, it felt...good. Like reclaiming something I'd thought

I didn't need but had missed more than I realized—having a life partner.

I fielded a few more questions, handing out business cards to those asking for them, saying, "The best way to stay updated is to follow me. I'll be sharing many more business insights and strategies on my various social media pages soon."

Once the crowd finally began to disperse, Maddie and I slipped away to head to our lunch meeting with one of my dad's long-time clients.

"So, it looks like you've officially decided to make this social-media-content-creation thing real then, huh?" Maddie glanced up at me, her smile teasing as we made our way toward the hotel restaurant where we would be meeting Mrs. Torres.

"Apparently," I said, pulling my phone from my pocket. "Guess I should let Kacie post one of those video's she's been stockpiling for me now, shouldn't I?"

"Absolutely." Her grin widened, her confidence in me settling something in my chest.

I tapped out a quick text to Kacie, my thumb hovering over the *send* button for a split second longer than necessary. Then I sent it, nerves buzzing faintly under my skin.

As I slipped my phone back into my pocket, Maddie looped her arm through mine, leaning into me as we walked.

"You're going to be amazing," she said softly, her voice filled with quiet certainty.

And as I glanced down at her, warmth spreading through me, I thought maybe she was right.

That maybe, with Maddie by my side, I might actually become the kind of man I'd always hoped I could be.

We were sitting at the restaurant, waiting for Mrs. Torres—the CEO of Opulent Beauty, a high-end makeup brand—to arrive when a thought suddenly struck me.

"You know," I said to Maddie, a casual smile tugging at my lips as I watched her fingers idly trace the edge of her water glass, "we've been cooped up in the hotel the last couple of days. I was thinking, after this lunch, maybe we could go out and explore Boston a bit."

"Really?" Maddie looked up, her expression brightening slightly.

"Yeah," I said. "You've never been here before, right? I thought it might be nice to go out, maybe do a little shopping."

"Oh...shopping," she said with a small nod. "Th-that sounds nice."

But there was some hesitation in her eyes, so I asked, "Do you not like shopping?" tilting my head, trying to get a read on her.

"I guess it's all right." She shrugged, her fingers stilling against the glass. "But I mostly shop for basic things, you know? Groceries, clothes for Grant, stuff like that. I'm sure it's not quite as exciting as the kind of shopping you do."

I frowned slightly, realization dawning on me. For me, shopping was often an indulgence, a way to celebrate or kill time. But for Maddie, it was more of a necessary evil—a chore and not a luxury since money had probably always been tight for her, especially as a young mom.

"Well," I said, shifting gears and leaning forward, "since I just announced our engagement to a ton of people back there, and you've been such a good sport about this whole thing, I think I owe you a bit of a shopping spree."

"Oh, no. You don't need to do that." Her eyes widened, and she shook her head quickly. "I'm fine, really. It hasn't been hard at all. Quite the opposite."

"No, I insist," I said firmly, holding her gaze. "It's the least I can do."

She opened her mouth to protest again, but I raised a hand to stop her. "In fact," I continued, a sly grin forming, "I think it can only help with our little ruse. Think about it. Margot knows I have money. She knows I love to pamper the women in my life. If you don't dress the part of the fiancée of a billionaire at that mixer tonight and the gala tomorrow, she's going to wonder if this is real."

"I don't know…" Maddie's lips pressed together, her brows drawing in slightly as she considered my words. "I feel like what I've worn so far has been fine…" She lifted her hand. "And this huge rock on my finger isn't exactly tiny."

"I know," I interrupted gently, leaning closer. "And I absolutely love your style. You dress beautifully, and it's perfect for work and for you—so please don't take this the wrong way. But for the events tonight and tomorrow, I think it might be fun to really lean into the part. Maybe something over the top. Gaudy, even. Let's stand out a little."

"Gaudy?" Her eyes narrowed playfully.

"Okay, maybe not gaudy." I chuckled, liking the spark of amusement in her tone. "But dramatic. The kind of dress that screams, 'My man has a Black Amex, and he loves to spoil me with it.'"

She laughed, though I could tell she was still trying to find a way to politely decline. "Ian, I really don't need—"

"Maddie, come on." I held up my hands. "It's all for the act. For Margot. This is a tactical move."

Let me spoil you just a little.

"Fine," she said, rolling her eyes even though a small smile tugged at her lips. "I guess I'll let you buy me a fancy dress." Then holding up a scolding finger, she added, "But only because you're forcing it on me."

"Good girl," I said, leaning back with a satisfied grin. "And don't worry, you're in good hands."

She shook her head, but I caught a hint of a blush on her cheeks. Like, even though she was trying not to look excited for this shopping trip, she might actually be.

Which, yeah, was so endearing.

Man, she was so different from all the other women I'd dated.

Most women I knew would have snatched the card out of my hand the moment I offered.

But not her. She was different—a refreshingly good kind of different.

And I couldn't wait to see what she picked out.

Because I had a strong feeling that this soccer mom who wore a T-shirt and cutoffs when she wasn't at work could also secretly rock a ten-thousand-dollar cocktail dress.

24

————

MADDIE

"ARE you sure you can skip the rest of the summit this afternoon?" I turned to Ian after we left the restaurant, unable to stop myself from asking the question that had been giving me anxiety all through our lunch with Mrs. Torres. "Won't they be upset if you're not there?"

"It should be fine." Ian glanced at me, his expression relaxed. "My keynote was the main event. As long as I'm at the mixers tonight, mingling and making connections, my dad and the board can't complain about me playing hooky this afternoon."

"Hooky?" I raised an eyebrow, smirking a little. "That doesn't sound very responsible of you, Mr. Hastings."

He chuckled, his smile easy. "You should try it sometime, Ms. Stevens. It's liberating."

I shook my head, laughing softly as we made our way back to the hotel. "All right, if you're sure you won't get in trouble."

"Positive."

Once we reached his room, Ian turned to me. "I'm gonna

change into something more comfortable, then we can head out. Meet me back here in twenty minutes?"

"Sure," I said, not remembering if I'd ever seen him wearing anything besides a suit in public—aside from the time we'd met in North Carolina. "What kind of clothes should I wear for this shopping trip? Should I just stay in this dress?"

"Just wear whatever you'd normally wear shopping," he said, giving me a good once over. But then his gaze landed on my heels. "But maybe wear something more comfortable for walking. The shops on Newbury Street are only about half a mile away, but I've heard something about stilettos being torture devices invented by men. I don't want you in pain all afternoon."

"How thoughtful of you," I teased.

"I try," he said, his grin crooked.

I couldn't help but smile as I nodded. "All right. Flats it is."

"And plan for a few hours," he added, pausing with his hand on his door handle.

"A few hours?" I blinked. "You think it'll take me that long to find a dress?"

"Two dresses," he corrected. "We've got the mixers tonight and the gala tomorrow."

"Okay, so...a few hours to find two dresses?"

He shrugged, but there was something in his eyes—a glint of mischief—that made me think he wasn't just planning to buy two dresses.

"What else are you planning?" I asked, narrowing my eyes.

His lips twitched, but he said nothing, just gave me a maddeningly vague look before slipping into his room.

As I walked into mine, I tried to tamp down the flutter of excitement in my chest. It wasn't like this was a real shopping date. Ian was just leaning into the ruse, helping sell the idea of us as a couple.

Still...it felt nice.

But then, another thought struck me. What if Ian wasn't planning to spend hours shopping for me but for himself? The man dressed like he'd stepped straight out of a fashion magazine, every piece of his wardrobe immaculately chosen, right down to his cuff links. He might be one of those super picky shoppers, like my sister-in-law Juliette who could spend hours debating between two identical shades of navy fabric.

Oh, no. I groaned inwardly, picturing myself sitting on a fancy couch in some upscale men's boutique while Ian agonized over tie patterns. If that happened, I'd die of boredom before we ever made it to the mixers tonight.

Shaking off the thought, I headed to the bathroom to freshen up and swap my heels for flats, trying to prepare myself for whatever this "shopping spree" had in store.

203-413-5517: Hey, this is Theo. I hope it's okay that I got your number from Sloan. But I was wondering if you'd mind sharing some of your potty-training expertise, since I'm apparently in over my head.

The text buzzed on my phone just as I was finishing up getting ready to head back to Ian's room. I smiled, touched that he'd think to ask me about parenting stuff since we'd only met the one time.

He'd mentioned at Sloan's party that he'd been parenting his two-and-a-half-year-old daughter on his own since his wife's tragic car accident a year ago. That couldn't be easy.

Me: Sure, I'm happy to answer any questions. I'm not sure I'm a potty-training expert since I only had to do it once, and apparently, Grant was pretty easy compared to most, but feel free to ask.

His reply came almost immediately.

Theo: Your kid was easy? Heck, maybe just tell me what you did then because I could definitely use an easy button if it's out there. Charlotte is just not getting it.

I laughed softly and texted back.

Me: Well, for starters, Grant was almost three when we finally got brave enough to start the potty-training process. So there's that. But long story short, we decided to bribe him with a toy.

Theo: Okay...I'm listening.

Oh...he was expecting more? He probably wouldn't like that for Grant, that was all it really took. But I decided to expound a little.

Me: So, we took Grant to the store, let him pick out what he wanted—a toy fishing pole so he could fish like my dad—and after that, it just...worked. He must have been super ready or wanted the fishing pole badly enough that as soon as he knew what he'd get, he went to the bathroom on the toilet every time after that. He even refused to wear diapers at night.

Theo's response came in quick.

Theo: You're making that up, right? That can't actually be real.

I grinned as I slipped my purse over my shoulder.

Me: Apparently, I got really lucky. But I think part of it was that we waited until he was ready. Like I said, he was almost three. I didn't want to worry about constant accidents—it was way easier to change a diaper than clean up a pee spot on the carpet.

After a quick glance in the mirror to check my reflection, I adjusted the black-and-white striped boatneck blouse I'd paired with white shorts—what Sloan had dubbed my "Audrey Hepburn outfit" when she saw it in my suitcase. Satisfied that I looked okay, I knocked on Ian's door, ready to head out.

Just as I let my hand drop, my phone buzzed again.

Theo: Yeah...I think I'm going to rip out my carpet and replace it once this is over. My little carpet cleaner only does so much.

I smirked and tapped out a quick reply.

Me: Oh dang. That sucks.

When no answer came from Ian's side of the door, I frowned and knocked again. Maybe he hadn't heard me the first time?

But then, there was the sound of footsteps, and a second later, the door swung open.

Ian stood there in a sage-green button-up with short sleeves that fit him perfectly, emphasizing his muscular arms in a way that was almost distracting. My gaze lingered for a second longer than it probably should have, and I couldn't help but wonder what kind of workout schedule he had to achieve arms like that. He'd paired the shirt with chino shorts and crisp white tennis shoes, the casual outfit somehow managing to look effortlessly polished on him.

His dark hair was slightly tousled, and when his sharp brown eyes met mine, an easy smile tugged at his lips.

"Hey," he said, his voice warm and inviting. "Ready to go?"

"Yep." I swallowed, my heart giving a little flutter as I smiled back. "Let's do this."

I followed him out of his room, and as we headed to the elevator, I couldn't help but think that Ian Hastings was, without a doubt, the most gorgeous man I'd ever seen.

And he probably knows it, too.

Which yeah...I really couldn't blame him if he did.

As soon as the elevator doors slid shut, my phone buzzed again. Leaning back against the wall, I unlocked the screen to read the new message.

> Theo: It's okay. She's only two and a half, so maybe I'll wait and try again later.

"Anyone interesting?" Ian asked casually, his eyes flicking to my phone. His tone was light, but there was a curious edge to it.

I glanced up, my lips tugging into a small smile. "It's Theo."

"Theo?" Something unreadable flickered in his expression. "What does he want?"

I slipped my phone into my purse. "He was just asking for potty-training tips. Apparently, his daughter has been making things tough on that front."

Ian chuckled. "Yeah, that doesn't sound like a very fun time."

"It's not," I agreed. The elevator arrived, and as we

stepped inside, another text buzzed in my purse. I pulled it out slightly to glance at it. It was Theo, asking if my son got into the summer program I'd told him we were hoping he'd get into.

Ian watched me type out my response, then asked, "So, did you give Theo your number at Sloan's party?"

I shook my head. "No, he must've asked Sloan for it recently."

He nodded, slightly lifting one eyebrow. "Oh, so you haven't been texting each other all week?"

I tilted my head at him, catching the faintest hint of something in his tone—jealousy, maybe? I bit back a smile. "I thought about giving him my number that night but didn't."

Ian's jaw clenched for half a second, and I couldn't help but laugh.

"What?" he asked, his brow furrowing.

"I was just kidding," I teased.

He rolled his eyes but then smirked. "Well, I guess I wouldn't blame you if you did. Theo's a great guy. Like we decided that night at the party, he's not quite as amazing as me, but still a good second choice."

I laughed. "Looks like you've figured a way around that whole 'We can't date because I'm your boss' thing though, haven't you?"

"You found me out." His eyes gleamed as he nodded. "I totally planned to tell Margot you were my fiancée as soon as you mentioned her email. I only pretended to panic at the restaurant. See what a good actor I am?"

I shook my head, laughing again as the elevator doors opened. "Well, your acting skills are impressive, I'll give you that."

Ian stepped aside, gesturing for me to exit first. "Glad you find me impressive in that way at least."

Oh...you are definitely impressive in so many other ways, Ian.

We strolled through the lobby, his presence at my side both steadying and electrifying.

"So," Ian said as we neared the entrance, his voice slipping easily back into that light, playful tone, "ready to shop like a billionaire's fiancée?"

"I guess I don't really have a choice, do I?" I laughed softly, though my heart fluttered at the way he said it, like it wasn't pretend at all.

"Nope." He opened the door for me with a mischievous grin. "It's time to show you off, Maddie Stevens. Let's make everyone at this summit jealous that I landed someone as amazing as you."

25

MADDIE

THE BOUTIQUE DOOR chimed softly as Ian held it open for me, his hand brushing lightly against the small of my back as I stepped inside. The air was scented with leather and something floral—luxury bottled and diffused into every corner of the store. Soft jazz music played overhead and racks of dresses stood like works of art.

"Let's find you something unforgettable," Ian murmured, his voice low, his hand lingering on my back, steady and warm.

I glanced up at him, catching the faint curve of his lips, the way his dark eyes glimmered with something playful and intent.

"Unforgettable might be a little ambitious," I teased lightly, trying to keep things casual even as the tension between us seemed to thrum like a live wire.

"Not for you," he said without hesitation, his hand guiding me toward the nearest rack of dresses.

I swallowed, glancing down at the racks, but my thoughts stayed with him. What was going on between us? This whole fake engagement had started as a ruse—a way to fend off

Margot and her meddling. But standing here with Ian, his attention solely on me, his touches lingering just a little too long... It didn't feel fake.

"Can I help you find something specific?" A bubbly brunette in a sleek black dress approached us, a bright smile lighting her face. "Are we shopping for a special occasion?"

"Kind of." Ian turned to her; his smile effortlessly charming. "We just got engaged, and I want to show her off at a business summit tonight."

The clerk's eyes widened slightly, her gaze flicking between Ian and me.

For a moment, I wondered if she recognized him. Ian wasn't a huge celebrity or anything, but with his billionaire status and a history of dating a few high-profile starlets, it wasn't impossible for someone to connect the dots.

But if she did recognize him, she didn't say anything.

"Oh, congratulations!" the clerk said, her tone genuinely enthusiastic. "That's so exciting! How did you two meet?"

Ian glanced at me, his smile softening into something that felt intimate, almost tender. "We got stuck in an elevator together," he began, his voice effortlessly sliding into the familiar story we'd crafted. But this time, he expanded on the details, adding small flourishes and moments that made it feel more vivid and real.

I watched, half in awe, as he charmed her completely, spinning the tale we'd told Drake the night before into something even more captivating.

By the time he finished, the clerk was pressing a hand over her heart, her expression soft. "That's such a sweet love story," she gushed. "You fell in love, and now you work together?"

"That's right." His gaze flicked to mine, warm and unguarded. "And now that she's mine, I want to make sure everyone knows it."

"Well then..." Her gaze shifted to me. "How about we find you something perfect?"

As she led us toward a rack of gowns, Ian stayed close, his hand brushing against mine. My pulse skittered at the light contact, and I couldn't help but glance up at him, wondering what he was thinking. His expression was unreadable, but every now and then, I would catch him sneaking glances at me—quick, almost shy. Like he couldn't help himself.

The clerk pulled a gown from the rack, a shimmering navy piece with a plunging neckline and an elegant, flowing skirt. "How about this one?" she asked, her eyes lighting up as she held it out for us to see.

Ian took the dress from her, his expression thoughtful as he held it up in front of me, tilting his head slightly as he studied it. "What do you think?"

I glanced at the dress, the luxurious fabric catching the light like ripples on water. "It's beautiful," I admitted.

His gaze shifted to mine, and something in his eyes softened further. "Try it on," he said gently, a small smile tugging at the corner of his mouth. "I think it'll look amazing on you."

Unable to argue when he asked like that, I took the dress and stepped into the fitting room, closing the door behind me. My fingers trembled slightly as I slipped out of my clothes and into the gown, the cool silk sliding over my skin like a whisper.

When I turned to face the mirror, I stilled, barely recognizing the woman staring back at me. The deep navy color made my skin glow and brought out the brightness of my eyes, and the way the fabric hugged my figure was nothing short of magical. I'd never worn anything so expensive, so refined in my life, but for some strange reason, I felt like I belonged in it.

A quiet knock on the door broke my thoughts, and Ian's voice drifted through. "How's it going in there?"

"It's...good," I managed to say, my cheeks heating as I smoothed my hands over the fabric.

"Can I see?" he asked, his tone curious.

I hesitated for a moment, butterflies stirring in my stomach, but then I took a deep breath and opened the door. "Okay," I said, stepping out slowly.

Ian's reaction was immediate, his gaze sweeping over me with an intensity that made me feel rooted to the spot. His eyes darkened slightly as they traveled from the plunging neckline to the flowing skirt, and his breath seemed to hitch for just a fraction of a second.

"You..." He stopped, his voice thick, before he cleared his throat and tried again. "You look stunning."

"You think so?" My cheeks burned under his unwavering stare. "You don't think it's too much?"

"No," he said, stepping closer, his hand brushing my arm. "It's perfect. You're perfect."

My heart stuttered at his words, the sincerity in his tone making it impossible to dismiss them as part of our act.

Was he pretending? Or was this something more?

Before I could figure it out, though, the clerk reappeared with another dress, a sleek black piece with a dramatic slit up one side. Ian didn't even wait for her to suggest it before nodding toward the fitting room. "That one too."

"Really?"

"Yes."

Dress after dress, Ian's reactions left me breathless. Each time I stepped out of the dressing room, his gaze would sweep over me, slow and deliberate, as if he was raking in every detail —taking in every single inch there was to see, like he couldn't get enough.

And dang, I'd thought the man was sexy before. But the way his eyes lingered... The look of hunger and approval in them... Well, I didn't think I'd ever had anyone look at me like that before.

"Turn around," he murmured after I tried on an elegant red dress with a low back. His voice was soft but firm, and when I hesitated, his lips quirked into a reassuring smile. "I just want to see the full effect."

I turned slowly, feeling the silky fabric glide against my skin. His silence stretched, his gaze practically a touch of its own, and when I peeked over my shoulder, I caught him rubbing his jaw, like he was trying to keep his thoughts in check.

"You're going to break hearts in that," Ian mumbled, his voice rough, lower than usual.

The words hit me like a ripple of warmth, spreading through my chest and down to my toes. I felt my cheeks heat, and I clutched the soft fabric of the dress, trying to ground myself.

"We're just trying to break Margot's heart, remember?" I tried to joke, but my voice wavered, betraying the unsteadiness I felt.

Ian didn't laugh right away. His gaze held mine, steady and searching, and something unspoken flickered in the dark depths of his eyes. The kind of thing that made my chest tighten and my heart pound in a way I couldn't control.

When he finally spoke, his voice was softer. "Honestly, Maddie," he murmured, the vulnerability in his tone cutting straight through me, "I'm starting to worry you'll end up breaking my heart before we're done with all of this."

What? His words hit me like a lightning bolt, leaving me momentarily stunned. *Did I hear him right?*

Did Ian Hastings—the man who had the world at his feet— really think *I* could break *his* heart?

It didn't seem possible. The idea that I could matter to him, that he could care enough about me for his heart to even be at risk—it didn't compute. Not when he was so far out of my league.

Not when I was just...me.

"I..." My voice faltered, my throat tightening. "I wouldn't want to do that." The words were barely more than a whisper, but the moment they left my lips, I realized how deeply I meant them.

The thought of hurting Ian in any way sent a dull ache through my chest. He'd been nothing but kind to me—thoughtful, patient, even protective. And the way he looked at me sometimes, the way he'd been looking at me this afternoon...felt like he saw something in me I wasn't sure I even believed in myself.

I glanced up at him, and the intensity in his gaze stole the air from my lungs. But then his lips curved into a small, almost hesitant smile as he said, "You say that now, but...what happens when Theo texts you again? I mean, how am I supposed to compete with a hot, single dad?"

I blinked at him, caught off guard by the comment. Was he actually worried about Theo?

Because as awesome as Theo seemed to be, there was literally no competition there. Not when I was already falling so hard for my boss.

But when I tried to tell him that, no words would come out.

And I wasn't sure if he could sense the words lingering on the tip of my tongue, the ones I was too afraid to say, but he sent me a carefree smile, stepping back as if to ease the tension and said, "Let's get the matching shoes and a clutch for that one, shall we?"

I blinked, my heart still racing, struggling to catch up with whatever had just passed between us. His shift back to practicality was almost disorienting.

Glancing at the growing pile of items Ian and the store clerk had already gathered, I swallowed hard. It was so much.

"I don't need all of this," I said softly, my voice tinged with uncertainty. "Really. It's...it's too much."

He tilted his head, his playful smirk back in place. "Maddie, I'm not just your fiancé—I'm your *billionaire* fiancé. Spoiling you is part of the job description."

"But—"

"No buts." He winked, cutting me off. "Besides, it sells the act. Margot would never believe I'd let you get away with just one dress."

Oh. His words brought me back to reality—the reality where this wasn't real.

I'd been letting myself get too caught up in the moment, in the way Ian made me feel, and had started to forget this was all an elaborate show. An act. For Margot. For everyone watching.

Probably even for the store clerk.

Was that why he'd said that thing about me breaking his heart? Because he knew she was nearby?

My stomach sank as the realization settled in. He was playing his part perfectly, but I was starting to forget that I was supposed to be playing mine, too.

I forced a smile and nodded toward the fitting room. "I'm going to change out of this, okay?"

"Okay." Ian nodded, stepping back to give me space. "But before you do, there's one more dress I'd like you to try on."

He held out another gown—a deep purple, floor-length piece that sparkled like a thousand tiny stars under the boutique's lighting. My breath caught when I glanced at the price tag.

Twelve thousand dollars.

"I can't wear this." I stared at it, my face draining of blood. "It's too much."

"Just humor me. Please." He shrugged, his gaze steady, unaffected. "I promise this is the last one. I just..." He trailed off, his voice softer now. "I just think it'll look really good on you."

There was something in his tone, something earnest, that made me pause. His eyes held mine, and for a moment, I couldn't tell what was real and what wasn't.

So, confused but unable to resist, I said, "Okay."

I took the gown and returned to the fitting room, my heart thudding unevenly as I slipped out of the previous dress and into the new one. The fabric was heavier, but the cut was exquisite, the shimmering material molding to me in a way that made me feel like I'd just stepped out of a fairytale.

Once it was on, I glanced at my reflection, stunned. This dress didn't just look expensive—it looked like it was made for royalty.

But as I reached for the zipper, it caught halfway up.

I twisted awkwardly, panic blooming in my chest as I tried to see what had happened.

But the zipper wouldn't budge.

Crap! Have I just ruined a twelve-thousand-dollar dress?

"Maddie?" Ian's voice came from outside just as I was trying to figure out how many months of salary I'd need to pay for this. "Everything okay in there?"

"Uh...I—" I hesitated, not knowing what to do. But since I literally couldn't get out of this dress without ruining it further, I said, "I think the zipper's stuck."

"Come out. I'll see if I can fix it."

I checked my reflection to make sure I was decent before stepping out.

Ian's gaze swept over me the moment I appeared, his eyes sharpening as they took in the dress. But he didn't say anything about that. Instead, he stepped forward, his expression shifting to concern as he examined the back of the gown.

I turned slightly, giving him a better view of my back, acutely aware of the gown's zipper caught halfway up, probably revealing too much of my lacy maroon bra.

I hardly ever wore sexy underwear. But of course, on the one day I had, my boss had to see it.

Hopefully, he didn't think I'd worn it with the intent to seduce him later.

The silence between us stretched, charged, as I felt his gaze settle on me. The heat of his nearness radiated like a quiet hum.

"It looks like it got stuck on this," he murmured as his fingers tugged gently on my bra, his voice soft, almost intimate.

"Yeah?" I managed to say, my throat suddenly dry.

"Yeah..." And when he moved closer, my breath hitched— the air around us seeming to thicken.

His fingers grazed my back lightly, warm and deliberate against the fabric of the gown. I could feel every point of contact. As if his touch carried a quiet electricity, surging through the thin barrier between his skin and mine.

"Hold still," he said, his tone low and intimate, a quiet command that made my pulse race.

His knuckles brushed the curve of my spine as he gently tugged at the zipper, and I couldn't stop the shiver that raced through me.

Why did this feel so good? So intimate—every second stretching as his careful movements drew out a tension I couldn't ignore.

My heart raced, thundering loud in my ears, and I was sure he could hear it. I stared straight ahead, forcing myself to breathe as the delicate pull of the zipper eased higher.

"Got it," he said, the words barely louder than a whisper. His voice was deeper now, softer, and instead of stepping back, he stayed close. His hand lingered at the base of my back, warm and steady, as if he wasn't quite ready to break the contact.

I turned slowly to face him, clutching the fabric at my waist to keep my hands from trembling. His eyes locked onto mine, dark and unreadable, and for a moment, it felt like the fitting room melted away. The world narrowed to just us.

"That dress," he said, his voice reverent, his gaze sweeping over me like a caress. "It's perfect. Like it was made for you."

The sincerity in his tone made my chest tighten, and I struggled to find words. "Y-you really think so?"

His brow furrowed slightly, as though my question didn't make sense to him. "Maddie," he said, his voice firm yet gentle, "how could I not?"

The words hit me harder than I expected, striking something deep and vulnerable inside me. After years of feeling like I wasn't enough, of being overlooked or left behind, hearing Ian say those words—seeing the way he looked at me—unraveled something tightly wound in my chest. It was as though he was trying to tell me that I was someone worth noticing. Someone worth more than I'd ever believed.

Before I could respond, he gently turned me toward the mirror, his hands steady on my shoulders. My reflection stared back at me, draped in the shimmering gown that hugged every curve. His hand drifted higher, brushing a stray curl from my shoulder, the light graze of his fingers sending a quiet hum through me.

"What do you think?" he asked, his voice soft but weighted with something I couldn't quite name. "Do you like it?"

I swallowed hard, staring at the woman in the mirror who didn't quite feel like me but who, for the first time, looked like someone who could be...enough.

"I love it," I admitted, the words quiet but honest.

"Good." His gaze met mine in the mirror, his expression warm, almost proud. "Because you look incredible."

"You don't think I look...like an imposter?" I turned my head slightly, catching his eye. "Like someone who doesn't belong in a dress like this?"

His expression softened, but the intensity in his gaze didn't waver. "No, Maddie," he said, his voice steady and full of conviction. "You don't look like an imposter. You look beautiful. Like you're much too good for the likes of me."

The words hit me with a force I wasn't prepared for. After years of feeling like I was never enough, like I was always second-best, it was hard to accept that someone like Ian could see me like this.

Not as someone forgettable or disposable, like my mom and Jaxon had made me feel when they left me behind, but as someone who mattered.

And that terrified me. Because with every lingering look, every gentle touch, Ian Hastings was making it harder for me to believe that this wasn't real.

By the end of our shopping spree, I wasn't just walking away with two dresses—I had shoes, jewelry, and even a designer clutch to complete the look. I tried to argue that it was too much, but Ian just waved me off, grinning as he picked out a tie to match my red dress in less than a minute.

"You're surprisingly decisive," I said, watching him pay with the effortless swipe of his black Amex.

He shrugged, his eyes meeting mine. "I know what I want."

And from the way he said it, the way his gaze lingered...it was impossible not to wonder if he was also referring to me.

Was it possible that I could be something he wanted?

26

———

IAN

THE MIXER BUZZED AROUND ME, the clinking of glasses and low hum of conversation filling the room. I held a champagne flute loosely in one hand, nodding absently to a man who'd introduced himself as Mr. Butler, one of the conference's sponsors. He was talking about his company's expansion efforts, something I should've been engaged in, but my thoughts were elsewhere.

On Maddie.

I'd spent the earlier part of the evening at a dinner for presenters and conference organizers, but I couldn't focus then, either. I'd decided to give Maddie the evening off from that part of the event. She deserved a break after how much time I'd monopolized her over the last few days.

From the summit's events to our shopping trip earlier, I'd barely given her a moment to herself.

Still, as much as I wanted her to relax, I'd been anticipating seeing her all night.

We'd decided earlier she would wear the red dress for

tonight's mixer, and I'd matched her choice with the red tie I picked up during our shopping trip. I still couldn't get over how stunning she'd looked trying it on. Heck, I couldn't get over Maddie, period.

The afternoon had only cemented what I'd already begun to suspect—I was falling for her.

Hard.

But unlike the whirlwind infatuations I'd had before, this felt different.

Deeper.

Calmer.

It wasn't about adrenaline or chasing the thrill; it was about her. The way she smiled. The way her laughter lit up a room. The way she didn't try to impress me and still managed to leave me breathless.

It was maddening. And exhilarating. And terrifying.

Mr. Butler chuckled, apparently at something he'd said. I forced a polite smile, raising my glass in acknowledgment. But then, out of the corner of my eye, I saw a flash of deep red.

Her.

My breath hitched as I turned, and the world seemed to tilt on its axis. Maddie stood at the entrance, scanning the room, her cheeks tinged pink as if she were nervous to enter the room alone. The red dress hugged her curves perfectly, the neckline revealing enough of her cleavage to make my throat go dry. My eyes wanted to follow the fabric down, to take her all in, but I reminded myself to be a gentleman and forced my gaze to stay on her face instead.

I could think about how good she looked in that dress on my own time.

Her eyes found mine a second later and she smiled shyly, the room going still as my chest tightened.

She really had no idea what she was doing to me, did she? No idea how she'd completely upended my world.

"Excuse me," I said to Mr. Butler. "My date just arrived."

And with that, I moved through the crowd, my pulse quickening with every step closer to her. When I reached her, I couldn't stop myself—I had to touch her, to make sure she was real. So I slid my arm behind her waist, resting my hand at the base of her bare back.

And wow, the contact of her smooth, soft skin against my palm sent an immediate rush of heat through me.

"Hello, darling." I leaned in, brushing a kiss against her cheek, trying to play it cool even though my heart was skittering around in my chest.

"Hi," she said.

"You look breathtaking," I murmured against her ear, my voice low and sincere.

"Thank you," she said softly, sounding almost shy.

And I couldn't help but smile, wondering how someone so effortlessly stunning could be completely unaware of the effect she had on everyone around her.

On me.

"Did you get some rest?" I asked, my hand still lingering on her back.

"I took a little nap." She nodded. "Got to talk to Grant, too."

"Good," I said, meaning it. I wanted her to feel as incredible as she looked tonight. "Can I get you something to drink?"

Her gaze flicked to my champagne flute. "I'll have one of those."

"Perfect choice."

So I led her toward the bar, stealing glances at her along the way. Every move she made, every flick of her hair, every soft smile she gave someone who caught her eye—it all drew me in deeper.

We grabbed her drink and were standing at one of the tall cocktail tables, chatting with Drake about the latest expansion plans he was spearheading, when I noticed Margot approaching from across the room. And when we made brief eye contact, a polished smile lifted her lips.

Was she headed our way, then?

I hoped not. We'd already seen too much of each other at this event. No need to keep interacting even though we'd once been close.

But she continued to move gracefully through the crowd, a wine glass in hand, her gaze flicking between Maddie and me as she closed the distance.

I straightened instinctively, sensing Maddie stiffen slightly beside me as well. But then, Maddie's hand brushed against mine—a seemingly fleeting touch that somehow grounded me more than I expected.

"Ian," Margot greeted smoothly, her voice light. "I know you're busy, but I would be remiss if I didn't tell you how incredible your keynote was earlier. You really have a way of wowing a crowd."

"Thank you, Margot," I said, her compliment taking me by surprise. "That means a lot."

"Of course. I know we have a complicated past, but I hope you understand that I can still appreciate how talented you are." Her smile stayed fixed, and I was just about to say something back when her attention shifted to Maddie, her gaze sweeping over her. "I love your dress, by the way. And those earrings—they're stunning."

"Thank you." Maddie returned the smile, her voice graceful but steady. "They were a gift from Ian."

"I thought they might be." Margot's lips twitched slightly.

"They looked so similar to the ones he bought me back in college that I figured he must still have the same taste today."

And there it was. The little jab I knew had to be coming.

But instead of lingering, Margot cast Maddie, Drake, and me one last smile before moving fluidly to the next group as though the exchange had been nothing more than a passing breeze—or more accurately, a fart in the wind.

Maddie and I exchanged a brief glance before Drake said, "Anyway, what was I saying again? Oh yes..." before picking up the conversation right where he'd left off.

His energy helped ease the moment's tension, and I found myself relaxing again. Maddie leaned in slightly, laughing softly at one of Drake's anecdotes. Her eyes sparkled in the warm light, and for a moment, I forgot we were even at the mixer since she had this way of making the rest of the world melt away, no matter where we were.

In fact, I was so caught up in watching her that I almost didn't notice Slade Jennings approaching us, his booming laugh cutting through the conversation. Slade was an acquaintance I'd crossed paths with during my last couple of years at this conference—a guy I barely knew but who seemed to think we were closer than we were.

"Man, Ian, you've come a long way from last year," he said, clapping me on the shoulder like we were old friends. "From living it up at the mixers to giving the keynote. What a step up."

"Yes—quite the shift," I said, feeling my face warm at his mention of what I'd done at last year's mixer.

"I'll say." Slade grinned, clearly relishing his walk down memory lane. "But I mean, just because you're this bigwig now, I hope you're still finding time for fun. Man, we had a wild time together last year, didn't we? I mean, you must've hooked up with what? Three different women in three days? That must be some sort of conference record."

Shut up, Slade. My jaw clenched as I tried to think of a way to get him to stop. Because while I knew that Maddie was somewhat aware of how promiscuous I'd been in the past, I really didn't want her to hear Slade's version of things.

But before I could stop him, Slade barreled on with a wide grin. "Wasn't one of them even a big social media influencer? What was her name? Nala? Man, she was hot. Probably a great lay, too."

My stomach twisted, a wave of panic washing over me as I saw any good opinion Maddie may have formed of me slipping away before my eyes.

I needed to get Maddie away from Slade before she could hear anything more.

But before I could figure out how to drag her away, Drake cleared his throat loudly and said, "Maybe we shouldn't talk about Ian's past indiscretions in front of his *fiancée.*" His tone was calm but pointed as his gaze flicked to Maddie.

Slade's grin dissolved instantly with Drake's words, his eyes going wide as he looked between Maddie and me.

"Oh crap," he said, clearly flustered. "I didn't realize. I thought she was just your assistant or...you know, your usual arm candy for the night. I didn't know you were engaged."

"Well, I am," I said, forcing a tight smile, every muscle in my body wound tight with frustration. "I've been more discreet —and hopefully matured—since we last saw each other."

I prayed that would finally shut him up, but Slade, true to form, wasn't done yet. He let out an awkward laugh, scratching the back of his neck. "Man, that actually surprises me. You were the last guy I thought would ever settle down."

My gaze darted to Maddie whose smile had grown brittle,

and it looked like she wanted to sink into the floor and disappear.

Slade, finally seeming to notice the discomfort he was causing, tried to backpedal. "Oh, but I'm sure he's been great with you. You seem like a nice girl. I mean, unless he got you knocked up and that's why all this is happening." He chuckled and shook his head as he looked back to me and Drake. "Yikes, can you imagine getting baby-trapped? What a nightmare."

"That's enough," I said, my voice sharp and cutting. "Really, Slade. Sometimes it's better to just shut your mouth."

Slade's eyes widened, clearly taken aback, but I didn't care. My focus was already on Maddie. She inhaled sharply, her expression paling as her crystal-blue eyes filled with a raw pain that twisted my stomach into knots.

Because even though Slade didn't know Maddie's history, he'd somehow managed to hit the exact nerve that would cut her the deepest.

"Hey," I said softly, leaning closer to her. "Let's get out of here, okay?"

She nodded, her movements stiff and automatic. "Okay."

I placed a hand on her back to guide her through the crowd. But as we stepped into the hallway, I thought I heard Slade mutter to Drake. "What crawled up Ian's butt?" he asked. "Is she actually pregnant or something? Is that why he's marrying her?"

I clenched my jaw, every muscle in my body going rigid. And when I glanced at Maddie, her lips were pressed together, her eyes closing briefly as she swallowed hard.

Yep. She'd heard it, too.

What a disaster.

Maddie and I didn't speak as we walked back toward the elevators, but the silence between us was thick. Every few seconds, I glanced her way, hoping to catch a glimpse of what she was feeling, but her face was unreadable, her expression carved from stone and carefully guarded.

When we reached our floor, I expected her to follow me into my suite as she had the last two nights. But instead of heading toward my room, she paused at the door to her suite instead, pulling out her keycard with trembling hands.

"Maddie," I said, my chest tightening as she swiped her card and pushed the door open. "I'm so sorry Slade was such an idiot down there. Please forgive me for ever being connected to someone like him."

"It's okay," she said softly, her gaze meeting mine.

And for a fleeting moment, I thought she might let me in. But then I saw it—the moisture gathering in the corners of her blue eyes, the slight tremble of her lips.

And I knew that it wasn't actually okay. None of it was.

She was barely holding it together and seeing her in so much pain broke something inside me.

"Hey," I tried again, stepping closer to the doorway. "Can we talk? Please. I—I hate what just happened down there. I hate that you had to hear it."

But she just shook her head, her eyes downcast. "Maybe some other time. I-I'm really tired, Ian. I think I'll just head to bed."

I wanted to argue, to say something that would make her stay and let me fix this. But the exhaustion in her voice left no room for debate. So I quietly said, "Okay," before stepping back so she could disappear into her room.

The door clicked shut, the sound far too final. I stood there for a long moment, staring at the closed door, frustration clawing at me.

Slade and his big, stupid mouth.

Why hadn't I stopped him sooner? Why hadn't I been

more careful in my past? My careless, reckless choices, always chasing the next thrill, had come back to haunt me.

And now, Maddie was on the other side of that door, hurting.

Because of me.

I went to my own suite, frustration simmering under my skin. Tossing my tie onto the dresser, I sank onto the edge of the bed, running a hand through my hair.

Had I just lost any chance I had at starting something real with Maddie?

27

———

MADDIE

THE LIGHT STREAMING through the hotel curtains didn't feel as cheerful as it should have when I woke the next morning. I blinked against it, my head pounding slightly from the restless night I had. Sleep had come in fits and starts, my mind replaying Slade's words over and over again like a broken record.

But even though all I wanted to do was stay in bed a little longer, I had to get up. Get up and face Ian and all the people at the conference who, after hearing Slade's words at the mixer, now probably thought Ian had only gotten engaged because I was supposedly pregnant.

Yay...it was like my senior year of high school all over again.

Dragging myself out of bed, I shuffled into the bathroom, flipping on the light. The reflection in the mirror stopped me cold. My eyes were swollen, puffy reminders of how hard I'd cried the night before. I pressed my fingers lightly under them, wincing at the tenderness.

Slade's voice echoed in my mind. His thoughtless laughter. The cutting way he'd joked about Ian's past escapades and thrown in that awful comment about the "nightmare" of getting stuck with a baby.

I gripped the edge of the counter, the sting of those words settling heavy in my chest.

Did Ian feel that way, too, then?

He *had* said before that birth control was always important to him, that avoiding fatherhood too early had been a priority. At the time, I'd thought he was just being responsible—kind, even—when he comforted me after I shared my fears about Jaxon feeling trapped by my pregnancy with Grant.

But had Ian been judging me all along? Thanking his lucky stars that he hadn't ended up with someone like me?

The thought cut deeper than I wanted to admit. And honestly, I couldn't blame him if he had. Not many guys would want to find themselves in Jaxon's shoes.

I let out a bitter laugh, the sound echoing in the small bathroom. How stupid had I been to get swept up in the romantic whirlwind of this week? To think, even for a second, that Ian might actually want something real?

He wasn't going to settle down. Not with me. Not with anyone.

I thought of the guilty look in his eyes last night. *Pity.* That was what it had been. He'd felt sorry for me. Sorry that I'd ever thought I'd have a chance with someone like him.

The realization sent a fresh wave of embarrassment crashing over me, and I dropped my gaze from the mirror.

Oh man, I can't face Ian today. Not after everything.

Would it be super obvious if I texted him to say I was sick?

Say I needed the morning off to recover—just a little more time to pull myself together?

No. That would only make things worse.

I was here for work, and even if the lines between boss and

assistant had gotten incredibly blurry over the past few days, Ian was still my boss and I still needed this job.

Grant and I still deserved our fresh start in Eden Falls, and I wasn't going to mess that up all because I'd gotten caught up in a fairytale and my feelings had been bruised in the process.

I took a deep breath, then stepped back from the mirror.

I could do this. I *would* do this.

One more day as Ian's fake fiancée, and then I'd be more careful.

Professional.

Detached.

Because even if listening to Slade's words had sucked, last night had at least made one thing abundantly clear: I didn't know Ian as well as I thought I did. And as much as I wanted to believe he'd changed in the ways he claimed he had, I couldn't afford to let myself be blind to the truth.

Not again.

I had a son to think about.

A life to rebuild.

And getting caught up in Ian's charm, no matter how genuine it seemed, wasn't worth the risk.

I turned on the shower, resigned to facing the day. After today, I'd guard my heart more carefully. I'd make sure to keep Ian at a distance where he couldn't hurt me.

Because I couldn't afford to be careless this time. Not when Grant was counting on me to get this right.

I was curling my hair—the final step before heading out to face Ian—when my phone buzzed against the bathroom counter. My sister Lexi's name lit up the screen.

Frowning, I set the curling iron down and grabbed the

phone. Lexi never called this early. Was she hoping for more details about my fake relationship with Ian?

Probably, since my last text to her and Juliette had been a picture of me in that gorgeous red dress from last night, accompanied by a playful, *Wish me luck!*

My stomach twisted at the thought of explaining how the evening had actually gone. The night I'd hoped would dazzle had ended in disaster instead. But I couldn't ignore Lexi's call, so I answered, pressing the phone to my ear.

"Hey, Lexi," I said, forcing a lightness I didn't feel. "What's up?"

"Maddie." Her voice was tight, panicked, and that single word made my heart lurch.

"What's wrong?" My voice rose.

Has something happened with her baby?

"It's Dad." She sucked in a shaky breath. "He had a heart attack."

The words slammed into me like a freight train, and my entire body went cold. "What?" My knees wobbled, threatening to buckle beneath me as my stomach churned violently. "Dad had a heart attack? Is he okay? Is he alive?"

"He's alive," she rushed to say, but her voice was trembling, shaky with emotion. "Sorry—I should've led with that. Yes, he's okay as far as I know."

"Okay, good." A small wave of relief crashed over me at her reassurance that he was alive. "What happened?"

"He went out for a jog this morning," she said quickly, "and Juliette's mom was driving past and found him on the sidewalk on the corner. She noticed he was struggling and was able to help him in time for them to life-flight him to the hospital in Syracuse. He's in surgery now."

"He's in surgery?" I closed my eyes, a wave of nausea sweeping through me. "Is he stable? Is he—will he be okay?"

"They don't know yet," Lexi said, her voice cracking. "I just heard about this a minute ago from Juliette and Easton, but I guess it depends on what they find. Noah and I are heading to Syracuse now to be there when he gets out of surgery."

"How can this even be happening?" I asked, my breath coming in shallow gasps, the edges of my vision darkening.

My dad.

My strong, indestructible dad. He couldn't—no.

"He's not even fifty," I choked out, tears welling up in my eyes. "He's not old enough to die."

"I know," she said softly, and I could tell she was holding it together for my sake. "We're going to be there, Maddie. He's in good hands. I'll call you as soon as I know anything, okay?"

"Okay." My voice wavered. "Please call me as soon as you hear anything."

"I will," Lexi promised. "Be safe and let me know if you're able to come, okay?"

I nodded, even though she couldn't see me. "Okay. Bye."

The call disconnected, and for a moment, I just stood there, staring blankly at my reflection in the mirror. My puffy eyes from the night before were nothing compared to the raw panic now etched across my face.

I burst out of the bathroom and started throwing my things into a suitcase.

I needed to leave. Now.

Ian would understand—I just had to tell him I couldn't stay.

As if knowing I was thinking about him, there was a knock from the adjoining door to his suite.

Hopefully, he wouldn't be upset with me for ditching out early.

As I stepped up to the door, I hesitated for half a second before turning the knob.

As soon as the door opened, Ian's gaze swept over my face. Then, seeing the suitcase on my bed, his brow furrowed as he asked. "What's wrong? Are you leaving?"

"Yes," I said, my voice cracking. "I'm sorry. I can't stay."

"Is it because of Slade?" He stepped into my room, concern flashing in his dark eyes. "Because I promise I—"

"No," I cut him off, shaking my head, tears spilling over. "It's my dad."

"Your dad?" His expression became serious instantly. "What happened?"

"He had a heart attack," I whispered, the words barely making it past the lump in my throat. "He's in surgery right now, and I—I don't know if he's going to be okay." My voice broke on the last word, and before I could stop myself, I was sobbing.

Ian stepped forward, his hands resting gently on my shoulders before pulling me into his arms. "Hey, hey," he murmured, his voice low and steady as he held me. "I'm so sorry, Maddie. I'm so sorry."

I clung to him, my tears soaking into his shirt as the fear and helplessness poured out of me. "I can't lose him, Ian. I just can't. He's my dad."

He's supposed to be invincible.

Ian's arms tightened around me, his hand smoothing over my hair. "You're not going to lose him," he said with quiet determination. "He's strong, Maddie. He's going to fight."

I pulled back slightly, looking up at him through blurry eyes. "I need to go see him, though. I need to get to Syracuse so I can be there for him."

"Then let me take you," he said without hesitation.

"But—don't you have meetings today?" I blinked at him, thrown off by his immediate offer. "And the summit—"

"I can reschedule everything," Ian said firmly, his gaze

unwavering. "They'll understand. Right now, you need to get to your dad, and I'm going to make sure you get there."

His words hit me like a lifeline, and I felt my knees weaken. Before I could stop myself, I fell into his chest again, clutching his shirt as the sobs wracked through me. "Thank you," I whispered. "Thank you so much."

"Anything for you, Maddie," he said softly, his lips brushing the top of my head. "Literally anything."

28

—

IAN

THE MOMENT MADDIE closed the door to her suite to finish packing, I darted into my room and threw everything into my suitcase. My thoughts were racing, bouncing between Maddie, her dad, and the plans I'd need to adjust for today.

I could apologize to the conference committee later about skipping tonight's gala. A fancy dinner didn't matter as much as getting Maddie where she needed to be.

After putting my suits in their bag, I texted Mr. Frankle—the client I was supposed to meet for lunch—and apologized for the short notice, explaining there was an emergency and that I'd be in touch next week to reschedule.

His company was just starting the onboarding process with Hastings Industries, so I knew he had a lot of questions for me to field, but hopefully, he'd understand.

Once that was taken care of, I slung my bag over my shoulder and headed down to the lobby to check Maddie and me out of our rooms.

When Maddie joined me a few minutes later, her face was pale, her shoulders tense.

"Ready to go?" I asked when the valet pulled up in my car, just outside the front doors.

"Yes." She nodded and then we stepped out into the warm morning air, putting our bags in my trunk with the assistance of the bellhop.

Maddie didn't say much as she slid into the passenger seat, but she didn't need to. I could feel her anxiety radiating off her.

Hopefully, her dad would be okay. Hopefully, he'd get through surgery and everything would be fine.

The drive to Syracuse was close to five hours, but according to the quick research I'd done on how long bypass surgeries took, we would most likely make it to the hospital before he was out.

I just hoped he was okay. I didn't know him, but Maddie's world revolved around the people she loved. Losing him? It would shatter her.

As we hit the highway, Maddie remained quiet, staring out the window as the landscape blurred past. Music played softly in the background—a mellow acoustic playlist I'd chosen—but it wasn't enough to fill the heavy silence.

I glanced at her occasionally, watching as she twisted her fingers together or wiped at her eyes when she thought I wasn't looking.

She just needs a little space, I decided. So I kept my focus on the road, even as my phone buzzed repeatedly in my pocket.

I'd missed a call from my publicist Bronwyn when I was checking out of the hotel and figured I'd just call her back later when we got to Maddie's dad. But she was apparently in a persistent mood today because my phone had been buzzing every fifteen minutes since hitting the road.

"Do you need to get that?" Maddie asked when Bronwyn's name lit up my phone once again about two hours into the drive.

I glanced at my phone, knowing that based on the persistence of her calls that Bronwyn probably had some kind of bad news for me. So I said, "I'll just call her back when we stop for gas."

Twenty minutes later, we stopped at a gas station to fill up. Maddie mumbled something about needing the restroom and headed inside. While the tank filled, I finally pulled out my phone and scrolled through the messages from Bronwyn.

> Bronwyn: Call me immediately.

> Bronwyn: Ian, you really need to see this.

> Bronwyn: There's a video from last night. You need to call me NOW.

I frowned, swiping to dial her number. She picked up on the first ring.

"Ian, have you seen the video?" she asked, jumping right in and ignoring her usual pleasantries.

"No," I said, my stomach twisting. "What video?"

"It's from the mixer you were at last night," she said. "You're standing at a cocktail table with your assistant—Maddie, right?—and Slade Jennings."

"What?" I asked, anxiety instantly flashing through me as I realized what the video probably showed.

"The audio isn't super clear," Bronwyn continued. "But it looks like you and Slade had an argument. Then it shows you pulling Maddie away, and as you walk out, Slade says something to another guy about you getting engaged to your assistant because you got her pregnant."

"Ah sh—" I said, stopping myself from swearing. "And a lot of people have seen it?"

"It's blowing up," Bronwyn confirmed. "And people in the

comments are talking about how you introduced her as your fiancée just earlier that day after your keynote. They're running with it, Ian."

"This is—" I blew out a breath as I ran a hand over my face. "This was not supposed to happen."

"No kidding," Bronwyn said. "Ian, did you really get engaged to your assistant? Because I'm pretty sure I saw a ring on her hand when I zoomed in on one of the photos someone shared."

"It's...complicated," I said, sighing as I glanced toward the gas station. Through the window, I could see Maddie browsing the shelves, completely oblivious. "I accidentally introduced her as my fiancée to get Margot off my back, and we just rolled with it for the summit. It wasn't supposed to be a big deal."

But of course it was a big deal. Because even if I seemed to forget it most of the time, there were other people out there in the world who liked to talk about me and whatever new trouble I'd gotten myself into.

And they all think I got Maddie pregnant!

This was not good.

"Well, it's a big deal now," Bronwyn said. "Which is why we need to decide how to handle this. Do you want me to release a statement?"

"I don't know." I hesitated, watching Maddie pick up a burrito and read the label. "This affects Maddie, too. I should probably talk to her first."

"Fine, but do it quickly," Bronwyn urged. "The sooner we address this, the better."

"I will," I promised. "But right now, her dad's in surgery after a heart attack. I'm not exactly sure she can handle this on top of everything else."

"I'm sorry to hear that." Bronwyn's tone softened immediately. "Okay, handle her situation first. But don't wait too long, Ian. This is already spiraling."

"I'll let you know."

We ended our call, and I slid my phone into my pocket, my chest tightening as Maddie walked back toward the car with burritos and coffee for both of us.

"Everything okay?" She glanced at me, her brows knitting together slightly.

"Yeah," I lied, forcing a smile. "Just work stuff. Let's get back on the road."

She nodded, climbing into the car without another word. As I started the engine, I couldn't help but wonder how I was going to break this news to her. Because while I didn't care about the rumors for myself, I hated the idea of Maddie's name being dragged into this mess.

She didn't deserve that—not after everything she was already dealing with.

As I glanced at her out of the corner of my eye, her face pale and her hands clutching the coffee cup, I made a silent vow. No matter what it took, I was going to fix this.

For her.

29

———

MADDIE

THE HOSPITAL PARKING lot blurred around me, a sea of concrete and cars that barely registered as I hurried toward the emergency entrance. Ian walked beside me, his steady presence the only thing keeping me grounded in that moment. The automatic doors slid open with a soft whoosh when we reached them, and a rush of cool, sterile air greeted us.

"My dad just had bypass surgery," I said when I stepped up to the volunteer at the information desk, my stomach twisting. "Which way do I go to see him?"

The man with barely graying brown hair glanced up from the desk. "Just down this hall." He gestured to the left. "The waiting room's at the very end on your right."

"Thanks."

Ian and I moved down the hall, the sound of our footsteps echoing in the quiet. When we reached a room with green carpet and mauve cushioned chairs, my eyes scanned the space, searching for my siblings. A moment later, I saw Lexi and Easton sitting together with their spouses in the corner.

"Maddie!" Lexi exclaimed, her eyes lighting up when she

saw me. She rushed over, throwing her arms around me. "You made it!"

The weight in my chest lightened just a little as I hugged her back, the warmth of her embrace grounding me. "Is Dad okay?"

"He is," Easton said, stepping up to me next, his voice calm but laced with relief. "They just told us Dad's out of surgery and in recovery."

"So...he's actually going to be okay?" My breath caught as the first sliver of hope slipped into my chest.

"He's doing well," Easton said, his voice steady but full of emotion.

Relief flooded me then, and I couldn't stop the tears as they spilled down my cheeks. Without thinking, I threw my arms around my siblings, and then a few seconds later, Lexi and Easton's spouses, Noah and Juliette, both joined us, their support wrapping around me like a blanket.

We stood there for a while, holding on to each other, letting the fear of the last few hours drain away.

"Ah, I can't tell you how relieved I am," I told my family when we finally pulled apart, wiping my eyes and chuckling quietly. "That was seriously the longest drive of my life."

"I know," Lexi said, removing the glasses from her face to dab at her eyes with a tissue. "I was panicking, too."

We all looked at each other again, seeming to feel the same relief as each other. There was a small movement behind me, and then I remembered Ian was watching all of us.

And when I noticed everyone's gaze flicking toward Ian, who looked a little out of place but still calm and composed, I stepped back to his side, saying, "I guess you guys are all probably curious who I came here with. But, uh, this is Ian Hastings." I cleared my throat. "He's my boss."

"Your boss?" Lexi's eyebrows shot up. Her gaze flickered

between Ian and me, probably remembering the story of how I'd accidentally kissed him at the club and the few details I'd texted her about our "engagement" story from the weekend.

Before she could say anything else, Ian stepped forward, extending his hand to Easton. "Nice to meet you all. I know it's probably weird for a boss to tag along for something like this, but we were at a conference together. And when Maddie got the call about your dad, I wanted to make sure she got here safely."

"We appreciate that," Easton said, his tone polite but with the protective edge of a younger brother sizing someone up. "Leaving your conference early to bring Maddie here."

"I'm glad I could do it," Ian replied, sounding sincere.

Noah stepped forward next. "Good to meet you," he said, his tall frame matching Ian's as they exchanged firm handshakes.

"You too," Ian said, his tone relaxed, though I could sense he was still a bit out of his element.

Juliette smiled as she introduced herself as my sister-in-law, the easy warmth in her voice helping to ease the tension. "Thanks for looking out for Maddie."

"Of course," Ian said, returning her smile. Then, glancing at me, his expression softened as he added, "She's been through so much lately. I just wanted to make sure she didn't have to face this alone, too."

The words were simple, but they hit me with an unexpected force. He didn't want me to have to do this on my own.

He wanted to be there for me.

I couldn't remember the last time someone who wasn't related to me had chosen to be there for me—without obligation, without being asked, without hesitation.

And it wasn't just that Ian had offered; he'd rearranged his life, canceled important plans, and dropped everything to make sure I wasn't alone in one of the scariest moments of my life.

That kind of care, that kind of selflessness...it was almost overwhelming. It made me feel seen in a way I hadn't felt in years, maybe ever.

And it terrified me, because I wasn't sure what to do with it —or what it might mean.

What I wanted it to mean, even though I'd been so sure this morning that I needed to forget all the feelings I'd been growing for Ian so I could focus on just doing well at my job and building a good life for Grant and me.

Ugh, there was so much going on right now. So many ideas bouncing around in my head. I just...I wasn't sure I even had the bandwidth to sift through everything that was happening right now.

We all moved back to the corner where I'd first found my siblings, sinking into the mauve chairs as the conversation shifted to lighter topics.

A nurse in scrubs approached us a little while later, her clipboard in hand. "Your father's awake," she said, her voice kind. "You can go see him now."

So my siblings and I filed into his room, leaving Ian and the in-laws in the waiting room.

"What are you all doing here?" Dad asked when he saw us, looking pale but alert, his tired smile tugging at my heart. "I'm fine."

"You're not fine," Lexi said gently, taking his hand. "You had a heart attack, Dad."

"I know." His eyes softened, and his voice was hoarse as he muttered, "Didn't mean to scare you all."

"Well, you did." Easton let out a quiet chuckle, though his voice was thick with emotion.

We spent the next little while catching up, laughing, and

sharing updates. And after the nerve-wracking day I had so far, it felt good to have my dad talking and smiling, even if he looked exhausted.

Later, a nurse came in, her ponytail swinging as she adjusted Dad's IV. And even though I hadn't seen her in several years, it only took a moment for me to recognize her— Amber Leighton, an old high school classmate.

"Maddie Stevens," Amber said brightly, her voice lifting with surprise and warmth as her gaze landed on me. "Wow, it's been years! How have you been?"

"I've been good, thanks," I said, blinking as recognition clicked. She'd been a year ahead of me in high school, a friendly overachiever who somehow managed to balance cheerleading with straight A's. "It's so nice to see you. I didn't know you worked here."

"I've been here a few years now," she said with a shrug, her smile unwavering. "How about you? What have you been up to?"

"Oh, you know," I hedged. "Just...life." My voice sounded off, even to me, but I tried to force a small smile.

Amber didn't seem to notice. "I heard you moved recently. I guess you're not in Ridgewater anymore?"

"No, I'm not," I said, unsure how much more to offer since we'd never been that close. Just had a P.E. class or two together.

"Your dad did great in surgery, by the way." Amber's gaze shifted to Dad, her expression softening. "A real champ."

"Thank you," I said, relief threading through my voice. "I was so relieved to see him again after getting the news this morning."

"I bet. Especially with everything you have going on right now." Her tone was kind, professional, and then she got a glint I didn't quite understand in her eyes before she said, "Oh, and congratulations, by the way."

Congratulations? I blinked. "Uh...thanks?"

What was she congratulating me on exactly?

Lexi and Easton had been standing nearby, quietly chatting while Dad rested. But seeming to realize this catch up with Amber might take longer than expected, Lexi gave me a quick hug. "We're going to grab something to eat. We'll be back in a bit."

"Okay," I murmured, still trying to process Amber's words as my siblings left the room.

For a second, I wondered if it was normal for nurses to congratulate family members after surgery. Maybe it was some sort of positive bedside manner thing.

But then Amber said, "I saw it on Instagram this morning. The engagement. So sweet how you two quietly dated all spring, and then you surprised him by getting a job in his building. A real-life fairytale."

What? My stomach lurched as I realized what she was talking about.

But before I could figure out what to say, Amber, clearly oblivious to my growing panic, turned to Dad with a wide grin. "And look at that ring!" She pointed to my hand, and my heart sank as I realized I hadn't thought to take it off before coming in. The massive diamond Ian had bought me for our charade sparkled obnoxiously in the fluorescent light. "It must feel good knowing your daughter's set for life. With a billionaire, no less."

"A billionaire?" Dad's eyes snapped to mine, his expression a mix of shock and something else—wariness? *"Engaged?"*

Oh no. This was not good.

Was he going to have another heart attack?

My pulse thundered in my ears. "Dad, I—"

But Amber, still cheerful and blissfully unaware of the emotional minefield she'd just detonated, gave a little laugh.

"Anyway, I'm going to need some privacy to take care of the catheter situation. If you could just step out for a bit..."

"Right. Of course," I managed to say, actually grateful for the excuse to leave and gather my thoughts.

I practically bolted from the room, my legs shaky as I stepped into the hallway. Leaning against the wall, I pressed a hand to my chest, willing my heart to stop racing.

What the heck was I supposed to do now? How could I possibly explain this to Dad without making his condition worse than it already was?

And how was I supposed to handle the fact that my so-called "engagement" to Ian was now officially out in the world?

30

—

IAN

"OKAY, yeah, let me know what the board suggests, and I'll take it into consideration before making any statements," I said into the phone, keeping my voice low.

"Just make sure you don't wait too long to respond." My dad's voice on the other end was steady but firm. "It's better to get ahead of this."

"Yeah, I hear you," I said, nodding even though he couldn't see me. "Thanks for the heads-up. I'll touch base with you later."

"Take care, Ian."

"You too," I said before hanging up.

I slipped the phone into my pocket, exhaling a breath. Turning around, I ran a hand over the back of my neck, the tension there refusing to ease. Then I saw that Maddie had just stepped back into the waiting room, her expression a mixture of uncertainty and exhaustion.

Her lips were pressed together, like she was trying to hold something back, and when our eyes met, I could tell she'd overheard the end of my conversation. "So," she said, crossing her arms and tilting her head, "I guess you heard that we apparently made the news?"

"Yeah." I nodded, my jaw tightening. "That's what Bronwyn was calling me about when we were driving here. I would've told you earlier, but with everything going on with your dad…" I sighed. "It didn't feel right to pile that on you, too."

She gave me a small, understanding nod. "It's okay. I get it." Then her brow furrowed slightly. "What exactly has been reported? The nurse in there—" She hooked her thumb over her shoulder toward the hallway. "—said she'd seen a story about our engagement. That we'd secretly dated for a few months. Is that basically it? Just what we were telling people at the conference?"

I shifted uncomfortably, licking my lips. "That's…part of the story."

Her eyes narrowed slightly. "What else is there?"

I hesitated, not wanting to drop this bombshell on her, but knowing I had no choice. "Well," I started carefully, "it sounds like someone posted a video of the conversation with Slade last night."

"What about the conversation?" She sounded wary, and her jaw tightened visibly.

I grimaced. "The video's audio isn't great, but apparently, you can hear Slade joking about us being engaged because you're…" I trailed off, reluctant to say it.

"Because I'm what?" she asked, her tone sharp now, panic rising in her voice.

I exhaled. "Pregnant."

"What?" Her jaw dropped, her face paling. "People— random people on the internet who I don't know—are saying I'm pregnant?"

I nodded, trying to gauge her reaction, but she was already

pacing, her hands running through her hair. "Oh my gosh. This is...this is insane."

"It's obviously not true," I said quickly, hoping to ground her. "So we can try to squash all the rumors with a statement."

"Have you talked to your family?" She stopped pacing and looked at me, her eyes searching mine. "Do they think...this?"

"No." I shook my head. "My dad knows the real story. I called him when you went to see your dad. I wanted to make sure they heard the truth before hearing anything else."

Her shoulders sagged slightly. "So he knows everything?"

"Yeah. He gets it," I said, trying to sound reassuring. "But before I even called him, he'd already gotten a few calls from people on the board who'd seen the story."

"And they're upset about it?" She winced.

"There have been pretty mixed reactions, actually." I let out a dry laugh, still wrapping my head around it. "Apparently, there are quite a few board members who are actually relieved to hear I'm settling down."

Her brows shot up. "What?"

"I know. I'm in shock, too. I mean, they've already been relieved that I stopped making headlines with my, uh, escapades. So while they're not thrilled to see my name popping up again—especially with a pregnancy rumor—I guess my dad's stories about how marrying my mom helped him focus stuck with them. They seem to think the same could work for me."

"And me?" She blinked, clearly trying to process that. "What do they think of me?"

"I don't know all their thoughts," I admitted, "but they know you're a hard worker, responsible. They probably think you're exactly what I need—someone grounded." Then I added softly, "Which you are."

She opened her mouth to respond, then closed it again, her

expression lost and overwhelmed. "This is just...a lot for me, Ian. I mean, I've dealt with gossip before—my last year and a half of high school was a nightmare with all the pregnant teen chatter—but this?" Her voice wavered as she gestured help- lessly. "This is all over the internet. How the heck are we supposed to handle something like that?"

"I'm so sorry," I said, my voice gentle. "This is all my fault. I wish you hadn't been dragged into my drama. But I promise I'll do everything I can to figure it out." I licked my lips, then hesi- tated as I recalled what she'd said about the nurse. I asked, "Did your dad's nurse mention the part about you being pregnant?"

"No. Thankfully, she didn't say anything about that. Just the engagement to a billionaire part." She shook her head like she still couldn't believe any of this was happening. "But still. He just had surgery. What if he thinks it's real? He's recovering from a heart attack, Ian. The last thing he needs is more stress."

"Maybe he didn't fully register it?" I offered weakly, knowing full well it was probably wishful thinking.

She let out a short laugh. "I guess it's possible. He is pretty hopped up on pain medication. Maybe he thought he was dreaming. If he even caught onto what Amber was saying at all."

"I'm crossing my fingers for you," I said. "But if not, I'm more than happy to help explain everything to him. Set the record straight. Let him know the gossip sites are wrong and I didn't actually impregnate his daughter just three weeks after meeting her."

Maddie's eyes widened, her expression a mix of shock and disbelief, and I immediately realized I'd been too blunt. Again.

Man, I really was great at sticking my foot in my mouth.

I cleared my throat, raking a hand through my hair as I tried to backtrack. "What I meant was—"

"Forget it." Her lips twitched, and for a moment, I thought

she might laugh. Instead, she shook her head, her gaze drifting around the waiting room. "Where's everyone else? Did they already head out to get food?"

"Yeah," I said, latching onto the change of subject. "They offered to pick something up for us, but I told them I'd take care of it."

Her gaze settled back on me, and for the first time in the conversation, a hint of relief softened her expression.

"You didn't have to do that."

"I wanted to," I said simply. "Are you hungry? Anything specific sound good?"

She hesitated for a beat before nodding. "Now that I know Dad's okay, I could definitely eat."

"Good. I looked up a few options earlier," I said. "There's a pub nearby. They've got a chicken salad that looked solid. Or a pastrami burger if you're in the mood for something heartier."

Her brows lifted slightly, and the corners of her mouth curved just enough to let me know she appreciated the effort.

"Chicken salad sounds great," she said. "Ranch on the side?"

"Perfect."

"And if they have potato munchers, I'd love some of those, too."

"I'll look into that, then." I couldn't resist the half-smile that slipped on my lips. As I pulled out my phone to order, I glanced at her. "Have you talked to Grant yet? Told him about your dad?"

"Not yet." She shook her head. "I didn't want him worrying when we didn't know anything. But now that Dad's okay, I think I'll call Jaxon and see if he can bring Grant to visit. Dad would love that since Grant's basically his best friend."

I smiled at that, imagining Maddie's son bringing some light to an otherwise stressful day. "That sounds like a great idea."

From how much she adored her son, I figured he'd bring Maddie some joy, too.

She gave me a small smile before pulling out her phone to make the call. As I stepped aside to place the food order, I realized something I hadn't expected: I liked taking care of Maddie like this. I liked being the one she could lean on.

And I wasn't sure what that meant, but I knew one thing for certain—I didn't want it to end.

31

MADDIE

I STEPPED BACK into my dad's room after eating my late lunch in the waiting room with Ian, deciding not to bring up the engagement stuff unless he did. He was already recovering from major surgery—the last thing he needed was more stress.

He looked better than before, though still pale and tired as he rested against the pillows. His eyes lit up when he saw me, the faintest smile tugging at his lips. "Hey, sweetheart," he said, his voice scratchy. "You doing okay?"

"Shouldn't I be asking you that?" I said softly, stepping closer to his bedside. I slid into the chair beside him, taking in the lines on his face, more pronounced than they'd been the last time I'd seen him.

"I'm fine," he replied, though the way his hand trembled slightly when he lifted it to adjust his blanket said otherwise. "They patched me up good as new."

I let out a shaky laugh, but it didn't feel right. My chest ached, and I couldn't hold back the guilt bubbling to the surface. "I should've been there this morning, Dad. I'm so sorry.

I should've been the one to help you, not Juliette's mom. What if she hadn't seen you? What if—"

"Maddie," he interrupted gently, his voice barely above a whisper. "Don't do that to yourself."

"I can't help it." The words tumbled out before I could stop them. "I shouldn't have moved to Eden Falls. None of us are in Ridgewater anymore. You're all alone now. Who's going to take care of you if something like this happens again? Who's going to be there to help you recover?"

He let out a soft sigh, his fingers weakly reaching for mine. His touch was so frail, it only made my chest tighten more.

Because my dad was getting older.

The strong man who had raised my siblings and me all on his own wasn't actually a superhero. He was in fact...human.

"Maddie, listen to me. You didn't do anything wrong," he said. "I'm okay. And you know what? Ever since you applied for that first job at your company and Lexi told me she and Noah were expecting their baby, I've actually been thinking it might be time for a big change myself."

"What do you mean?" I asked, searching his face.

"I've been thinking about moving," he said, his words slow but steady. "Lexi and Noah are in New Haven. Easton and Juliette are only an hour from there. And you... I'd love to be closer to you and Grant in Eden Falls. I miss that boy so much. It makes sense for me to come to all of you. I want to be around my grandkids while I still can."

"You'd leave Ridgewater?" I blinked, his words sinking in. "Sell the house?"

"That house is just walls, Maddie. Family is what matters." He nodded, the movement subtle but resolute. "And besides," he added, his lips curving into the faintest smile, "I can't ask you to leave your fiancé now, can I?"

My heart stuttered. "Oh...uh..."

He arched an eyebrow, a flicker of amusement in his tired eyes. "Were you afraid to tell me? Think I'd react badly? PTSD from when you told me you were pregnant?"

I swallowed hard, my pulse quickening. "I—I didn't..."

"Sweetheart," he interrupted softly, his gaze warm and steady. "This is different. I trust your judgement. You're an adult, and if you're in love with him, I'm happy for you. I've been so worried about you and Grant being on your own, it's nice to know you've got someone good by your side. You deserve that. You deserve to be loved."

The lump in my throat swelled, making it almost impossible to speak. "Thanks, Dad," I managed, the words barely audible. And in that moment, I knew I couldn't tell him the truth now.

Not after seeing the relief in his eyes, the hope on his face. Not after the scare he'd just had.

He'd been worried about me moving away on my own, and even though I hated to let him believe a lie, it almost seemed wrong to take away the hope he suddenly had of having his daughter finally taken care of after so many years of worrying about me.

So, even though it was probably wrong and twisted to let him believe it, I'd let him.

I'd pretend. Just for now.

And later, when he was stronger, if he asked me about my plans with Ian, I could tell him we had gone our separate ways.

It would be fine.

"Okay," he said after a long pause, his eyelids fluttering. "You should go get some rest, Maddie. You've been worrying too much."

I leaned down and kissed his forehead. "I'll check on you soon, okay? Get some rest."

He nodded, and as his eyes closed, I lingered a moment

longer, watching his chest rise and fall, each breath a reminder of how close I'd come to losing him.

When I stepped back into the waiting room after my conversation with my dad, my eyes immediately landed on Grant, who was perched on a chair next to Jaxon. His blond hair was slightly disheveled, his legs swinging as he grinned up at me.

"Mom!" he called, and before I could respond, he jumped up, running toward me, his little legs pumping with all the energy I loved about him. I crouched down just in time to scoop him up, hugging him tightly. His arms wrapped around my neck, and the familiar weight of him against me was like a balm to my frayed nerves. A few Band-Aids adorned his scraped knees, telling me he'd been his usual rambunctious self while I'd been in Boston. But he was well and happy, which was all I ever hoped for when he was with his dad.

"I missed you so much, buddy," I murmured, squeezing him tighter.

"I missed you too, Mom," he said, his voice muffled against my shoulder.

Jaxon had followed Grant over, standing a few feet away now with his hands shoved into the pockets of his shorts. His blond hair caught the fluorescent light, and his brown eyes held a touch of tentativeness.

There had been a time when I couldn't look at him without feeling that magnetic pull—his looks had been so striking to my sixteen-year-old self, his charm intoxicating. But now? Now, he was just Jaxon, the father of my child. That spark, the one that had once burned so brightly, was gone.

"Hey, Mads," he said carefully, his voice low. "How're you holding up?"

"I'm okay." I smoothed Grant's hair and stood, tucking him against my side. "My dad's doing a lot better now, and the doctors think he'll be fine."

"That's good news." Jaxon nodded, his expression softening slightly. "I was worried when you called."

"Yeah, it's been an intense day," I admitted. "Thanks for bringing Grant, though. My dad is going to be so happy to see him."

"It's no problem." His gaze flicked around the waiting room briefly before settling back on me. "Glad I could do it."

For a moment, we both seemed unsure of what to say. The weight of our shared history hung between us, a presence that was always there.

I cleared my throat. "Do you want to see my dad? He's just resting now, but I'm sure he'd be okay with a quick hello."

But Jaxon shook his head. "If he's resting, I don't want to bother him. Just tell him I stopped by."

"Okay." I nodded, knowing it was probably for the best. My dad wasn't exactly Jaxon's biggest fan after everything he'd put me through. "He'll appreciate it."

"Okay." He hesitated for a beat, then stepped forward, his movements slower than usual, as if he were unsure. Wrapping his arms around me, he murmured, "You're doing a great job, Maddie. With Grant, with everything. I hope you know that."

His words caught me off guard—they were soft and unexpected, carrying a weight that felt like a glimpse of regret for what we'd lost, for what he'd walked away from.

But as his arms tightened briefly around me, I realized something I hadn't before. His embrace felt different now—foreign, distant. When he let go, I was struck by the stark truth:

I didn't feel anything anymore for the man I'd once thought might be the love of my life.

That chapter of my life, the one where Jaxon had been everything, was truly closed. And for the first time, I was okay with that.

"Let me know if you need anything, okay?" Jaxon stepped back, his expression somber but kind. "I can take Grant tonight if you need more time here."

"No, it's okay," I said, glancing down at Grant who was now playing with the zipper on my purse. "I think having him with me will be good. He's kind of my home now."

"Yeah." Jaxon's lips twitched into a faint, sad smile. "He's the best."

He reached out to ruffle Grant's hair, earning a laugh from him, before saying goodbye.

As I watched him leave, I felt a bittersweet mix of emotions. Gratitude that he'd stepped up for Grant, sadness for what we'd lost, and relief at the realization that I really was no longer tethered to the complicated feelings I once had for him.

Some people come into your life for a season, a chapter, I thought. And while Jaxon had been a huge part of my life once, now he was simply the man I shared a son with.

But that was okay. Life was like that sometimes. You lived, you learned, and if you were lucky, you came out stronger on the other side.

32

___

IAN

"LET'S TRY 'PARTY' next," Grant's voice said from across the room where he was perched next to Maddie's brother, Easton, deeply invested in the game of Wordle they were playing together.

"You think that's it?" Easton asked, smiling at Maddie's son, his adoration for his nephew apparent in his eyes. "Because we try it every time and it's never right."

"It might work this time, though..." Grant looked up at his uncle. "Just do it."

"Okay..." Easton shrugged before making a big show of typing in the letters. And he must have pressed the *enter* button because a moment later, Grant's shoulders fell and he said, "Dang it."

Maddie's smile lit her face at her son's investment in the game, and I liked seeing it. She needed this moment—this reprieve with her family—after the emotional rollercoaster she'd been through.

I stuffed my hands into my pockets, unsure what to do with myself. Maybe this was my cue to leave. The day had been long for everyone, and while I'd wanted to be there for Maddie, I wasn't sure how much help I could still be. She was with her family now, surrounded by the people who knew her best.

And yet...I continued to stand awkwardly off to the side, pretending to scroll through my phone because even though it was close to nine o'clock in the evening, I didn't want to leave.

There was something grounding about being here, about watching Maddie interact with the people who clearly meant the world to her. It made me want to know her more, to be part of that world in a way I hadn't anticipated.

I shoved my phone into my pocket, my thoughts flickering back to the whirlwind of the last two days. The news about our so-called engagement was still buzzing somewhere out there, no doubt gaining traction.

I'd avoided scrolling through social media all day, knowing exactly how these things played out. Today's viral sensation would be forgotten by next week, replaced by some other headline or drama. I wasn't exactly a household name, and the corner of the internet that actually cared about my life wasn't all that big.

Honestly, as long as the board didn't have a problem with my name in the headlines again, I wasn't too concerned about it.

At least...I wouldn't have been, if the stories were only about me.

Sadly though, Maddie's name was also being dragged through the mud.

And that changed everything.

She hadn't signed up for this kind of attention. She hadn't asked to be dragged into internet gossip or have strangers speculating about her life.

She'd been holding it together so far, probably because her

dad's heart attack had taken up all her focus. But I knew that as soon as she had a moment to breathe, it would hit her.

The stories. The rumors about her being pregnant. The assumptions about our so-called engagement.

It was all complete nonsense, and it was my fault she was caught in the middle of it.

I was such an idiot for thinking I could get away with a fake engagement at such a big conference and not have it come back to bite me in the butt.

"Yay! We did it!" Grant cheered, bringing my attention back to the present. "I knew it was 'thumb'!"

And when I looked over to the group to see them giving each other high-fives for figuring out today's Wordle word, I caught Maddie's eye.

From her somewhat surprised expression, I wondered if she'd forgotten I was even here. But then she smiled faintly and excused herself, weaving her way over to me.

"Sorry you've been here so long," she said softly, tucking a lock of hair behind her ear. "You must be bored out of your mind."

"No, I'm good," I said, not wanting her to be worried about me. "I've been keeping busy."

"Yeah?" she asked, like she didn't believe me. "Because you can head out if you want. I know you have a lot of important things you can be doing instead of hanging out in a hospital waiting room."

"No, it's really fine. I want to be here." I didn't want her to think I was put out at all. "But I was wondering what you wanted to do tonight. I know your dad's place is about an hour from here. Were you and your siblings planning to stay there tonight? Because I'd be happy to book hotel rooms for everyone if you'd rather stay close by."

"Oh, you don't need to do that." She shook her head,

waving the thought away. "We were hoping to stay in town, but we can take care of our own arrangements. You've already done so much."

"It's no trouble," I said quickly. "Really, I have so many points on my credit card that I'll never use them all."

"I'm sure you probably racked up a bunch of points with our shopping spree yesterday," she said, laughing lightly. "But we can take care of our hotels."

Was it weird that I found her independent stubborn streak attractive? Because I did.

And because I'd known she'd probably turn down my offer before I even asked, I brought out my phone, pulling up the booking app where I'd already selected four rooms at a nearby hotel. Then, with a single tap, I finalized the reservation I had queued up.

"Oops," I said, holding up the screen so she could see it. "I accidentally booked them. Non-refundable. Guess you guys better stay in them so they don't go to waste."

"You're impossible." She narrowed her eyes at me, but the corners of her mouth twitched. "But thank you," she said, her voice softer. "You really didn't have to do that."

"Well," I said, slipping my phone back into my pocket, "I don't know if your family has heard anything about us yet, but it's the least I could do for my future in-laws."

A laugh escaped her and she shook her head. "Oh, man, we're in a mess, aren't we?"

"Yeah, sorry about that." I scrunched up my nose, a wave of guilt washing over me. "D-did you talk to your dad about...that particular subject?"

She grimaced, then let out a long sigh. "I wasn't going to bring it up. You know, I was banking on the hope that maybe he didn't register the news in his medicated state." She paused. "But then he brought it up."

"And how did it go?" I asked cautiously. "Was he mad? Did you tell him it was made up?"

"I probably should have..." She sighed again, her shoulders sinking a little. "But before I could explain anything, he started going on about how he trusted my judgment and was relieved to hear I'd found a good man who could take care of me since he'd been worried about me moving away on my own."

"Oh." I was speechless for a moment because that was definitely not the response I'd been expecting. "Well, that's... something."

"I know, right?" She gave a half-laugh, half-sigh. "It's crazy. He's never even met you." She shook her head. "And I'm sure if he were his usual self, he'd be asking all the questions, probably demanding I bring you in so he could give you the third degree about your real intentions with his daughter. But apparently his softer side is coming out with all the pain meds because he just seemed so happy for me."

"Does he think you're pregnant, too?" The words tumbled out before I could stop them.

"Oh, gosh, no!" Her eyes widened. "At least...I don't think so. I'm sure that would be a whole different story."

"Probably," I agreed, relieved to hear that wasn't part of the equation.

"So, what are you going to do now?" she asked. "Have you decided what you're going to do about the board?"

"I think I'm going to tell the board the truth about what's going on," I said. "Honesty is the best policy there since I don't want them to distrust me. Not when I'm hoping to take over my dad's position one day."

"That makes sense." She nodded.

"But as for making an official statement...I kind of wanted to talk to you about that before I said anything."

"Oh..." she said, as if only just then remembering how big

this thing had blown up today. She probably still hadn't even looked online with everything going on.

"Do your siblings think I'm your fiancé?" I asked, wondering what she'd told them if her dad thought she was engaged.

"No, they already knew everything was fake," she said. "I told Juliette and Lexi about the whole fake engagement stuff back when we were in Boston."

"Okay, good..." I said, my stomach twisting a little when she said the part about *everything* being fake.

I'd at least hoped that *some* of what had happened with us had been real.

"But with my dad..." she continued. "I think I'll just let him believe it for a little while. He's happy. And after everything he's been through, I don't want to take that away from him. Once he's fully recovered, I figure I can just tell him we broke things off."

"Okay," I said, not really liking the idea of us breaking things off. Even if we weren't really a couple, I kind of wanted to be one. But I didn't want to look like I was the only one hoping for more out of the arrangement I'd basically forced her into, so I tried to keep things light by saying, "Just make sure to tell him a really good breakup story, okay? Something like, 'I realized I could do way better than Ian Hastings and completely shattered his foolish little heart.'"

"I'll keep that in mind." Maddie laughed, a soft, breathy sound that eased some of the tension between us. "Maybe we can come up with a story as epic as the one we came up with when we were at the conference."

And even though she was talking about our breakup story like it would be a funny, light-hearted event, I couldn't help but think that if this all ended—if we went back to being nothing more than colleagues—it wouldn't be just another crazy conference story for me to tell my friends about.

It would actually sting. Much more than I cared to admit.

Because even though I'd been the one to push for this fake engagement, the truth was becoming clearer with every passing moment: there was nothing fake about the way I felt. And if this ended? A broken heart would feel like an understatement, since I was pretty sure I'd be devastated.

33

MADDIE

THE NIGHT AIR was cool as we stepped out of the hospital to head to the hotel, the faint scent of freshly cut grass lingering on the breeze. The moon hung low in the sky, casting a silvery glow over the parking lot. Grant walked beside me, his small hand clasped in mine, his energy seemingly untouched by the long day.

"Are we taking *The Lambo* or is your friend, Ian, driving us?" Grant asked, his voice curious and bright as he tilted his head up at me.

I glanced at Ian who was walking on my other side. His brow furrowed, his lips twitching like he wasn't sure if he should laugh. "Wait," he said, "do you guys have a Lambo? And you've just been driving that old Subaru around so no one guesses you're secretly rich?"

"No, no, definitely not." A laugh bubbled out of me before I could stop it. "We only have one car, and it's *not* a Lambo. That's just the nickname Grant and I gave it one day. Something silly."

"That's actually fun." Ian grinned, his face softening in the moonlight. "I like it. The Lambo."

Grant beamed, clearly proud of our little inside joke, but I crouched slightly so we were eye to eye. "You actually get to ride in Uncle Easton's car tonight," I told him. "The Lambo's still in Eden Falls since I caught a ride here with my friend."

"Oh, okay," he said, sounding a little disappointed.

I ruffled his hair and pointed to Ian. "Ian's car is even fancier than a Lambo, but it only has two seats, so we'll just meet you at the hotel, okay?"

Grant nodded, seemingly placated, and reached for Easton's hand as my brother caught up with us. "Come on, buddy," Easton said with a smile, leading him toward his car. Juliette followed close behind, the four of us heading in different directions.

The hotel wasn't far, just a few blocks away, and Ian's sleek car hummed quietly as we made our way there. Once we arrived, Ian went straight to the front desk to check us in. A few minutes later, he returned with a handful of key cards, handing them out.

"Here you go," he said, holding mine out to me with a small smile. "Room 215."

"Thanks," I said, taking it from him.

"Want me to help you and Grant get settled?"

"That would be great," I admitted.

We headed upstairs, and once we reached the room, Ian carried my suitcase and Grant's small bag inside before setting them down near the bed. "I'll let you two get settled," he said, his voice low and warm, lingering for a beat as though he wasn't quite ready to leave. "I'm just next door if you need anything."

"Thanks," I said softly, watching him as he stepped back toward the door. He gave me a small, reassuring smile before heading out, quietly closing the door behind him.

Turning my attention back to Grant, I focused on getting him ready for bed. He'd been bright-eyed and full of energy when we'd left the hospital, chattering nonstop and soaking up the buzz of being surrounded by family. But now, as I handed him his pajamas and helped him brush his teeth, I could see the tiredness creeping in.

By the time I tucked him under the covers, his eyelids were heavy, and he yawned, snuggling deeper into the pillow. Within minutes, his soft, steady breaths filled the room—a peaceful rhythm that never failed to make my heart swell. I lingered by the bed, smoothing his hair back, whispering a quiet, "I love you, baby," before stepping away.

Slipping into the bathroom, I let the cool water rinse the day's weight from my face. The familiar routine was grounding, a small moment of calm after the whirlwind we'd been through. As I dried my face, I reached for my phone, hesitating for only a moment before typing out a quick message to Ian.

> Me: Thank you again for all you did for me and my family today. I really appreciate it so much.

I hit *send* and started applying my nighttime moisturizer, half-expecting him to take a while to reply. But my phone buzzed almost instantly.

> Ian: I'm glad I could help. Glad your dad is doing better.

I smiled faintly, typing back.

> Me: Me too.

After flossing and brushing my teeth, I stepped into the room and paused. My eyes caught on a door next to the mini-fridge—an adjoining door. A flicker of amusement danced through me as I remembered sharing a similar setup with Ian in Boston.

How was it possible that so much had happened since then?

Curiosity got the better of me, so I texted him.

> Me: What room are you in?

A moment later, his reply came.

> Ian: 217

I walked to the hallway, opening my door to check. Sure enough, Ian's door was just left of mine. Grinning, I knocked lightly on the door connecting us.

A few seconds later, it opened, and Ian stood there, leaning casually against the doorframe. He was in a white T-shirt and gym shorts, his dark hair slightly tousled. He looked effortlessly good—just like the last time I'd seen him in pajamas. How had that been only two nights ago?

"Fancy seeing you here," I said, my voice lighter than it had been all day.

"Yeah..." He chuckled softly, running a hand through his already tousled hair. "I may have asked the hotel clerk for adjoining rooms." A sheepish smile tugged at his lips. "I just wanted to be close by, you know, in case you needed anything."

My heart gave a little flutter. "That's really sweet of you to watch out for us," I said, softly.

With his gaze steady on mine, he sincerely said, "I can't really help it now."

Warmth bloomed in my chest, spreading to my toes. There was something so deeply comforting about knowing someone was looking out for me—really looking out for me—not because they had to, but because they wanted to. It was a feeling I wasn't used to, and I didn't quite know what to do with it.

I peeked my head into his room, eyeing the modest layout. "How does it feel to be in a regular room? Must be quite the downsize from the suites you're used to."

He chuckled. "It's just fine," he said, crossing his arms in a way that emphasized his muscular forearms. "I'm really not as high maintenance as you think."

"Good to know." I turned toward the open door that connected our rooms, gesturing toward mine. "I should probably head back," I said reluctantly. "It's late, and I should get some sleep."

"Yeah," he said, his voice low and steady. "You probably should." But his eyes lingered on me, a glimmer of something unspoken making it clear he wasn't quite ready to let me go.

So, needing to fill the silence—and maybe delay leaving—I asked, "Do you really think those fancy dresses will be okay in your trunk tonight?"

"Yeah," he murmured as he stepped closer, his gaze flicking to my lips before returning to my eyes. "I think they'll be fine."

"You sure?" I pressed, my pulse quickening from the way he was looking at me, the way the air seemed to thrum between us. "I mean, what if someone sees your fancy car in the parking lot and gets the idea that there might be some really fancy things inside to steal?"

"I'm not worried about it." He sounded calm, sure.

"You're positive?" I asked, my voice wavering slightly as his nearness sent a rush of heat through me.

"The most precious cargo is already safe inside the hotel, staying in the room next to me tonight."

For a moment, I was speechless. My breath hitched, and

my mind raced for a response, but before I could find one, he winked. "And his mom is pretty cute, too."

It took me a second to catch on, and when I did, I swatted his arm, laughing despite myself. "And here I was thinking you were talking about me!"

"Of course I was talking about you." He chuckled. "But yeah, your son seems pretty awesome, too."

I smiled, warmth spreading through me. "Glad you think so."

He nodded, his expression softening. "I do."

He leaned in closer, and for a heartbeat, I thought he might kiss me. But instead of pressing his lips to mine like I hoped, he brushed a featherlight kiss against my cheek.

Then, resting his forehead against mine, his breath warm and minty against my nose, he mumbled, "This is probably breaking some sort of rule we didn't talk about when we started this whole thing, but...I like you, Maddie." He sighed as he lifted a hand to brush his thumb over my cheek. "Probably way more than I should."

And despite all the misgivings I'd had last night and this morning—the worries that I might just be another fleeting chapter in his long history of conquests...I believed him. I really did.

The sincerity in his tone, the look in his deep brown eyes— it made my heart ache in a way I couldn't explain.

"I don't know what's going on," I admitted, my voice trembling as I let out a shaky breath. "Just this morning, I was so determined to stop all the...flirty vibes between us. To keep things professional. To forget everything that happened this week because I didn't want any messiness or drama in my life. But..." My breath caught, and I shook my head. "I'm not sure I actually want to forget everything."

The air between us thickened, charged with an electricity

that felt almost tangible. His lips brushed my cheek again, featherlight and gentle, and then my forehead, lingering just long enough to make my heart constrict. The tenderness of his touch unraveled me, thread by thread, making me feel cherished in a way I hadn't in years. When his lips moved to my temple and then to my other cheek, each kiss was deliberate, reverent, leaving me breathless and trembling.

"You make it impossible not to fall for you," he murmured roughly, the words grazing my skin like a promise.

The sincerity in his tone, the way his deep brown eyes held mine as though I was the only thing he saw—it sent a deep pang through my chest. I felt like I was standing on the edge of something monumental, something I wasn't sure I was ready for but desperately wanted to leap into anyway.

How was it possible that he was even real? That this man, who had once been infamous for his fleeting romances and trail of broken hearts, now held me as though I was the most precious thing in the world.

Logic told me it was too good to be true, that I should guard my heart because once he'd had his fill, he'd move on like he always had.

But the way he was looking at me, the way he touched me—it didn't feel like the man from the headlines. It felt like someone entirely different. Someone who wanted more than just a fleeting moment.

Someone who maybe, just maybe, might even want *forever*.

I mean, he'd told his interior designer to make him a house that "looked like a family could live there."

That wasn't something a man who intended to always be a perpetual playboy would say, was it?

Of course, the only way to know if he was actually being sincere would be to trust him—which could put my heart at risk at being hurt again. But right here in this moment, I wanted to. Against all reason, I wanted to trust him.

So, reaching up, I placed my hand gently against his chest, feeling the steady, reassuring beat of his heart beneath my palm. "You know," I murmured, my voice soft but steady, "you're making it really hard for me to remember why I was trying to keep my distance."

His eyes searched mine, his expression unreadable at first. But then, a warmth bloomed in his gaze, his lips curving into the faintest hint of a smile. For a moment, the world seemed to pause, the air between us growing heavier, more charged. I could feel the tension pulling us closer, as if some unseen force was drawing me toward him.

His head dipped slightly, and my breath hitched as his lips hovered over mine, the anticipation sending a shiver down my spine.

And then, finally, he kissed me.

Softly at first, like he was testing the waters, his lips brushing against mine in a way that sent my senses reeling. But then, the gentle pressure quickly gave way to something deeper, more urgent, as though he couldn't hold back any longer. His hands moved to my hips, pulling me closer, and I melted into him, letting myself get lost in the heat of the moment.

When he stepped forward, pressing me against the wall, a soft gasp escaped my lips. The cool surface at my back only heightened the warmth of his body against mine, firm and unyielding. I threaded my fingers into his hair, holding him close as his mouth weaved a spell over my mind and body, leaving me breathless.

His lips traveled down to my jaw, then to my neck, pressing hot, open-mouthed kisses that left a trail of fire in their wake. My head tipped back against the wall, a soft sigh escaping me as his mouth found the sensitive hollow just beneath my ear. He lingered there, pressing a kiss that sent a jolt of heat straight through me, and then he continued his path downward, his mouth warm and teasing against my skin.

I clutched at his shoulders, trying to anchor myself, my breath coming in shallow gasps as he kissed along the curve of my neck, his stubble rasping lightly against me in the most delicious way.

"Ian..." His name escaped me, half a sigh, half a plea.

He murmured something low against my skin—something I couldn't quite make out.

But the sound of his voice sent a shiver racing down my spine. His hands slipped beneath my cami, roaming higher, his thumbs grazing across my ribs as though he couldn't decide if he wanted to hold me tighter or explore further.

And all I knew was that I wanted more. More of his touch. More of the way he was making me feel.

More of the way he made me forget everything but this moment, this connection, this overwhelming need that neither of us seemed able to resist.

But then, almost as if he could sense that I was ready to leap headfirst into uncharted waters with him, to dive into the unknown, he slowed our kisses. Guiding me instead to a soft, fluffy cloud that could carry us down gently, letting us drift toward the sandy shore instead of plunging headlong into the depths.

His lips lingered on mine, warm and unhurried, melting into something tender, something that felt like an unspoken promise. A promise that we didn't need to race toward the horizon—that maybe we might actually have all the time in the world.

When he finally pulled back, his eyes met mine, dark and warm, filled with an emotion I wasn't sure I was ready to name.

His hand came up to cup my cheek, his thumb brushing softly against my skin as he leaned forward and pressed a gentle kiss to my forehead.

"Goodnight, Maddie," he murmured. "I'll be in here if you need anything."

I nodded, unable to form words, as he stepped back, giving me space to slip back through the door and into my own room.

My heart was still racing as I leaned against the closed door, a hand pressed to my chest like it might help me make sense of the emotions coursing through me.

The day had been so long, so draining—full of worry and fear and raw emotion. But somehow, in the quiet of this moment, as Ian's care and kindness settled over me, it felt like the world had steadied itself.

I finished getting ready for bed in a blissful haze, my thoughts circling back to the way he'd kissed me, the way he'd touched me as though I mattered. As though I was precious.

And as I climbed into bed beside my sleeping boy, the events of the day fading into the background, I realized that even though it had been one of the hardest days I'd faced in a long time, it didn't feel quite so heavy anymore. With Ian by my side, somehow, it felt like everything might just be all right.

34

———

IAN

"KEEP ME UPDATED, OKAY?" I said to Maddie as we stood outside the hospital doors the next morning, the warm air brushing against us. The chirping of birds in the trees above filled the silence between us. "And don't rush back to work before you're ready."

"Okay." Maddie smiled, soft but tired, her warmth shining through despite the long week she'd had. "But I'll try not to be gone too long."

I reached for her hand, my fingers brushing against the large diamond ring still on her finger. She glanced down, her brows lifting slightly. "Oh," she said, twisting the ring as if noticing it for the first time. "I guess I should probably give this back now, huh?"

She moved to slide it off, but I stopped her with a light squeeze of her hand. "No, hold on to it for now. Your dad still thinks you're engaged, right?"

Her lips parted, and she hesitated. "Right..."

"So just hold on to it while you're here taking care of him," I said. "When you're back in Eden Falls, we can worry about returning it then. Believe it or not, I don't have much use for it in the meantime."

Her mouth quirked into a faint smile. "Not planning to hire a new assistant while I'm away and asking her to pretend to be engaged?"

"Nope." I chuckled, shaking my head. "I'm pretty sure you're the only assistant I'd want doing things like that with me."

Her cheeks flushed a light pink, and I couldn't help but think how beautiful she looked.

Man, I was going to miss her.

Way more than I probably should.

"You're sure I'll still have a job to come back to once things settle down here?" she asked, her tone half-teasing, half-serious.

"Absolutely," I said without hesitation. "Although, if you stay away for a month or two, I might start to worry you're not actually coming back. That maybe I scared you off with every-thing happening."

"I'll be back." She smiled, her voice reassuring. "We've already had neighbors reaching out to offer help, so I think Dad will be okay once he can move around on his own."

"Good." I nodded, though the idea of not seeing her for a couple of weeks already felt like an eternity. After a beat, I asked, "And you're sure you don't want me to make any sort of official statement on social media? About...us, or the pregnancy rumors?"

"It can't be worse than the teen pregnancy rumors I dealt with in high school." She gave a small shrug, her lips twitching with the faintest hint of amusement. "Plus, at least this time, people think I upgraded to a billionaire baby daddy."

"Fair point." I laughed, appreciating her ability to joke even when the situation wasn't ideal. "But are you sure you don't want me to address it?"

She shook her head. "Only if you want to. I deleted Instagram from my phone this morning, so unless someone comes up to me in person, it's like it never happened."

"Interesting logic, but I guess it could work," I said with a chuckle, filing away the idea of deleting social media from my phone as well. "Who knows, maybe this will actually work in my favor. All those eyes on my accounts might see my posts about helping small businesses grow."

She grinned. "Some people might even think we started the rumors ourselves to drum up buzz."

"If only I were that much of a genius," I teased.

"Pretty sure you are." Her gaze softened, and she tilted her head slightly. "But I like that you're using your genius to help others instead of purposely creating drama for yourself."

Her words settled over me, warm and grounding. She actually saw me—the version of me I was trying to become—and didn't hold my past against me.

I sighed internally, grateful in a way I couldn't put into words. *Ugh, I don't want to leave her here.*

But I didn't want to reveal the full extent of my growing obsession with spending all my time with her because it might scare her away for good. So I forced myself to say, "I should let you get back to your family."

"Okay," she said softly, though the quiet reluctance in her tone mirrored my own. Neither of us seemed ready to let go just yet.

I stepped forward and pulled her into a hug, wrapping her in my arms and holding her close. For a long moment, I just let myself feel her warmth, the way she fit against me with her head against my chest, like she belonged there.

Pressing a kiss to the top of her head, I closed my eyes and inhaled the sweet, familiar scent of her shampoo. "Take your time with your dad," I murmured against her hair, my voice low. "But don't take too long to come back, okay?"

"I'll be back before you know it," she said softly, looking up at me with a smile that was warm and steady yet held an emotion I couldn't quite name. "I'll keep you updated on my timeline for coming back, but...hopefully, I'll be back in two weeks."

I nodded, even though two weeks already felt like an eternity. "Good."

With that, I reluctantly let her go, letting my hands drop to my sides. I took a step back, then another, until I finally forced myself to turn and head to my car.

When I reached the driver's side door of my Bugatti, I hesitated, glancing back toward the hospital entrance. My chest tightened—and then swelled—when I saw Maddie standing there in the doorway, watching me.

Our eyes met, and she raised her hand in a small wave, her smile filling me with hope.

I raised my hand in return, lingering for one last moment. And it wasn't until she turned and disappeared back into the hospital that I finally climbed into the car and started the engine.

Two weeks, I told myself as I pulled out of the parking lot and onto the road back to Eden Falls. *I just have to make it through two weeks.*

35

———

IAN

"SO YOU THINK I should address everything with the board?" I asked my dad, leaning forward in the chair across from his desk in his home office that afternoon.

"I think it's a good idea," he said, sitting back as his thoughtful blue eyes locked on mine. "Personal lives usually stay personal, but since this happened at a work conference and involves your assistant...it complicates things."

His home office matched his polished persona—mahogany bookshelves lined with awards and thick, leather-bound books, the faint scent of aged wood and success hanging in the air. It was a powerful space, perfect for such a powerful man.

But his tone wasn't the commanding one he used in board-rooms. Right now, he wasn't just the CEO. He was my dad, and he was genuinely trying to guide me through this mess.

"So, transparency?" I sighed, dragging a hand down my face. "You really think that's the way to go?"

"With the board, yes." He nodded. "It's better to face these things head-on. Avoiding it will only raise more questions."

"And HR?" I asked, the question heavier than I wanted it

to sound. Just the thought of hashing this out with Human Resources made my stomach twist.

"You'll need to address that, too," he said in a steady but firm tone. "The company has a responsibility to ensure there was no undue pressure or coercion, given your position. We need to confirm Maddie feels safe and that this arrangement wasn't something she felt she couldn't refuse."

A wave of unease hit me, sharp and immediate. I pressed my hands to my thighs, hoping it didn't show on my face. "I think everything was fine there," I said quickly, my voice tight. "At least, I never got the feeling that she felt like she couldn't say no."

"I believe you." My dad's gaze softened, and he leaned forward, resting his elbows on the desk. "But it's important that we follow protocol, Ian. It's not just about protecting the company—it's about protecting Maddie."

"Of course," I said, nodding. "I-I'll make sure she gets a heads-up about all of that."

"Good." He stood, patting my shoulder as he walked around the desk. "You're handling this well. And don't beat yourself up too much. You're not the first Hastings to stir up a little controversy." A half-smile tugged at his lips. "I mean, if I was able to make CEO after everything with Carter and his mom came out, you should be fine." He winked. "And if they do have a problem with this, thankfully, I'm not retiring anytime soon. So you've got time to rebuild trust with any board members who might be clutching their pearls."

"Okay, good." I chuckled. "Thanks for the pep talk."

"Anytime. Now let's go eat before your mom starts sending out a search party."

We headed into the dining room where the smell of roast and mashed potatoes greeted us. The long table was already buzzing with conversation; my siblings—Carter, Nash, and

Cambrielle—were seated with their significant others, Ava, Kiara, and Mack. My mom, ever the picture of poise, sat at the head of the table, smiling warmly as we entered.

"Finally," Nash teased. "Thought Dad was giving you a semiannual review in there."

"Something like that," I said, taking my seat.

Dinner was lively, the conversation shifting from work to Carter and Ava's upcoming wedding.

"I can't believe it's just over a month away now," Ava said, her eyes glittering with excitement. "It seems like we've been planning it forever."

"And you only turned into Bridezilla twice," Carter teased, putting a hand on his fiancée's leg. "How did I get so lucky?"

Ava made a face at him and everyone chuckled.

"So, Ian," Mack said as he smirked from across the table, leaning back in his chair, "with all the buzz about your recent engagement, does that mean you'll actually have a plus-one for the wedding?"

Laughter rippled around the table, and I shook my head, grinning. "I'll have to get back to you on my plus-one status. Seems like the news isn't always accurate these days."

"Oh, don't I know it," Cambrielle said, rolling her eyes. "I went to lunch wearing a baby doll dress a few weeks ago, and by dinner, I had hundreds of DMs from people asking if I was pregnant."

"That's...fun." Ava grimaced.

"Yeah, usually I'd be mad but..." Cambrielle's smile widened. "...they actually weren't wrong this time so I couldn't be too offended."

"What?" Kiara asked, her jaw dropping as the rest of the table erupted into shocked gasps and cheers. "You're actually pregnant?"

Cambrielle and Mack exchanged a beaming look before nodding. "Yep. Just made it into the second trimester."

I glanced at my mom, noting her serene expression. "You already knew, didn't you?"

"Of course she did." Cambrielle chuckled, leaning back in her chair. "I needed someone to complain to about my morning sickness."

"Was it bad?" Kiara's brows lifted, her curiosity evident. "I've heard it can be horrible."

"Mine hasn't been as bad as some people have it," Cambrielle admitted, resting a hand on her stomach. "But let's just say I've been carrying around saltine crackers like they're drugs for weeks now."

The table erupted into more laughter and congratulations, and the conversation quickly shifted into an enthusiastic mix of baby talk and wedding plans. Yet, as the lively chatter swirled around me, my gaze flicked to the empty chair beside me. And even though I'd always been fine attending these family dinners without a girlfriend before, the absence of someone sitting there suddenly hit me—a longing for someone to fill the gap I hadn't even realized was there.

My siblings had all found their life partners. Someone to share whispered jokes and stolen glances with during family dinners. But me? I was the oldest of all my siblings—older than Carter and Nash by almost five years—and yet, I was still a bachelor.

They'd all been able to grow up and mature in relationships in a way I never had.

Sure, I'd had my own life experiences that had made my life full and meaningful. But I couldn't help but think it would be nice to have someone sitting beside me during events like this.

A permanent plus-one, so to speak.

An image of Maddie sitting there and her son Grant charming everyone at the table suddenly filled my mind.

And even though becoming a husband and father had always been more abstract in the past—things that would be nice to have someday—it was suddenly all I wanted.

And even though I was probably jumping a hundred steps ahead, at least for today, I couldn't help but think that Maddie and Grant were exactly who I wanted that future with.

Hopefully, after she talked to HR, I wouldn't discover that the future I was starting to picture with Maddie and Grant was never even a possibility.

"Ian," my mom said as she stepped into my office on Monday morning, her long brown hair swept back into a sleek bun, her expression calm but serious. "Your dad and I just spoke to HR. Marsha's ready for your interview."

A flicker of nerves tightened my chest, quick and sharp. "Okay," I said, blowing out a low breath as I pushed back my chair and stood.

For all the times my name had been splashed across tabloids, most people would assume I'd been through countless HR interviews. But the truth was, this was uncharted territory for me. And while I was sure—or at least mostly sure—that things would turn out fine, the stakes felt higher than ever.

I loved my job here, didn't want to risk it, or have any of this reflect badly on the company. More than that, I didn't want Maddie to face any fallout because of my choices.

The walk down the hall was quiet, save for the click of my mom's heels against the polished floor. The office buzzed faintly with the sounds of phones ringing and keyboards clacking, but it felt distant, muffled.

As we approached Marsha's office, my mom reached over and gave my hand a quick squeeze. "Things should be fine," she said, using the same soothing tone she'd always used when I was a kid and nerves got the better of me. "Just be honest, and it'll all work out."

I glanced at her, searching for any doubt in her brown eyes. "Do you really believe that?"

"I do." She stopped in front of Marsha's door, turning to face me fully. "Your dad and I went through something similar when I started working for him and it came out that we were dating. The scrutiny, the questions... It's not easy, but as long as you were respectful with Maddie—and from what you told me last night, it sounds like you were—then it'll be okay."

"Thanks, Mom," I said, her words steadying me more than I expected.

She pulled me into a brief hug, patting my back. "Good luck. I'll be waiting when you're done."

I nodded, releasing a breath I hadn't realized I'd been holding, and stepped into Marsha's office.

Marsha greeted me with a professional smile, gesturing to the chair across from her desk. "Have a seat, Ian."

The leather chair was stiff and unyielding, a fitting match for the clinical air of the room. My palms rested on my knees, slightly clammy, as Marsha shuffled some papers. The hum of the overhead light filled the silence, making my nerves prickle.

"So, Ian," Marsha began, her tone neutral as she peered at me over the rim of her glasses. "Let's start from the top. Can you explain, in your own words, what happened at the summit last week that led to this...situation?"

"It started with a misunderstanding." I cleared my throat, shifting slightly in my chair. "We were at a restaurant, waiting to be seated for dinner with a client, when one of my exes came up to us and...well, I panicked. Without thinking, I introduced Maddie as my fiancée."

"Okay." Marsha nodded, her expression remaining steady, giving nothing away.

So I continued, explaining how what had seemed like a small, spur-of-the-moment decision had spiraled into something much bigger. How what we'd only thought would be a tiny blip at the conference had turned into the whole spectacle that was now in the gossip news.

By the time I finished recounting everything, my palms were damp, and a knot of tension had settled in my chest. I found myself searching Marsha's face for any indication of what she might be thinking, but she was an expert at keeping her expression unreadable—probably honed over years of handling situations like this.

"And you said Maddie agreed to go along with this?" Her tone was even, revealing nothing, and it left me feeling as though I were standing on a cliff, waiting to see if the ground would crumble beneath me.

"She did," I said quickly, but then hesitated, wanting to be as transparent as possible. "I asked her, and she agreed. But I made it clear that she didn't have to. It was completely her choice."

"Did she seem hesitant at all?" Marsha asked. "Is there any chance she felt pressured because of your position as her superior?"

The question made my stomach churn. I forced myself to stay calm, though. "No. At least...I hope not. I never wanted Maddie to feel like she didn't have a choice. I thought it would be harmless."

Marsha nodded slowly, making a note. "Were there any moments during the summit where Maddie expressed discomfort or reluctance about continuing the charade?"

"No," I said firmly, shaking my head. "She seemed okay with it. If she'd told me otherwise, I would've stopped immediately."

Marsha's gaze remained steady, piercing, as she asked her next question. "And your interactions with her—would you classify any of them as romantic or physical?"

My heart stuttered, a quick, uncomfortable rhythm as memories surged forward—the kisses we'd shared, especially the one in my hotel suite where I'd barely restrained myself from taking her to my bed.

"There were moments," I admitted, my voice low, cautious. "A few kisses. But they were mutual. Consensual. And I was careful to keep things from escalating to a more intimate level."

Marsha nodded, her pen gliding over the notepad in front of her. "You understand why this situation raises concerns, don't you?" She leaned back slightly, her calm professionalism doing little to ease my nerves. "The power dynamics alone complicate things."

"I do," I said, holding her gaze, hoping she could see the sincerity behind my words. "And I hate that I might've put Maddie in a position where her integrity—or her professionalism with the company—could be questioned. That was never my intention."

"Intent matters, Ian." Marsha's expression softened, just slightly. "But so do perceptions."

"I know." I sighed. "And I feel bad that this could reflect badly on the company if it got out that the relationship was fake. Really, I had no idea we'd end up here."

Marsha asked me a few more questions. When we were done, she said, "Thank you for your honesty, Ian. I'll be speaking with Maddie as well to get her perspective, but your transparency is appreciated."

I nodded, the weight of the conversation settling heavily on my shoulders. "What happens next?"

"After my interview with Maddie, my team and I will evaluate everything and make a recommendation to the board," Marsha said. "But I don't anticipate any drastic measures, as long as Maddie's account aligns with yours."

Relief flooded through me, but it was tempered by a lingering unease. "Thank you, Marsha."

She offered a small smile. "Hang in there, Ian. It sounds like it's been a long week."

"It has." I nodded, though I held back the truth. The last two days had been the hardest—but strangely, the days I'd spent pretending to be engaged to Maddie had been some of the most fun I'd had in a long time. Probably not the kind of confession Marsha needed to hear right now.

I rose from the chair, offering her a polite nod. "Thank you, Marsha."

As I stepped into the hallway, the tension I'd been holding in my shoulders began to loosen—just slightly. My mom was waiting for me a few doors down, just as she'd promised, her steady presence a welcome balm to my frayed nerves.

"It went okay," I said, keeping my voice measured, though my thoughts were already spinning in a hundred different directions. What would Maddie say in her interview? Had I done enough to keep things steady for both of us? And, most importantly, had I protected her from any fallout my careless actions might have caused?

I exhaled, following my mom down the hall, praying I hadn't messed things up for either of us.

36

____

MADDIE

"HEY, IAN," I said, balancing the phone against my ear as I folded one of the blankets in my dad's hospital room. The nurse had wheeled him out a few minutes ago, saying they would be gone for about fifteen minutes to get some fresh air.

"Hey. I wanted to give you a heads-up." Ian's voice came through steady, though there was a faint edge of concern. "Marsha from HR might try calling you today. I just had a meeting with her and I think she's going to want to meet with you when you get back to work in a couple of weeks."

"Oh, I actually already heard from her this morning." I paused, smoothing the folded blanket and setting it on the foot of the hospital bed. "We have a video call scheduled for this afternoon when I'm at my dad's house and have decent Wi-Fi."

"You're heading to your dad's house?" There was a beat of hesitation in his tone, like he wasn't sure if that was a good sign or not.

"Lexi and Noah are taking over the next shift here so I can go back and get his house tidied up and ready for when he comes home."

"Does that mean you know when he's getting discharged?"

A small smile crept onto my lips, the weight in my chest lifting slightly. "The nurses said tomorrow, as long as he behaves and takes it easy."

"That's amazing," Ian said, the warmth in his voice like a balm to my frayed nerves because he actually cared—not just about my dad, but about what this meant for me. And that care, so genuine and unforced, made my heart ache in the best possible way.

"Yeah," I said softly, my fingers brushing over the corner of the blanket. "It's such a relief."

A moment of quiet settled between us before Ian's voice came through again, lower now, more serious. "Listen, Maddie...I just want to say I'm sorry for dragging you into all of this. You've already been dealing with so much, and then I go and make everything worse. If you're mad at me—or if you want to quit—I get it. I'll give you the best recommendation I can...though, with the headlines, I'm not sure how much that would help."

I let out a small laugh, even as a knot of tension twisted in my stomach. "It's fine, Ian. Not fun or ideal, but I'll survive. I just hope people don't think I was trying to, you know, sleep my way to a big raise."

The other end of the line went completely silent, and for a moment, I thought maybe I'd shocked him into speechlessness. A smile tugged at my lips as I teasingly added, "It's nice to be the one throwing the shocking comments around for once. Usually, that's your job."

His chuckle came a second later, awkward and warm, and I imagined him running a hand over the back of his neck. "You caught me off guard, that's all."

His voice, his laugh, everything about him made my heart squeeze, and for a moment, I let myself revel in how much I liked talking to him. Even with everything going on, it was moments like this—easy, light, filled with something I couldn't quite name—that made the world brighter.

I considered asking if "sleeping my way to a raise" was actually on the table, just to see how Ian would respond, but I held back. That was a line I better not cross—not when my mind was already doing a poor job of keeping things professional. Thinking about Ian in strictly work-related terms had become almost impossible, thanks to the way his kisses had burned themselves into my memory.

The thought of our last kiss—the way his hands had gripped my hips, his body pressing me firmly against the wall—flashed vividly in my mind. Heat surged up my neck, and I had to force myself to focus. "So, uh...exactly how much detail did you have to go into during your interview with Marsha? Does she know the...full extent of our interactions? Or did you keep it mostly about the fake engagement?"

There was a pause, and I could hear Ian exhale softly before he answered. "I told her how the situation came about. And..." His voice dipped slightly, like he wasn't thrilled about what he had to say next. "And I mentioned that we kissed. A few times. But that it didn't go further than that."

"Okay." The word came out quieter than I'd intended, and my cheeks burned as my heart thudded harder in my chest. This was the first time we'd actually acknowledged those kisses out loud.

Had he thought about them as much as I had? Had they left the same lingering effect on him, the same spark that felt impossible to extinguish? I hoped so.

But then again, I'd been wrong before. I'd let myself believe things were one way when they weren't—like I had with Jaxon, spending nearly a decade thinking he might someday love me enough to marry me. That he'd see me as something more than the mother of his child.

The memory stabbed at me, but I shoved it aside. I couldn't dwell on that now. Not when there were more pressing things to worry about, like keeping my job and salvaging my reputation. I just hoped Ian's family and the people at work didn't look at the shopping spree, the ring, and the headlines and think I was trying to gold-dig my way into the Hastingses' family fortune.

"Thanks for the heads-up," I said finally, my voice steadier than I felt. "I better get going. I need to head to my dad's house and prep for the call."

"Of course." Ian's tone softened. "Good luck with it. And... let me know how it goes, okay?"

"I will."

As I hung up, I exhaled a shaky breath and stared at the screen for a moment, my thoughts swirling. If I could just get through this call with HR without losing my job, then maybe I'd have a chance at figuring out if I had a future with my boss.

I sat at my dad's kitchen table later that afternoon, the faint hum of the air conditioner the only sound in the otherwise quiet house. My laptop sat open in front of me, the camera angled just right, though I'd already checked it at least three times.

I'd told myself to stay calm, but as Marsha's face appeared on the screen, my stomach twisted into knots.

Hopefully, I don't screw this up.

"Good afternoon, Maddie," she said, her tone calm but focused. "Thank you for taking the time for this meeting today."

"Of course," I said, clasping my hands in my lap to keep them from fidgeting. "Thank you for being flexible with the video call."

"No problem. We want to make this as smooth as possible." She smiled slightly, adjusting her glasses. "Now, if you're ready, we'll go ahead and begin."

I nodded, my heart thudding against my ribs.

"First," she began, glancing at her notes, "can you explain how the decision to go along with the engagement story came about? Did you feel pressured or obligated to agree?"

I exhaled slowly, my mind flashing back to that first moment in the restaurant when Ian had introduced me as his fiancée. "It was spur-of-the-moment," I said, keeping my voice steady. "Ian ran into someone he knew—an ex—and it seemed like he panicked. He introduced me as his fiancée before I could process what was happening. Later, he asked if I'd be okay playing along for the duration of the summit to keep things from getting awkward. I didn't feel pressured exactly. He asked, and I agreed."

Marsha's pen moved over her notepad as she nodded. "Did Ian at any point suggest, imply, or directly state that this was necessary for your job or advancement at the company?"

"No," I said firmly. "He made it clear that it was entirely my choice."

Her gaze lifted, steady but not unkind. "Were there any instances where you felt uncomfortable or unsure about your role in this arrangement? If so, how did Ian respond?"

I hesitated, chewing the inside of my cheek. "There were moments," I admitted. "It's not every day you pretend to be engaged to your boss, so it was a little weird at times. But Ian was always respectful. If I'd said I wasn't okay with something, I believe he would've listened."

She nodded again. "Can you confirm whether any physical

or romantic interactions occurred between you two during the summit? If so, were they consensual?"

My face heated. "There were...a few kisses," I said, my voice quieter now. "But they were consensual."

Marsha made another note. "Do you feel that Ian's position of authority influenced your decisions during this past week?"

I thought about it, running my finger over a scratch in the table's surface. "I don't think so," I said finally. "I didn't agree to this because he's my boss. I agreed because I thought it was harmless at the time."

"Were there any moments where Ian acted in a way that made you feel pressured or uncomfortable?"

"No," I said, shaking my head. "He was...considerate. I never felt pressured."

Marsha looked at me carefully, as though trying to gauge my sincerity. "Do you believe this situation has impacted your ability to perform your role effectively?"

I hesitated, then nodded. "It's been a distraction, for sure. And with the rumors spreading, it's hard not to worry about how people at work will perceive me now."

"Have you experienced any backlash or unprofessional treatment from colleagues because of this situation?"

"Not yet," I admitted. "But I haven't been back to work since the summit, so I guess I don't really know what to expect."

"Do you feel safe and supported in your position at the company?"

"Yes," I said. "I've only been with the company a short time, but I've never felt unsafe."

"And how would you like to proceed professionally after this situation?" Marsha leaned back slightly, her pen pausing mid-air before she folded her hands on the desk. "Are there any accommodations or changes you'd request?"

I considered the question, the weight of it settling heavily over me. "I just...I want to do my job. I want to move past this and not have it hanging over me—or Ian—for the rest of my time at the company."

"Thank you for your honesty, Maddie." Marsha gave a small nod, her expression still neutral. "I'll be reviewing this meeting with the board, and you can expect a follow-up call in the next day or two to go over their findings."

"Okay." I nodded, managing a small, tight smile. "Thank you."

The call ended abruptly, the screen going blank before I could even process the past fifteen minutes. Marsha didn't mess around—she'd gotten straight to the point, just like she had in my previous two job interviews and during the hiring process. No fluff, no wasted words. And, really, what else should I have expected?

I reached for my phone, the familiar weight of it grounding me as I typed a quick message to Ian.

> Me: Just finished the HR interview. Wow, they really wanted to dig into everything, didn't they?

Of course, I understood why HR had to ask all those questions—it was to make sure I was safe, that nothing inappropriate had happened. But wow, having to tell the person who'd interviewed and hired me just weeks ago that I'd turned around and kissed *my boss* in his hotel suite?

Probably not a great look.

Maybe I should just save everyone the awkwardness and quit.

If I moved back to Ridgewater, I could help my dad recover without him feeling the need to uproot his entire life and move to Eden Falls. And it would save me the trouble of finding a place for Grant and me, especially since I hadn't gotten far in that process anyway.

Sure, I had wanted to move away from Ridgewater for a fresh start. But now, after making headlines, I'd probably just get the same whispers and weird looks in Eden Falls—or even New Haven. So, what was the point?

I sighed, setting my phone down and leaning back in my chair. The kitchen was quiet, the faint ticking of the wall clock the only sound. I pressed my fingers against my temples, trying to push away the spiraling thoughts.

I was still trying to sort through my thoughts when my phone buzzed. Ian's name lit up the screen.

"Hey," Ian said, his voice steady but with a slight edge of concern. "I saw your text. I've got a few minutes between meetings and wanted to check in. How are you doing? Was Marsha rough on you?"

"She wasn't too bad," I said, closing the screen on my laptop. "Just asked all the same kinds of questions she probably asked you."

"Yeah," he said, his voice tinged with something I couldn't quite place. "Do you know how long it'll be before you get any updates?"

I hesitated. "She said they'd follow up in the next couple of days. But...do you really think I'll still have a job after this?"

"They can't fire you for this," he said firmly.

"Can't they?" I let out a humorless laugh. "I saw a few of the headlines before I deleted my social media apps, Ian. If the board saw any of those suspicions that I conned you into proposing because I had my eyes on your money, don't you think they'll be worried about my trustworthiness?"

"That's ridiculous," Ian said. "Since the board will know the actual truth—that the engagement was fake. And it was *me* who actually conned you into playing along."

I pinched the bridge of my nose, a headache forming as I tried to keep the different versions of our story straight.

"But what if the board finds out about the part where I kissed you at the club before I knew you were my boss? Someone could've taken a video, Ian. If that goes public, it's going to look like I knew exactly who you were and that I was attempting to seduce you before we even had the whole forced-proximity/forbidden-boss-romance trope going on."

There was a short pause. Then in a confused tone, he asked, "What do you mean by us having the forced-proximity trope going on? What are you even talking about?"

"Sorry, I forget our social-media algorithms are different." I chuckled. "I'm not just in the 'fall enthusiast' algorithm. I'm deep into 'Bookstagram'—specifically, the romance-book-lover world. We describe love stories with tropes."

"Okay..." Ian sounded bemused.

"So I'm guessing that you don't know what a book trope is?"

"I mean..." He hesitated. "There was a girl who threw a paperback at me during a breakup, yelling that I was nothing like the hero in her billionaire romance novel. Does that count?"

I laughed, the tension in my chest easing. "Not exactly, but close enough."

"Well, I guess I've been stuck in the business non-fiction section too long," he said. "Not much romance in quarterly earnings reports."

"That checks out," I teased.

"Hey," he said, his tone lightening. "I just made it back to my desk. Can I FaceTime you?"

I glanced at my reflection in the mirror across the room. I'd cleaned up a bit before my interview with Marsha, but if I'd known Ian would be wanting to see me, I probably would have taken the time to add another coat of mascara.

But I should probably care less about how attractive my boss found me since just having a job should be my main concern at the moment. So I smoothed down my hair quickly and said, "Sure."

His FaceTime request came through a second later, and my heart did a little flip when his face filled the screen. His sharp features and warm brown eyes looked as handsome as ever, and his easy smile made something in my chest flutter.

"Hi," he said, his voice softening. His gaze flicked down, and his grin widened. "Wearing the green dress again?"

I glanced down, realizing I was wearing the emerald-green dress I'd worn on Friday. "All my other work clothes are at Sloan's," I said, suddenly self-conscious.

"I like it," he interrupted, his tone sincere. "That color looks really good on you."

A memory of the morning I'd first worn this dress flashed in my mind—the day he gave his big presentation and took me shopping. It had been a good day.

"So," he said, leaning slightly closer to the screen, "since you're into book tropes and romance novels, have you read anything good lately?"

I laughed. "I just finished a boss romance I'd started before the summit. It was pretty good."

"Boss romance, huh?" His grin turned teasing. "Would you say that's a favorite trope?"

"It has a certain appeal, I suppose." My cheeks warmed.

His smile deepened. "Good. Because if I was going to pick up a romance novel right now, I'd want one about a cute single mom moving to a new city and getting into a fake relationship with her boss."

I gasped. "So you *have* heard of book tropes."

"Maybe I did a little research in college." He shrugged, a

playful glint in his eyes. "Wanted to know what women are looking for in an ideal man."

"Of course you would!" I laughed.

"Hey," he said, his grin widening. "It's like a cheat sheet on how to get the girl to fall in love with you."

"Which you've clearly been a master student of," I teased. "Considering how many girls have fallen for you."

He shrugged, his gaze softening. "Now I just need it to work on the right girl."

His words, paired with the way he looked at me through the screen, sent goosebumps racing over my skin.

And oh, how much I wanted that girl to be me. The realization was so sharp, so visceral, it left me breathless. I wanted it so much it physically ached.

Ian cleared his throat and his expression shifted to something almost hesitant, as if he was choosing his next words carefully. "So, uh...I've been curious about your plans for lodging in Eden Falls."

"Lodging?" I asked, his sudden change in topic catching me off guard.

He winced slightly, as if he knew how awkward that sounded. "I mean...are you still looking for a place there?"

"Yeah." I nodded, brushing a strand of hair behind my ear. "That is, as long as I still have a job to go back to, then yeah, I think Eden Falls is where I want to stay. The twenty-minute commute to work isn't bad, and Grant seems to really like it there. It's just about finding the right kind of place."

"What are you looking for, exactly?" Ian tilted his head, his brows pulling together slightly.

"Two bedrooms would be nice." I shrugged, leaning back in my chair. "Since sharing a bed with an eight-year-old who has wrestling matches in his sleep isn't exactly restful."

"Yeah, I get that." He chuckled, the warm sound making my stomach flutter.

"And I guess I've been hoping for a place with a yard," I continued. "We probably won't be able to get any pets like Grant wants until I buy a place, but...having some space for him to run around in would be nice."

Ian's expression brightened slightly. "Cool. If you'd like, I can talk to my parents. They own a few properties in town and might know of something coming up."

"Oh, no," I said quickly, shaking my head. "You don't need to ask them to help me. I mean...they probably don't exactly like me right now, considering I'm involved in all this drama with you."

"Drama *because* of me," Ian corrected, his voice firm but kind. "And they're not as scary as they seem, I promise."

I gave him a skeptical look. "Yeah...you billionaires aren't intimidating at all."

His chuckle was low and genuine, and despite myself, I couldn't help but smile.

He glanced at his watch, his expression softening with regret. "Ah, my two-thirty appointment starts soon. I better let you go. But I'll make sure to call as soon as I hear anything from HR or the board."

"Okay," I said, nodding. A swell of nerves tightened in my chest, but his steady gaze made it a little easier to breathe. "I'll talk to you later."

37

———

IAN

I GLANCED up from my desk on Wednesday afternoon to see my mom stepping inside. She wore a sleek, structured black dress with a gold zipper running down the back, her usual composed elegance radiating even in the middle of the workweek.

"Well?" I asked, my voice tighter than I'd meant for it to be.

"Your father and I just finished our meeting with Marsha and the board," she said, crossing the room and taking the chair across from me. "And aside from Mr. Mendez making a comment about how the youth of today are so willy-nilly with engagements these days—" A small smile lifted her lips. "—they don't see any reason to suspend anyone or reconfigure positions."

"Thank goodness." I exhaled sharply, the tension I'd been carrying for days finally easing. "That's...that's great news."

Mom studied me, her blue eyes sharp but warm. "You really care about Maddie, don't you?"

I froze for a beat before rubbing the back of my neck. "Yeah," I admitted quietly. "I really do. A lot."

Mom tilted her head, waiting for me to continue.

"And I'm worried I'm going to screw it all up," I confessed. The words tumbled out before I could stop them. "She's been through so much already. She's a single mom raising an incredible kid on her own, and she deserves...everything. But what if I'm not what she needs? What if I just make things harder for her?"

Mom's gaze softened and she reached across the desk, resting a hand over mine. "If you want to pursue this, Ian, you need to be careful. Maddie isn't like any of the girls you've dated before. She has a son. And I'm not sure how much you remember about when your dad and I took a break before we got back together, but it was really hard. You can give her the world, Ian. You can swoop in and change everything for her and Grant. But you can also hurt them."

Her words landed heavily, and I nodded slowly, the weight of what she was saying sinking in.

"You've only known her a few weeks and...I just want to make sure you're sure before you get their hopes up," she continued. "And I know it's a two-way street, so if she's what you really want, then I hope she feels the same way."

I swallowed hard, the knot in my chest tightening. "I don't want to mess this up."

"Then don't," she said simply, her smile gentle but knowing.

An idea flickered in my mind, and I leaned forward. "Has anyone moved into Vaughn's cottage yet?"

Mom raised an eyebrow. "It's still empty. Why?"

"Maddie's looking for a house," I said, the words coming quickly now. "And since I'm trying to be good and not just invite her to move in with me—" I gave her a wry smile. "—I was wondering if I could offer her the cottage. It would be perfect for her and Grant."

"That's a great idea, Ian." Mom's smile widened, her approval evident. "I think she'll love it."

"Thanks." A small flicker of hope warmed my chest. "I just...want to make things easier for her."

"And that's a good place to start," she said, squeezing my hand briefly before standing. "Now, go make it happen."

"Will do," I said, watching her head toward the door. Then, picking up my phone, I added, "Just after I let Maddie know the board's decision—and that we're both in the clear."

"Good idea." Mom winked and then left to head back to her office.

38

MADDIE

THE SCENT of coffee lingered in the air as I sat cross-legged on my dad's well-loved couch, my laptop balanced on one knee and Ian's emails open on the screen. It was Saturday, and technically, I wasn't on the clock, but I didn't want to let anything slip through the cracks. I needed to prove I was a good employee—someone who could handle her job despite the mess of headlines and gossip.

My phone buzzed beside me, interrupting my focus. I glanced at the screen to see Ian's name and an attachment. My heart gave a little flutter as I opened the message.

> Ian: I finally got a chance to drop by that place I was telling you about and took a few photos. What do you think? Does it look like a place you and Grant could live in?

Swiping open the text, I studied the attached photo. It was a charming little house with white siding, a dark shingled roof, and a neat, welcoming yard. My gaze lingered on the swing set in the corner, a detail that immediately tugged at my heart.

It was perfect. Too perfect. My chest tightened with longing as I stared at the image, already imagining Grant playing on that swing set or running barefoot through the grass.

But just as quickly as the image formed, reality doused it because a place like this was probably way out of my price range.

Ian lived in an entirely different stratosphere than I did. He probably didn't realize that regular people couldn't drop thousands a month on rent without breaking a sweat.

I sighed, setting my laptop aside. Glancing at Ian's calendar to make sure he didn't have a random Saturday-morning meeting, I decided to video call him. Yes, I could probably just text him back about the house, but it had been a week since he'd gone back to Eden Falls and I had missed seeing his face.

The call connected, and Ian's image appeared, looking as sharp and effortlessly handsome as ever in what looked like his living room.

He wore a sleek golf shirt, his tan skin glowing like he'd just come off the course, and his dark hair was freshly cut. The sight sent a flutter through my chest, though I tried to tamp it down.

"Hey," I said, smiling despite myself.

"Hey," he replied, his voice warm. "What's up?"

"Am I bugging you? You look like you just got back from golfing."

"I did." He chuckled. "Went a few rounds with Owen and Evan on my parents' course this morning. But I've got time. What's on your mind? Did you like the house?"

"I did. It's beautiful. Like, way prettier than anywhere I've ever lived before. But...I'm pretty sure it's out of my price range."

"Oh..." Ian frowned slightly, leaning closer to the camera. "What price range are you looking for?"

"Um..." I hesitated, feeling a little embarrassed to say it out loud. "I was hoping to stay under two thousand a month. Less would be even better. But I know that's probably wishful thinking."

"Well, you're in luck," he said, his grin returning. "This place is only a thousand a month."

"What?" My jaw dropped. "How is that possible? Is it missing windows or something? No furnace?"

He laughed, the sound rich and warm. "Nope. It's in great condition—recently remodeled, actually."

"Then what's the catch? Terrible neighbors? Is it next to a landfill?"

"It's actually a cottage on my parents' property," he said, a note of amusement in his tone. "Their driver, Vaughn, lived there for years, but he just moved in with his partner in town. So it's vacant."

"And your parents don't have any other employees they want to rent it to?"

"You're technically an employee," Ian said with a teasing glint in his eye. "So they'd like to rent it to you."

I looked at the photo again, my resistance wavering. It really was perfect.

"I can take you to see it when you're back in town," he said. "If you want."

"Really?" I asked, my voice soft with disbelief.

He nodded. "Absolutely."

Before I could say anything else, something in the background of Ian's video feed caught my eye. A little black cat sauntered across the couch behind him.

He had a cat? When did that happen? Because I was pretty sure he'd told me before that he didn't have any pets.

"Since when did you get a cat?" I asked, narrowing my eyes at the screen.

"Oh. Yeah." Ian glanced behind him and smirked. "I forgot

to tell you. A couple days after I got back, I saw this little guy out back. He looked hungry, so I gave him some meat."

"Oh no," I said, shaking my head with a laugh. "You fed him? Such a rookie mistake. That's basically a binding contract. You're his now."

"I figured that out pretty quick." Ian chuckled. "Rookie mistake, indeed. And well...now I have a pet cat."

He set his phone on the coffee table, propping it up against something before reaching behind him to grab the little black bundle of fur. The cat squirmed briefly but then settled into Ian's hands, its green eyes blinking curiously at the screen. Ian sank onto the carpet, holding the cat in front of him, his long fingers gently stroking its head.

"This is him," Ian said, his tone oddly fond.

"Oh my gosh," I breathed, unable to stop the grin spreading across my face. "That is the cutest kitten ever."

"I know." Ian's lips quirked into a boyish smile. "I haven't had a cat since I lived at my parents' house, but apparently, I'm a cat person now."

And I didn't think it was possible for my heart to swell any more than it already had. But seeing this big, strong, manly businessman sitting cross-legged on the floor, cradling a tiny black kitten, well...it was almost too much to handle.

I mean, I'd been doing my best not to let my feelings for Ian spiral out of control, but how was I supposed to keep my cool when he was so...adorable?

"Mom, what are you looking at?" Grant's voice pulled me back to the moment as he plopped onto the couch beside me.

"Ian has a new cat," I said, turning the screen toward him. "Look."

Grant's eyes lit up as he leaned in. "Oh, he's so cuuute!"

"I know, right?" I said, sharing a conspiratorial smile with my son.

Grant looked at me. "Can we get a cat? I really want a cat."

I sighed, already knowing where this was going. "I know, buddy. I want one, too. But we need to find a place to live first—one that allows pets."

"You always say that." Grant folded his arms with a pout, his lower lip sticking out dramatically.

"Because it's true," I said with a shrug, trying not to laugh at his theatrics.

"If your mom lets you," Ian said, his voice cutting in, "you can totally come see my cat sometime. I know it's not the same, but Satan would love to play with someone besides me."

"Wait...what did you just say?" My heart stuttered, and I blinked at the screen. "Did you just call your cat *Satan*?"

"I thought it fit." Ian's expression faltered only momentarily before he nodded. "He's been a little devil."

I stared at him, my mind racing. This couldn't be a coincidence, could it? My suspicion that Ian was the guy from the beach had been growing for weeks, but this...this was just too much.

Grant, oblivious to my internal spiral, turned to me with wide eyes. "Isn't that so silly, Mom? Ian has a cat named Satan, and you always said if we got a cat, we'd name it Satan."

I opened my mouth but no words came out. Instead, I glanced back at Ian on the screen, searching his face for any sign that he was putting the pieces together. But he just chuckled like Grant, apparently finding it all a funny coincidence.

"That's hilarious," Ian said, shaking his head. "Looks like you really do need to come see my cat when you're back. Maybe you can even take him for a walk."

"You can't take cats on walks." Grant burst into giggles. "They aren't like dogs!"

Ian feigned a sheepish look. "Oops. Guess that explains why he was so mad at me when I tried to last night."

Grant giggled harder, and I couldn't help but smile. Ian's easy way of talking to my son warmed something deep in my chest. I'd never pictured him being so good with kids, but he'd surprised me—again.

The kitten climbed onto Ian's shoulder, looking ready to make its way to his head. Ian winced, flinching slightly as tiny claws dug into his skin. "Okay, buddy," he said, lifting the cat down. "You're a busy little devil, aren't you?"

Grant leaned against me, his eyes glued to the screen. "Your cat is so silly."

Ian grinned, his gaze flicking to me. "He's been keeping things interesting, that's for sure."

I cleared my throat, glancing at the time. "We better let you go. We've got to head to the store. I'm making heart-healthy lasagna for dinner tonight."

"Sounds delicious."

"I hope so," I said. "Trying to find some good, easy recipes that go along with my dad's new eating plan."

"That's sweet of you to do that for him," Ian said, his voice warm and steady. "He's lucky to have you."

The way he looked at me, his deep brown eyes soft with sincerity, made my chest flutter. How was I supposed to keep my guard up when he said things like that?

"Anyway..." Ian cleared his throat, his tone shifting slightly. "Have fun with your grocery shopping."

"We'll try."

For a second, I considered making a joke about how no shopping trip would ever compare to the one we'd shared, but I held back.

Before we could hang up, Ian asked, "A-are you still coming back in a week? No plans to come back a little sooner?" His tone was casual, but there was a faint edge of hope that tugged at my heart.

I hesitated, glancing over at Grant who was now sprawled on the floor, watching TV. "Yeah," I said. "Probably next Saturday or Sunday."

"Do you need a ride?" he asked quickly, almost like he'd been waiting to say it. "Since your car is still sitting in my driveway."

I bit my lip, unsure of how to answer without it sounding awkward. "Jaxon offered to give us a ride," I said finally.

"Oh." Something flickered across Ian's face—disappointment, maybe? But just as quickly, he smoothed his expression and nodded. "Awesome. Let me know when you're close. Maybe you and Grant can stop by and see Satan."

I blinked, momentarily caught off guard by the name. "I'm sure Grant would love that."

"And maybe after," Ian added, his tone light, "I can show you the house. It's pretty close to my place. We could even walk there."

"Sure," I said, trying to keep my voice neutral even though the idea of spending extra time with him sent a little thrill through me. Probably more than it should.

We ended the call, and as the screen went dark, I let out a long breath and leaned back against the couch. Being here for my dad had been good, grounding even. But as much as I hated to admit it, part of me was already counting down the days until I'd be back in Eden Falls.

Closer to the man who was starting to feel like home.

39

———

MADDIE

"TAKE CARE OF YOURSELF, DAD," I said, wagging a finger at him. "And don't even think about bribing Lexi into sneaking extra cheese into your meals while I'm gone."

My dad chuckled, propped up in bed with a blanket over his legs, a twinkle in his eye. "I'll try to be a good boy, but you know Lexi—she's a sucker for a well-placed puppy-dog look."

"Don't even try it," I said, smirking.

"Okay, fine." He softened, his expression turning more serious. "I appreciate you taking such good care of me, Maddie. I know you've got that new life and fancy fiancé of yours waiting in Eden Falls..."

"I'll always have time for you," I said, my voice steady even as my chest tightened. I hated that he seemed to feel like he was a burden when, in reality, he was one of the most important people in my life. "I hope you really know that."

"I do, sweetheart." He gave me a soft smile, his eyes warm. "I just want you to have your own life, too. But once I'm all healed up, I'm heading your way to meet this mystery man of yours. Gotta make sure he's good enough for my girl."

"He's not perfect," I said, unable to keep the affection from my voice. "But I think you'll be impressed. And happy."

"Well," Dad said, his tone light but firm, "I already like that you two haven't moved in together yet. I know we see things a little differently there, but it's nice to know this guy's a gentleman."

A hint of surprise flickered through me, but I managed a nod. "Yes, very gentlemanly."

Maybe a little *too* gentlemanly, considering I was fairly certain I'd have jumped into his bed if he hadn't kept our kisses firmly PG... Okay, edging toward PG-13.

Yeah, I had the hots for my boss, and my usual self-control seemed to vanish into thin air when Ian was involved.

"Jaxon and Grant just pulled up out front," Noah said, poking his head into my dad's room. "Want me to carry your bags out?"

"That would be awesome," I said, smiling at my brother-in-law. "Thank you."

Noah grabbed my suitcase while I turned back to my dad, leaning over to give him a hug and a kiss on the cheek. "Call me if you need anything. I know Lexi and Noah will take good care of you, but I'm just a phone call away."

Dad patted my hand and smiled. "Just take good care of my best friend," he said, referring to Grant. "And don't you dare elope with that billionaire fiancé of yours before I can meet him."

"Okay." I laughed lightly, though his words settled uneasily in my chest.

How was I going to tell him that Ian and I were never actually engaged?

Maybe I could convince Ian to hold a fake wedding ceremony in a couple of years...and then keep dodging my dad's attempts to meet him. *Sorry, Dad. Ian's on a work trip...again.*

Yeah, that was a terrible idea. Probably shouldn't have let him believe it in the first place.

My gaze dropped to the ring on my finger, and I swallowed hard. As strange as it was, I'd gotten used to wearing the huge thing. But I'd need to give it back to Ian when I got to Eden Falls.

After saying goodbye to Lexi and Noah, I stepped outside to where Jaxon and Grant were waiting in the truck. Grant waved eagerly from the backseat, his grin wide and infectious.

"Ready, Mom?" he called out.

"Ready," I said, climbing into the passenger seat and buckling up. As Jaxon pulled out of the driveway, I glanced in the side mirror, watching my dad's house grow smaller and smaller behind us.

Eden Falls was waiting. And so was Ian.

———

"Now I see why you were fine pretending to be this guy's fiancée so soon after meeting him." Jaxon let out a low whistle, his gaze sweeping over Ian's sprawling property as his truck came to a stop in the circular driveway. "He's loaded."

"You know, not everything I do is about money, Jaxon," I said, unable to keep the edge entirely out of my voice. "But yes, Ian has a very nice house."

"Just saying, it's quite the upgrade from Ridgewater." Jaxon raised an eyebrow.

"Yes, it's been a good move for me," I said, trying my best to keep my tone steady. "But since we're currently staying at Sloan's house, and it's just my Subaru that's been staying at this property, my boss's living situation doesn't really affect me that much."

And while I wanted to say a lot more, I left it at that. Jaxon had been nice enough to drive Grant and me all the way here. It wasn't worth getting into an argument when we'd been on pleasant terms most of the drive.

Still, his assumption that I was after my boss's money did sting a little—a reminder of how easily people could misinterpret my choices.

I'd told Jaxon the truth of my "fake engagement" after his friend sent him the gossip article the day after the story broke. He'd called me, asking if the headlines were true. Since we shared a son—and I didn't want Grant hearing half-truths—I'd laid it all out for him. The fake engagement, the way it had spiraled out of control...everything.

Apparently, though, even with the truth, Jaxon still thought there was more to it. That maybe I'd seen an opportunity and taken it.

But before Jaxon could say anything else, the front door to Ian's house opened, and Ian stepped outside. His presence shifted my mood instantly, the weight of irritation lifting as I took him in. Dressed casually but still exuding that effortless confidence, he made me feel lighter. Happier.

I climbed out of the truck, giving Ian a smile.

"Hey," he said, returning my smile with a warm one of his own as he strode toward us. "Do you need help carrying your things to your car?"

"Sure." I motioned toward the back of Jaxon's truck. "They're just in the back."

I stood by, watching as Ian lifted our bags with ease. Grant ran over to his dad, wrapping his arms around him in a tight hug.

"I love you, Dad," Grant said, his voice muffled against Jaxon's chest. "I'll miss you."

"I love you, too, bud," Jaxon said, his hand resting lightly on Grant's back. "You be good for your mom, okay?"

"I will." Grant pulled back, and a pang of guilt hit me, watching them say goodbye. It wasn't easy living an hour away from Jaxon and having Grant split his time between us.

But since Jaxon had been the first to move away from Ridgewater, and his new place was actually closer to Eden Falls than it was to Ridgewater, my move here had at least made it slightly better. Still, I knew the distance was hard on Grant sometimes.

"Thanks for driving us," I said to Jaxon, giving him a small smile. "I appreciate it."

"Anytime," he said, his tone even. "Take care of yourself, Maddie."

"You too," I said, taking Grant's hand and walking toward my car. Ian was waiting near the trunk, a sheepish expression on his face.

"I guess I need the keys to actually put these inside," he said, holding up the bags.

"That might help." I chuckled, fishing my keys out of my pocket and unlocking the trunk.

Ian loaded the bags inside, then closed the trunk with a soft click. "Before we head out, do you guys want to meet my cat? Satan's been waiting for you."

"Yes!" Grant's face lit up with excitement, and I couldn't help but smile at his enthusiasm.

We followed Ian inside, walking down a wide hallway toward the living room. The house was every bit as grand as I'd remembered, but it somehow felt even warmer this time.

Ian stopped in the middle of the huge living room with vaulted ceilings, his hands resting on his hips as he called out, "Here, Satan. Come here, kitty kitty. I have a friend who wants to meet you."

And the sight of this confident, successful businessman—

towering in his perfectly tailored clothes—calling for a kitten was almost too much.

"There you are," Ian said suddenly, his gaze locking on the little black cat perched on a stuffed chair.

But Satan wasn't about to make this easy. The moment the kitten spotted us, he darted off, disappearing under the couch in a blur of fur and whiskers.

Ian crouched down, lowering himself to the floor to peer under the furniture. "Sneaky little guy," he murmured, then turned to Grant with a conspiratorial smile. "Do you think you're up for a special secret mission?"

"Yes!" Grant's eyes widened, sparkling with excitement.

"Okay." Ian motioned for Grant to come closer. His tone dropped into something playful, almost like he was sharing a top-secret plan. "We're going to need one of us on each side of the couch. If we work together, we can catch him before he gets away."

Without hesitation, Grant scrambled into position, dropping to the floor and lying flat on his stomach. His small hands braced against the carpet as he peeked under the couch, his face serious and determined. Ian mirrored him on the opposite side, his long, muscular frame folding effortlessly to the floor.

"Ready?" Ian asked, glancing across at Grant.

"Ready," Grant whispered, his tone matching the intensity of a soldier preparing for battle.

"All right," Ian said, nodding toward the tiny shadow under the couch. "Let's get him."

In perfect synchrony, they both reached under the couch, their hands moving carefully but with purpose. Satan let out a tiny, indignant meow as the two worked together to gently corner him. And then, a second later, Grant sat up, triumphant, the kitten squirming lightly in his small arms.

"I got him!" Grant beamed, his grin stretching from ear to

ear. He held the kitten close to his chest, his whole body practically glowing with pride.

"Good work!" Ian said, his expression one of genuine delight as he got to his knees and gave Grant a high five. "You saved the day."

Grant giggled, his cheeks flushed with happiness as he nuzzled the tiny black ball of fur. "He's so cute," he said, his voice filled with wonder.

"He's a busy little devil, that's for sure." Ian chuckled, brushing a hand through his hair before sitting back on the floor.

And seeing Ian like this—so natural, so completely at ease with my son—stirred something deep inside me. It was a side of him I hadn't expected, and yet, it felt so perfectly him. He was thoughtful and playful in ways that seemed almost impossible for someone with his world of responsibilities.

And yet, there he was, sitting cross-legged on the floor like he had all the time in the world.

We watched as Grant and the kitten played, Grant's laughter filling the room as he waved a little laser pointer across the floor. Satan pounced after the green dot with boundless kitten energy, his tiny body leaping and twisting in pursuit of his elusive prey. Ian sat beside me on the couch, his arm resting casually along the back, a soft smile curving his lips as he observed the scene.

It was such a simple moment, but it felt perfect. The kind of Sunday afternoon I craved—watching my son giggling and carefree, basking in the presence of a man whose quiet strength and warmth seemed to anchor everything.

I let myself get lost in it, the comfort, the joy, the aching possibility of more afternoons like this. Afternoons where laughter and contentment filled the air, and Ian was a steady presence at my side.

"Want to take a look at that house real quick?" Ian asked after the kitten flopped onto his side, clearly done for the moment.

"Yes," I said, unable to keep the smile from spreading across my face. "I'd love to."

Ian stood, offering me a hand to help me up, and my heart did a little flip as our fingers brushed. Once Grant had given his new kitten friend a quick goodbye pat, we headed outside.

"It's just this way." Ian led us through his expansive backyard, past a beautiful pool to a gate tucked into the hedge. Beyond it, a stone walkway meandered through a patch of trees.

"This is so pretty," I said, taking in the charming path. "Has this always been here?"

"My parents had it put in when I started building my house," Ian said. "Figured it would come in handy for walking back and forth between our houses." He paused, a small smile tugging at his lips. "One day, I think it'll be the perfect little path for my kids to ride their scooters and bikes when they want to visit Grandma and Grandpa."

I stopped walking, glancing up at him. "Hearing you talk about your future kids...it's interesting."

"Do you not see me as the future dad type?" He raised an eyebrow, his expression curious.

"No, it's not that," I said quickly, hoping I hadn't accidentally offended him.

"Then what is it?" He studied me, his gaze steady and patient.

"I don't know." I shrugged, my lips curving into a small smile. "I guess it's just...kind of sweet." I examined his face, the strong jawline softened by a hint of vulnerability in his expression. "You keep surprising me."

"Hopefully, good surprises," he said.

"Very good," I said softly, feeling the truth of it settle in my chest.

We continued down the path, and soon Ian's parents' estate came into view. Their sprawling country manor that could rival Mr. Darcy's house in *Pride and Prejudice* stood in the distance, stately and impressive. But my attention was drawn to a smaller, more charming building off to the side. The little cottage sat nestled in a corner of the property, its quaint architecture framed by a tidy yard.

"This is it," Ian said, unlocking the front door and gesturing for me to step inside.

The moment I crossed the threshold, my breath caught. It was even prettier than I'd imagined. The open-concept living area was bright and airy, with large windows that offered a stunning view of the backyard. The kitchen gleamed with state-of-the-art appliances, its modern design tempered by warm, inviting touches. There were two cozy bedrooms and two pristine bathrooms, each thoughtfully designed.

And the yard... Oh, the yard. My heart swelled as I took in the open space, perfect for Grant to run around and play. There was even a little garden patch, just waiting for someone to plant something in it next spring.

"This is incredible," I said, turning to Ian. "I love it."

He smiled, his satisfaction clear. "Good." He pulled a set of keys from his pocket and held them out to me. "Here."

I blinked, staring at the keys in his hand. "What about a deposit? Or a background check?"

"Not necessary," he said simply. "Just the first month's rent. And you don't have to worry about that until you're ready to move in."

"How soon can I move in?" The words tumbled out before I could stop them.

"Whenever you like," Ian said, his smile widening.

I stared down at the keys, a wave of disbelief washing over me. This was perfect. Too perfect. I was going to need to pinch myself later to make sure this wasn't a dream.

"Thank you," I said softly, meeting his gaze. "Really. This means so much to me."

"You deserve it, Maddie." He nodded, his expression warm. "You and Grant both."

The late afternoon sun filtered through the trees as we stepped out of the cottage. Grant bounced beside me, clearly excited about the house. My thoughts were a tangle of gratitude and disbelief as I imagined us living there.

We started walking toward Ian's house, but as we approached the stables nestled just beyond the edge of the property, we ran into Ian's parents. His mom carried a basket, and his dad had a relaxed yet purposeful stride, both heading toward the barn.

"Well, hey there," Ian's mom greeted us with a warm smile. "We were just heading out to check on the horses."

"Is the mare doing okay?" Ian asked, falling into step beside her.

"She's doing well," his mom replied, her expression softening. "But I like to keep a close eye on her, especially after surgery."

Ian nodded before gesturing toward me. "I was just showing Maddie the house. She likes it."

"That's wonderful!" Ian's mom said, her eyes lighting up. "We're so glad you could use it. It's a darling little place, isn't it?"

"It's beautiful," I said, unable to keep the awe from my

voice. "Thank you so much for offering it to us. It's perfect for my son and me."

Ian's mom glanced down at Grant who was holding my hand but eyeing the barn curiously. She crouched slightly, meeting his gaze. "And what's your name, young man?"

"Grant," he said with a shy smile.

"Well, Grant, it's nice to meet you," Ian's dad said warmly. "How old are you?"

"I'm eight," Grant said proudly.

"Eight is a great age," Ian's dad said, his tone thoughtful. "Tell me, do you like horses?"

Grant's eyes widened, and he pointed to the barn. "Are there real horses in there?"

"There sure are." Ian's dad chuckled. "In fact, we have one that's just the right size for an eight-year-old to ride. If it's okay with your mom, maybe you could ride her sometime."

"Really?" Grant's voice rose with excitement, his whole face lighting up.

I hesitated, glancing at Ian, unsure of how to respond.

Ian grinned and stepped in smoothly. "I'd be happy to give him a few lessons if you like. Only if it's okay with you, of course."

Overwhelmed by their generosity, I managed a shaky smile. "Th-that would be amazing. But we definitely don't want to put anyone out just because we'll be living here."

"Oh, we'd love it." Ian's mom straightened; her expression filled with kindness. "With all our kids grown and out of the house, we could use someone young to help liven things up again."

"Th-thank you." I nodded, swallowing hard. "That's so generous."

"Well—" Ian's dad gave Grant a little wink before tipping

his head toward the barn. "—we'd better check on that mare before she wonders where we are."

We exchanged goodbyes, and Ian's parents continued toward the stables while we headed back toward his house.

Grant skipped ahead a few steps. Seeming to notice my son's enthusiasm, Ian glanced at me, his lips curving into a gentle smile. "I think Grant's already in love with this place."

"I think you're right." I looked at my son, his joy practically radiating from him, and couldn't help but smile back. "I think I might be, too."

Might even be a little in love with the man who showed it to me, too.

40

MADDIE

THE GOLDEN GLOW of the porch lights illuminated the sleek lines of Ian's home as Grant ran ahead of us, his energy seemingly endless. I trailed behind with Ian, still buzzing over the idea that I was going to be living in that cottage soon.

It was already fully furnished, so if I really wanted to, I could probably just drive my Subaru right over there tonight and live out of my suitcase for another day.

Eek! This was so surreal. Like, what even was my life right now? It was like I'd hit the jackpot and was just staying on a winning streak.

"Have you guys eaten recently?" Ian asked when we got back to his house. "Any dinner plans?"

"Not yet," I admitted, ruffling Grant's hair as he started to tug at his shoes by the door like he was readying for round two with the cat and the laser. "We were probably just going to grab some leftovers at Sloan's house."

"Well, I haven't eaten yet, either," Ian said, his lips curving into an easy smile. "I was planning to grab something from this Mexican place downtown, but I'd love some company..."

I hesitated. He'd already done so much for us today—showing me the house, offering to teach Grant to ride horses. Saying yes felt indulgent.

But before I could politely decline, Ian raised his eyebrows and added, "You'd actually be doing me a favor. The last time I grabbed takeout there, the owner looked like she felt really sorry for me ordering for one."

"Okay, fine." I laughed despite myself, shaking my head. "Mexican food sounds pretty good."

"Perfect," Ian said, his grin widening. "And if you're in the mood for Italian instead, they've got you covered, too."

I frowned, confused. "Mexican and Italian?"

He winked as he grabbed his keys. "You'll see what I mean when we get there."

———

"It's one of a kind, isn't it?" Ian said, his half-smile tugging at the corners of his mouth as he caught my amused expression the moment we stepped inside the restaurant.

He'd told me that they served both Mexican and Italian food, but I had not been prepared for the unique experience that was The Italian Amigos. There were traditional Mexican decorations hung alongside Italian frescoes. But the real pièce de résistance was the pair of *David* statues—one wore a sombrero and Italian flag swim trunks, while the other was draped in a vibrant fiesta serape with a pizza balanced on the slingshot in his left hand.

"I love it!" I chuckled, unable to stop the soft laugh that escaped me as I checked out the black mustache perched above the upper lip of one of the *David* statues.

"Just wait till you taste the food," Ian replied.

We followed the hostess to a booth at the back of the restaurant and Grant scrambled eagerly onto the seat beside me, his little hands immediately grabbing the menu. His wide eyes darted across the pages like he was preparing to make the most important culinary decision of his young life. I bit back a grin, watching his enthusiasm as he frowned in concentration, clearly debating his options.

We placed our orders—fettuccine Alfredo for Grant, fajitas for Ian and me—and as we settled into the soft hum of the restaurant's atmosphere, I felt an unexpected calm wash over me. It was easy being here. Comfortable.

"Excuse me for a minute," I said to Ian and Grant after the waitress brought us our waters, sliding out of the booth to find the restroom.

When I returned, the sight before me stopped me in my tracks.

Ian and Grant were leaning over the table, their heads close together, a small deck of cards spread out between them. Grant's cheeks were flushed, his eyes lit with excitement as he clutched his hand of cards like they held the key to his next great victory. Ian's brow furrowed in mock concentration, his lips quirking into a smirk that told me he was enjoying himself just as much as Grant was.

"Do you just always carry a pack of cards with you?" I asked as I slid back into the booth, my voice teasing.

"Not exactly." Ian glanced up at me, his smile bashful. "I may have grabbed it from my game closet before we left. It's something my dad used to do when he first started dating my mom."

I stared at him, my chest tightening. It was such a simple gesture, and yet it carried so much weight.

Jaxon had always handed Grant his phone during moments like this, which I understood. Parenting was hard, and sometimes you just needed a break. But Ian... Ian had taken the time to think ahead about what might make a little boy smile.

To make him feel seen.

And watching the way Grant lit up under his attention made me feel like my heart might burst.

"You're so good at this game!" Ian said, his voice tinged with exaggerated surprise as Grant laid down a card triumphantly.

Grant giggled, his entire face glowing with pride. "I told you I'm good at Uno!"

"You did," Ian said with a wink, ruffling Grant's hair before drawing another card. "But I didn't realize you were this good. I'm going to have to step up my game if I want to keep up."

I smiled, unable to stop the warmth blooming in my chest as I studied Ian. The way his shoulders filled out his shirt, the way his arms flexed subtly as he shuffled the cards. The way his hands moved with steady precision, deft and strong, yet somehow gentle when he dealt the cards to Grant.

And his laugh—deep, rich, and so unguarded—it tugged at something deep inside me.

Was it strange to be so drawn to a man's laugh?

Maybe.

But there it was, settling into my chest like a melody I didn't want to stop listening to.

The game ended, and Ian gathered the cards. "All right, Grant," he said with a playful grin. "Do you think we should let your mom play a round of Uno with us?"

"I guess." Grant glanced at me, his face scrunching up in exaggerated skepticism. "But she's really bad at it. She always loses."

Ian chuckled, his deep brown eyes flicking to mine, warm and teasing. "Well, maybe this time will be different."

And as he handed me the cards, his fingers brushing mine for the briefest moment, I couldn't help but hope that he was talking about more than just the game.

41

———

IAN

"THANKS FOR TAKING US TO DINNER," Maddie said when we drove back toward my house in the Range Rover I kept on hand for when I needed to transport more than one person. "I had a really good time. Pretty sure Grant even liked it more than McDonald's."

"Now that is a big compliment," I said, remembering back to what she'd said about McDonald's being their typical go-to place for eating out. "I'll have to tell Rosa that The Italian Amigos has a couple new fans."

"They totally do," she said. But then, a sudden shyness filled her expression as she added, "But as nice as it was there, I think my favorite part was seeing how much fun Grant had with you."

Really?

Warmth spread through my chest at her words, my hand tightening slightly on the steering wheel as I glanced at her. "I had a great time with him, too," I said, the wholesome fun we'd had together at dinner making something inside me settle.

"He's an awesome kid. Smart. And ruthless when it comes to Uno."

"He wasn't exaggerating when he said he always beats me at Uno." She smiled, her eyes lighting up in that way that always made it hard to look away. "He's just...strangely good at the game."

"Oh, don't I know it?" I said, letting out a low laugh. "He has no mercy. The kid barely lets me put my second-to-last card down before he's calling out 'Uno!' on me."

I glanced in the rearview mirror, catching Grant's reflection as he fiddled with a toy dinosaur. I grinned as I turned back to Maddie, hoping she could tell from the way I couldn't stop smiling all afternoon just how much I genuinely enjoyed their company.

Because yep, I was an addict. Hooked on this sweet single mom and her cute eight-year-old boy.

As we drove through the sleepy streets of Eden Falls and got closer and closer to my house where her Subaru waited to take them back to Sloan's house, I felt the urge to take several wrong turns, just to delay the inevitable goodbye we'd have to say at the end of the drive.

I knew it was absurd since I'd be seeing her again at work in less than twelve hours...and yet, I was already going through the withdrawals.

Spending time with her and Grant tonight had felt so right. Easy in a way I wasn't used to.

These last two weeks while she'd been at her dad's, I'd missed her.

Missed seeing her through my office window. Missed the little smiles she'd send my way while we worked. Even now, with her sitting beside me, I was already starting to miss her. Missed the hours I wouldn't have with her between now and the sunrise.

Sure, I knew she hadn't been to Sloan's house for two and a half weeks and probably had some unpacking and catching up to do before the morning came, but I was a selfish man. And if it wouldn't make me seem completely obsessed, I'd probably tell her that if she wanted, she and Grant could just stay in the spare bedrooms at my place.

I could have some fresh pajamas and extra toiletries delivered within the hour—heck, they could have a whole new wardrobe and everything else delivered with a single call to my head of staff and she'd take care of everything so they'd never have to leave again.

Okay...so maybe that was a bit overboard.

But I couldn't help it. I'd missed her so much that only having a few hours with her today wasn't nearly enough.

I'd spent way too many nights alone in my big, empty house. I didn't want another.

It was a new feeling for me—this pull to stay, to stretch out every second I had with her. In the past, my relationships—or flings, if I was being honest—burned hot and fast. Three days in, and I'd be itching for a clean break. A little space, a little distance, and I was good as new.

But with Maddie?

The thought of space felt unbearable. Being with her didn't suffocate me the way it had with anyone else. It did the opposite. It made me feel lighter. Happier. Like maybe, for the first time, I'd found something worth holding on to.

Was it logical? Probably not. But love wasn't logical, was it?

Wait... The word *love* stopped me cold.

Love.

Was that what this was? Was I...in love with her?

The realization hit me like a gut punch, knocking the breath out of me as I stared straight ahead at the empty road.

It wasn't something I'd let myself think about in years. Love didn't happen to me—not when I'd spent the last nine years keeping everything and everyone at arm's length to avoid the kind of pain I swore I'd never go through again.

But as I glanced over at Maddie—her head tilted toward the window, a faint smile on her lips as the glow of the streetlights traced her profile—I felt it. A tightening in my chest, a swell of something I couldn't name but instinctively knew was real.

If someone had asked me a few months ago how long it took to fall in love, I probably would've shrugged and given some vague answer like, *As long as it takes.*

But now?

Now, I knew.

Because if my math was correct, I was pretty sure it only took thirty-seven days.

Give or take the nine years in between.

42

—————

MADDIE

WHEN WE PULLED BACK into Ian's driveway after dinner, Grant unbuckled his seatbelt and leaned forward between the front seats. "Can I play with the kitten one more time before we go?"

I glanced at Ian to see what he thought, and after searching my face as if to assure himself that it was okay with me, he turned back to Grant and said, "Of course."

Grant was already off, calling for Ian's cat as he darted into the living room, and I stood in the archway by the kitchen, watching him with a smile.

As the kitty pounced on the toy mouse Grant dangled in front of him, I couldn't help but feel...content. Happy. The kind of deep, steady happiness that had been elusive for so long.

And then I felt it—Ian's hand slipping into mine.

I blinked, startled by the warmth of his touch, but as I looked down at our fingers intertwined, I realized how natural it felt. Like it had always been this way, even though it hadn't.

A flutter spread through my chest, light and soft, and I glanced up at him.

Ian didn't say a word. He didn't break the moment or let go. He just stood beside me, his quiet smile directed at Grant as he played, as if he belonged here just as much as I did.

And oh, this was *nice*. Peaceful, even.

It struck me, in that quiet space, how strange it was that this man—who could make my heart race wildly and leave me breathless—was also the one who made me feel calm. Safe.

That word—*safe*—settled over me like a revelation, making my throat tighten. Safety and security were the very things I'd been chasing for so long, always just out of reach. I'd spent years treading water, constantly on edge, waiting for the next wave to knock me under. Then just when I thought I had things figured out, something would shift—Jaxon, bills, work, life—and I'd be scrambling again, trying to hold it all together for Grant.

But with Ian? I didn't know how he did it, but being around him made me feel like I could let go of that constant vigilance. I could take a breath. I could stop scanning the horizon for the next storm and just...*be*.

It was like taking a vacation from my problems, knowing I could lean on him for a moment, let him take the reins—and when I came back, everything would still be okay. Probably even better than before.

And that was what did it. That was what really got to me. Sure, Ian was the most physically attractive man I'd ever met— *let's be real*—but his capability? The way he stepped up, the way he was so steady and reliable? That might just be the sexiest thing about him.

Years spent with someone I couldn't rely on had chipped away at me, made me suspicious of everyone and everything. But with Ian, I felt...held.

His thumb began tracing gentle circles over my knuckles, the gentle motion pulling me back to the present. And when I realized he was running it over the large diamond ring I still wore, I stiffened slightly, remembering I was supposed to give it back today.

"Oh," I said, pulling my hand from his and twisting the ring free. "I guess I should probably give this back to you now."

I held it out, expecting him to take it right away.

But he didn't.

His gaze lingered on the ring, then shifted back to me, a flicker of hesitation crossing his face. "You can hold onto it a little longer if you need," he said after a beat. "I mean, what if your dad tries to FaceTime you and notices you're not wearing it?"

I smiled faintly, touched by the suggestion—by the fact that he didn't seem to want me to stop wearing it, either. "He did mention wanting to meet this mysterious fiancé of mine when he comes to Eden Falls in a few weeks," I admitted. "But I think he'll be feeling good enough by then that I can let him down gently about the engagement being called off. I don't think he'll be too disappointed."

"Okay." Ian exhaled, a quiet chuckle slipping out as he finally opened his hand. I dropped the ring onto his palm, watching as his fingers curled around it. For a moment, it seemed like he wanted to say more, but then he cleared his throat. "I'll just put this away in my room for safekeeping."

"Good idea," I said, forcing a casual tone to hide the strange sense of loss I felt at no longer wearing it. "You'll stick it in the jewelry safe you probably have in your closet, right?"

He let out a real laugh at that, the kind I could feel in my chest. "How did you know I had one of those?"

I shrugged, letting my smile widen. "It just seemed like something you'd have."

"You're not wrong," he said, shaking his head with amusement. "I'll be right back."

As Ian disappeared down the hall, I found myself glancing after him, curiosity stirring. What did his bedroom look like? I'd only seen the main rooms of the house so far—the sleek, modern living room, the gorgeous kitchen—but I had no doubt the rest was just as exquisite.

It was the kind of space I could've spent hours admiring. My degree in interior design had given me a front-row seat to some incredible homes over the years, but none of them compared to this one.

I'd always had a vague idea of what my dream home would look like if I ever managed to save enough money to buy it. But after spending a little time in this home, I was pretty sure it was literally my dream home now.

Especially if Ian Hastings came with it.

Before I could get too lost in the thought, Ian returned, his steps light as he rejoined me. I hesitated, considering asking him for a tour—partly because I was curious, and yes, partly because I wanted to stretch out this time with him.

But since that would probably be weird, I turned back to Grant instead and called out, "Hey buddy, we should head back to Aunt Sloan's. She's probably wondering what happened to us."

"Aw, okay." Grant sighed, scooping up the squirming kitten for one last hug before setting him down gently on the carpet.

Ian walked us to the door, stepping out onto the driveway as I unlocked my car. Grant climbed into the backseat, and while he was buckling in, I turned back to Ian, suddenly unsure of what to do.

Should I just wave and leave? Should I hug him? Should I—?

I was still overthinking it when Ian stepped closer, his

strong arms slipping around me like it was the most natural thing in the world.

And just like that, I melted.

His embrace was warm and steady, his chest firm beneath my cheek, and for a short moment, I let myself breathe him in. He just felt *right*—safe and comforting and everything I hadn't even realized I'd missed.

His head dipped lower, his lips brushing next to my ear as he murmured, "I'm not sure what the protocol is for kissing in front of eight-year-olds, but since he's just a few feet away and I don't want to shock him by kissing his mom, I figure I'll stick to this for now."

A smile tugged at my lips as I leaned back just far enough to look up at him. "You're very considerate, you know that?"

"Only sometimes," he teased, his voice low.

I tilted my head slightly, giving him space to kiss my forehead. The gentle press of his lips against my skin was soft but lingering, sending a shiver through me that I felt all the way down to my toes.

When he pulled back, I didn't let go right away. I wrapped my arms around him again, possibly holding on a little too tightly. But I couldn't bring myself to care. I needed this—him— just for a little longer.

After a moment, Ian's hands slid to my back, giving me one last squeeze before letting me go. "Drive safe," he said, his voice steady and quiet, though there was something unspoken in his gaze. "I'll see you tomorrow at work."

"Okay," I whispered, my chest tightening as I forced myself to take a step back.

I turned and climbed into the car, glancing back one last time before shutting the door. Ian stood there on the driveway, hands tucked into his pockets, watching us with a soft, thoughtful expression.

As I pulled out and onto the quiet street, I stole one last look in the rearview mirror. He was still there, standing like he wasn't quite ready to let us leave either.

And as I drove toward Sloan's house, a warmth lingered in my chest, soft and steady—a reminder of him, and the way his arms felt like home.

43

———

MADDIE

I COULDN'T STOP SMILING as I watched Ian and his friends carry the last of my things into the cottage on Wednesday night. Miles and Bash were taking boxes two at a time like they were weightless, Owen was hoisting a bookshelf on his shoulder, and Ian was unloading the heavy furniture with Evan, both of them barely breaking a sweat.

I hadn't been prepared for this level of muscle, to be honest. All of Ian's friends were ripped—absurdly so. Especially Evan, who, despite being freshly back from his honeymoon, looked like he'd spent those two weeks lifting cars for fun.

"Where did you find these guys?" I teased Ian as he passed by, carrying a chair in each hand like they were folding lawn chairs.

"Don't let their muscles fool you. They're all soft on the inside," Ian said with a smirk. Then he called out to Bash and Miles, "Watch the walls! We don't want Maddie regretting letting us help."

"Wouldn't dream of it, boss," Bash shot back, dropping his boxes with an exaggerated thud.

By the time everything was unloaded, my storage unit was empty, and I was blinking back tears of gratitude. I didn't even have to ask for help—they'd all just shown up with Ian and done it with the kind of easy camaraderie that made me feel like part of their group, even if I wasn't.

"Okay, pizza and drinks are ready!" I called from the front porch, pointing to the boxes of pizza I'd set up on a folding table.

The guys gathered quickly, grabbing slices, beers, and waters, and sprawled themselves out in the yard like it was a lazy summer afternoon. Grant was already settled on the grass, devouring a slice of pepperoni and making friends with Miles—who I'd just learned was a literal NFL quarterback—by challenging him to a race across the lawn. I smiled at the scene, warmth filling me as I went to grab some more napkins from a box inside.

I stood in the little kitchen, sifting through the haphazardly labeled boxes until I found what I needed. The window above the sink was open, letting in the evening breeze, and as I pulled out the napkins, I heard the low rumble of voices drifting through from outside.

"Okay, okay," Owen was saying, his voice laced with humor. "So none of us have dates for Carter and Ava's wedding next weekend, huh? That's pathetic. Well, except for Mr. Honeymoon over there."

"That's right," Evan replied, his tone smug. "I've got my plus-one for life. But I'm sure you'll all follow in my footsteps eventually."

"You think?" Bash said, a challenge in his voice. "Who do we think is next, then?"

There was a beat of silence before Owen chimed in. "Well, I *wish* it was me. But apparently, my future wife has been praying I don't meet anyone before I meet her because it's working. Seriously, she can stop praying now. Like, *please,* it's working a little *too well.*"

The group erupted into laughter, and I couldn't help but grin to myself. Owen really was a cutie. If I had a younger sister who wasn't already married, I'd totally try setting her up with him.

I grabbed the napkins and turned to head outside, but Bash's voice made me pause in my tracks.

"I'm pretty sure Ian's on his way to matrimony, though," Bash said casually, his words tinged with mischief. "From the way he's been looking at Maddie all night."

My heart stopped.

Still holding the napkins, I froze, eyes widening as I hovered near the window. I peeked out through the curtain just enough to see Ian's reaction.

And there he was, standing in the yard, a sheepish smile tugging at his lips.

And he didn't deny it.

Didn't even deflect.

"Hopefully, I'm lucky enough," Ian said finally, his voice quiet but steady, like the words carried more weight than he was willing to show. "Just gotta convince her I'm not a complete doofus after introducing her to you idiots."

The guys erupted in laughter, teasing him with a chorus of "Oh, you've got it bad, man," and "Ian Hastings, smitten? Never thought I'd see the day."

"Yeah..." he admitted, rubbing a hand along his jaw. "I was pretty much a goner the first time I saw her."

The words hit me like a bolt of lightning, sending warmth rushing through me, melting me from the inside out.

"But she's got a kid," Bash said, his tone curious but not unkind. "Would you really want to be an instant dad?"

The yard fell quiet, all the joking and banter fading as the question hung in the air.

I held my breath, suddenly terrified of his answer, because it felt like the kind of moment that could shatter everything.

But Ian didn't hesitate, his voice steady and sure as he said, "I know it's probably strange for you guys to hear me say it, but if they'd take me, I'd love to be Grant's stepdad. He's the best."

I pressed a hand to my chest, my heart thudding so hard I was sure they'd hear it all the way outside.

Ian's words—simple and honest—knocked the air right out of me.

My hand pressed lightly against the fabric of my shirt as if that could steady the intense swell of emotions rushing through me.

He meant it.

I could hear it in his voice—no hesitation, no careful phrasing, no joke to deflect the gravity of what he'd just said. Just pure honesty.

My throat tightened, and I closed my eyes for a beat, needing a moment to pull myself together. How had this man—this unexpected, wonderful man—come into my life and completely changed everything? Not just for me, but for Grant, too?

The guys' voices shifted to another topic, their laughter easy and natural, and I took a steadying breath before stepping outside, hoping my face didn't reveal that I'd just overheard their conversation. "I finally found some napkins if anyone needs them," I said, placing the stack next to the paper plates and pizza boxes.

"Perfect timing," Bash said, reaching for another slice.

Once the guys had finished their pizza and drained their drinks, they turned their attention back to me. "Anything else you need, Maddie?" Miles asked, brushing his hands on his jeans. "We're happy to help."

I glanced around, taking in the stacks of boxes and scattered furniture, and shook my head. "I think I'm good now. I just need to figure out where to put everything, but you guys have done more than enough already. Thank you so much for your help."

"No problem at all," Owen said with a grin. "And hey, don't hesitate to call if you need more muscle. We're just a phone call away."

Ian gave each of his friends a quick fist bump as they said their goodbyes, and soon it was just the three of us—Ian, Grant, and me.

I grabbed a slice of pizza and took a seat on the front porch, savoring the quiet hum of the evening as Grant swung happily on the little wooden swing in the yard. There was something so perfect about seeing him like that, laughing and carefree, and I leaned back against the railing with a contented sigh.

Ian joined me, settling into the space beside me, and for a moment, we just sat there in companionable silence.

"Do you have any plans for July thirty-first?" he asked suddenly, his voice casual but tinged with something more.

I furrowed my brow, thinking, before reaching for my phone like I needed to check my nonexistent social calendar.

"It's a Saturday," he said, watching me with a faint smile.

"Well, if it's a Saturday, then I'll probably just be hanging out here alone since Grant will be at his dad's," I replied, setting my phone back down. "Why do you ask?"

"It's Carter and Ava's wedding that day, and I don't have a plus-one yet," Ian said, shifting slightly on the wooden porch. "And I was wondering if you'd mind going with me." He paused, his gaze steady as he added, "As my date."

"As your date..." I repeated slowly, letting the words hang between us as I pretended to consider them.

His smile deepened, and there was something so charming about his confidence mixed with that hint of vulnerability. "I know we've been spending a lot of time together," he said, "but I haven't actually asked you on a *real* date yet. So I was hoping you'd be up for it. You know, if going on a date with your boss is okay with you."

I couldn't hold back the smile that spread across my face. "I think it's more than okay with me."

His expression lit up with that boyish grin I'd grown so fond of. "So you'll go with me, then?"

"I'd love to," I said softly, feeling my heart flutter. "It'll give me an excuse to wear that twelve-thousand-dollar dress I have sitting in my closet."

"Yes!" He laughed, his eyes sparkling with amusement. "I've been kind of hoping you'd wear it to work one of these days, just so I could see it again. But I guess wearing it to the wedding is probably a better idea."

"Yeah," I teased, "I mean, it's not like we don't already have enough people at work wondering if I'm just there to get my hands on your money. Me showing up in that dress would only confirm their suspicions."

"Has it been bad?" His brow furrowed with concern. "I thought everyone was good about everything. Thought it settled when we squashed those pregnancy rumors and it came out that Margot was the one who leaked the video of Slade. If not, I can talk to Marsha and issue another public statement."

"No, it's been fine." I waved a hand, brushing it off. "Everyone's actually been great. That was just me being insecure."

He nodded, seeming reassured, and I finished off my pizza before standing. "I need to grab something to drink. Want anything?"

"Sure," he said, leaning back lazily against the railing. "I'll have whatever you're having."

"I was just going to make a Moscow mule."

"Sounds perfect."

I went inside, pulling limes and ginger beer out of the fridge and setting them on the counter. As I started slicing up the lime, I heard the soft creak of the floorboards behind me, followed by the unmistakable warmth of Ian's presence.

Before I could turn around, his hands found my hips, his touch gentle yet firm as he stepped up behind me. My breath caught as he leaned down, his body pressing softly against mine. I felt him nuzzle the curve of my neck, his lips brushing just below my ear.

A shiver ran through me, and I closed my eyes briefly, a smile tugging at my lips as I savored the feeling.

I liked this—Ian pulling me close, touching me like he couldn't help himself.

We hadn't talked about what was happening between us, hadn't defined it, but this...this said enough.

It said he wanted me.

And I liked that I didn't have to question it.

Tilting my head slightly, I let out a soft laugh. "You know, you're very good at distracting me."

"Is that a bad thing?" he murmured, pressing a light kiss to the spot just below my ear.

"Not at all," I whispered, smiling as I turned my head slightly to catch his gaze.

For a moment, we just stared at each other, the air thickening, charged with unspoken words neither of us seemed ready to say.

And then Ian closed the distance between our lips and kissed me.

Slowly at first, his lips brushing against mine with a tenderness that made my knees weak. My breath hitched as I turned toward him, my hands finding the front of his shirt to steady myself. But when I kissed him back—deeper, more certain— something shifted.

His hands slid up from my hips to my waist, pulling me flush against him as the kiss grew more passionate, more consuming. A low moan escaped him, almost like he'd been holding back and couldn't anymore. I felt the counter at my back as he moved closer, the space between us disappearing entirely.

He reached out, sweeping a box aside on the counter with a soft scrape of cardboard, and before I knew it, his hands gripped my waist again—strong, steady—and lifted me effort-lessly. I let out a quiet gasp as he set me on the counter, my legs naturally bracketing his hips as he stepped between them, his mouth never leaving mine.

And then there was nothing but the kiss. The heat of it. The way his hands roamed—up my thighs, over my waist, to cup my face as if he couldn't decide where to touch me next because he wanted it all.

My fingers tangled in his shirt, pulling him closer, wanting to feel more of him, to explore. My hands skimmed over his shoulders, down the broad planes of his chest, and I ached to slip them beneath the fabric, to feel the hard muscles beneath his bare skin.

His lips traveled down to the corner of my mouth, along my jaw, before finding that sensitive spot just below my ear. A soft sigh escaped me, and I tilted my head, giving him more access as a deep flutter built low in my stomach.

But then—

Footsteps. Small ones. On the porch.

Grant.

Reality snapped back into place like a splash of cold water, and we both froze, our breathing heavy and uneven as we broke apart like two guilty teenagers about to get caught sneaking around.

"Oh my gosh," I whispered, my cheeks blazing as I slid off the counter in a rush. I straightened my shirt, smoothed my hair, and shot Ian a wide-eyed look as if to say, *What just happened?*

Ian scrubbed a hand over his face and took a step back, looking equally disheveled and entirely too attractive for his own good.

The screen door creaked, and Grant came bounding into the kitchen, completely oblivious to the lingering heat in the air.

"Mom! I just saw an eagle!" he burst out, his face alight with pure excitement as he pointed back outside.

"An eagle? That's amazing!" I said, my voice pitching a little too high as I quickly tucked a strand of hair behind my ear —desperately trying to look like I hadn't been just seconds away from ripping Ian's shirt off.

"It was *huge!*" Grant spread his arms as wide as they could go, practically bouncing on his toes. "Like, this big!"

"That's awesome, bud," Ian said, his voice smooth and casual—far steadier than mine—as he reached out to ruffle Grant's hair. "Eagles don't show up every day, so you've got pretty great timing." Then with a teasing grin, he glanced at me and added under his breath, "Honestly, the kid's got a knack for showing up exactly when I shouldn't be trusted."

"Ian!" I hissed, shooting him a scandalized look that was half-laughter, half-plea.

He shrugged, entirely unrepentant. "I'm just saying..."

I glanced quickly at Grant, who, thankfully, had his nose pressed against the window again, scanning the sky for his elusive eagle. I let out a small breath of relief, but Ian's grin only widened, sending another rush of warmth straight through me.

Yeah, great timing, I thought wryly. But maybe, *hopefully,* someday soon we'd find time—real time—where we wouldn't get interrupted.

And if Ian kept looking at me the way he was looking at me now?

Well, I was pretty sure I'd have no complaints about how that time would be spent.

44

——

IAN

THE SHARP, clean snap of my cufflinks echoed faintly in the quiet of the groomsmen's room as I finished buttoning my tuxedo jacket. My reflection stared back at me in the mirror—dark suit, white shirt, black bow tie—but all I could think about was Maddie.

The past couple of weeks had been some of the best of my life. Having her so close—just a short walk through my back gate—felt like the kind of happiness I hadn't even known was possible. Every evening was something I looked forward to: cooking dinner together, teasing her about burning garlic bread while Grant bounced around the kitchen with endless energy. Taking long, lazy walks around the neighborhood while Grant sped ahead on his scooter, laughing in that carefree way only kids can.

Even introducing them to the horses had been something special. I could still see Maddie's smile when she trotted for the first time, Grant cheering her on from the fence line.

It had been magical. That was the only word for it.

And while I hadn't said it out loud yet—that big, weighty *L* word—I was pretty sure Maddie knew. The way I looked at her...the way I found any excuse to touch her hand or kiss her forehead...how I wanted her to stay longer every night. How I had to tear myself away from her every time we said goodbye.

I wasn't exactly subtle. But I knew I needed to tell her. Soon.

I shook off the thoughts as I headed back into the room where Carter, Mack, and the other guys were already gathered, finishing the last touches on their tuxedos. Mack—Carter's best man—stood with a glass in his hand, already starting in on a little toast.

"It's about time you married my sister, man," Mack said, grinning at Carter as he raised his glass. "Now you two just need to catch up to me and Cambrielle and get pregnant already, so my kid can have some cousins to play with."

Everyone laughed and Carter rolled his eyes good-naturedly. Then, turning toward Nash who had gotten married last summer, Mack added, "And that goes for you and Kiara, too, okay? Your parents want grandbabies."

More laughter rippled through the room, Nash shaking his head with a chuckle.

I smirked as I listened to them, but something tugged at me as I adjusted my jacket again. Something I hadn't really thought I'd be ready for until this summer: I wanted to join them.

The idea hit me out of nowhere, but it settled deep in my chest, steady and unshakable. I wanted what they had—the love, the family, the life they were building together. I wanted that with Maddie. With Grant, too.

My phone buzzed in my pocket, snapping me back to reality. It was a text from my driver.

Alex: On the way with Maddie. Be there soon.

Perfect timing since the ceremony would be starting soon.

I told the guys I'd meet them outside and made my way to the front doors of the venue, pacing a little as I waited.

A few minutes later, Alex's car eased to a stop in the driveway, and my heart did this ridiculous, anticipatory thud as I stepped forward to open the door for Maddie.

And when she stepped out...

My brain short-circuited.

She was *stunning*. Absolutely breathtaking.

Her hair fell in soft waves over her shoulders, the kind of effortless elegance that made my chest tighten. The glam team I'd sent to her house that morning had clearly outdone themselves, but it was the dress that nearly knocked me flat. That deep purple, floor-length gown—the one we'd picked out together in Boston—shimmered in the fading sunlight, catching every movement and making her look like she'd stepped straight out of a dream.

It hugged her perfectly, every curve, every line, just *so*. I had to blink, as if my brain needed a moment to catch up to how unfairly beautiful she was.

She smiled up at me, her eyes bright, and for a second, I forgot how to breathe.

"You're..." I swallowed hard, the words catching in my throat. "You're breathtaking, Maddie." My voice came out a little rougher than I intended, my heart thudding like a freight train. "No offense to Ava, but I'm pretty sure you're about to outshine the bride tonight."

Her laugh was soft and warm, brushing against me like a touch. "You're too much."

"Can't help it," I murmured, grinning like a complete fool. Because I really *couldn't* help it. Not when it came to her.

She slipped her arm through mine, the feel of her so natural, so right, that I didn't want to move. But together, we walked toward the rows of white chairs, the soft notes of a string quartet threading through the air as guests settled into their seats.

We found a spot near the front next to my parents, Maddie's hand resting lightly on my arm. I wasn't sure if she realized how much that simple touch affected me—how much it anchored me, even as my thoughts swirled with everything I felt for her.

The ceremony began, and soon everyone rose, the hush of anticipation settling over the garden like a blanket. I turned, along with everyone else, and saw Ava appear at the end of the aisle.

And my breath caught.

Ava practically *floated*, the soft fabric of her white dress trailing behind her as she moved. She looked radiant, her face alight with a joy so pure, it was impossible not to feel it. All eyes were on her, but Carter's expression said it all.

He watched her like she was his entire world, his love for her written so plainly across his face that it hit me right in the chest.

I didn't take my eyes off them, but I *felt* Maddie lean into me, her shoulder brushing mine in a way that was as subtle as it was grounding. It wasn't much—just a touch—but it tethered me to the moment, to *her*.

Carter took Ava's hands beneath the wedding arbor, their voices soft as they exchanged vows. And as they spoke promises about forever, about building a life together, I couldn't help but glance at Maddie.

She caught me looking, and after studying my expression and seeming to read what was in my gaze, her lips curved into the faintest smile, her eyes soft and knowing.

And right then, as the string quartet swelled and my brother slid a ring onto his bride's finger, it hit me all over again.

This.

This was what I wanted.

Maddie. Grant. All of it.

A future where they were *mine* to love, to protect, to come home to.

My throat tightened, but it wasn't fear. It was knowing. Clarity.

Because I loved her. I *loved* her.

And maybe, if I could stop being such a coward about it, maybe tonight would be the night I told her.

45

______

MADDIE

AVA AND CARTER'S wedding reception was straight out of a fairy tale. Lights strung across the garden sparkled like stars, casting a warm golden glow over the guests. Soft music floated through the air, blending with the hum of laughter and clinking glasses. It was magical, the kind of night that made even the biggest critic believe in love stories and happily-ever-afters.

I sat next to Ian at one of the round tables, my heels kicked off beneath my chair for some relief. The energy of the night buzzed around me as I took a sip of my drink and watched Ava and Carter make their rounds through the crowd, hand in hand, completely wrapped up in each other.

The ceremony earlier had been beautiful—simple, heartfelt, and full of love. Even though I didn't know Ava and Carter all that well yet, it was obvious they were meant for each other. The way Carter looked at her, like she was his entire universe, made my heart ache in the best way.

It was the kind of love I'd always hoped for. I wanted that, too. One day.

Hopefully.

I let out a soft sigh, shaking off the wistful thought as I picked at the dessert on my plate—some decadent chocolate cake that probably cost more than my weekly grocery bill. These billionaires really knew how to throw a party. Every detail was perfect—from the food to the music to the gorgeous floral centerpieces that looked like they belonged in a magazine.

"This cake is insane," I murmured, glancing over at Ian who sat beside me.

"Worth every calorie." He grinned, his eyes crinkling slightly at the corners.

"No arguments here." I set my fork down with a happy sigh, feeling the buzz of contentment in my chest.

Ian was quiet for a moment, his gaze distant as he swirled the ice in his glass. Finally, he looked at me, his expression casual but with a flicker of curiosity in his eyes. "Have you ever heard of the whole 'right person, wrong time' idea?"

I paused, frowning as I thought about it, the question catching me off guard. "Like, the book trope?"

"I guess it could be a book trope." He chuckled softly. "But I meant more like...the concept. In real life."

His words made me go still. The idea wasn't foreign, and now that he'd brought it up, I realized it was something I might actually have a bit of experience with. "Yeah," I said slowly, "I've heard of it."

Ian nodded, his focus still on me. And while his tone stayed light, there was an undertone I couldn't quite place. "What do you think about it?"

I tilted my head, studying him, trying to read the intention behind his question. "Is that part of Ava and Carter's story?"

"No." He shook his head. "They've been together pretty much since high school. They only had a minor blip in their timeline."

"Then why are you asking?"

"I don't know." He shrugged, the movement almost too casual. "I guess I was just curious about it."

My brow furrowed as I studied him, sensing there was more to his question than he was letting on. Was he tiptoeing around something? Trying to test an idea without actually saying it?

"I think..." I started, choosing my words carefully. "I don't know how often it really happens. I mean, people can know each other—maybe be acquaintances or friends—before falling in love. Like the brother's-best-friend trope, or boy-next-door romances."

"Uh-huh." A faint smile tugged at his lips, clearly amused by my tendency to reference life through books, but he stayed quiet, listening intently.

"But if you're talking about something like that movie *Serendipity*," I continued, "where two people have a chance meeting, lose complete contact, and then somehow fate brings them back together..." I paused, my gaze drifting to Ian's face, searching his eyes for any flicker of acknowledgment, any sign that he might know I wasn't just talking about a movie. That I was talking about us—about that night on the beach so many years ago. "I don't think that happens too often. That feels rare. Really rare."

"*Rare.*" Ian licked his lips, his expression thoughtful as he nodded. "I like that word for it."

I stared at him, waiting—*hoping*—for more. What was he thinking? What was he trying to say?

Was he hinting at what I hoped he was?

But before I could ask, the music changed and a hush fell over the crowd. Ava and Carter stepped into the center of the garden, all eyes turning toward them as they began their first dance.

"We should probably go watch them," Ian said, offering me a hand.

So I placed my hand in his and let him lead me to the edge of the dance floor to watch the bride and groom enjoy their first official dance as a married couple.

Ava glowed as Carter pulled her close, the two of them moving together like they were in their own little world. And it was impossible not to feel the love radiating from them, to not be moved by the sweetness of it.

As the evening carried on, Ian pulled me onto the dance floor a few times, his hand warm against my back, his touch sending shivers through me every time he pulled me close. We swayed and spun, my dress catching the lights as I laughed in his arms, the magic of the night wrapping around us like a blanket.

Later, as the party began to wind down, Ian and I stood together at the edge of the reception, watching Ava and Carter twirl beneath the strings of lights.

"Hey, how did you two meet, anyway?" the voice of Evan's wife, Addison, broke through the moment as she approached, arm in arm with her husband.

"Oh," Ian said, his expression suddenly playful, like he might be considering telling them a juicy story like the ones we'd told everyone in Boston. But instead of making up a random story, he gave me a gentle look before saying, "We actually met on a beach in North Carolina. A little over nine years ago..."

And that was when the world tilted, the weight of his words hitting me like a wave. I gasped, my heart lurching as I turned to him, my voice trembling. "So you knew?"

His smile softened. "Yeah," he said, his eyes meeting mine with steady warmth. "Of course I knew."

My throat tightened, tears pricking at the edges of my

vision. "H-how long?" I whispered, barely able to get the words out.

"Since we were in my hotel room, looking at those engagement rings together."

The breath left my lungs in a shaky rush. "Really?"

He nodded, his gaze never wavering. "Really."

Out of the corner of my eye, I caught Addison exchanging a quick glance with her husband, her brows lifting slightly. Evan murmured something low, and without a word, they turned and slipped away with quiet grace, clearly sensing they'd stumbled into something private.

For a moment, the emotions surging through me were too much—shock, disbelief, and something deeper, warmer, that took root and spread through my chest. I stared at Ian, trying to process the revelation, the enormity of what he was telling me.

His fingers found mine, threading through them with a gentle certainty, and that small gesture anchored me.

He had known. This entire time, he had known who I was. And not once had he said anything—not until now.

"Why didn't you tell me?" I asked, my voice breaking as I searched his face.

"Because I didn't want you to question why I fell for you," he said, his expression full of something that made my chest ache. "I didn't want you to think it was because of some idea of fate or because I couldn't let go of a memory. I needed you to know that I fell for you because of *you*. Because I couldn't help it."

The weight of his words settled over me like a warm, grounding blanket, wrapping me in something steady and real. "Oh Ian..." I whispered, my voice trembling.

"I know..." he murmured, a faint smile playing at the corners of his lips. He reached up, his fingers grazing my temple as he tucked a strand of hair behind my ear, the gentle touch sending a shiver of warmth across my skin. "And the fact that we met on that beach all those years ago? It's incredible, and I love that it's part of our story. But it's not *why* I fell for you, Maddie. I fell for you because of who you are now. And I needed you to see that."

The truth of his words hit me with a force I hadn't expected, tears slipping free as I tried to blink them away. "I wanted to say something so bad when you named your cat Satan," I admitted, my voice cracking with emotion. "I thought maybe...maybe you remembered that girl from the beach, but you didn't realize she was me."

"You have no idea how hard it was to keep a straight face when Grant said you two wanted to name a cat Satan." Ian chuckled. "I barely survived it."

"You should've just told me." A laugh bubbled out of me, wet and shaky.

"I could have," he said, his smile turning tender, "but I kind of loved doing it this way. Seeing it all click for you in person. Getting to see how special it was to you, up close... It made it worth the wait."

My chest ached with so many emotions I could barely breathe. Gratitude, happiness, love. I tightened my grip on his hand, giving it a squeeze. "You're worth the wait, too, you know."

His gaze met mine, the depth of his feelings shining in his dark eyes, and I didn't need him to say another word. It was all right there, unspoken but so loud I could feel it.

Ian stepped closer, his free hand lifting to cup my cheek, his thumb gently brushing away the tear that had slipped free. "I love you, Maddie Stevens," he said, his voice low and raw, thick with emotion. "I started falling for you that day. Always wondered what happened to that beautiful girl on the beach. Hoping you were okay...wishing I'd thought to get your name or number so I could check in, to see how things went with your dad."

He'd thought about me? Worried about me?

Tears spilled over, but I didn't care. I smiled through them, my heart so full it felt like it might burst. "I love you, too," I whispered, the words tumbling out so easily because they were true. "Pretty sure part of me fell for you that night on the beach."

His lips curved into a smile, the kind that reached all the way to his eyes.

And then he bent his head, his lips finding mine in a kiss that was slow and unhurried yet brimming with everything we hadn't said until now. Every touch of his mouth spoke of love, of longing, of the connection we'd shared from the very beginning.

I gripped the front of his tuxedo jacket, pulling him closer, needing him closer. His arms wrapped around me, anchoring me to him as the kiss deepened.

His hands slid down my back, fingers pressing into the fabric of my dress as if he couldn't get enough of me. I felt his heart pounding against mine, a frantic rhythm that matched my own.

Ian pulled back just enough to rest his forehead against mine, his breathing uneven. "Maddie," he murmured, his voice rough with restraint, "we need to leave. Now."

I nodded, my chest heaving as I tried to catch my breath. "Okay."

Without another word, Ian took my hand, lacing his fingers through mine as he guided me away from the reception. The sounds of laughter and music faded into the background as we slipped out the side gate. My heart raced as we reached his car, the urgency between us palpable, electrifying.

He opened the passenger door for me, his touch lingering

as he helped me inside. The moment he slid into the driver's seat and started the engine, the world outside blurred into insignificance. My skin buzzed with anticipation, every glance he shot my way sending another wave of heat rushing through me.

Somehow, we made it back to his house, though I barely remembered the drive.

The instant we stepped inside, Ian's hands were on me, his touch igniting a fire that burned through me, fierce and consuming. His lips found mine again, leading me into a kiss so intense, so utterly unrestrained, that it stole my breath. His kisses had always brimmed with desire, but this was different—this wasn't just *want*. It was hunger, need, desperation, like he'd been holding back a dam of emotion that had finally broken free.

He backed me against the door, his body pressing into mine as his hands framed my face, his thumbs brushing along my jaw. The kiss deepened, his lips demanding, coaxing me to give him everything. And I did. My fingers tangled in his hair, tugging him closer as my body arched into his, craving every inch of contact.

Ian's name escaped me in a soft moan, and the sound seemed to ignite something deeper in him. He pulled back just enough to let me catch my breath, his forehead pressing gently against mine. His warm breath mingled with mine, uneven and ragged, matching the pounding rhythm of my heart.

"Maddie," he murmured, his voice low, rough, and trembling with desire. "I've wanted this for so long."

"Then don't hold back," I whispered, my voice shaky yet firm, the anticipation simmering between us too much to contain. My hands slid up his chest, pulling him closer. "Take me."

A growl rumbled in his throat, raw and primal, sending

shivers down my spine. His hands slid down to the small of my back, guiding me to turn until I faced the door.

His fingers found the zipper at the back of my dress, tugging it down with an ease that made me gasp, a mix of surprise and excitement flooding me. I stood still, letting him peel the fabric from my body. The dress pooled at my feet, leaving me in the silky black slip I'd chosen, the fabric clinging to me in a way that left little to the imagination.

Ian stepped back, just slightly so I could face him again. And when I looked at him, his gaze traveled over me like a slow, deliberate caress, the moonlight streaming in through the windows illuminating the hunger and reverence in his dark eyes.

"You're so sexy, Maddie," he said, his voice thick. His hands returned to my waist, sliding upward, smoothing up my sides and over my ribs, leaving a path of molten lava in their wake.

He bent down, his lips finding mine again, and this kiss was deeper, hungrier. His tongue danced with mine as his hands roamed, exploring every curve as if memorizing me, worshiping me.

My fingers trembled as I reached for the bow tie at his neck, fumbling slightly in my urgency to rid him of the layers separating us. Ian chuckled, low and rough, and with an impatient tug, he yanked the tie loose himself, the strip of fabric landing carelessly on the floor.

I wasted no time unbuttoning his shirt, my fingers grazing the smooth, warm skin beneath. As each button gave way, I pushed the fabric aside, revealing the hard lines of his torso. My hands explored him, tracing the ridges of muscle with unrestrained curiosity. And as I cupped and squeezed his chest, the heat and feel of his body beneath my palms sent sparks racing through me, making the muscles in my abdomen clench and swirl.

He felt so good. So strong. So perfect.

Ian's breath hitched as my hands wandered over his shoulders, my fingers combing through the hair at the nape of his neck. And when his jaw clenched and his fingers tightened around my waist, as if to ground himself, I knew he was feeling everything I was in that moment.

"Maddie..." His voice was hoarse, and I could feel the tension thrumming through him, like he was teetering on the edge of control. "You have no idea what you're doing to me."

I swallowed, my heart racing as his words sank in. "I think I have an idea," I breathed, my voice trembling slightly as I leaned in closer. "And I really don't want you to stop."

As if that was all the permission he needed, in a swift, fluid motion, he slid his hands down my thighs and lifted me effortlessly. My legs wrapped around his waist instinctively, and I held onto him as he carried me through the house, every step deliberate and steady. The door to his bedroom opened, but as he crossed the threshold, I barely noticed the beautiful decór—the soft glow of the fireplace, the lush bedding. My entire focus was on him, on the way his body moved with purpose, how he made me feel like the world had narrowed to just the two of us.

He set me down gently on the edge of his bed, his gaze locking with mine. And as he slowly took me in, the intensity in his gaze, every track of his eyes, felt like a heated caress.

I'd never had a man look at me like this before. Like I was special, beautiful—*enough*.

He leaned down, his lips finding mine in a kiss that was both soft and searing, stealing the breath from my lungs. Then, with an almost aching tenderness, he guided me backward, laying me down against the cool sheets before he climbed in beside me, his arm going behind my back and pulling me against him.

He slowly dipped his head, his lips brushing against my

forehead—a fleeting, reverent touch. Then my cheek and my jaw, each soft kiss leaving trails of goosebumps that made me ache in ways I couldn't name. When his lips returned to mine, the kiss was slower, deeper—an unspoken vow that left me trembling in his arms, every part of me alive and attuned to him.

His hands explored me reverently, sliding along my sides, tracing every inch and curve as if committing me to memory. My skin burned under his touch, my body arching into him as I craved more, needed more.

"I love you so much," he whispered against my lips, the words so raw, so full of emotion that they made my heart stutter.

"I love you, too," I breathed, my voice shaky but sure, my fingers threading through his hair as I pulled him closer.

His lips found mine again, our tongues and bodies tangling together as the world around us fell away. Time didn't matter. Nothing mattered except this moment, this man, and the way he made me feel like I was everything he ever wanted.

Every touch, every caress felt like a crescendo, building and building until I was drifting off into the clouds. His hand slipped beneath the hem of my slip, his touch leaving a trail of fire in its wake as his fingers rose inch by inch, his gaze never leaving mine.

"Are you okay with this?" he asked, his voice a low rasp as his fingers paused on my ribs, his eyes searching mine.

"Yes," I whispered, sliding my fingertips along his jaw, my thumb brushing against the stubble there. "I've never been more sure."

He smiled then, a slow, tender smile that made my heart swell. And as his weight settled over me, pressing me into the soft mattress, I knew I was his completely—and he was mine.

As the night unfolded and we became one, every touch,

every kiss, every whispered name carried us closer, binding us together in a way that felt permanent, unshakable. The passion, the connection, the love—it was all-consuming, leaving no room for doubt or hesitation.

And when the world finally stilled, and I lay in his arms, his heartbeat steady against my ear, I knew I'd found my forever. Ian Hastings wasn't just the man I loved—he was the man I was meant to spend my life with.

EPILOGUE
IAN

I LAY on my side on Thanksgiving morning, watching Maddie sleep, her features soft and peaceful in the morning light that filtered through the curtains. Her hair spilled across the pillow in messy waves, and her chest rose and fell in a steady rhythm that matched the calm I felt just being near her.

And I couldn't help but smile.

The fact that she and Grant were here, living with me now, still felt surreal. They'd moved in just after Grant's birthday in October and it had been amazing. There were no more nightly goodbyes at the door, no waiting until the next day at work to see Maddie again.

Now, I just got to say goodnight and wake up to this—the woman of my dreams, right here beside me.

It was everything I could have hoped for.

She stirred, her hand twitching slightly before she shifted on the bed, her eyes fluttering open. A soft, sleepy smile curved her lips when her gaze landed on me. And man, I'd never get tired of seeing her smile at me like that first thing in the morning.

"Morning," I said warmly, my voice low.

"Morning," she murmured back, her voice still thick with sleep.

"How'd you sleep?"

"Pretty good." She yawned and stretched slightly. "How about you?"

"I slept okay," I said, though honestly, I'd barely slept a wink. I'd been too amped up, buzzing with anticipation over my plans for today.

"Just okay?" she asked.

"I think I was just a little too excited for my brain to settle down." I shrugged, a small smile tugging at my lips. "It's a big day today."

She blinked, briefly confused, before realization dawned. "Oh, right. Thanksgiving. My family will be here soon, won't they?"

"Yes. Though we've still got a few hours," I said, knowing how much she had planned to do before they arrived.

When Maddie first said she wanted to host Thanksgiving this year, I'd offered to have it catered and let my staff handle all the setup so she wouldn't have to stress.

But Maddie being *Maddie* apparently looked forward to the chaos of cooking a big meal and crafting centerpieces. So she'd politely declined all the help, insisting she wanted to do most of it herself.

Granted, we were still having the turkey and several pies delivered—there was only so much she could take on—but Maddie's homemade sweet potatoes and hot apple cider were sure to steal the show.

"I should probably get started on decorating the table," she said, sitting up and readying to climb out of bed.

But before she could slip away, I reached for her hand.

"Wait," I said, my heart thudding in my chest. "Just...hold on a sec."

She paused, her brow arching. "What's up?"

"I, uh..." My voice faltered as I shifted under her gaze. "I just wondered if you noticed something...different."

"Different?" She searched my face, clearly puzzled. "What do you mean?"

"It's something small," I said, trying—and failing—to keep the nerves out of my voice.

She let out a sigh, her eyes darting around the room as if expecting to spot some new decoration or trinket. "What am I supposed to be looking for?" She turned her attention back to me, her lips curving into a faintly amused smile. "You're being weird."

"I know," I admitted, blowing out a low breath.

Apparently, the nerves bubbling in my chest weren't doing me any favors.

She leaned in slightly, her impatience growing. "Can you at least give me a hint?"

I glanced down at her left hand, trying to keep my smile from turning into a full-blown grin.

Maddie caught the movement, frowning slightly as she looked from me to her hand, clearly trying to figure out why I was looking at it. Then realization finally hit her and she froze.

Her eyes went wide, a soft gasp escaping her lips as she lifted her hand closer to her face. The light glinted off the ring, delicate yet sparkling.

"Ian," she breathed, holding her hand up. "Did you put this here while I was asleep?"

"I did," I said, unable to stop smiling now.

"Why?" Her mouth fell open slightly. "Is this because my dad's coming and I never told him we called off our fake engagement? Because I promise I'll get around to it."

"No." I chuckled and shook my head. "I put it there because I thought you should have it. It's been sitting in my closet, all lonely, and I just thought...it could use a friend."

She laughed, the sound soft and full of disbelief. "So you thought I should wear a huge engagement ring around because it was lonely?"

"Well, I mean, it only makes sense," I said, my tone playful.

She shook her head, still laughing. "Ian, if I wear this, people are going to start asking questions. And since everyone at work is just now getting used to the fact that we're dating and not actually engaged, I think this would only add to the confusion."

"Hmm..." I pretended to think it over, rubbing my jaw with my thumb. "Yeah, I guess that *could* be a problem."

"You think?" Her eyebrows shot up.

"Well, I guess that means I should probably ask you a question, then," I said, unable to hold back a grin as I climbed off the bed and walked over to her side of the bed.

Her eyes widened as I lowered myself down on one knee, and I watched a kaleidoscope of emotions flit across her face—excitement, anticipation, and a flicker of hope that made my chest swell.

I reached for her hand, my thumb brushing over her knuckles. Her skin was warm beneath mine, the ring on her finger grounding me as my heart thundered in my chest.

"Maddie Elizabeth Stevens," I began, trying to infuse every syllable with the depth of my emotions. "I love you. More than words could ever fully express. I want to spend every single day proving to you just how much. You've shown me what it means to love and to be loved, and I never want to let that go." I paused, drawing in a shaky breath, the weight of the moment pressing against my chest. "So, Maddie...will you marry me?

Will you make me the happiest man in the world and marry me?"

Her hands flew to her mouth, and a choked sob escaped her as the first tears filled her eyes, trailing down her cheeks. She nodded frantically, unable to speak at first.

When she finally found her voice, it was soft and trembling. "Yes," she whispered, her words breaking with emotion. "Yes, of course, Ian. A million times, yes."

Relief and joy surged through me as she climbed off the bed and launched herself into my arms, her tears dampening my shirt as I held her close.

"I love you," she murmured before kissing me, her fingers curling into my shirt as if anchoring herself to the moment.

"I love you, too," I replied, my forehead resting against hers. The warmth of her acceptance settled deep in my chest, filling every corner of me with happiness.

But there was something else I needed to do.

"There's just one more thing," I said, pulling back slightly, my tone lighter now but no less serious.

"What do you mean?"

I reached for her hand, pressing a kiss to her knuckles before meeting her gaze again. "I need to ask someone else a question."

She blinked, momentarily confused, before she seemed to understand. Her lips curved into a smile as I stepped toward the door and called, "Grant? Can you come in here for a minute, buddy?"

"Okay," he called from the living room.

A moment later, Grant bounded into the room, his curious gaze darting between us. He climbed onto the bed, flopping down beside Maddie who smoothed a hand over his hair.

"What's up?" he asked, his eyes alight with curiosity.

"I need to ask you something important," I began, sitting

down on the bed so I was facing him. "What do you think about me joining your family? Do you think it'd be okay if I married your mom?"

"Hmmm," Grant said, scrunching his face into an exaggerated expression of deep thought. "Let me think about it..."

He tapped a finger to his chin, dragging out the moment like a pro, clearly savoring the attention.

Finally, after peeking at both Maddie and me to make sure he had us on the edge of our seats, he broke into a mischievous grin. "I guess you could marry her...but only if you promise to get her a real Lambo someday."

A surprised laugh burst out of Maddie, and the infectious grin spreading across Grant's face had me chuckling, too.

"A real Lambo?" I teased, ruffling his hair. "You drive a hard bargain, kid."

"I think the original 'Lambo' is just fine." Maddie shook her head, laughing as she wiped her eyes. "Don't let him swindle you, Ian."

"Okay, okay, how about this—" Grant put his hands out, his face utterly serious. "Maybe you can get *me* a Lambo when I'm older."

"I'll have to talk to your mom about that one before I make any promises," I said, loving this kid and his antics so much.

"Aw, man!" Grant groaned, throwing his head back dramatically. "I already know she's gonna say no!"

We all burst into laughter and then Maddie pulled both of us into her arms for a family hug. I wrapped my arms around the two people I loved most, letting the sweetness of this moment sink in.

It was perfect—they were perfect.

And they were mine.

OWEN

"WHAT'S THAT FACE ABOUT?" Ian asked, leaning toward me as Maddie's family chatted happily around the table in his formal dining room.

Yep, it was Thanksgiving dinner, and like I'd done every year since college, I was crashing Ian's dinner plans.

But unlike the previous years when we'd both been the cool and aloof bachelors among his family members, this time, I was the only bachelor in attendance.

And feeling far from cool.

"What face?" I asked, trying to school my expression so he wouldn't guess how much of an odd man out I felt today.

But Ian was way too good at reading me after two decades of friendship. And instead of letting my bad mood slide, he said, "You've got that brooding 'I'm too cool to care' thing going on, but I know you better than that."

"I'm not brooding," I said, probably a little too defensively. "Just...observing."

"Sure..." His tone dripped with skepticism.

So deciding to be honest, I gestured at the table full of his future family and said, "I don't know. You've got this whole cozy family thing going now, and I'm just realizing how much being single actually sucks."

"Oh, yeah..." Ian nodded, a hint of understanding in his eyes. "It does suck. I've definitely been there. But...you could find someone, too." Then shooting me a crooked grin he added, "It just, you know, starts with asking someone out on a date first."

"Oh, that's how it works? I had no idea," I shot back, my voice dripping with sarcasm.

Ian snorted, shaking his head, but his words stayed with me.

Yeah, I probably should be more proactive. It wasn't that I didn't want to date—it had just been hard to find the time. Between working two jobs and grinding away at my PhD over the past few years, dating had felt like an impossible luxury.

But now that the PhD was taken care of, I really didn't have an excuse anymore.

Did the thought of diving into dating apps make me cringe? Yes.

Big time.

They felt so superficial, like playing a game I wasn't equipped to win.

But since my current go-to of just going to work and hanging out with my buddies here and there wasn't exactly helping me land dates, maybe that was what I needed to do.

I mean, it wasn't like I'd magically find my dream girl in one of my chemistry classes since dating a student was definitely off-limits.

Especially for a first-year professor just hoping to earn tenure in a few years.

I sighed and pulled up my phone, opening the app store.

And even though it pained me, I searched for "Meet Your Match," the dating app I'd used back in college.

Who knows, maybe it was better now than it had been the last time I'd used it.

And as the app downloaded to my phone, I found myself watching Ian and Maddie—the way they smiled at each other, sharing little glances and whispering sweet nothings in each other's ears as everyone chatted happily around them.

I wanted what Ian had found.

Because, despite what all those James Bond movies had taught me growing up, the bachelor life wasn't everything it was cracked up to be.

And for the first time in a long while, I knew I was ready to change that.

Who knows, if I actually put myself out there and took a chance, maybe I could find my own person to share next Thanksgiving with.

Want to read a **bonus epilogue** that shows where Ian and Maddie are four years later? Snag it here: https://BookHip. com/PDGFTQA

I hope you enjoyed *Say You Remember Me*. The Kings of Eden Falls Series continues with Owen's professor/student romance! Coming soon!

To stay up to date on news, sales, and releases from Judy, join her newsletter here: https://subscribepage.com/judycorry

While you wait for Owen's book to release, read about Ian's

siblings and their love stories in Judy's Eden Falls Academy series, starting with Carter and Ava in *The Charade*.

Read about Maddie's siblings' love stories in Judy's Ridgewater High Series, starting with Lexi and Noah in *It Was Always You*.

Dear Reader,

I want to thank you for taking a chance on Say You Remember Me, and for giving me the opportunity to share this story with you. I couldn't do my dream job without you!

I would also be so grateful if you could take the time to leave a review. It's amazing how such a little thing like a review can be such a huge help to an author! Even a sentence or two counts!

Thank you so much!!

-Judy

AUTHOR'S NOTE

Want to hear the story behind why I decided to have Maddie tell Ian that she wanted to name a future cat Satan?

Well, it actually comes from a funny story my dad told us at the dinner table growing up—one that still makes us laugh to this day!

Apparently, there was a family in our neighborhood back then who had two dogs, one named Satan and the other named Lucifer. One day, some missionaries from a church were walking up to this family's door to talk to them about their faith. But just as they approached the house, the dad called out the door for the dogs to come inside, yelling, "Satan! Lucifer! Get in here!"

Understandably, after hearing such a declaration, the missionaries stopped in their tracks, turned around, and decided to head the other way. They even told some neighbors down the street about their *very strange* experience!

It's one of those stories my dad loved sharing over the years, and it always gets a laugh in my family. I hope it gave you a chuckle too!

ACKNOWLEDGMENTS

After writing one of the toughest books of my career so far, I'm beyond grateful that Ian and Maddie's story practically wrote itself. It's a story I've been waiting several years to get to—ever since introducing Ian in *The Charade*—and I'm so happy with how it turned out. (Hopefully you enjoyed it, too!)

And apparently, I kept my complaining to a minimum this time too, because when I announced to my family that I'd finished my manuscript, my oldest daughter said, "Wait, you were writing another book?" (In her defense, she's practically lived at her school this year since her extracurricular activities have kept her extremely busy. 😊)

So, aside from wanting to thank Ian and Maddie for being two of my most cooperative characters yet, I want to thank my husband, Jared, and my kids—James, Janelle, Jonah, and Jade—for supporting my author career. A writer's mind can be a chaotic place, and I appreciate them understanding that I'm not actually crazy when I talk about my characters like they're real people.

I have to give a special thanks to my daughter, Jade, who was so invested in Maddie and Ian's story that she'd ask to go on walks with me and the dogs just so we could chat about my latest writing sessions. She loved brainstorming what should happen next, and it's been so much fun seeing her excitement for the *Kings of Eden Falls* books grow right alongside mine.

(And yes, she *insists* she deserves most of the credit for this book because of all the great ideas she shared with me. 😌) So thank you, Jade, for your brilliant ideas and for being just as excited about Ian and Maddie's story as I was!

To my author friends—Anne-Marie Meyer, Kelsie Stelting, Kelsie Rae, Kali Hart, Tia Souders, and Kimberly Loth—thank you for all our chats. Being an indie author can be intense at times, and I love having such great friends in the trenches to learn from and navigate this journey with.

A huge thank-you to my amazing beta readers, Crissy Holland, Meredith Logan, Sarah Constable, and Kera Butler. I'm always insecure about my books in the early stages, and having you read along and offer feedback and ideas has been invaluable.

Many thanks to my incredible editor, Precy Larkins. I feel so fortunate whenever you fit me into your schedule. Your meticulous eye for detail never fails to impress, and when my pre-publishing jitters hit, your calm assurance is exactly what I need. Thank you for being the perfect editor for my work and always going above and beyond.

A heartfelt thank-you to my proofreader, Jordan Truex, for being so accommodating with this book's timeline. I'll never fully trust my own grasp of grammar rules, so relying on your sharp eye before publication truly saves my sanity!

To my wonderful ARC and Influencer teams, thank you for getting excited about this book from day one. Your encouraging DMs and emails kept me motivated as I sprinted to the finish line—truly, I couldn't do this without you!

I'm also incredibly grateful to every reader, Bookstagrammer, BookToker, blogger, and reviewer who picks up my books and shares them with the world. It warms my heart each time I see someone connect with my stories, and I deeply appreciate the care you put into your posts and reviews. Recommending and reviewing my books is truly one of the best gifts you could ever give me.

And finally, thank you, dear reader, for taking a chance on Ian and Maddie's story. Because of your support, I get to do my dream job every single day, and I couldn't be more thankful.

Also By Judy Corry

Eden Falls Academy Series:

The Charade (Ava and Carter)

The Facade (Cambrielle and Mack)

The Ruse (Elyse and Asher)

The Confidant (Scarlett and Hunter)

The Confession (Kiara and Nash)

<u>Kings of Eden Falls:</u>

Hide Away With You (Addie and Evan)

Say You Remember Me (Maddie and Ian)

Rich and Famous Series:

Assisting My Brother's Best Friend (Kate and Drew)

Hollywood and Ivy (Ivy and Justin)

Her Football Star Ex (Emerson and Vincent)

Friend Zone to End Zone (Arianna and Cole)

Stolen Kisses from a Rock Star (Maya and Landon)

Ridgewater High Series:

When We Began (Cassie and Liam)

Meet Me There (Ashlyn and Luke)

Don't Forget Me (Eliana and Jess)

It Was Always You (Lexi and Noah)

My Second Chance (Juliette and Easton)

My Mistletoe Mix-Up (Raven and Logan)

Forever Yours (Alyssa and Jace)

Standalones:

Protect My Heart (Emma and Arie)

Kissing The Boy Next Door (Lauren and Wes)

ABOUT THE AUTHOR

Judy Corry is the Amazon Top 12 and *USA Today* Bestselling Author of Contemporary and YA Romance. She writes romance because she can't get enough of the feeling of falling in love. She's known for writing heart-pounding kisses, endearing characters, and hard-won happily ever afters.

She lives in Southern Utah with the boy who took her to Prom, their four awesome kids, and two dogs. She's addicted to love stories, dark chocolate and chai lattes.